# MOONBOW

# MOONBOW

Part of the triptych of novels

SCENES of ENGLAND

*Russell Bower*

*FORGOTTEN TIMES PUBLISHING*

Works by Russell Bower include:

| *FICTION* | *PLAYS* | *BIOGRAPHICAL* |
|---|---|---|
| The Girl Who Painted Moonbow | Mr Kett | A Childhood of the Mind |
| I'm Thinking of Arabella | | A Thousand Thirsts |
| Who Steals a Goose | | Please, Sir! |
| Five Faces of Love | | |

*MOONBOW was a prize-winner in the Heinemann/Eastern Arts Novel Writing competition, 1992.*

© Russell George Bower, 2017

Published by Forgotten Times Publishing

All rights reserved. No part of this book may be reproduced, adapted, stored in a retrieval system or transmitted by any means, electronic, mechanical, photocopying, or otherwise without the prior written permission of the author.

The rights of Russell George Bower to be identified as the author of this work have been asserted in accordance with the Copyright, Designs and Patents Act 1988.

A CIP catalogue record for this book is available from the British Library.

ISBN 978-0-9996803-0-8

Book layout and cover design by Clare Brayshaw

Cover image released under Creative Commons CC-BY-NC-ND (3.0 Unported)

Cover illustration A Rainbow with Cattle" c. 1815, Joseph Mallord William Turner (1775 - 1851). Accepted by the nation as part of the Turner Bequest 1856. Photo (c) Tate, London 2017

Prepared and printed by:

York Publishing Services Ltd
64 Hallfield Road
Layerthorpe
York YO31 7ZQ

Tel: 01904 431213

Website: www.yps-publishing.co.uk

This book is dedicated to my sister Olive
With love

1919 - 1921

# CHAPTER 1

"Why me? Why is it always *me!*"

Maudie sighed, stared out of the window.

Her job was "doing the salt", which meant scraping away at a block of salt with a dinner knife on to a cooking-board, then tipping the grains into a bowl. When the bowl was full it had to be emptied into a skep. You had to have *four* bowlfuls to have enough salt for when they killed the pig.

"Make sure you keep it flat," the bitches had said, meaning not to get a hollow in the salt block. And then Muriel had gone cycling off to Beckthorp when everyone knew she couldn't stand Beckthorp, and Barbara had gone out to look after her old cows.

"Keep the damn salt flat yourself!" Maudie exclaimed to the empty room. "What do I care if it's flat or hollow?"

She scooped up a handful of salt grains, let it trickle out of her hands like sand on the beach. Some went in the bowl, some on the floor. She didn't care. If she heard anyone coming she would sweep it up and flick it back in the bowl, dust and all.

She was on a beach. A child. Had shiny black shoes on. Her mother was calling, *"Mau-die!"* She was never told off by her mother. Mummy used to say, "Come along, little dreamer!"

If only her mother was alive and her sisters were dead! She'd swap the bitches ten times over to have her mother back.

She watched the salt edge out of her hands like sand, down, down into the bowl, build up into a little white pyramid.

The knife lay in the salt, forgotten.

The two of them, the Major and her. He'd got down from his pony trap, they were chatting, his lovely dark eyes close to her eyes, his moustache –

The door banged open. The dream died; Major Dawson had only looked and smiled as he drove past.

"Everything ready?" her father asked.

Muriel came in at the same time.

"Copper's been on the boil ages."

"I'll get the pig, then."

While her father was gone Muriel measured out the salt Maudie had scraped.

"Not even three! I told you to do four!"

Maudie brushed the salt off her hands, her skirt.

Barbara came in from the dairy.

"She's hardly done three," Muriel told her.

Maudie sighed. "What's it matter? Pig won't care."

"Pig won't *keep*, you mean," Barbara said. "Got to have salt for the brine."

"I'll do some more," Muriel said. "No good relying on her."

Muriel set to. Salt showered down. This was how it *should* be done!

The shrieks of the pig got louder. Edges of sound, like tearing metal. Enough to deafen you. Muriel opened the door. Her father and Sammy, each with a board either side of the pig, Sammy with the chain from the pig's snout round his wrist. A tall pig, eyes distended, eyelashes pale, the curtain of lip round its upper jaw drawn back like a grin. It seemed to know which door was the slaughter-room. It hung back, tried to turn away, screamed like a file across metal.

Muriel kept scraping. Barbara opened the bottom door. Sammy dashed in, swung the pig round, steered it to the post where the hooks were, lashed the chain to the ring, and Barbara held the bowl so when her Pa stuck the throat with the knife she was able to catch the spurt of blood.

Maudie closed her eyes. Heard the blood pouring against the metal, someone stirring to stop it clotting, the pig shrieking enough to pierce your eardrums, and Barbara remarking as if she'd never noticed it before, "This bowl's getting really hot!"

The shrieks softened. Ceased. A sort of sigh. The pig was dead. Maudie wanted it to recover, wanted it to snort its way back to its sty and lie down fat and comfortable in its mess and straw.

"Go and get the water," Barbara told her. "No good you standing there with your eyes shut."

Maudie lifted the lid off the copper, sniffed the clean smell of the steam, scooped out a handbowlful of boiling water. They told her where to pour it, a little at a time over the pig while they scraped off the bristles and muck and blood and scum with the scraper, scraped the skin of the poor dead animal instead of leaving it in peace. She had to bring more hot water till the scraping was done and the bristles were off and Sammy was hooking out the toenails. The creature looked almost comical, its great mouth open, that dreadful red flap in its throat, its snout flattened as if it had run into a wall.

Maudie banged the bowl down on the animal's side.

"I hate it! I hate this place and everyone in it! And I hate myself!"

"Steady!"

He always spoke quietly, her Pa. "Go and get some fresh air, Maudie."

But Barbara sniffed, said as Maudie had done next to nothing all morning she'd better go and bring a few buckets of water from the pond to wash things clean.

It was a relief to be away from the stench of blood, out in the sunshine and walk across to the pond. She breathed the smell of grass, the pondy air. At the end of the platform she looked at her reflection in the water, the dark shape of herself, the sky behind her blue and sunny. She splashed the bucket down. The image splintered.

"Serve you right!" she told it.

She plunged the bucket in, hoped she'd captured some of the sunshine to wash over the pig.

It hung head down, suspended by hooks from the beams. Its belly was slit from crotch to throat, its insides a mass of tubes and pipes steaming from the tub. From a tube that was yards long her Pa squeezed green-brown stuff out, his forearms streaked with blood and mess. More bucketfuls of water, the cavity washed out, blood and slime broomed away along the open drain across the floor and out through a hole in the wall.

Then she was sick. Was glad she was sick. Served her right for hitting the pig. She sluiced water into the drain, broomed the sick away along with the slime.

"Now I'm like the pig. Cleaned out."

She stood by the wall at the end of the garden. Fields, autumn hedgerows, trees with brown and yellow leaves, the landscape stretched away beyond the neighbouring parish. This was where, two or three years ago, she'd stood with her Pa and heard the farmhouse windows rattle from the rumble of the guns in France. She used to pray for Herbert to come home safe and well. Now he had come home. And then left and gone to Yorkshire.

But her prayers for her mother hadn't come true.

"The dead can come back," she whispered. "If you try hard enough."

*"Can even meet Major Dawson,"* a voice in the dream said, *"if you try hard enough."*

# CHAPTER 2

"Nothing to worry about, dear. The war's over."

Wilfred recollected himself.

What a fool, he thought. On an evening walk, for heaven's sake! In a country lane! The flare he had been afraid of, only the glow of the sinking sun! Wheel ruts underfoot made by farm carts, not gun carriages!

"Must be a bore, Jenny. Always having to coax me back!"

She stroked his hand. It was what she had done the best part of a year since he came home from France, what she had to do to keep him normal. She knew what the night-time part of him knew, that the dead come home. Every night they unfolded out of his brain, as they had been in life, as he had seen them in death. Lately they called in the daytime, men with their souls ripped out, he, their chaplain, bearing what comfort he could.

"It isn't you the dead hold guilty, Wilfred."

"But guilt there ought to be. Somewhere."

The couple were walking down Church Lane on their way to St Matthew's Hall, a Georgian house Major Dawson had bought in 1914, and to which he had recently returned.

"Oh-ho! Rector! Oh-ho!"

A well-built woman in her late thirties brandished a pruning rod at them the other side of a gate in the hedge. "And Mrs Jackson! Oh-ho!"

She waved them closer, blue floppy hat pitched forward, straw and hedge clippings on her hair and clothes.

A suddenness, almost excitement in the voice. Yet the eyes were sleepy, her features unexcited.

"We're just on our way to the Hall now, Mrs Dawson," Wilfred said. "Some idea your husband's got. Wants to talk it over with us."

Rose Dawson's attention had flitted to the branch of an oak tree which reached out over the lane. She raised the pruning pole, snipped at a clump of twigs overhead.

"Thought I'd lost one the other day, you know," she told the intersecting boughs. "I told Richard the day he came home, 'I think I've lost one of my tits!' Then I counted them again. Everything normal."

She seemed pleased at that, ignored the leaves and bits that had fallen on her, but Wilfred had a feeling of being observed, of eyes wide awake under their lids.

"May see you at the house then, Mrs Dawson," Jenny said.

But the Major's wife was back at her work, tidying more twigs in the oak tree. The rector raised his hat, the couple continued their walk.

They knew about Rose Dawson. Everyone in the parish knew about Rose Dawson.

St Matthew's Hall stood at the end of a box-bordered driveway. Richard Dawson opened the door wide, ushered them in.

"Good of you to come, Wilfred. Jenny."

A sweep of his arm showed them through to a room at the back.

Tall, with brown eyes, military moustache and well shaped features, the Major was most people's idea of a World War One army officer.

"Almost a year, Rector," he said, "since the war ended, and not much done for those who came back. The Americans have set up the American Legion. The least we can do is set up something similar here. Don't you think?"

What he had in mind, he said, was a dance on Hallowmas Eve. Time, seven-thirty; place, the great barn next door. Object one, to raise funds on behalf of the wounded; object two, to provide a focal point for a social get-together for the parish, a celebration of a year at peace. He wanted to sound people out on the idea.

"Anything that reinforces a feeling of peace," Jenny murmured.

"I've had a look at the barn," Richard said. "Damn good wooden floor in the middle. Used to thresh corn there, people tell me."

Would do a treat if he got the lumber out, had the place cleaned up. Need lights, lanterns and so forth. Volunteers'd be needed to bring a bit of food and drink. As for music, Jacksons know anyone who could play?

Well, actually, Jenny said, she did. The thing was though, it was the piano.

The Major had got a piano. He'd get it tuned – organize a bit of transport – four or five strong men – horse and cart – "Anyone else in the village play?"

Wilfred admitted to still doing a bit on the violin. Was how he and Jenny had met, as a matter of fact.

"And who knows," the Major said, "could be others in the parish with a bit of talent."

He'd leave the music side for the Jacksons to deal with.

And publicity? Was there anyone at the heart of the parish, someone who could spread the word? Someone everyone would take notice of?

Jenny and Wilfred each had a name. Came out with it together like a chorus. *Stanley Chatham!*

A tap at the window. Mrs Dawson grinned at them. She was holding a hen by the neck. She shook it to emphasize its deadness, undulated it up and down, simulating flight across the window, one wing hanging, head drooping. Then there was only the empty window, the orchard beyond in the greying light.

Richard seemed unconcerned. "Stanley Chatham it must be, then. I'll have a word with him."

Rose came in, fluff and down floating away from her clothes, her grin lopsided as if her face had forgotten it.

"We're trying to organize that dance for Hallowmas Eve," the Major told her. "Don't know if you've had any thoughts on the matter, Rose?"

"Dance? First I've heard of it."

Rose pulled open a small drawer, fudged about till she found a jewellery box, took out a small gold wrist watch. "Did I tell you about my dream last night?" she asked her husband. "Dreamt you'd died in the war." She fastened the watch, held her wrist up to the Jacksons.

"He brought me this when he came back. Don't know if it tells you how much time we've got left, Richard?"

"We were discussing the dance, Rose."

Hallowmas Eve. In the Great Barn. The profits to help the wounded.

"Oh, the wounded!" she said. "Of course we must help the wounded. If we knew who they are."

She shook the watch, held it up to her ear. "Not so much time as there was, do you think?" She held it for the

Jacksons to hear. "Seldom had time to come home, you know. All those years he was away!"

The last of the sunset had gone by the time the Jacksons left. There was no moon, cloud obscured the stars. Wilfred was glad to walk home in the dark. He felt part of the night, part of the shadow under the bush beside the bank. How should a man be unwounded, he asked himself, and his comrades slaughtered?

He and Jenny walked hand in hand. Occasionally a pheasant croaked, a blackbird chattered alarm. Across the fields a cow lowed in the darkness.

"We'll have to practise." The prospect seemed to please him. "Do us good. Something to aim at."

They'd have to go to Beckthorp music shop, Jenny reckoned. Buy a few suitable pieces people could dance to. Nothing too out-of-date. Younger generation would have to be catered for as well, of course.

They recalled music they'd already got, discussed which item might follow which, and by the time they paused at their wrought iron gate they had the makings of a programme.

It was Jenny who voiced the other thing.

"I wonder what Rose was trying to tell us."

"Our Father is aware of the fall of a single sparrow," Wilfred smiled. "I suppose we must allow Rose to number her tits amongst her losses."

"Good idea, this dance," he added. "With the Lord's help it'll heal a few wounds."

"Amen to that, dear."

Not for the first time she wished her faith was as strong as her husband's.

# CHAPTER 3

By the time the sun was up Stanley was easing his horses through the narrow gateway between barn and ditch. The great necks of the Suffolks arched over him, their hooves crushed clods he had stood on, and as they nodded their heads and swished their tails he set up the markers for the first draw. A long day's work was ahead. The first furrow had to be the best of the day.

Richard Dawson slept alone. Even so he moved quietly, not wanting to disturb Rose. He went downstairs, boots in hands, let himself out at the back door.

A relief to be outdoors. The sun was above the tops of the oaks at the end of the field. Stanley and his team were about to set off on a draw towards the far hedge, a strong-framed young chap and his pair of Suffolks, a black and grey-white tumble of rooks and seagulls around the turned-up soil.

"Mornin' Major."

Exhilarating to hear the thrust of the share, see the rush of turned earth against the mould board. Major Richard Dawson wondered at the harnessed power of the beasts that could rend the soil as if it was water. He felt its roughness under his boots, smelt its rawness as the layers turned and poured themselves along the furrow. He was the legal owner of the field, had the deeds to prove it, though it was rented out to Stanley. Regarding ownership, the land was in his gift, he could neglect it, sell it, leave it to whom he wished, but regarding its fruitfulness he knew it belonged to the likes of Stanley and the long generations before him.

"In good heart, is it?"

Richard watched them, the horses, the man who mastered them, mastered the plough and the living field.

"I was thinking of holding a dance."

"Dance?"

The last Friday of the month, Hallowmas Eve. "Wondered what you'd think of the idea, Chatham?"

Stanley shook the traces, the horses leaned into their work, the wave of soil rose from the plough, fell to the top of the furrow.

He liked the idea. Couldn't think of a place to have one, though.

"I thought of having it in the barn."

"*That* barn?" The plough didn't quiver, Stanley didn't quite turn and stare at him. "Take some work to clean that bugger out!"

Hall Barn, one of the huge old barns of England, was a flint, brick and timber structure older than the Hall where the Major lived. It had gone out of use, was now a storehouse for farm implements and waggons and horse gear.

"Wonderful old floor in there, under the muck."

Stanley kept his eye on the depth and straightness of the furrow, sometimes called a friendly word to Diamond or Dolly leaning their strength against the collar. Richard strode alongside, this man whose strength kept the plough steady.

"Where they used to thrash the corn," Stanley told him. "Before the war."

They reached the headland, the horses slowed, turned, the plough was set for the next draw across.

"I suppose," the Major asked, "everyone in these parts was bred and born here, apart from myself and Mrs Dawson?"

"Except the Stelfoxes," Stanley joked. "Only been here twenty years."

Richard's step quickened. This would be Joseph Stelfox, he asked. Farmed Beck Farm? Had two or three daughters?

"There's Muriel Stelfox. There's Barbara Stelfox. Then there's Maudie."

*Maudie!*

She was the reason! All this to-do he'd dreamed up about a dance! Young Maudie Stelfox! That young country girl, black hair, blue eyes, waiting near the gate! She was the one! She'd dance!

"All the family would come?" he asked.

"If it was in the barn, I daresay Muriel might."

Elevenses. He gave the horses their bait, unwrapped his sandwiches.

The others two?

Stanley thought they might. Couldn't be sure. "We're just friendly, Muriel and me."

The way he spoke it seemed a comfortable friendship.

Richard said he'd be getting some invitations done. "But I was thinking, if Muriel's a bit shy, hers might be better coming from you?"

It didn't fill Stanley with dismay, the prospect of writing to Muriel, inviting her to a dance.

The mother was dead, he said. But there was the father, Joseph. Was the Major going to ask him too?

"Everyone. I want them all to come. All the parish."

Stanley knew how big the parish was. "Be an expense, Major."

Richard laughed, picked a stone up, flung it high into the blue. "Money's no good to me, Chatham. Won't buy what I want."

Stanley pushed the last of the sandwich into his mouth, wiped his face on his forearm. Didn't understand such talk. What he'd got he'd had to work for. Didn't intend to let the Government have it – or fling it away into the blue.

"You'll spread the word – about the dance, will you?" Richard asked. "I'm told you're the man people listen to round here."

Stanley lifted the nosebags away from the horses, checked the harness ready for the start-up. "Be a full house, I should think."

The team drew away, man and horses battling with the earth, seagulls and rooks wheeling, waiting for what chance might turn up.

Market days were the worst, drovers prodding the cattle and pigs with sticks, hitting them between the legs, treating them like helpless money. And Briggs's shop! Muriel hated the shop-girls making knowing little signs behind your back as if they knew everything. Beckthorp people had been nowhere and knew nothing – except the colour of someone's privy door half a mile away. She hated Beckthorp itself, was only sorry the pretty little beck that flowed through Beck Farm was unlucky enough to have to flow through Beckthorp on its way to the sea.

The road home climbed up towards St Matthew's and the open sky. At the top of the hill stood the ivy-covered barn, and that great bush like some old god of the hedgerow, its bare branches like outspread arms. Best of all was the church tower in the distance, wallflowers growing up its sides, yellow and red against the flint-grey walls. Now she was away from Beckthorp she could enjoy the morning, its leaves yellowing in autumn sun, stubble fields golden brown.

She stopped at a gate. The approaching horses and plough and horseman put her in mind of a bride and groom, a bridesmaid in attendance, the aisle stretching away to the far hedge. Though anyone less like a bridesmaid than Stanley she couldn't imagine. He'd seen her. She could tell by his face.

When he reached the headland he drew the horses to a halt. He smelt of horses and hard work, the look he gave her was like sunshine.

"What's that you've got there, Muriel?"

He meant the couple of blue paper packets in her cycle basket.

"Rice. Father's killed a pig."

"What's the rice for? Going to stuff it?"

She laughed, told him it was to make black puddings with. They stood, only the farm gate between them, had known each other all their lives, and made their meetings last as long as possible.

"Haven't shown you my scar yet, have I?"

"What do you mean *yet?*" she laughed. She sensed he had been told something. Stanley always had a fund of interesting news.

"Gate's quite warm in the sun," she said.

His hand brushed hers. Feeling its coolness he enclosed it in his.

"You know what they say about cold hands?"

She didn't respond, content to leave her hand where it was.

"I spose you've been pottering about," he said.

"As women do. Passing the time."

She watched him, his eyes alive with something he'd heard. After a while she said, "You've got some news, Stanley Chatham. Haven't you?"

People liked to tell Stanley things. He wasn't a gossip, but it seemed to give tittle-tattle more status if Stanley knew it.

He cleaned his boot on a bar of the gate.

"Might have."

"Well, tell me."

He scraped the earth off the other boot.

"Had a word with the Major."

She waited. "Seems a nice man, the Major."

She kept her voice low, as if what was said was between him and her only.

"So the girls tell me."

She knew what he meant. Major Richard Dawson, best-looking man in the parish.

"Lovely old house, the Hall," she said, her voice no louder than the grasses brushing against each other on the headland.

"Lovely old house," Stanley agreed, equally softly.

It was the moment to whisper a secret to a waiting girl. No secret arrived. There he was, silent. With a grin on his face!

She withdrew her hand, didn't see why he should hold it if he wasn't going to confide in her. She wasn't going to be treated the same as everyone else, not by Stanley Chatham.

"You shall be the first to know, Muriel."

His voice was so quiet, so manly and confiding, she almost forgave him, almost leaned close for one of the little kisses they had started enjoying lately. But he hadn't told her. She was dying to know, and he hadn't told her! She wasn't going to stand there and be made a fool of, least of all by Stanley Chatham.

"Why can't you tell me now?"

"You'll know soon."

He wasn't altogether clear why he wanted to keep it a secret, except that he fancied the idea of writing her a letter asking her to come to a dance with him on Hallowmas Eve.

"You'd better get on with your ploughing, then," she said, wheeling her cycle back to the road. "I've got to be getting back."

"That's a pity, Muriel."

"Yes, it is a pity, Stanley Chatham."

She cycled off. Heard him talk to the horses, heard the plough rattle, the birds scream as they searched the furrow. By the time she got as far as the next field she still hadn't forgiven him, wasn't going to look back for their parting smile.

# CHAPTER 4

The sun hadn't yet risen. The air was colder, mud crackled underfoot. Barbara was glad to get into the cowshed where the air was warm from the cows, odorous with cowpat and milky breath. This was her family, the one she preferred. These creatures welcomed her, mostly in silence, sometimes with lowing or a snuff of the breath. She loved this time of day, cobwebby windows turning grey in the first of the morning, the glint of the lantern in the cows' eyes as they turned to see her.

She hung the lantern on the nail in the window, started as always with Buttercup. She patted the creature's bony back, pushed her round so she had room to get the stool down beside her, then leaning into the cow's side she found the teats, squeezed the milk out into the pail. She knew she spoilt the old cow, talking to her as she milked, but she didn't mind. Buttercup was part of her family.

When the cow was finished she moved to Betsy the other end of the row; then it would be Daisy's turn in the middle of the opposite row. She always milked in the same criss-cross sequence, starting with the most senior and finishing with Spot whose calf had now been put in a pen by itself. She felt sorry for cows whose calves were taken away, but she knew it was necessary. What was not necessary, was downright unfair, was that the farm – the cowhouse, the cows and everything else – would be left to her brother Herbert when her father died. These animals wouldn't be a family to him; they'd be a herd to be kept or sold – as he wished. That was how her father had written his will.

The tumbril draw up outside. The cowshed door opened.

"Where do you want the beet?"

A small-built man, a new-moon face curving out at the nose, back at forehead and chin.

"Where do you think I want them? In the bedroom?" She carried on milking, her pale blue milking-gown tight on her back as she leaned into the cow. "Put some through the slicer."

She moved her stool across to a cow the other side. "What are you standing there for? Been turned into a pillar of salt?"

"Why do you keep moving round like that?" Walter asked. "Carting your stool and pail about, first this side then that."

"Cows'd be upset if I milked them out of order. Wouldn't give so much milk."

"I wouldn't take any notice of a few old cows."

"That's your trouble. You don't take notice where you should take notice."

"You want to milk all this side first," he insisted. "Then do the other side. You'd save half an hour a go. That's an hour a day." He calculated on his fingers. "That's seven hours a week. That's half a day's work a week. Twenty-six days a year. Three and a half weeks. What do you want to work three and half weeks for nothing for?"

Barbara switched to the other two teats, tossed her hair back off her face.

"If you thought a bit more about work instead of how to get out it, you wouldn't have fetched up in court like you did, Walter Leggett."

Walter's face wore the grin he hid behind when Barbara got going. He knew what her tongue was like. Twenty years old, a farmer's daughter and hardy with it. He was younger, not fit enough to get into the forces, in trouble with the police.

"And I'd put that old slicer where it was needed. You want to have a lean-to built against the cowhouse and shift the slicer into it, then you could do all the beet you want without having to hump them all the way from the barn."

He didn't wait. He saw the flash of her eye, knew it was time to go and put the beet through the slicer.

Barbara settled down at the next cow, drew at the teats, milk jetted out into the pail. Leggett knew how to organise other people's lives! His own was in a big enough mess! Though it might help to have the slicer closer to where the beet were needed. Not that she'd ever admit as much. Wouldn't do let the likes of Legget have the last word.

By the time she had taken the pails across to the dairy the milk was cool enough to put through the separator, a machine with two spouts, a handle and a container at the top that held the milk. She leaned on the handle to turn it, heard the hum reach the note that told her she was turning at the right speed, skimmed milk rattled out like water into a bowl. From the other spout a trickle of cream, coiling down into the smaller bowl. When cream and milk had finished dripping from their separate spouts Barbara stopped turning the handle, the hum of the separator subsided. She removed the cream container, emptied it into an earthenware bowl already half full of cream from previous milkings, gave it its daily stir to keep it right for butter making. Then she washed and dried the separator components, reassembled them ready for the evening's milk. It was cold work, lonely, but she loved it. She loved the dairy, the bare stone floor, she loved the scrubbed wooden shelves and cupboards. Loved the pots of cream, the butter churn, the whole paraphernalia of milk and cream and butter. And, little as it was, she loved the profit she got from selling at Beckthorp market, the money in her hand, fruits of her labour. Slavery, some might call it. She knew different. She called it freedom.

She loved living where she lived, the farmhouse, barns, cowhouse, the meadows that were lovely in the summertime, and the beck that ran through them where the cows drank. She knew she'd always live there. If brother Herbert chose to live elsewhere that was their affair. Why on earth her father bothered with him! It had been Herbert's decision to go and learn butchering in Yorkshire. Seldom wrote home. In her opinion Herbert wasn't worth bothering over.

The yard in front of the farm was as big as a paddock. Maudie had been told to tidy it up.

"First thing people see when they come down the cartway."

Her father always spoke quietly, and because it was for him she set about hoeing the weeds, raking them up and taking them by the barrowful to the midden. Then cleaned round the line of big stones in front of the house so she could give them a coat of whitewash later.

She realized she was bursting. The privy was in the elder bushes. It had two wooden seats side by side, one for children, the bigger one for grown-ups. Once she'd sat on the wrong seat, had nearly fallen in. Barbara had hurried in to see who was screaming.

"It's always you, you little bitch! Wish you had fallen in! Where you belong!"

Mr Athorp the postman was cycling down the cartway when she came out.

"Mornin' young Maudie! Two today."

He fetched the letters out, his eyes flickering over her as if she ought to give him a reward. She took the letters, studied the postmarks. The silly man had brought one for Barbara and one for Muriel. Nothing for her!

"You'll get letters one of these days." His eyes licked at her. He knew about young girls.

She ignored him, went indoors.

She could guess who Barbara's was from, but Muriel's was a mystery. Hadn't seen that handwriting before.

From the dairy came the hum of Barbara's separator starting up. Maudie pressed the envelope to her forehead, tried to will the contents into her brain. She felt where the letter was, traced its outline with her finger.

The separator was going full speed. Barbara wouldn't stop now. Even if the roof fell in Barbara wouldn't stop now.

Maudie pushed the kettle further on the fire, got a pointed knife out of the drawer. Knelt in the hearth, held the envelope in the steam till the gum softened. Got the knife point under the flap, gradually worked the knife along till it was all unstuck.

Pulled the letter out.

*Dear Muriel*

*Major Dawson is going to hold a dance on Hallowmas Eve in that barn of his. So he can raise money for the wounded. He's writing to everyone, but he asked if I'd write to you. If you and your family would like to go to let me know and I'll come and pick you up.*

*Yours truly, S Chatham*

Maudie read it, read it again. Hallowmas! Muriel and Stanley! Quiet little cat! Never a word to anyone!

The kettle was still boiling, the knife soon opened the other envelope. Boring letter. Cousin Kate up in Yorkshire. Hardly seen anything of Herbert, she wrote, even though he was up in Yorkshire in lodgings, and learning to be a butcher – -

Maudie put it aside, read the other one again. And again.

*"If you and your family would like to come -"*

The separator had stopped. Barbara was washing down, could walk in at any moment.

She whisked the letters back in, moistened the gum in the steam, pressed the flaps well down. She smoothed the envelopes out, stood them on the mantelpiece by the clock.

Back in the yard she went over the soil again and again with the rake, took hours over it so it looked new and fresh as if it had never been walked on. She wanted her father to see how well she had done it – and then she was at the gateway with the Major. Like a prince in a story book. No-one had smiled at her like that! His face, his moustache, his eyes –

"I don't spect she wants any dinner today!"

It was the bitches' way of telling her it was ready. She put the gardening things away, went indoors.

"Here she is!"

She knew from the voice something was wrong.

She dried her hands. "Now what?"

"Why did you open my letter?"

Maudie took her outdoors shoes off, got her indoor ones out of the cupboard. "What *are* you talking about?"

"You know what I'm talking about. You opened my letter!"

"What letter?"

"You know what letter."

Maudie squeezed her feet into the shoes, winced at the pressure on her toes. "These shoes!"

"I said, you know what letter."

"Oh, do I? One for you, one for Muriel. I put them on the mantelpiece for you."

"After you'd steamed them open first."

Maudie laughed. "I wonder your tongue don't fall out! All them lies."

"And you let the kettle boil dry after you'd steamed them open."

It stood in the hearth, blackened from bottom to handle, one side burnt away.

"Oh, you liar!"

If her sister had been smaller Maudie would have hit her, but Barbara was tall and hardy, and the look in her eye cooled any such thought.

"You put it on to open my letter and forgot to take it off. So now you can buy a new kettle."

Maudie glared at the burnt-out object. As if it need have let her down like that!

"I couldn't bear to read anyone's letter. You spend too much time with your old cows. No wonder you're starting to look like one!"

"You could bear to read someone's letter, Maudie."

Muriel spoke gently, as if to someone she felt sorry for. "Don't try to pretend, dear, because you read my letter too."

Muriel's voice was soothing, forgiving, like a mother to her child. Maudie laughed in her face.

"You're as crazy as she is! I don't know why I stay with you two bitches."

"Tell me why you did it, dear."

Maudie wasn't going to be tricked by a pleasant voice. Many a time she'd been tricked by that little cat.

"I didn't open the letters! Do you think I'd tell a lie?"

"Course you'd lie," Barbara said. "You lie all the time."

"I swear to God -"

"No good you swearing to anyone, dear," Muriel said. "When you put the letters back you put them in the wrong envelopes."

Maudie stared at the letters a long time. She turned away, chin high.

"Sooner I can get away from you two bitches," she said, "the better."

# CHAPTER 5

"So tell me about the war, Richard."

Richard put his glass back on the table, brushed a trace of potato from his lips.

"War?"

"The one you were in," Rose said. "That kept you away so long. Even when it had finished."

He could tell by her face, that too-bored-to-ask look. She was at her sharpest like that. She knew he had been seconded to the new protectorate territories, had come home less often than he might have done. He didn't explain, would only make things worse.

The war was dreadful, he said. But England and the Empire had *won*. Whatever the French or the Americans might think, Britain had won it.

"No-one came out the same as he was before."

He'd said too much. She'd be thinking he was making excuses. For being what he was?

"So you're holding a dance to celebrate!"

Not the war. To raise funds for the wounded. Celebrate a year of peace.

"Celebrate the Bramleys while you're doing," Rose said. "Been a wonderful year for Bramleys."

"I'll have to get in touch with a piano tuner."

"Don't know about the piano." She rang for the maid.

"It always looked beautiful, whatever it played like. Have you met *people* like that, Richard?"

Miriam came in.

"I don't suppose I was much of a loss to all the things I never managed to do. Was I, Miriam?"

"Oh, ma'am. Shall I bring the pudding in?"

Richard was aware of a shapeliness. The girl had a cast in her eye, a nose that belonged to a bigger face. She looked better leaving a room than entering it.

"Don't know if you'd like a new dress for it, Rose?"

"Be the belle of the ball?"

And maybe go to pictures while they were out, he said.

"And see other people's lives? I don't care about other people's lives. Mine's quite enough for me."

Miriam brought in a treacle pudding and a bowl of custard, checked the table to see if she'd forgotten anything.

"Looks a nice big pudding, Miriam."

"Yes, sir."

"You'd like me to make an entrance?" Rose said. "I shan't let you down, Richard."

"If that's all, ma'am?"

"By the way, Miriam, I shall be having a word with my saucepans. I want them to think of you as a friend."

"Oh, I hope they do, ma'am."

The girl had come with a good character. No background to speak of, the Warburtons had written, thoughtful young woman, twenty times as bright as that husband of hers. Miriam, yes, the reference said. Raymond, at your peril.

"She up to the job?" Richard asked when she'd gone.

"I've no idea what she's up to, Richard."

The Major wound his way through a slice of the pudding. He'd pictured this room when he was in France, these green plaster walls, the beams edging the ceiling. Had once thought rural life would suit them both; now it was like living with foreigners. The war was different. Life had been worth living during the war. Now it was over.

"Thoughtful today, Richard."

"I've started clearing out the loft. Ready to store your Bramleys."

"I found a coat in the hedge yesterday. Amazing what people throw away."

*Maudie Stelfox!*

Young figure, blue eyes, black hair. The merest whim. This dance, all the organisation, all the work, an excuse to dance with her? Folly. Even to think of her was folly. But what was life without folly? Maybe it was why he had done well in the war.

"So I brought it home and hung it up," Rose said. "Ready for the great occasion."

"Have a word with your Bramleys, Rose. Tell them the loft'll soon be ready."

# CHAPTER 6

"Remember when we used to send Herbert his bits of ham when he was in France?"

Joseph Stelfox was butchering the pig, Barbara was cutting meat from the head – ears, chops, snout, lips. She put the knife down, reached for a saucepan large enough to take the rest of the head.

"Funny thing he didn't want to stay at home when it ended," she said.

It was early evening, the dairy already gloomy, its single window facing north. In the light of two lanterns Joseph sawed down the pig's backbone as the animal hung by the hind legs, the shadow of butcher and carcase across the whitewashed walls. The carcase, waxy-pale outside, pink and red inside, became joints, some for the brine tub, some for the hooks across the chimney breast.

"What if he decides to live in Yorkshire, Pa?" Barbara asked. "Will you still leave him the farm?"

Joseph stopped sawing. "Can't forget him, Babs. Just because he's away from home."

"Don't you think it's unfair, him to be left so much?"

"Just because a thing is unfair doesn't mean it's wrong."

That was what hurt, the one who had gone away counting for more than the one who'd stayed at home. Day in and day out she'd done the work, had put up with the cold and the toil, yet it was always *Herbert* with her father. It almost made her sympathise with Walter Leggett, the Stelfox family owning land, crops, animals and barns when all he'd got was a bed in his parents' tied cottage on Howletts' farm. She didn't like him, but guessed how he felt. Which was why she'd let him have a bit more pig's fry than he ought to have had.

"I've had a letter from cousin Kate."

Joseph's face brightened.

"Thinking of changing her job. She's back in Yorkshire for a while."

Did she say if she'd seen Herbert? her father asked.

She'd seen him once. "Said she thought he was good-looking." Barbara laughed. "Takes all sorts, I suppose."

She put water and salt in the saucepan, stood it on the kitchen range. "I didn't realize Herbert was in lodgings. I thought he was still living at Uncle Arthur's."

Joseph went back to his sawing. The halves of the carcase swung apart, he and Barbara heaved one half on to the bench to be cut up. She was as good as a man on the farm, better than many. The two got on well together. Barbara wasn't his favourite. She didn't need to be. Wasn't a person who needed favouring. But he knew who he could turn to if he needed help.

"I shan't leave you unprovided for, Babs. You could have it now, for all me."

She told him about the dance Major Dawson was going to hold at the barn.

"Will you girls be going?"

Couldn't. Hadn't got anything to go in.

Joseph was surprised to hear it. Thought the girls were pretty well turned out.

Not to go to a dance in, Barbara told him. Perhaps he

could take them to Beckthorp so they could get something suitable.

"Can't you take the trap yourselves? I don't know anything about dresses."

"We don't want you to know anything about dresses, Pa. We just want you to pay for them. So you might as well come too."

There was no point resisting. He had three good daughters, none of them a patch on their mother, but good enough in their way.

"Let me know when you want to go."

The other thing he ought to know, Barbara said, was she'd had to buy a new kettle.

"No need for you to notice it's a new one. I'll tell you the story one day."

"Just as you say, Babs."

The kitchen door was barged open. Maudie came in backwards, dumped a basket of apples on the table.

"Whatever's that awful stink?"

Pig's head, Muriel told her. In the saucepan.

Maudie went closer, peered at it.

"Aren't going to eat it, are you?"

"You've always liked brawn well enough."

"Is that what it's made of?"

Muriel raised a finger. "Thought I heard the tumbril."

"What time's he coming?"

"Not till the cakes are done, I hope."

Maudie leaned closer, looked up at her sister. "You love Stanley, don't you? I can tell by your face."

"Love?" Muriel tried not to look pleased at the word. "Don't you get your hair in my cooking."

"And Stanley loves you. Doesn't he. Don't deny it."

Muriel mixed rice and bread crumbs together in the bowl, wiped her fingers, added sage and seasoning. She seemed so content, doing ordinary things. And Barbara, milking cows and making butter as if it was all there was to do in life. Her Pa was the same. Her own life was *empty*. She worked all day long, but only at what she was told to do, not at what she wanted to do.

Already dark. Wasn't even winter. Nights were going to get longer and darker, life was going to get duller and duller. For months. Nothing to do indoors. No-one to talk to. The bitches had their own lives and her Pa had his, all wrapped up. What did they think about, all those hours working? What did they want to happen?

Muriel added pig's blood from a jug, stirred a spiral of crimson into the whiteness.

Maudie sniffed.

"Everything is blood in this house. Blood and more blood. Makes me feel sick!"

Muriel scraped the mixture out into a couple of baking tins. Then she took the cakes out, left them on one side to cool, put the tins in the oven

"Everybody's full of blood," Maudie said. "Old people, little babies – full of horrible blood."

Muriel put the dishes and cooking things in the sink, poured hot water over them from a saucepan.

"You *always* look happy!" Maudie told her. "Even when you're washing up! I wish I was like you."

"I wish you were, Maudie."

Maudie took her sister's arm, waited till she turned and looked at her.

"What did our Mother die of?"

Muriel's face changed. She shot a glance at the door between them and the dairy where their father was.

"Why do you ask?"

Maudie turned away. "I knew you'd be like that."

"Like what?"

"Nobody talks about it, how she died."

"You know how she died. It was an accident with a knife. You know that!"

Muriel washed a bowl up, then some cutlery.

"Died of shortage of blood?"

Muriel didn't reply.

Maudie took the cloth, dried the bowl and cutlery.

Always the same: something you wanted to know about, bitches never talked about it. Boring things they'd talk about all the time.

"Can't we have another lamp?" she asked. "It's as dark as a pit here."

Wasn't enough paraffin, her sister said. Because of the war.

"Not enough coal, not enough oil, not enough food -"

"I managed to get a box of matches in Beckthorp," Muriel said.

"They should keep us warm, I must say!"

Muriel and Barbara – couple of old hens – scratching at a piece of land till it was bare, like old women at a jumble sale picking over second hand clothes, clucking over something as if it was going to change their lives. She'd never get like that. Would if she stayed on the farm! She'd turn into an old hen and see nothing but other old hens till the day she died.

"That's why I opened the letters!"

"What did you say!" Muriel was seeing to a saucepan that had come to the boil. "What did you say about the letters?" She put the lid over the firehole, slid the saucepan back.

33

Maudie dug her nails into her temples. If there was enough pain she could forget she lived in a place where a poor old pig had had its throat cut, and no-one let you do what you wanted to do, and her mother was no longer there to say she loved you. The harder you dug your nails in, the better, because pain was better than emptiness.

Her wrists were wet but she couldn't stop the tears even when Muriel told her she'd make her face bleed and Stanley would be here any minute. She wanted someone to make her heart feel better, but Muriel was only a sister.

"What *have* you done to your face!"

Muriel wiped her forehead and fluffed the hair over her forehead so the marks hardly showed.

"You're a funny one," she said, and patted her head and told her to go and dab her eyes in cold water.

By the time she had dried them Stanley's horse and tumbril had pulled up outside.

Muriel opened the door.

"Maudie'll give you a hand."

Stanley was seeing to the horse. He didn't want one of Maudie's hands, he said, he'd got two of his own. It made Maudie laugh so much Muriel handed her a basket and told her to take it out and fill it with wood. Then their Pa came out, and Stanley spent his time talking to him instead.

They backed the horse, tipped the sawn wood off the tumbril outside the woodshed. Joseph wouldn't hear of them stacking it at this time of night. He'd just have a couple of basketfuls indoors in case it rained.

Maudie brought them in, heaped the logs either side of the fireplace, put one on the fire to boil the kettle

"You mind you don't do too much, Stanley Chatham," Muriel warned, looking out of the door at the great heap of wood he'd brought. And when she heard him catch his breath as he sat down she said, "Ploughing all day and now loading all this wood!"

Stanley said he was as sound as a bell. "Show you the scar if you like."

Muriel asked if he'd like a cup of tea. "Got a brand new kettle, Stanley. As you can see!"

No-one actually looked at Maudie, but she felt they all knew about it.

"More than you can say about farming, Stanley," Joseph said. "Can't say that's as sound as a bell."

Talk turned to the depressed state of agriculture and the farms up for sale. Howlett's was the latest, Stanley had heard. The bank wouldn't give them any more time. And corn down to seventy-one shillings a quarter, whereas last year it was seventy-six – yet there was less corn this year.

"America." Joseph blew on the tea in his saucer. "They grow good corn, bring it all the way here – still sell it cheaper than ours."

"They say wages are going up next year," Stanley said.

"If there's anyone left to pay them."

"Don't think they care about that."

Joseph finished his saucerful, poured another. As usual the girls left farm chat to the men, and as usual farm chat was depressing. When Maudie heard *they say* in a conversation she knew things were going to turn gloomy, as if *they* were a gang of robbers. Tonight *they* felt close. The other side of the door. In the dark.

Joseph finished his tea. Time for him to do his nightly round of the buildings. When he'd gone the mood room turned more cheerful.

"We got the invitations, Stanley," Muriel said. "Thank you."

Maudie expected to hear them tell him how she'd opened her sisters' letters. But all Muriel said was, "I think the three of us would like to go."

"We'll have to squash up together, then."

Muriel gave him one of her disapproving looks. "That'd just suit you, Stanley Chatham, wouldn't it?"

Barbara called her into the dairy, asked her if Stanley would like a bit of fresh butter to take back with him.

While she was gone Stanley murmured, "Someone'll be pleased to see you at the dance, Maudie."

"Me?"

"Got a moustache. Just come home!" He winked. "Between me and you."

"Me!"

"I could tell." He gave her another wink. "True!"

Muriel and Barbara came in.

"You'll have to get the milking done early that night, Barbara," he said. "Or put clothes pegs on them cows of yours. Turn the old things cross-eyed."

Maudie laughed, could hardly stop laughing. She felt lighter, even the lamp seemed brighter. She loved Stanley, she loved her sisters, all the world.

*Someone'll be pleased to see you...*

She remembered the day. He'd come home in his pony trap past the top of their roadway. He'd raised his hat. Smiled. Then he'd gone. But his lovely brown eyes! Moustache! The way he'd smiled!

*Be pleased to see her at the dance!*

She sat up on her chair the way she thought *he'd* sat. Smiled a little, returned *his* smile, inclined her head slightly, like you would to a gentleman. Not like a country bumpkin. But graciously. Like so.

"Whatever is the girl at *now!*" Barbara said.

They were all looking at her.

She faced them back. She'd never tell them. They'd never see inside her head. It was different now. Somebody loved her. Life had been dull and now it was bright. The Major had been away, but as soon as he was home he had noticed her. Life was going to be different now.

And because it was different, because she was going to leave these bitches soon, she gave them a wave. Just lightly, with her fingers. Like saying farewell. Goodbye! Like so.

Barbara gave her a look enough to fry her, but with company present she talked about Mrs Dawson, how peculiar she was, going about in an old coat anyone would think she'd found on a heap.

"What the Major must think, God only knows!"

Maudie found herself agreeing with her. That silly old fool of a woman didn't deserve a husband like the Major. Nobody did. Except herself.

# CHAPTER 7

Miriam Whatling laid them out on the attic floor. Had to be laid in rows on newspaper, close together but not touching. She loved the patterns they were forming, green apples, yellow apples, red apples, pretty as a picture. She'd never done any painting, never held a brush, but one day – if things turned out right.

She emptied the basket, sat back on her heels. The attics were oak floored, doors fitted snugly into their frames, the rafters, good sound timber – and all the place was used for was to store apples! She and Raymond had to store everything they owned in a few boxes under the table.

She loved the view from the window, willows round the pond, fields stretching away for miles, farms, cattle, the clusters of cottages – and all of it the property of other people! Every place in Suffolk *belonged* to someone, every lane, every hedge, even the verges beside the road, – and she and Raymond didn't own single blade of grass. But one day – if things turned out right!

She came away the window. Tongues would ask who *Miriam Nobody* thought she was, gawping out of the Hall windows as if she was *Lady Somebody*! There was gossip enough about them already, what with her funny eye and big nose – and the silly remarks Raymond came out with. *"Huh?"* he'd say after every remark. *"Huh?"* as if he'd said something clever. If he ever said anything only half sensible it was like a miracle.

She was happy here at the Hall, here up in the loft on her own. When she was with Raymond she had to listen to what he'd said a hundred times before.

The Major was bringing up the next load of apples. Miriam pictured him coming up the servants' stairway, crossing the landing below and up the stairs to the attic. The thought of him approaching pleased her, what with his good looks and his quick way of doing things.

The door opened, Richard backed in, put the basket down and tossed her a cushion.

"Don't want you to spoil your knees!"

He left the full basket with her, took the empty one away. How inept, she thought, not thanking him, not making conversation.

She worked quickly, gave each apple a wipe with a cloth, planted it in its row, and by the time the Major brought the next lot up she'd emptied the basket.

"They look nice," he said. "You seem to make the best of everything."

He stood the basket down for her to take. The handles were warm from his grip.

"Hard work, I expect, Major? Up all those stairs."

"Not when I can see a nice young woman at the top, it isn't."

She liked the way he said it, liked the way he smiled.

She asked how the preparations for the dance were progressing.

"Pretty well," he said. "You and Raymond will be there, I trust?"

She seemed doubtful.

"I hope you will," he said. "Everyone'll be there."

"*I'd* go. It's just that Raymond -"

She didn't know what to say about Raymond, didn't want to be unkind about him.

Richard knelt beside her, touched her arm. "He's got to be there. You can get round him – young woman like you."

He got to his feet, took the empty basket. "I shall want a dance, you know."

The door swung shut behind him. She heard his footsteps down the stairs, hoped he'd soon come back. She set to work, knelt on the cushion the Major had thrown her, held apples he'd held.

*"Shall want a dance, you know!"*

His face close as in dancing, his round brown eyes, his clipped moustache.

"Be for you too, Raymond," she promised. A thought she didn't articulate was that it might benefit Raymond more if he *didn't* go to the dance.

In the shed at the edge of the orchard Rose was sorting apples brought in by the pickers.

"Blemished," she'd pronounce every now and then to an apple, dropping it in the cider sack. "No mercy for you." When Richard arrived, his basket empty, she was telling the better ones, "You're the chosen ones. Judgement Day for those who fail."

There'd been a time when Richard would have worried about her – but not now. Sometimes she was like a child, upset if a bird seemed to be missing of a morning, pleased as punch if she came across someone's old hat in a ditch; other times he wondered if it was a facade, that she was goading him, trying to make him lose patience. He didn't care. To the Hall, the barn and the land behind it, to Rose herself, he felt he was beginning to say good-bye. Yet the thought that this might be his last season for storing apples made him catch his breath.

"Not tiring, are we?" Rose asked. A couple more bramleys filled the basket. The next half dozen went in the cider sack.

"You're the one doing the work," he told her. "Making the decisions."

He heaved the basket up and set off. After a step or two he looked back to estimate how many more basketfuls he might have to carry. Rose happened to be looking at that new watch. He was surprised she treasured it. He felt more tender towards her.

He climbed the stairs, reached the attic, swung round to open the door with his back. Miriam, hearing his approach, swung the door open to save him having to push it, and suddenly having nothing to check his momentum he lurched backwards. Miriam tried to save him and the two of them fell, Richard still gripping the basket to save the apples.

They landed on the floor. Still hugging the basket he turned to see how she was, found himself kissing her and being kissed back.

They were apart, startled. She touched her mouth.

"Oh Major!" she gasped. "Thank you!"

He put the basket down, took her hand.

"I do beg your pardon."

She turned away. Her mouth! Her servant's hand!

He took the empty basket, went downstairs.

He was in the shed before Rose heard him. Saw her checking her watch, realised she was timing him.

"You pass," she suddenly told some apples. "And you. And you. Fail *you*."

But he knew she had resumed, that it was part of some game.

She was aware of his quicker breathing.

"Getting tired, are we?

"Had a bit of a fall on the threshold."

He filled another basket, wound his way upstairs again. Part of him hoped Miriam wouldn't be there, wished the kiss hadn't happened. He had the sensation of climbing through a house he didn't really own, of climbing out of a marriage he ought never to have got into, yet part of him regretted what he was doing, whether he wasn't letting himself down thinking of a servant woman. But when he got to the attic, with its cosiness and emptiness and its smell of apples, and when he saw Miriam kneeling there, her arms bare because of the warmth under the pantiles, her hands polishing and placing the apples so easily and quickly, at the sight of her his doubts vanished.

She didn't turn, didn't acknowledge him, kept her face averted, her attention on apples.

He rested the basket on the floor, knelt beside her, let his fingers caress her bare arm.

She shivered. "We mustn't," she whispered.

"Is your life so wonderful?"

He let his hand rest on her back, felt her body move as she worked.

"You know it isn't," she said.

He touched her neck where the dress hung away at the top, let his fingertips move over her neck, her throat.

She stopped. Seized his hand, held it tight to her. She turned, looked at him with the eye that held him in focus.

"What's the matter?" he whispered.

"You're a gentleman. I'm only – !"

It was what she had heard from mother and grandmother, the centuries-old warning to keep to her class.

He picked up the emptied basket, leaned across and kissed her neck.

"Major!"

It was a whisper, mostly appalled. But its excitement echoed under the cobwebby pantiles, across the dust on the floorboards.

Richard Dawson, aware he was being timed, that note was taken of his breathing, didn't sing as he went downstairs. He'd fallen through a door Miriam had opened, was falling out of his old life, didn't know where he would land.

# CHAPTER 8

A feature of the farmhouse, that old semi-circular tank, like half a hollow wheel. In its time it had held water to house a whetstone for sharpening ploughshares and other things. Now it was used as a water tank for washing people and other things. And now it was in need of a repaint.

"Mind you scrape it down well," Barbara told her. "Then rub it down and brush it clean."

She showed Maudie the paint tin, full of brown stuff.

"You'll have to stir it till the white comes through the oil," Barbara added. "And keep stirring till it all turns white. If you don't, it'll be brown – then you'll have to do it all over again."

"Thank you for telling me," Maudie said. "I want to do it ever so well."

As a further encouragement Barbara added, "You'll want to put an old pinny before you start. And don't get any paint round your mouth or it'll kill you because it's got lead in it. But that's up to you."

"Oh, Barbara, I'm so glad you told me. It's ever so kind of you."

"Oh, is it! The brushes and paint are in that shed, back of the barn."

"I'm really going to make a good job of it, specially for you, Babs."

"And you'd better get a move on or it'll be dark."

"I'm so glad to have a chance to help you, Babs."

"Don't you come Little Miss Goody-Goody with me, my girl!"

Barbara stared at her. But when she went back hours later the tank had been cleaned, the front was as white as a patch of snow.

"I'm really enjoying painting this, " Maudie told her. "I want to blot out all the bad things I've done."

"Good! I"ll have to see what else you can do."

"Anything to help you, Babs."

The garden was on the south side of the house, the air was warm. When she'd finished the front of the tank she started on the side. Difficult to get to, under the curve under the tank. But it was more private. And because it was hidden she daubed M D for Major Dawson, and above it a heart and kisses.

A movement caught her eye. A young woman in a loose dress and purple-red cardigan was at the gate in the box hedge.

Everyone knew about the Whatlings. Lived in a poky little rented place – and now this Miriam Whatling had gone and got herself a place at the Hall. Maudie hated her, hated that this woman's feet walked on floors the Major walked on, her hands cooked the food the Major ate. Couldn't bear to look at her, couldn't take her eyes off her, this woman – that great nose – that eye that looked in the ditch. She wriggled further under the tank, hoped she wouldn't be noticed.

Miriam unhitched the gate, walked across.

"Excuse me, Miss Stelfox. Is the other Miss Stelfox in the dairy?"

"I should think so. She lives in it."

Miriam knocked and went in. Maudie wriggled out, left the brush and paint pot against the wall, peered through the window.

Barbara was knocking Miriam up half a pound of butter, smiling and chatting as if they were old friends. As she always did when she'd got a customer!

"Mrs Dawson leaves it to me what to get," Miriam Whatling was saying. "You know how it is -"

Barbara seemed to know exactly how it was, seemed to know how a lot of things were.

Miriam paid, left with the butter.

Barbara caught sight of her. "Have you seen your clothes, you little fool?"

Her pinny had come undone, the front of her dress was smeared with white paint.

"Must have been that Miriam Whatling. I did the rest all right. She'd put a spell on anything."

"Drew a heart with an arrow through it!" she heard Barbara telling Muriel later. "What are we to do with her!"

Next day the weather was raw. The wind was northerly, the air damp, too cold to snow, people said, the sort of cold that got into your bones.

She hardly spoke, ate what she was given, wore what they told her to wear. She didn't care about the cold, set about painting the tank till her hands ached.

When she'd finished she made her way across the fields into Church Lane and the churchyard. She knelt beside her best friend in the world, the headstone on her mother's grave. She could talk to her mother and know she was listening, tell her things that were going wrong, and know her mother would say, "Never mind, little dreamer. It'll all be all right."

Like she used to – before –

Before what?

She knew what before. Dreaded it coming out into the daylight. Wanted it to sleep in the darkness at the bottom of her mind.

"Let it lie there!" she prayed. "At peace there!"

"Maudie! Is that you?"

Muriel's voice cut like a whip.

Maudie turned back to the headstone, whispered, "Help me, Mummy. Help me get away."

"Must be out of your mind! Almost dark! Out here without a coat! Must be perished!"

Maudie blew her mother a kiss, drew a kiss on the headstone with her finger.

Muriel took her arm, pulled her away. Maudie looked at her as if at someone she used to know.

"Good bye, Muriel."

Muriel stared. "You want to come in and have something to eat, my girl. You're frozen through."

"Won't have to put up with me much longer, Muriel. Be better when we're strangers."

Muriel let go her arm as if she was already a stranger.

"What are you talking about, child!"

"I don't want to be a trouble," Maudie said. "You'll get on better without me."

"Talk so daft. I've just been and got the dresses."

As if ordering dresses and collecting dresses was another chore.

Maudie, suddenly all smiles, climbed into the trap. "Do they fit?"

"That's what we've got to find out," Muriel said. "Or back they go to Mrs Beckett. Can't make out what you were doing hanging about in the churchyard."

"Talking to Mother. Didn't know you'd gone to get the dresses."

"Because you don't listen."

Muriel shook the reins at Dainty. The trap rolled forward. Maudie looked up and down the lane as if people were already crowding towards the barn, as if she might get a glimpse of Major Dawson. And because it would only be a matter of days before she did, she put her arm round her sister.

"I'm sorry to be such a trouble to you both, Muriel. Won't be for much longer."

# CHAPTER 9

There was music from a crimson-horned gramophone, the threshing floor was cleaned and polished for dancing, there were rows of lanterns on the wall studs in the flint-brick wall, and although the cathedral loftiness of rafter and beam remained in shadow, at lantern level and below all was light and cheerfulness. There were chairs from the Hall, there were tables loaded with cakes and sandwiches, teacups and glasses, there were jugs of lemonade, a barrel of cider and a barrel of ale, there was a platform for the musicians with the piano in position, and lanterns either side of the entrance lit the way for the parishioners of St Matthew's and neighbouring parishes. It was Hallowmas Eve, the night of the dance.

Come seven o'clock country roads and lanes were rumbling with people making their way on foot, by pony trap, by omnibus. Well might the start of the dance have been advertised as seven thirty; as soon as the populace was ready it was on the move. Some might have had milking or feeding to detain them, most did not. No sooner were they washed and changed than they were on their way, dozens of vehicles had parked, a crowd of people stood chatting, joking, smoking outside the barn in the excitement of standing about in their Sunday best in the company of others on this unusual night.

Stanley drew up, tethered the pony, helped Muriel out of the trap. Then Barbara. When it was Maudie's turn her new tight dress caused her to stumble into Stanley's arms and had to be lifted down, at which she giggled and tossed her head at her sisters to show she didn't care what they thought.

People of importance arrived, were let inside: Mrs Cousins and Mrs Bailey who did the tea, young Fred Barber, son of the landlord of the Kings Head who had supplied the ale, Jimmy Catchpole the shoemaker who was acting as MC for the evening, the Reverend and Mrs Jackson who were doing the music. And Walter Leggett.

"Who does Walter Leggett think he is?" Barbara wanted to know.

"You should know," Muriel told her. "You're the one who talks to him."

"No more than I can help. He's said nothing to me."

Attention turned to Stanley.

"Stanley Chatham," Muriel demanded. "What have you heard about Walter?"

"They say," Stanley coughed, cleared his throat,"Well, you saw as well as I did what he took in with him."

"I saw a case on his shoulder."

"They say," Stanley spoke with a certain carefulness, "it's an accordion."

"Who for? Walter Legget can't play an accordion!"

"They say – he can. Picked it up real quick."

"They say! They say!" Muriel mimicked. "Who're all these they says?"

"Well, that I can't say."

For which he endured a cuff on the arm from his lady love.

There wasn't a queue, but people took their turn, bought their tickets from Fat Tydeman and his wife at the door. Maudie and Barbara had their own money, but a squeeze on the shoulder from Stanley persuaded Muriel that he and she were going as a couple. It was the first time a young man had paid for Muriel to go anywhere, and the sight of Stanley paying two shillings instead of one was romantic enough to cause her to take his arm.

Major Dawson had done well. People said it again and again, looking round at a barn they had known all their lives. The dust, the straw, the obsolete machinery, the bits of harness and ancient implements, all had been cleared out and taken away, and here was the old elm floor again, swept and polished and ready for the dance. The Major had put his back into it, they said, had done a damn good job. And seeing it was now a dance floor people kept to the sides and walked round the edge, as if what the man had done deserved respect.

The Major was at the door, chatting with the Tydemans about the sale of tickets; he was having a joke with Mrs Cousins and Mrs Bailey and their helpers at the refreshment tables; he was checking the lanterns; he was having a word with the Jacksons, seeing that her music stool was the right height and Wilfred's music stand was close enough and the lantern behind him bright enough; he was having a special word with Walter Leggett who had shown such an aptitude for the accordion. And wherever he went the gaze of a certain young face followed him, willed him to look at her. Then suddenly he turned, looked deep into Maudie's eyes across the floor. She thought he smiled, had to turn away, scarcely able to bear it that the handsomest man in the world was looking at her.

An arm round her shoulder, a voice against her ear.

"You can take your eyes off him, dear. He's married!"

Her friend Eva Briggs.

"Who ever do you mean?"

Eva laughed. "You know who I mean. I've been watching you."

The two looked into each other's eyes, young girls whose secrets over the years had travelled in whispers from this one's mouth to that one's ear.

"Did you see the way he looked at me?"

"Don't think so."

"Looked right into my eyes." Maudie held a hand to her chest. "Made me quite breathless."

Eva, her brown hair touching Maudie's black hair, their faces only inches apart, was concerned.

"Don't you go getting tangled up with a married man."

"Course I won't! What do you think I am?"

Richard Dawson made his way to an upturned beer crate beside the piano. People fell quiet. Fat Tydeman closed the outside door.

Tonight, the Major said, the dead were here in the memories of the living. Thousands of men had given their lives, many of those who had survived would never dance, never even walk again. What the families needed, what the wounded needed, was help. Whatever funds were raised tonight would go towards setting up a British Legion to give help to the wounded and to the families of those who had made the ultimate sacrifice.

He studied the slip of paper in his hand.

"I know you'd like me to mention each of our local heroes by name."

There was Will Barber, Ted Catchpole and Tom Catchpole, Jack Cousins and John Bailey, Charlie Beamish.

He completed his list of those wounded or had been killed, thanked all who had in any way contributed to the evening, and declared that the dance was about to begin. The MC took over.

The violin sounded well, the piano sounded well, and to Barbara's irritation the accordion sounded well. In fact, watching Know-all Walter Leggett swaying himself about to the dance tunes, she had to concede that it looked as if he had absolutely got the hang of the thing.

"Works on our farm," she told young Mrs Pegsby. "We often have a chat in the cowhouse."

"Wouldn't mind him helping me in the wash-house sometimes!" Oona eyed the young man up and down.

A war widow, Oona Pegsby had found her own ways of coping with bereavement, and Barbara began to wonder if she herself hadn't slightly underestimated the young man.

It was the most natural thing in the world, holding Stanley's hand in public, feeling his hand spread out across her back, his gentle pressure keeping their bodies close as they figured out how to move to the music. And pleasant enough to persuade Muriel there was no reason why the feeling should end with the dance. Nothing was said, but by the time a waltz and a foxtrot had taken them round and about the floor her mind was made up. Which meant nothing needed to be put into words.

Another matter, however, had to be put into words. In fact, her new relationship with Stanley laid a duty on her to ascertain exactly why Stanley Chatham's name hadn't been read out in the list of those who had fought in the war.

"So why didn't he mention you?" she asked, when, drinks in hand, they found themselves away from the crowd.

It wasn't inquisitiveness, it was merely that if Stanley needed help Muriel could help him better if she knew in detail what the trouble was.

Stanley had no idea what she was talking about.

"He mentioned all the others."

Stanley cleared his throat again. "Well, I spose they were killed, y' see."

"Some of them were wounded. So were you."

"You sure he missed me out? I thought he said my name too."

"You know he didn't. I want to know why."

Stanley took a swig of his lemonade. Was silent. Cleared his throat. Took another swig.

"So you told Major Dawson not to say your name?"

"I don't know as I exactly told him -"

Muriel didn't press. She had broken through. It was enough. She knew how to wait.

She stood their glasses back in the tray, her eyes clear and untroubled as a summer pond. "Might as well get our money's worth," she smiled, taking his arm. "Don't want to stand about here all night."

As naturally as if it was what she had done all her life, she led him on to the floor for a quickstep.

Couples glided, twirled and glided again, bodies close, legs intertwining, a man's cheek against a girl's cheek or lightly against her hair. Maudie felt excluded as she always felt excluded, an onlooker at the luckier ones who knew about partners and where to find them. So when a voice said, "Come on, my dear. No good standing looking at it," she was on the floor almost before she realised it was only old Mr Athorp the postman.

A strange-looking little man with a round body, a sharp face and a forehead that stretched from eyebrows to back collar stud. Not that Mr Athorp considered himself old. He took her round the floor at a lick, as if he was late on his round and had better get a move on or he wouldn't be finished by bedtime, overtaking couple after couple until the pink in his cheeks extended up his forehead and over to the little tuft of hair at the back.

"Get lots of mail from London nowadays," he confided when the dance ended. "Mostly from gals who go there to work. I say to meself, 'Another one'll be home soon. In trouble.'"

His hungry little eyes looked Maudie up and down as if there were things he could tell her if she wanted to know.

"I can always tell a gal's writing."

He had narrow cheeks, a small mouth, and large front teeth.

"Like at the Hall," he said. "If I took half a dozen letters there the whole of the war, that'd be the outside. Now the Major's back, I take half a dozen there a week."

The music resumed. She let him take her round again.

"Know who from?" she asked.

Mr Athorp leaned closer, let his fingers move down her back so he could feel its curves as she moved. "You'd be surprised."

Maudie pulled herself away. The man's teeth looked as if they had gnawed their way into many a secret. "Don't open his letters, do you?"

"Open his letters!"

Mr Athorp stopped dancing, glared at her as if he had been accused. Maudie glared back, couldn't bear to think the Major's private affairs had been looked at by this horrible little rabbit.

"Me? Open people's letters! You want to watch what you say, young lady!"

He strutted off, left her to find her own way off the floor. His forehead, she noticed, had gone quite pale. Yet she'd said no more than everyone else said.

"You'll be going to the dance, Miriam?"

Mrs Dawson had thrown open her wardrobe, was studying her dresses.

"Well, ma'am, it depends on Raymond. He's hurt his knee again. Shall you go ma'am?"

Mrs Dawson had dresses ancient and modern, had never bothered to sort them through. She gazed at them as at people she had met once or twice in the past and couldn't quite place them.

"I'm told I'm expected. Though I shouldn't have thought that was quite the word."

She brought a dress out, twirled it round and laid it on the bed. Then out came another, and another.

"I think I'd better go now, ma'am. Unless you need me?"

Another dress swirled round and lay on the bed.

*Oh my darling, mine alone, alone...*

Rose hummed the tune to herself, held a dress up to herself, did a few steps and a twirl.

"Nothing needed, Miriam. Nothing needed, thank you."

*You have never older grown ...*

"Very good then, ma'am."

Miriam went downstairs, let herself out of the house. The moon lit her way down the lane to the stile and along the footpath, yet she was uneasy at leaving Mrs Dawson. She edged round the side of the Hall, looked up at the uncurtained bedroom window. Mrs Dawson, in underclothes and a hat, moved about as if to music, smoothed a dress on a hanger down her body to see if it suited. Miriam set off home, determined to go to the dance whether Raymond would or no.

The waltz ended. Major Dawson escorted old Mrs Cousins off the floor, attentive to her advice on how to take up beekeeping and store honey, and it seemed quite by chance that he was standing next to Maudie when the next dance was announced.

It was like a dream. No man in the world was like this man. She felt as light as a spray of flowers in his arms. She felt him ease her closer, his cheek against her hair, his hand warm round her hand, she and the Major gliding away to the music, his leg glancing across hers as they turned, his hand gentle against her back.

She hardly dared look at him. But when she did, when she saw herself close to those smiling dark eyes, she knew there was no face on earth she could love as much. That he was older, or married, or came from a different class, or had been through a war, these were things her sisters would delight in pointing out, would tell her what a perfect little fool she was even to think such a crazy idea as to want to marry him, were she to tell them. Which she never would. She settled herself lightly against him, could feel the way he would turn or hesitate or surge them on to the music, could feel when to twirl away under his hand and then come close up to him again, and presently she was aware that people were looking, that some had stopped dancing to watch her and the Major dance.

"What a perfect pair!" they would be thinking. "As if they've danced together for years!"

There was little conversation between them. On the few occasions Maudie felt she had something to say the thought died on her tongue, too trifling to say to a man like the Major; for Richard it was a relief not to have to make small-talk, pretending to be interested in pigs or the weather, but just to dance with a pretty child with nothing to say.

The irony amused him. For this slip of a country girl he had organised this get-together. Not for the parish to celebrate the peace, nor to raise money for the wounded. All this effort, all the organising, merely to have a few minutes with a little country bumpkin with nothing about her except her face and figure. He almost laughed, and Maudie knew he was glad to be with her.

"Do you always go to dances on Hallowe'en?" she asked.

*Hallowe'en*!

The word recalled the trenches, men who had been alive at the end of that first October and were not alive now –

"Or are you afraid of the spirits?"

Had any single one of those who survived the war, he wondered, benefited from all that slaughter? On either side? All that effort, all that expense, all that courage – for nothing.? Those years had been the top of his life.

"Spirits?" he asked.

She seemed urgent, as if the answer was important to her.

"Have you ever seen one? A ghost I mean? Have you?"

What he had that moment seen was Miriam, standing beside a lantern the other side of the barn, the light shadowing her face.

Maudie could tell by the way he hesitated that he had.

"Was it near here? Near the church? You needn't keep it secret. I'd never tell anyone."

"Probably wasn't a ghost."

But the girl was so eager he didn't want to be dismissive. "Can't be sure about these things."

"Will you show me where you saw it?"

The face in the lantern light across the room had caught him. Miriam had come to the dance to see him, married woman that she was, servant, lover that she was. It was the old game. He couldn't resist it.

"Please?"

He disliked the girl's insistence, harping on the trivial. "Maybe later, Maudie."

The dance ended. He offered his arm, walked her off to rejoin her sisters.

"Any sign of Mrs Dawson, Miriam?"

It was the last interval of the evening. Things had gone well, people were enjoying themselves, there was still food and drink to be had, the raffle tickets had sold well. And Miriam Whatling had made herself up to look almost attractive. He was reluctant to leave her.

"Told me to come along without her, sir. Said she'd be along later."

"I shouldn't want her to miss it."

"Oh, I'm sure she'll be in, sir."

"In the meantime we may get another dance in, Miriam."

He spoke quietly, his eyes holding her eyes.

They did what people generally do at such times, fell in with groups they felt comfortable with. Farmer chatted with farmer, farmworker had a drink with farmworker, tradesman ate his sandwiches with other tradesmen. And Doctor and Mrs James, the Reverend and Mrs Wilfred Jackson and Major Dawson discussed the success of the evening. But Maudie wanted to be on her own. She slipped away from the crowd, wandered along the lane.

Hallowmas Eve. Almost a full moon. Richard would be thinking of her. Beside the pond opposite the church she sensed his spirit float like a leaf from the hedgerow, like the moonlight in the sparkle on the pond.

The water was dark, unrippled, the surface further out broken, catching the brilliance where spirits flew in the moonbeams. She raised her arms, a tree, as if she could catch at his presence in the night when he looked for her. She wished she could stand all night like the trees, bare branches raised up for a spirit to slide through as easy as moonlight.

No sign of him. He'd be desperate to see her, but he was the most important man in the parish. Everyone would be wanting to talk to him.

The moon slid amongst the clouds, washed their edges like the sea washing the beach. That was where he would be when they were apart, in the moonlight, the moon itself, not with old Mrs Dawson who was as mad as a hatter.

If only the woman would die! One day she would! One day the crowd of people who were keeping him talking would be gone, the bitches would be gone, everything that kept her and the Major apart would be gone. The door of the Hall would open, Richard and she would be arm in arm, Richard and herself, the real Mrs Dawson at last!

"Mrs Whatling. I wonder if I might have the pleasure?"

The interval was over, the music about to start. Miriam, nervous, went with him into the music. They talked a little, how well attended the dance was, how fine the night was in spite of the showery day. He asked her whether Mrs Dawson would be coming and Miriam said she thought she would be. But it was in the squeeze of his fingers against her hand, the answering squeeze against his that their conversation lay. The expression on their faces was perfectly proper, as was the distance between his cheek and her cheek – the music faltered, the accordion produced a couple of extraordinary chords, the music stopped.

Heads turned towards the door. Gasps. Walter Leggett was heard to exclaim, "Bloody wars!"

Rose Dawson had come in.

Wearing the coat she had found in the ditch.

And a hat that twenty years earlier had been the height of fashion, turned up at the back, with flowers and gauze on the crown.

The Major walked over to her.

"You've got a good crowd here, Richard."

The tone was personal, as if there were only the two of them in the room.

"I'm glad they're enjoying themselves." She sounded amused. "We all like to enjoy ourselves sometimes, don't we."

"May I take your coat?"

She turned, allowed him to take it over his arm.

"What do you think, Richard?" It was a bedroom scene, her voice scarcely raised, addressing him in the bedroom.

"Tell me whether you like it, Richard."

She was wearing a long oyster dress with a tight waist and a full lace bodice with a high neck and sleeves tight below the elbow. It was as if she had stepped out of a museum.

She twirled it a little to show it off to him, intimate, amused.

"What do you think, Richard?"

Richard, apparently unmoved, looked across to Wilfred and Jenny, his lips framing, "Waltz?"

The music under way, he offered his wife his arm, and with Rose wearing her antique hat they took the floor.

She was a good dancer. She lay back against his arm with almost a smile, as though newly in love. Other couples took the floor, but Rose was the centre of attention, sometimes poised, sometimes whirling around making a fool of the occasion.

Richard remained calm, neither amused nor annoyed, accommodating her steps.

The melody changed to *"Silver Threads Among the Gold."*

Rose removed her hat, twirled it across to the edge of the floor. Her hair was up in the late Victorian style fashionable when she was young. Suddenly she danced apart, swaying in front of him, mocking, singing to the music:

*With the roses of the May*
*I will kiss your lips and say*
*Oh! my darling, mine alone, alone,*
*You have never older grown*
*Yes, my darling, mine alone – -*

Over and over, till the words were indistinguishable in laughter.

Chairs were stacked, crockery and glasses had been put away to await collection, most of the lights were out. In the lane, except for a lantern by the door, the barn was lit only by the moon.

Rose had been escorted home by Miriam and Raymond, the one carrying her hat, the other her extraordinary coat.

The Reverend and Mrs Jackson shook hands with the parishioners as they left, thanked them for coming, wished them good night. Gradually the parish dispersed, most walking, some getting into traps or the omnibus, a few like the doctor, cranking their cars and driving away. Muriel and Stanley stood about waiting for Barbara who was collecting up a few bits of her butter that hadn't been used, Stanley happy enough with his arm round Muriel's waist and Muriel taking it for granted as if his arm had been around her waist for years.

Time passed. Barbara came out of the barn with her bundle of butter, got up into the trap.

"Where's Maudie?"

Maudie edged closer to the tree, her chance with the Major slipping away. A breeze sprang up, clouds covered the moon. Old Mrs Chatham shivered, said it was time they were getting their beauty sleep. Stanley saw his parents into their trap. As they drove off the Major happened to look in Maudie's direction.

He went across to her, shook her hand.

"Didn't go quite as planned," he murmured.

Maudie knew he meant more than he said. She wanted to comfort him for having to live with a wife trying to make a fool of him, wanted him to know who really cared about him.

"Perhaps some other time," he smiled.

At that moment the moon reappeared and lit his face. It was like a vision, as if he'd come down in glory to see his bride-to-be.

"Oh, I hope so!" she said.

He took her hand again, seemed to wait for her to say something. She wanted to tell him she would wait till he was free, would wait for him. For ever.

"Well, good night," he said.

It was only the slightest pause, but she had missed her chance.

He went over to the barn to lock up.

"What *ever* were you doing! Under a tree!"

Maudie ignored her. The trap seats were wet with dew. Muriel and Barbara buttoned their coats because of the wind getting up. Stanley shook the reins, the trap rumbled on up the lane.

"You want to do your coat up," Barbara told her. "You'll get the pip."

Maudie felt neither warmth nor cold. Why, she asked herself, why had she talked about *spirits*? Just because the word had popped into her mouth, no need to go on badgering the man to show her where he might have seen spirits! And then fall silent when she could have talked about love!

Couldn't understand it. Couldn't understand herself. She'd wasted her chance with him.

"I wish I hadn't!"

"Hadn't what?" Barbara asked, suspicious.

"Oh, I wish hadn't!" she cried in her mind. "Wish I hadn't wasted it!"

She twisted round in her seat to see the place where she'd had such hopes. The lantern by the barn door was out, the crowd had gone, the lane empty.

# CHAPTER 10

Herbert Stelfox paused at the break in the dry-stone wall. He usually paused there on his Sunday morning walk. To his left the Yorkshire moors reached away till heather became distant mist, to his right the road wound up behind the hill where sheep wedged themselves against its steepness, trying patch after patch of poor feed before finding grass worth eating. No wonder they kept an eye on him, the sheep, as if they knew he was looking at them as a butcher might, shoulders of mutton, saddles of lamb, meat to be sliced and jointed, all for the moment wrapped in wool.

He ran his tongue round his mouth, wished he was in the Hadale Arms. He longed to be at the counter, a mug of fresh-drawn beer set down in front of him. Looked forward to lifting it up, studying its golden-brown light against the window, and the moment he could put the glass to his lips and take the first long pull.

An hour to wait. Come twelve he could get in the pub, knock back a pint, knock back another, maybe three or four. He liked the company in the Arms, liked the talk, the laughs, he liked the sensation of drinking pint after pint so that come the afternoon he could sleep it off and not have to think about work, what life had come to, and what he was doing up here in Yorkshire in the first place.

It was a twenty minute walk back to the pub. He didn't want to be late, didn't want to get there early and stand about outside the pub. He liked to time it exactly, get there just as the doors opened, old Jarvis red in the face straightening up from undoing the bottom bolt and saying, "Thowt it'd be thee, young Herbert!"

He sat down, leaned back against the wall, made himself comfortable. Took out the weird little letter he'd had from Maudie. Did Herbert think she was too young to marry? Not that she was going to get married yet, of course, but if someone asked – did Herbert think she ought to say yes? Couldn't talk about it here at home, couldn't even mention it. All you could talk about here was cows and housework, what the neighbours were up to. But *what if* someone asked her? Someone she liked? Please, she begged, don't say a word, even breathe it! Or she'd run away from home, away from the bitches.

To him, Maudie was the kid she'd been when he joined up in 1914. Took an effort to realise she was five or six years older now. Still sounded like the strange little child she'd always been. Miles too young to think of marriage. Just as well there wasn't anyone suitable.

He put the letter back in his pocket, decided to walk up to the barn at the top. Then a brisk walk down would take him outside the pub just right.

At the bend near the barn a horse was cropping the grass at the side, its rider immersed in a book. Herbert crossed the road, walked the other side so as not to disturb her.

The horse sensed him, shook its ears, continued lipping the grass. Then sneezed at something against its nose.

"Morning," Herbert said.

He walked on, checked his watch. Another twenty minutes and he could set off down to the pub.

"Herbert?" The girl dismounted. Stuffed the book in her pocket. "Or are we in too much of a hurry?"

He knew her! Suddenly knew her!

"Kate?"

Her tailored riding jacket, breeches, hat, the best materials. And a figure to carry it off!

His cousin! Who used to visit Beck Farm before the war. Who he used to be sweet on!

"Kate Stelfox!"

Never a face he'd liked as much as this.

"Going somewhere nice?" she asked. "Dashing along, ignoring people."

Going up to the barn at the top, he told her.

"And then?"

"Going down again, I suppose."

"I see."

She laughed, not unkindly.

"I understood you were working in London."

Had been, she said. As a junior nanny. With a family in Belgrave Square.

"Sounds posh."

Might sound posh. But posh people had problems like the rest of us. And posh children were no nicer than poor children.

"You're home on holiday?"

She'd decided to do something else. Till then she was living at home. "And you? Still butchering?"

Still with Walter Bumford.

"Like it?"

Things were getting easier now in the meat line, he said. The government had allowed delivery rounds to be started up again after the wartime restrictions.

"So Doris Bumford's probably started calling at Werndby House for your orders."

Why, when he'd got the chance of talking to a girl he couldn't take his eyes off, did he have to make himself sound like a butcher touting for business!

"Never mind Doris Bumford. It's *you* we'd like to see. Mother says you've hardly been round since you've been up here."

He'd made a couple of visits to his aunt and uncle shortly after getting lodgings in Hadale, hadn't been since. He didn't like to tell her, couldn't stand her father, Uncle Arthur Stelfox.

"Anyone would think you didn't like us!"

It took him back to their childhood. Had always loved her, always been unable to show it. Wondered if she liked him. Been afraid to ask.

She was going to give Beauty a run on the moor, she said, as far as Riggs's farm. So if Herbert would like to walk that way Beauty would be pleased. "What's an extra three or four miles to a strong young man?"

*Or three or four hundred miles, to be with a girl like you?*

But she was a stranger now, well off, educated. He felt old, out of her class. Didn't have the nerve to tell her so.

The road curved away across the high moor, the pink and violet tussocks either side merging to a twilight of purples.

Kate shaded her eyes. "A road like that ought to lead to somewhere significant. Don't you think?"

"It has. It's led to you."

"By 'eck, lad!" she laughed.

He tried to laugh too, amazed his heart dared say such a thing.

They talked about visits her family used to make to Beck Farm before the war. Herbert recalled how on one stay she'd wake up early and get into his bed.

"Oh, I must have been an absolute infant!" she declared. "If there's even a *grain* of truth in the story."

He used to push her out of his bed with his feet, he said, but next morning she'd always be back. "Mind you," he added, "I wouldn't be so unkind now."

Kate turned her back on him, stroked the horse's nose. "Beauty!" she murmured. "What *will* he be telling us next!"

He asked her how long she was home for.

Till she could go away again and train to be a nurse.

"Couldn't you train round here?"

She wanted to get away. What would it amount to, living off her father? Wearing nice clothes, taking the horse for a walk once a day?

"What would a life like that do for me?"

"You could marry," he said. "And have children. You could have any man you wanted!"

"Herbert Stelfox! Do you hear what you're saying? *Have* a husband. *Have* children. It's all *having*. What about *doing*? What does a woman *do* with her life?"

He had nothing to say. Marvelled at the way she talked.

Kate offered him the reins. "She's very quiet."

He'd rather walk, he said. "Then I can watch you."

He watched them, a girl and her horse, wanted to look at nothing else.

It was opening time. The bar would be filling up. Old Jarvis would be wondering where he'd got to, friends would asking where he'd had got to. But, watching horse and rider going like the wind down a grass-covered slope, seeing her rein in at the bottom and turn and urge Beauty up the incline amongst the scrub and bushes, he didn't care what old Jarvis was wondering, what his friends would be saying. Kate was poised over the shoulders of the horse, her shape, her face, everything about her –

He quickened his pace, wanted to be at Riggs's driveway so as not to miss a moment of her.

The warmth, the smell of the horse as they trotted up took him back to the stable at Beck Farm after a day's ploughing, the horses tired, wanting their feed. He patted Beauty's nose, held the bridle as she got down.

"What would you have been doing if you hadn't seen me?" she asked.

Her eyes were grey rather than blue, he noticed. Her hair neither fair nor brown, more the colour of certain feathers of a kestrel he had shot recently.

"In the Hadale Arms. Trying to get drunk."

He recalled it later, the disappointment in her.

"Every Sunday?"

"If possible."

"How drunk?"

"So I can forget."

It was a new experience, having his life concentrated on, thought about.

"Forget what?"

For a moment the smell of it, the corpses, the shells – he couldn't disturb it now, even for Kate.

He stroked the horse's neck. Wiped his hands on a bit of dry grass.

"What were you reading, when I saw you back there?"

"Was it the war? What you want to forget?" she insisted.

They were walking the long way down to Hadale.

"Shouldn't be surprised."

"Wish you were in the pub now?"

He wanted to tell her the pub meant nothing compared to being with her, nothing compared with being with her.

"Not particularly."

They walked on, Herbert on the road leading the horse, Kate walking with him on the grass. The verge widened, became an open piece of grass in front of a tumbledown cowshed. They sat down on a dilapidated horse roller.

"Book of poems," she said, taking the volume out of her pocket. "Keats. I was looking at his *Ode to Autumn*."

She handed it to him.

"It's this way up."

"Don't know anything about Keats," he admitted. "Any poet, really."

She indicated the poem, he watched her lips as she read.
*Think not of them, Herbert, thou hast thy music too –*
*While barred clouds bloom the soft-dying day,*
*And touch the stubble plains with rosy hue;*
*Then in a wailful choir the small gnats mourn*
*Among the river sallows, borne aloft*
*Or sinking as the light wind lives or dies;*
*And full-grown lambs bleat from hilly bourne;*
*Hedge-crickets sing; and now with treble soft*
*The redbreast whistles from a garden-croft;*
*And gathering swallows twitter in the skies.*

She said it without a glance at the words, as if she could hear the swallows, see the colours of autumn skies.

"You know it by heart."

She pointed to the title.

"Sounded like this time of year," he agreed.

He read the poem through.

"Sad time of year, autumn. Swallows flying away. All the nice things going away. Like you."

Kate took the bridle, led the horse back to the road.

"You'll hardly have time for a sip," she said, looking at her watch. "I've kept you talking all this time. You'll never be able to drop off this afternoon."

"Never hear the end of it."

The Hadale Arms had become irrelevant. Everything was irrelevant, except Kate. But as they made their way down from the moor it was easier to chat about lighter matters, the scene around them, the little myths and jokes of family recollections.

At the bottom of the hill one road led to Werndby, the other to nearby Hadale. They said the things relations say to each other at such times, wished each other good luck, hoped it wouldn't be so long next time before they met again.

Kate mounted the horse, smiled good bye.

He stood looking up at her. He wanted to ask when he could see her again, wanted to say how much she meant to him, couldn't move his mouth to do it.

The moment passed. He raised a hand, she wheeled the horse round, trotted beyond the curve of the bushes, was out of sight. He stood still, the sound of horseshoes died. With no hurry in the world he made his way back to Hadale.

# CHAPTER 11

A morning or so after the dance Richard Dawson opened the dining-room curtains. Outside the window was a witch's broomstick, a besom broom, stabbed down into the grass.

He was outside in a moment, pulled the broom out, snapped it in halves. Pushed among its twigs a piece of card, the words ROSE DAWSON WITCH heavily scrawled in pencil.

He tore the card up, put the bits in his pocket. Took the broom pieces round to the rubbish heap he was making for the Guy Fawkes' Day bonfire and pushed them into the middle of it.

He glanced up at Rose's bedroom curtains. So far as he could make out they remained undisturbed.

# CHAPTER 12

Even those still abed knew the sound, the ringing of iron wheels up the Beckthorp road, the rumble of machines, the pulse of compressed steam. The thrashing team was on its way to Beck Farm.

Before it was properly light Joseph Stelfox watched the engine draw towards his farm gateway, the driver spinning the steering wheel ten or twenty times to set up the approach. There was a thudding of pistons, a grinding of great wheels across the road surface, then engine, drum, straw pitcher and cabin trundled between the gateposts with barely a hand's thickness to spare either side. Joseph marvelled at the skill of a man who could nurse the monsters through with such judgement; and marvelled also that he could summon such a caravan to his farm. It was an annual event, yet Joseph still tingled with wonder at seeing the great red drum, the yellow straw pitcher with its endless belt of spikes, the blue sleeping cabin, and the engine itself sweating steam and smoke and drawing the whole huge outfit past the farmhouse and down to the stackyard. It seemed like a touch of the fairground.

Once in the stackyard, Tom, the driver and owner of the outfit, positioned the drum so that when its sides were raised to form a platform at the top it could receive sheaves from the wheatstack which were fed into the vent and thrashed. Thrashing produced four products: corn, be it wheat, barley or oats, which poured out heavy and golden from the drum via a spout into sacks; chaff, the light crisp husk of the seed, which rushed out into more sacks the other side of the drum; coulder, or poor quality damaged straw which was strewn out loose in huge quantities from the drum by means of a sideways-shaking shelf; and finally long, yellow, good quality straw which was conveyed up the great straw pitcher or elevator erected to whatever height the forming straw stack required. Tom's job was to see that everything went properly, and see to the running, fuelling and watering of the steam engine and the proper working of drum and pitcher. When, some days later, the threshing was completed it would be his job to guide his caravan safely off the farm to his next place of work. After all of which he might have to wait months or years for the farmer to be minded to pay the bill.

The last and smallest vehicle of the outfit was the cabin, a simple four-wheeled vehicle with a bunk and coal-fired stove. This cabin was for Henry.

Local girls had heard of Henry. Short, well-built, with a saucy face and humorous eyes, Henry lived for work, drink, and women. He had the sort of reputation that made young men grin, young women glance a knowing glance at other young women, and older women declare that Henry was no good to anyone. Older men, in the interests of a peaceful life, generally ventured no opinion at all about Henry.

Tom turned the engine round to face the drum, looped a huge metal and fabric belt from the engine flywheel to the flywheel of the drum, another belt from the drum to the straw pitcher, checked that there was a man for the chaff and coulder, another to sack the corn, a couple to pitch sheaves to the drum from the corn stack, two or three to stack the straw, and a man and a waggon to take the corn to the barn. And finally there was the feeder, the man on whose work the entire process depended. It was the feeder's job to receive the sheaves on the top of the drum from the corn stack, sever the twine holding the sheaf together and feed sheaf after sheaf through the vent to the blades beneath. However fast the sheaves were fed in, the drum was always hungry for more. It was the feeder's job to work at breakneck speed hour after hour to supply it without a pause. That feeder was Henry. He was as good and fast a feeder as any in East Anglia, and Tom knew it.

So he paid him over the odds for his work, and turned a blind eye to other matters.

Walter Leggett was the man who should have kept an eye on another matter, but it wasn't till a waggon wheel started squeaking that they noticed how hot the hub was. They found it hadn't been greased for ages, and then they found there wasn't so much as a dab of grease in the can in the barn.

"Axle grease?" Walter jeered. "I don't bother about damned old axle grease."

Maudie was sent with a canful up to the barn. The quickest way was across the meadow, but what with the smoke and steam and noise she preferred to go through the stackyard.

Time for elevenses. The machinery slowed, the flywheel came to a stop, the engine sighed itself into something like silence. Men made their way behind a stack to relieve themselves, then sat the other side out of the wind to eat their bread and cheese and swig their bottle of cold tea. Walter Leggett, chaff and coulder man for the next couple of days, spat a mouthful of dust and tea out into the straw, belched, took another swig.

"Seen Pa?" Maudie asked him.

Walter nodded towards the engine where Joseph was having a word with Tom. Maudie transferred the can to her other hand and walked on. She had a message for her father from her sisters, but it would do on the way back.

"Seen Pa, la-di-da?" Walter mimicked.

But Henry was on his feet, catching her up.

"I'll carry that for you, my love," he called.

His hands were warm. It was easy to let him carry it.

"It's to go up the top barn."

"You just tell me where you want it."

Everything about Henry was warm. His eyes looked into her, friendly eyes – like his face and his saucy turned-up nose. She liked him, felt she had known him ages. He wasn't a wet blanket, always saying no to whatever you wanted to do.

"Doing your good deed for the day, Henry?" someone asked.

"Hope to," he said. The others laughed.

She liked it, the way Henry made the men laugh. Everyone liked Henry.

Away from the shelter of the stacks the wind was keen. What leaves there were shivered in the hedge, but Henry's hand was warm on her arm.

"Aren't you hungry?" Maudie asked. "Didn't you want your elevenses?"

"Shouldn't mind a little nibble."

"Shouldn't think you would," Maudie said. "Pa says it's hard work up on that drum."

Henry hurried her along the ruts of the cart track, his hand on the inside of her arm, the back of his hand interested in the curve of her breast.

"No wonder you keep warm," she said. "You go so fast."

"Who's been telling you about me?"

She loved it, the way she could make him laugh, how light-hearted he was, and she loved the way he made her laugh. She didn't care what her sisters said. She was going to do what *she* wanted to do.

It was a traditional East Anglian barn, with tarred claylump walls and a pantile roof, and double doors facing south. These looked towards fields where there wasn't a soul in sight, but Henry pulled the doors to, just in case.

When her eyes adjusted to the darkness the barn was lit by streaks of light from the roof where tiles had slipped from their battens.

"Where do you want it then, Maudie?"

"Over there."

He made out a bench littered with tools, bits of tumbril wheels, broken metal tyres, stuff collected over the years and kept lest one day it came in handy. Beside the bench, on a couple of brick supports, a solid stone slab. Here stood paraffin, cans of lubricating oil, an empty grease can, the floor around stained with the drips and spillages of years.

Henry dumped the can up on the slab, rubbed his hands on his sleeves to get the dirt off, all the time looking her up and down as she'd never been looked at before

She was excited, wanted to laugh.

"What do you want?"

"You know what I want. Same as you do."

She felt his hands on her back, her bottom, her body drawn to his body, drawn close, his lips on her lips. His searching mouth, unshaved chin on her neck, her throat. She gasped for breath, excited. Knew what she didn't know she knew.

The engine in the stackyard started into life, the steam whistle shrieked. Henry gave her a squeeze on the bottom and made for the door.

"Come and see me tonight," he whispered. "About eight."

She rearranged her clothes. What her sisters would say! She imagined the look on their faces – but one way or another she'd find a way to get out and see him tonight.

She made herself useful, helped Barbara clean the separator, helped Muriel wash the eggs, then surprised them by announcing she was going outside to see if there were any eggs she'd missed when she collected them earlier. She thought she'd heard a fox last night, wanted to make sure it didn't steal any.

Muriel and Barbara looked at each other.

"What's come over her?" Muriel wondered. "Turned over a new leaf?"

Barbara sniffed. "Some hopes!"

Maudie searched. Filled a basket, knew there were plenty she hadn't bothered to look for other nights.

"God knows how old some of these eggs are!" she thought.

The other side of the hedge in the stackyard a couple of men were pulling a tilt over the newly-made strawstack to keep the dew off. The wind cut through the hedges, hurrying smoke and sparks away from the funnel of the steam engine. In his cabin Henry stoked the shovelful of coals he had brought across from the engine furnace, threw in new coal to bring the cabin fire to cheerfulness.

The last of the men were setting off home.

A cockerel stalked over the flattened soil, picked up a morsel, dropped it at Maudie's feet. Then strutted away, comb and lobes glowing in the twilight.

Smoke from the banked-up furnace of the engine drifted out of the smoke stack. It smelt of iron, of men.

It was starlight. She shivered, pulled her coat close. Bits of straw crackled underfoot, great shadows from the machines darkened the stackyard, the engine hissed, there was a smell of smoke and metal. Dust hung in the air, mingled with thoughts of Henry.

His cabin half-door was open, a figure leaning out, smoking. Behind him light flickered from the fire inside.

"Someone there?"

"Me," she whispered.

He came down, squeezed her arm.

"Knew you'd come."

She was in his arms.

"Let's go in," he whispered.

She stiffened. Hung back.

"I mustn't."

"Course you must."

He held her, kissed her as she turned away, kissed her neck, her cheek. Her heart thumped like a rabbit's, knowing what going up the steps would lead to, wanting to, afraid to.

"Mustn't."

His lips were close to her ear. He smelt like an unwashed animal, coaxing her.

"Only for a minute. Warm in here."

She hesitated.

"Watch out for the dust." He swept her coat away from the steps and ironwork, kept it clean as she went up.

"Only for a minute," she insisted.

He closed both halves of the door behind them. The glow from the fire under the stove lit the low curved roof, flickered on the pinewood sides and the bit of newspaper he had fixed over the window. She sat on the bunk beside him, told herself she wasn't going to lie down, but he knew her body better than she did. All afternoon she had longed to be with him, and when the newspaper slipped down off the window and he got out to fix it up again she longed for him to be back with her. She eased herself to the wall to give him room beside her.

"Maudie!"

Muriel's voice.

Almost into the stackyard.

Maudie sat up. Was off the bunk.

"Maudie! You're wanted."

Henry swore, told her to ignore it. But she was at the door, pushing her feet into her shoes.

"Mind your coat, then," he whispered. He eased the door open. When she'd slipped out he opened the top door for a smoke.

She ran to the strawstack, came round the other side as if to search the hedge, saw the shape of someone near the straw pitcher.

"Why, Muriel!" she exclaimed. "Is that you!"

Her sister hurried towards her.

"Where *ever* have you been, girl! It's the police!"

The firelit cabin, the bunk bed, Henry himself, all became a whirl, a dream she had just woken up from. She was back in the real world, her sister nagging her, something frightening about to happen.

# CHAPTER 13

They were waiting for her when she went in, Barbara, her Pa, Stanley. And PC Philips.

"Says she was looking for a fox," Muriel said. "Something's been taking the eggs."

"Fox!" Barbara scoffed. "I haven't seen anything of a fox!"

"Fox took one of our turkeys last week," Stanley said.

They were in the living-room. The table had been cleared, washing up taken out to the kitchen. Joseph was in his armchair by the fire, his daughters and Stanley around at the table. PC Philips sat in front of the dresser on which his helmet rested as if it was on duty, black, stern, the badge facing into the room.

Muriel and Maudie sat down like a couple of children late for school. The room was different with the policeman in it. The armchair he sat in, the end of the table he was sitting at seemed his territory, hostile ground in their own house.

Something terrible had happened. He'd got to go round all the parish. To every house. Someone had got questions to answer!

He stared at the family as if waiting for them to own up. Maudie wondered how he could be so nasty about it, walking into someone's house and talking as if he had the right to suspect everybody, whoever they were.

"Was anyone here in St Matthew's church today?"

He waited, eyed each of the daughters in turn.

"Hardly got time to go on a Sunday," Barbara said. "Let alone on a weekday."

The policeman ignored her.

"Or yesterday?"

Again the scrutiny, this time including the men.

He sounded impatient, took out his notebook and pencil. Made a note of the time and the people present.

"You all sure about that? No-one been in the church today or yesterday?"

Another pause. As if he waited long enough someone was going to confess. But Maudie wasn't going to confess anything, not to PC Philips or anyone else. What a fool he looked, sitting there with that purple dent all round his head where his helmet came off, the top of his head pale and bald, his great pig chin all red and veiny.

"Something happened?" Joseph asked.

"What's happened, Mr Stelfox, is a baby was found there this afternoon. Dead."

It was what he liked about his job, frightening people, making out he knew more than he was letting on, terrible details they hadn't better know about.

"Dead?"

"Dead and cold, Mr Stelfox. Wrapped in a newspaper."

"Whereabouts in the church?" Stanley asked.

"Wrapped in newspaper, Mr Chatham. And placed on the altar."

"How old was it?" Maudie asked.

"Ah!" He shifted on his chair and studied her. "I'm glad you asked." He sounded as if she was the very one he wanted to question. "The baby was new born, Miss. Wouldn't know a young lady who's been expecting lately, would you?"

Maudie thought of her friends. Thought of Henry. Hoped she hadn't blushed. Stare at her as he might, and wait as long as he might, PC Philips got no response. Her clear eyes had weathered many a storm from Barbara and Muriel.

He cleared his throat, said he hoped she didn't have to find out later what the penalty was for concealing information.

"Strange thing to ask," he said, "anyone here know anything about witchcraft? Anyone here – think they're a witch?"

"Plenty o' tales of witches," Stanley said. "But a dead baby on the altar! Something damn strange there."

Maudie pictured one of her friends – and a screwed-up little face – but the girl and the babe had gone away, and the girl had come back alone.

"What about that old Mrs Barnes?"

"Dead, Muriel," Stanley told her. "Died last night."

"There's that Mrs Dawson -" Maudie said.

A look from her Pa silenced her.

"Up at the Hall you mean!" The policeman busied himself with his notebook and pencil. "I may be back later." It sounded like a threat. "More in this than meets the eye." He lifted his helmet off the dresser.

Policeman, notebook and helmet had gone, but the thought of a new-born babe, dead, alone and in a cold church, stayed with them.

The view from Maudie's bedroom window of a daytime was of the garden, the stackyard and the meadow that fell away towards the beck. Now, with only stars for light, Maudie gazed across to the stackyard. She caught the smell of the engine, the drift of a coal fire. Sometimes a spark or two from the smokestack rose, glowed, slipped away into the night.

The events of the evening throbbed through her, raised goose pimples on her skin. Her mind raced with images – the firelight, her shadow and Henry's on the pinewood sides of the cabin, Henry on the bunk with her. She closed her eyes, gave herself back to sensations she had scarcely dreamed of, realised she was panting, the palms of her hands damp on the window sill. Recalled Henry helping her into the cabin, her protests at getting into the bunk with him – that weren't protests at all – how she lay there, Henry lying on her.

Then that voice!

*Maudie! Wherever are you!*

That was the finish of it. Whatever she did that was nice, her sisters were always the finish of it.

*Maudie! Where have you got to?*

She could have cried with disappointment, rearranging her clothes, racing to open the door before Muriel got closer. And then – she saw it all in a memory – that piffling little – thing! On the shelf where he kept his food! Her eyes had got used to the darkness in the cabin, saw it clear. Half a small cheese!

It hadn't registered at the time because of scrambling out of the cabin before Muriel caught her. But something Barbara had been moaning about that morning disentangled itself, about a bit of cheese. You couldn't listen to Barbara for long and not go crazy. Worse than the gut ache, her sisters finding fault, picking, pecking like a couple of old hens.

She tried to dismiss it, wanted to get back to her dreaming – but every time she pictured the cabin she saw this damned cheese, small, with that orange-coloured rind Barbara was so proud of. On Henry's shelf!

She wanted to make sure, wanted to settle it now. She was too wide awake to get into bed. She listened if anyone was still up. If anyone heard her go downstairs she'd say she wanted to go out to the lav. No, she didn't want to use the chamber pot. She wanted to go out to the lav. Wasn't she allowed to go out to the lav now?

She went down in her bare feet for quietness. The floorboards creaked. The stairs creaked. The latch snapped up with a crack. She stopped. Wondered if she'd heard a movement. Stood on the bristly doormat in her bare feet, listening. Everything seemed still.

She unlocked the back door, went out down the step on to the path to the dairy. She knew whereabouts under the tank the key was. Found it, unlocked the door. It swung open into darkness. She pulled the door to behind her. Felt for the candle and matches at the end of the shelf, struck a match, held it to the candle. The wick lit, the flame grew large enough to see the whitewashed walls, the settling pans, the skimmer, butter bats, the cheese press, the stuff Barbara made so much fuss about. And there, on that old green dish – there it was! The same round shape. The same colour rind. Half a cheese! Those complaints she had had to close her ears to came back, *half a cheese has vanished – must have been between milking and midmorning!*

Henry's piece had come off this bit on the green dish!

Suddenly the candle glow was brighter. She shot round to look. Holding another candle, someone was standing at the doorway.

"So now we know who the thief is!"

She knew the voice. Had heard it every worst moment of her life.

"What are you doing in here!"

"I thought you'd be on the prowl."

"Just as well I am," Barbara said, "or there'd be more gone by the morning."

Maudie wanted to tell her where the other bit of cheese was, wanted to say who she suspected. But there was no-one to confide in, no-one to listen and understand, except her poor old Pa, and she wasn't going to take her troubles to him.

She pushed past her sister, put the candlestick back on its shelf, blew the candle out.

"Don't know what Pa's going to say," Barbara hissed. "When he knows we've got a thief in the family!"

Maudie waited for her to go out, locked the outside door, put the key back under the water tank.

"And you aren't even undressed yet!"

It amused her, the way Barbara had to whisper when she wanted to shout. Like an old goose. Hissing!

"Undressed yet!" she echoed back.

She let her sister into the house, tried not to giggle, Barbara pale with anger and all up a gum tree. Maudie wished she could tell her where the stolen cheese was. Glad she couldn't. Be a pity to explain what had really happened. The bitch could stew all night, thinking she'd got to the bottom of it, but not sure, and boiling, not being able to say anything.

"Good night, Babs, dear," she said at the top of the stairs. "Hope you sleep well."

"Good night?" Barbara hissed. "You'll know what a good night it is in the morning."

"Be good morning then, Babs," she said, and couldn't stop herself laughing out loud.

Back in her room the smell of the engine on the night air recalled the cabin. Henry. The bunk bed. Heaven.

Then the other thought! If she'd done what Henry wanted her to do, she might have had to do what that other poor girl had done – might have been her baby lying cold and dead in the church, its little body wrapped in newspaper. Nine months on she could have felt like that mother felt now. And no-one to turn to.

It was how life was. Only a little of it was nice. Even what was nice had its nasty side.

# CHAPTER 14

The wood store was the best place. An L shaped building, its shorter part being where wood was stored on racks for logs to dry, its longer part both coke store and workshop. A forge, no longer used, was the reason for the coke heap. Over the years coke dust had covered the windows so you could hardly see out, let alone in. After their first time Miriam put an old coat on to protect her clothes when pushed back against the ironwork. This she folded up and hid between some wood piles ready for future meetings. Their encounters were warm, whispered, a pleasure to look forward to.

One day Miriam had news. She was pregnant.

She'd well and truly missed. Looked as if she'd have it next July.

"Say something. Aren't you pleased?"

"I'd never thought I'd be a father."

"You'll be a sort of father. You won't be the dad. Raymond'll be the dad, but it'll be your child. Always will be. And I'll want you to choose its name, you know!"

The thought of not bringing the boy up didn't depress him. His concern was to prevent Rose finding out; her peculiar mind could sometimes hit a nail on the head all too quickly. Yet it was surely nothing unusual for a married woman to get pregnant later rather than sooner.

He wondered where the boy would go to school. Hoped he wouldn't have Miriam's eye or nose. Wondered whether Rose would continue to employ her when she knew she was pregnant.

Miriam saw he was doing it wrong, the way he was hoeing the beetroot.

"My Raymond!" Pointed to what he was doing.

Raymond stopped. "'S'up?"

"Beetroot," she said. "You'll let the fly in, hoeing."

"Damn thing!" He threw the hoe away. Served the damn thing right!

A long-limbed man, awkwardly put together, an emptiness around the eyes. Miriam read his face at a glance.

"What's up, my Raymond?" She took his arm, led him indoors. "Sit down and tell me all about it." She undid his boots, pulled them off his feet, stood them as a pair on the mat.

"Got the sack."

It was always a stab to the stomach. Not that it was a new thing with Raymond. He was a man employers seemed able to dispense with. Miriam had known when she married him what she was taking on – a man with few gifts. But not given to deception. The employer who had suddenly deprived himself of Raymond's labour was the vicar of St Luke's church in the next parish. The Reverend Griffin had taken him on as a gardener, and with the post went Charity Cottage, a rented church property in the gift of the parson. It was in Charity Cottage that they were now living; Raymond losing his job meant the couple had lost their home.

"When do we have to get out by?"

Raymond, hunched up in his chair, shook his head. "Dunno."

"It'll either be Christmas or Lady Day. Didn't he say?"
"Dunno."

Miriam sighed, glanced around at their few sticks of furniture.

"Christmas, I expect, seeing it's the Reverend Griffin."

Later, over a meal of bread, a scrape of butter and a few bits brought home of leftovers from the Hall, she told him she was going to have a baby. Seeing by her face that it was good news he cheered up.

"Boy or girl?" he asked.

She laughed. "We shall have to wait and see."

"I suppose we shall manage?"

"I think we shall, my Raymond."

In fact, she thought, their future was more assured now than it was before she'd got pregnant. As a couple they hadn't many assets, but their main one, recently well used, had brought home the bacon. Or, if things turned out as she hoped, would do so presently.

She washed up, did a little cleaning round the house and, with the autumn weather turning cold, suggested an early night.

"Might as well enjoy ourselves," she said.

Raymond, surprised, caught her meaning.

She wanted to please him. Life was never easy with Raymond but with the Major in love with her and a child on the way she was finding it easier to be affectionate. They had had years of coolness. Tonight, what she was used to doing with the Major for love she was happy to do with Raymond out of kindness.

Afterwards, before turning over to sleep, she said, "If we could get a few young turkeys to fatten up for Christmas we might make a bit of cash."

"That we might," Raymond said. "If we had somewhere to keep 'em."

"I'll think about it," she said.

Which wasn't strictly true. She'd already thought about it, thought of the very place. All she needed were the turkeys.

She wondered why Raymond had been sacked this time. She hadn't asked, didn't want to depress herself. It would be like all the other times: something he forgot to do, or did badly, or hadn't understood. She thanked God for Richard Dawson. He'd opened more doors than one.

# CHAPTER 15

PC Philips cycled up the drive to St Matthew's Hall, leaned his bike against a bush, took off his cycle clips, rather wished he'd left this little visit till the morning.

Man of mystery, this one, parish couldn't quite get the measure of Major Dawson, in spite of that dance everyone spoke so well of. Man of medals. Had made his name in the war. Might be in for a knighthood, some said. Wealthy enough to buy a fine house like this. Made you feel a bit out of place. Different matter from your common or garden farmhouse, Major not the type you could come the heavy hand with. More the sort it was better to have with you than against you.

It was this baby, the constable explained. Found on the altar at St Matthew's church. Dead, unfortunately. Wrapped up in last Sunday's newspaper. Peculiar thing to do, no fathoming some people. He didn't suppose either the Major or Mrs Dawson could shed any light on the matter?

"Baby?" Rose exclaimed. "I put it there."

"You, ma'am?"

The Major, he was interested to note, appeared as surprised as he was at the news.

"Best place, in the circumstances," Rose said.

"I see, ma'am."

The constable, who had hardly expected to make many notes here, took his notebook out, laid it ready on the mahogany top of a chiffonier. A lucky intuition on his part, coming up to the Hall. Had saved himself hours of work.

Looking at the eccentric figure of Mrs Dawson he felt the witchcraft theory might be justified.

Care needed, though. Seemed to shine out from the mahogany veneer his notebook rested on. Even the family photographs on the walls seemed to be saying, "Better be careful here, old mate. Use your sense. Only a dead baby."

But questions had to be asked, replies had to be noted.

"Found it in the hedge," he wrote.

And what had made her look at that particular place rather than another?

"Because the brambles were out of place."

He repeated her words as he wrote. "*Because the brambles were out of place!* Have I got that right, ma'am?"

"So were the hazel and the hawthorn, but not to such an extent."

So, he said, to understand the matter clearly, she usually carried secateurs about with her on her walks to tidy up the hedgerows round fields?

"Just a snip here and there," she told him. "I'm not a fanatic."

And could he ask, he said, what made her open the package of newspapers?

"Because it was asking to be opened," Rose said, as if it was obvious. "Like a hedge asking to be snipped – or boots asking to be cleaned."

PC Philips involuntarily glanced down at his own boots, was gratified that in that respect they asked nothing.

The interview was easy enough. Woman gave every impression of answering truthfully. No signs of life in the body, he recorded, no sound, no breathing, no warmth, and the limbs felt stiff. And what sort of state generally, he asked, would she say the baby was in when she saw it?

"Oh, a state of serenity, constable. It would never be abandoned any more."

The Major stirred the ashes between the bars of the grate, tapped the poker gently on the hearth.

"And you didn't think," the policeman made the point with some delicacy, "you didn't think, ma'am, it necessary to inform the police because you knew the flower ladies would be in the church shortly afterwards. One of the ladies comes by bicycle, I believe, and lives closer to the police station than you do, so you knew she could easily inform the police. And that was what you expected would happen?"

"Sounds a very fair interpretation, Constable," Richard said.

"I told its Maker," Rose said, "and put it on the altar. It was quite safe there, you know."

"Quite, ma'am. You had done everything that could have been done, and you removed the infant from the hedge without delay."

He wrote for a while, made it clear that Mrs Dawson had acted as any reasonable person would have acted. He read aloud what he had written and, assured of the accuracy of his report, put pad and pencil away.

There was just one more thing, he said. Late as it was, he would like to suggest that they all went along now to see the exact place where Mrs Dawson had found the parcel.

"Save us going tomorrow," he explained. "Won't draw so much attention in the dark."

Rose went to get her topcoat. Richard and PC Philips exchanged a glance.

"Very competently done if I may say so, Constable," Richard murmured. He seemed to give him to understand that those who dealt with such matters would get to know that Constable Philips was, in the opinion of some, deserving of commendation.

Rose drifted back, her coat as yet unbuttoned.

"I've just wondered," she said to Richard, "whether the officer may have caught a glimpse of my tits. Has he?"

PC Philips straightened up, red in the face from putting his cycle clips on.

"We'd best be off now, ma'am," he said. "Before the pub turns out, so we don't attract attention."

"Attention?" Rose said. "Oh, I don't think I've ever attracted much of that, have I, Richard?"

# CHAPTER 16

Smoke spurted from the smokestack, steam was up, the belts started the machinery into life. Threshing had started early, to finish by mid-afternoon and move away to another farm. The wind was brisk, a blessing to the threshers because it blew the dust away.

"Must have blown the eggs away too," Maudie thought. "Unless someone's already been and got them."

She searched around for some, managed it so that she was a yard or two from Henry's cabin. The upper door was open. She took her chance.

Tiny! Dirty! The stained mattress, dingy blankets! And the smell! Stale food, sweat, sour breath – yet none of it quite blotted out the pleasure. What if she'd gone and got herself pregnant! By a man like Henry! Wouldn't have been able to bear herself. Yet she could wish she was back in the cabin, in the firelight, Henry's face touching her face, his lips on her lips -

She shuddered at the loveliness, the horribleness of it!

She shut it out of her mind, recollected why she had come. She looked along the shelf and there it was, that piece of cheese she'd thought about in the night. She took it, put in her basket.

She went out, the lower of the half doors slammed behind her. A workman on the steadily growing strawstack glanced at her, carried on pitching straw. She neither looked away nor hurried, didn't care whether she'd been seen or not. She was going to come back again later. Was going to have words with somebody.

Before going in for his dinner Frederick washed his boots in the metal bath by the kitchen door, brushed them clean with the handbrush and took them off. From indoors the usual sound of argument. Nine times out of ten it would be because Maudie hadn't done something – or hadn't done it properly. He didn't know what to make of the girl. He got on well enough with her, got on well with all the girls. He went into the kitchen. Maudie and Barbara, unaware he'd come in, were at it in the next room. The voices were spiteful, intending to hurt. He sat at the partly laid table, tried not to hear the details of the row, hoped it would stop.

"Trouble is," Barbara was saying, "no-one knows what to make of you. You don't act like anyone normal."

"I shan't stay here any longer than I'm obliged, don't you worry! I know where I aren't wanted."

"Good, I shan't lose any more cheese then, and that'll be a blessing."

"If you want to know where your cheese went, you take a look in there!"

Joseph heard the creak of wicker, guessed it was a basket.

"Where did you get that from?" Barbara asked.

"Never mind where I got it from. What you want to find out is who took it out of the dairy."

"I know who took it. You did!"

"You know so much, you do! Praps you ought to blame someone you're a bit sweet on. Someone beginning with W."

There was a hiss. "You little bitch! You stupid little bitch!"

Much as Joseph tried to distance himself from the quarrel, what Maudie implied struck him. Could Walter Leggett still be thieving?

"That's who you want to keep an eye on," Maudie mocked. "Just because Pa's given him a job doesn't mean he's given up thieving."

Incidents came to mind. Things missing! He'd thought giving the chap a chance would be the making of him, help him to turn over a new leaf. Yet why should it? You can put a pig in a different sty. You can't stop it rolling in filth.

Muriel came in from ironing in the living-room, saw her Pa at the table.

"Pa's here, if you two can stop arguing!"

The meal was quiet, bitterness not far from the surface. Joseph's thoughts drifted to Maudie. She'd been no more than a child when Annie died. He'd left her sisters to bring her up, had supposed it wasn't his place to interfere, in spite of ructions from time to time. He wondered whether he hadn't neglected her, stood back too often, let her grow from childhood to womanhood without the attention she ought to have had. If truth be told, he had given more time to pigs and horses than to Maudie. Yet this dinner time she'd put two and two together about Walter, made him wonder about the chap – when the family ought to have seen it for themselves.

Later he made a point of chatting to the girl. Pretty features, eyes that could fasten on your face – as if she wanted – he didn't know what she wanted, didn't know much about the girl at all. She'd never asked about her mother. Maybe it hadn't occurred to her to ask. Maybe her life was so full that what had happened to her mother didn't bother her. He felt easier, believing that.

The farmhouse was built in traditional Suffolk style, the rooms in a linear arrangement upstairs and down, almost all the windows facing south. Joseph did his accounts in the study. Situated between the living-room and the best room at the end, the study was the room from which the stairs went up to the bedrooms. His bureau was near the window, and when Maudie went there to steal money she had to make sure she kept down below sill level.

She slid the chair away as usual to get into the kneehole under the bureau, unhooked the key from behind the leg and unlocked the lid. Her father kept his sovereigns in a narrow mahogany box hidden amongst some papers. It had a lid that had to be pressed and slid simultaneously, an operation Maudie had little difficulty with. She took a sovereign, and left the bureau as she found it. Then she slid the chair back into position and crawled away until out of sight from the window.

She put the coin with the other sovereigns under a floorboard in her bedroom, took herself outdoors on the pretext of looking for eggs.

The threshing had finished. Tom was manoeuvring the engine round to pull the equipment away, the men were tidying up, getting a tilt over the strawstack, rolling the belts up, pulling the engine hose out of the pond.

"What did the police want, then?"

Henry had come up behind her. He ran his finger down her arm, his face close to her hair.

"Police? What police?" She was feeling about for eggs in the dry grass under a bit of galvanized iron.

"What your sister said. Last night!"

He kept his voice low, confidential. It took her back to the cabin, the warmth, just the two of them, the bunk bed ready. It thrilled her, the way he spoke, his mouth close to her hair, hardly raising his voice.

"Police?" she echoed, still feeling about in the grass. "What are you on about?"

"You know what I'm on about," he said. "Last night. You and me. In the bunk."

His eyes were on her body, and against her will Maudie wished they were back in the firelight, the warmth, the rough rank smell, but she knew the game she was going to play, the game she wasn't going to lose.

She straightened up. "Henry, I don't know anything about a cabin! Or a bunk in a cabin! You been dreaming?"

"You know what we'd a' been havin', if your sister hadn't turned up! So do I!"

"You keep on about my sister! I don't know what to think about you, Henry."

"You know what I mean," he grinned. "You were begging for it as much as I was."

Over his shoulder she noticed Walter Leggett making his way towards them, guessed Walter had been told everything.

"Can't make you out," she said. "I begin to wonder if you're nice to know."

"You thought I was nice enough last night," he laughed. "Nice enough to get into bed with."

Walter joined in, grinned at Henry, jerked his head as if she was the lowest of the low.

"Get what you wanted, Henry?"

Maudie ignored him. "Police came round about some cheese. What someone's been thieving off our farm."

"Cheese?" Henry shot Walter a look. "Don't know nothin' about thievin' cheese."

"I happened to look in your cabin dinner time," Maudie told him. "Happened to notice a bit of cheese – exactly like what my sister had had stolen. Thought I'd better take it so you didn't get caught with it."

"You took it!"

"That I did! So no-one'll think you did. Unless PC Philips hears about it!"

It was only momentary, the glance the two men passed, but it signified. PC Philips was definitely not a person they wanted business with.

"Why should old Philips hear about it?"

"Why!" she jeered. "You ought to have seen my sister when she found out someone had stolen her cheese!"

"Do she know?"

"Might do."

"Is she going to tell him?"

"Depends," she said. And eyed Walter as if thieving was all he was good for. "All depends! Whether there's any more lies about that cabin! One more word – be the worse for you two!"

She walked off, felt the the pair of them looking at her, sizing her up. She'd bested them. For the time being.

The autumn sun hung lower in sky, its light coloured the fields, the yellowing trees. Last night's adventure was over. She was safe, out of it, not a fool of a girl any more.

Yet when the caravan huffed its way past the farmhouse and up the driveway she was sorry to see it go, those fantastic red and blue and yellow machines. And when the engine stopped at the far gate and screeched its whistle of cheerio she wished she could climb aboard and travel with it, along unknown roads, free as the smoke, carefree as the trundling wheels and rattling frames.

# CHAPTER 17

He was cycling home from Beckthorp Railway station. Occasionally from a farmhouse or cottage window light flickered, but mostly night meant an absence of light, except for the glow of the stars, sometimes a flare of moonlight.

He turned into Church Lane, aware of the looming church, and amongst the shadow of surrounding trees the deeper shadow of the Hall. This lane, these ancient buildings were what he had come to know as home, were what he was saying goodbye to. He'd miss their everlastingness, as he missed the glamour of military days.

"And Rose," he told himself in the relief of leaving her, "I shall miss you, Rose. Maybe most of all."

As for Miriam – impossible for him to stay now even if he wanted to, his own flesh and blood in the belly of another man's wife, the boy growing up in another man's house, playing on the village green, sometimes visiting the Hall, a child it would be impossible to look at and look away from, and pretend they were squire and poor man's son.

He turned his cycle lamps out, went on past the Hall down to the barn. From inside it, the sound of turkeys. He smiled to himself. Stanley had come up trumps.

He pulled up at the barn, went inside. In the paraffin-lit turkey warmth Miriam, a scarf over her head because of the fleas, was making her way through her bronze-feathered flock to the feeder troughs, into each of which she poured, as best she could with turkeys attempting to perch on hands and arms and bucket, a measured amount of grain. She straightened up, knew whose arms encircled her from behind. She rested her head back against him, and by the glow of the all-night burner they two of them watched beaks hammer down and down and down until soon all troughs were empty.

"Stanley?" he asked, meaning the turkeys.

"Knows a farmer who's selling up. So he bought them. Said you'd had a word. Bless you."

She thanked him with kisses. "I must try to pay you back."

"I settled up before I went."

He warned her against giving any details to Rose, except that she'd got them off Stanley. She settled back against him, and in the warmth and dimness they watched the birds that would turn dry bread into bread and butter and cheese and meat for her and Raymond.

"Have a nice time in London?"

"Mostly business." He rested his hand on her belly. "All going well?"

She held his hand against her.

"You think it's mine?" he asked.

"If you knew what my marriage is like." She turned and faced him. "But I've told him it's his. All my young life, no-one would look at me. Then I meet someone like you! You've given me so much. Love. A baby. And now these."

Turkey noise filled the barn, the sound of grooming, preening, the cackles, croaks of contentment.

He held her, this woman full of gratitude, full of his child in her. He pitied her for the shock when she knew he was leaving.

He kissed her. She was intelligent, was shapely in body and mind, wanted to give him pleasure.

It wouldn't do. He couldn't stand it, seeing boundaries. It was how his life went, searching for the unexplored, unable to live in it when he'd found it.

"I hardly know how I'll live till I see you again," she whispered.

"You've got to live. We've all got to *live!*"

Outside again he breathed the coolness, away from the suffocation of heat of the burner, the atmosphere of turkeys.

"All agreed, then?"

He read the draft terms to her, passed the contract to her to read. She didn't look at it.

"This really what you want?" she asked.

Because it was very much what he wanted he said, "Why don't you come too?"

Any other time, except this moment of ending, she would have said, *Go! Leave me in peace! I long to see the back of you!*

She said it in her thoughts. In a few weeks she would look at the far wall and not see him. She'd walk through a room, wander in the garden, and there'd be nothing of him, not so much as a footprint on the lawn or the smell of his clothes. She pictured bundling up anything of his he'd neglected to take, and getting it out of the house. And savouring the scene she smiled, saw him as a guest who had stayed overlong and would shortly be packing his bags.

Richard's family had an old-established import-export business in London's dockland. He was pleased with the way the negotiations had gone. He hoped she would think the arrangement he had come to would be satisfactory.

"I'll be based in London," he said.

"At the family firm."

He was glad she said that. Rose was no fool. There was no need for gossip or village whispers.

"I shall want you to write to me, you know," he said.

A sleepiness stole across her face. "Maybe when my mind comes back I'll write you a memorable letter."

Because he was getting what he wanted he asked if she would give him a memento of some sort, a little something for a keepsake he could look at sometimes.

The smile vanished. Just for a moment the guise of secrecy left her, the eyes sharpened. A moment later she was as she always was, distant, her attention unengaged.

"Snapshot, perhaps?" he said.

A frown as of something unrecalled came and went.

"I gave you something once," she said.

Later, before going to her bedroom, she said, "I think it was my life. I gave it to you one day and you lost it somewhere."

Earlier than usual next morning she was up and dressed. It wasn't till the New Year, he reminded her. Till then he'd be here at the Hall.

"I couldn't go unless I knew you were being looked after," he said. "I think Miriam ought to move in with her husband when I go. As tenants."

But only for as long as Rose wanted them. They could have a room or two at the back. An agreement could be drawn up by a solicitor so Rose could kick them out when she wanted to. But that way they'd be on hand if Rose needed them.

Rose brushed a few crumbs off the tablecloth into her hand.

"What does Miriam think of the idea, Richard?"

"She doesn't know."

Rose didn't answer. She couldn't help but punish him as long as he stayed.

She went outdoors to brush the crumbs from her hand on to the bird table. A blue tit darted away.

"Would save them rent, I suppose," she said when she came in, "if they lived here."

Her tone was more kindly.

"We must look at the Will," Richard said. "I should want you to have everything. As for an allowance you must let me know what you want."

He wondered if she had the remotest idea of what she would want; then as if to show him she had a very clear idea of what she wanted she rang the bell. Miriam came in.

"Miriam," she said. "Come and sit down. The Major's got something to tell you."

He could hear by the way she spoke, the ridicule, the loosened mouth.

"The Major's going away. Going to leave us for ever. Isn't that a shame?"

Miriam sat still, scarcely took it in.

After all their loving!

Her countrywoman's mind told her to be careful, told her to keep what she'd got. She'd got a job, a husband, a baby on the way and turkeys in the barn.

She sat still, knew her place. She was a servant, they were the master and mistress.

"He'll tell you the details," Rose said.

"We're offering you and your husband accommodation here," Richard said. "To look after Mrs Dawson when I've gone. If you and he decide to accept we shan't have to advertise. There would be a properly drawn up contract, of course."

He was saying words he had rehearsed. He knew what his wife was up to. Under those droopy lids, under her foolery, she was as deceitful as he was. But she had deceived him as to herself.

"Leaving for London," she said. "Soon after Christmas. He'll tell you better than I can."

If Mrs Dawson expected a heartbroken reaction from the girl because of his departure she was disappointed. Miriam had no money, no skills, a fool of a husband and a baby on the way. Life had made her a realist. She knew good luck when she saw it.

"Oh, ma'am," she said. "Raymond and I accept with pleasure."

Richard left them to it. He had arranged what he wanted to arrange, Rose in good hands and Miriam secure. And the two of them well matched.

For himself, he knew what he didn't want, he didn't want too long an acquaintance, didn't want his days mapped out like King's Regulations, didn't want his weaknesses known, inspected like troops on parade.

One day perhaps, if he lived long enough, he might find out what he did want.

# CHAPTER 18

The letter was from Herbert. He'd managed to persuade Mr Bumford to let him have a day or two off at Christmas, so would be home some time Christmas Day and stay till the Sunday.

It was wonderful news. He must have done ever so well, the family said, must have made a marvellous impression on Mr Bumford. Herbert could easily run a butcher's on his own. Maybe one day he'd come home and buy a butcher's shop locally.

Barbara's opinion was that if one day Herbert did come home he needn't think he could interfere with the milk! Her cows were *her* cows. The butter and cheese were her affair, not Herbert's, even if he was the only son!

The others had no such reservations. The thought of having Herbert back with them at Christmas for a couple of days cheered them up. Joseph went about the farm a happy man, Maudie felt she wanted to help rather than hinder, wanted to do something without being told to. One thing she could do, she decided, was cut some chaff for Barbara's cows, *chaff* being a term for chopped-up straw, which was mixed with hay for feed now the cows were indoors for the winter.

The chaff cutter was a cast iron machine with a wooden hopper into which straw was fed while another person turned the handle. Maudie had sometimes seen the men use it single-handedly, spinning the flywheel fast with one hand, packing straw on to the spiked rollers in the hopper with the other. She tried it a time or two, managed to chop a little, she worked the wheel up to a faster speed, and chopped a little more. Then tried turning the wheel continuously with one hand and feeding the straw in with the other.

It being a cold morning, the iron handle was icy to the touch. A pair of men's gloves lay on the framework under the hopper, too big by half, but at least they'd keep her hands warm. She fixed a sack to the mouth of the hopper to catch the cut straw, she spun the wheel and fed the straw in. The sack began to fill, Maudie gained confidence, sped up the process. A finger of a glove trailed into the cogs, was caught, glove and hand were dragged into the machinery.

Screams were heard in the house.

When Muriel found her the left hand was trapped, Maudie was bending over as though to lessen the pain.

"Keep away!" she screamed. "Don't touch!"

The only way to free her was to turn the wheel back. Muriel turned, the cogs rolled over the hand again, the glove came free, her fingers ran blood.

Muriel held her wrist, ran her into the kitchen, filled the handbowl with cold water and plunged the hand in.

The next bowlful they cut the glove off. The side of the hand and the little finger were like meat. But the screams had stopped.

When Barbara came in Maudie was still sitting quietly, her hand in cold water, holding her wrist to slow the bleeding.

Elmsfield hospital was run by nuns. The building was in secluded grounds in Beckthorp, away from noise and traffic. The wards were quiet, even the daylight angling through the arched windows came in on tiptoe.

The nuns were efficient, knew what to do. By the time Joseph and Muriel left her Maudie was sedated and near to sleep, her face pale amid her black hair.

"Can't think what came over her!" Barbara said. "Not like her to do anything without being told. Can't understand what came over the girl!"

If the girl had been more careful, she told them, had kept her mind on what she was doing she wouldn't have got injured.

Joseph blamed himself. He'd known the chaff cutter was dangerous. The box housing the cog wheels had long been broken, ought to have been repaired. An hour's work would mended it. But it wasn't only the chaff cutter. All his life he'd never quite had time for the girl, had seldom swept her up in his arms, seldom listened to her childhood tales. Now here she was, a young woman, his chance of knowing her almost gone. There'd been so many calls on his time. But the tenderest call of all had gone unheard.

"I think I do," he murmured. "Poor child."

# CHAPTER 19

"Four for a penny, ma'am?"

Lovely herring, he said. Last of the voyage. Last for him, any rate. He couldn't stand it any more, seasick every trip, stomach turned inside out days at a time.

He looked ill, face thin, hair straggly with salt and wind. He showed her the herring in the box, their blue-green backs, silver underneath, a little redness round the gills.

"How you can tell they're fresh," he said. "That and the eyes."

"I'll have twopennorth," Miriam said.

He put them on her plate, full fish, the scales silvery on his fingers.

"Thank ye, ma'am," his face grateful.

He asked whether there were more houses down the lane, and being told there weren't, trudged away with his box towards the village.

But when she came to fry them she found she'd used all the lard. She was about to cycle into Beckthorp to see if Briggs would let her have a little when the Major came through.

He wouldn't hear of her going. There was a nationwide shortage of fat, he was sure he'd stand a better chance of getting some from Briggs than Miriam would. He'd see what he could do. He'd never tasted herring, would like to try one.

Mr Briggs told the girl to serve another customer, saw to the Major himself.

'Can't let everyone have it," he murmured, passing a package across the counter, his hand covering it. "But seeing it's you, Major."

It was a windy night, the cloud broken, the moon already up and bright. Richard push-biked back up St Matthew's hill, the wind in his face, and by the time he reached the top he was glad of a rest. He paused at a farm gateway, leaned his bike against a post. The moon glistened on a farm roof or two, lit the field and hedgerow vagueness that patterned the countryside. It was a landscape he was about to leave, had never known well, but a landscape his son would know, names of the fields, names of the farms, the rhythm of how things were done in the country. The boy would explore the local lanes with the other boys, go to the local school, speak the way the locals spoke. Maybe it would be no bad thing, the boy making his own way in the world, his own flesh and blood, his only son, at home here, where he himself had never been at home.

Miriam was wearing a headscarf to keep the smell out of her hair as she prepared the fish. She put them one by one in a bowl of water, scraped the scales off with a knife from the tail towards the head, ripping the silver off so they sank like discs of moonlight into the water. Richard stood away a little in case Rose padded in.

"I can't begin to thank you," she murmured. "Even though it'll break my heart when you go."

"I wanted to tell you myself. But you see how I'm fixed."

Miriam cut the heads and tails off the fish, then held them one at a time, slit the belly and took out the dark red tangle of guts.

"So since I can't thank you," she said, "I'll show you how to do the herring."

She rinsed the insides with clean water and showed him the silver bit to remove, and while she worked he watched the way she moved, her sleeves rolled up, her hands and wrists wet in the blood streaked water.

"I hope you're paying attention to the herring, dear Major."

She cut three slits in the back of each fish, two in the broad part and one where it narrowed towards the tail.

"One for you," she said, "one for me, and a little one for the little one!"

While the lard melted in the fish pan she coated the herring in flour, took them over to the stove and placed them in the hot pan, and with the fat sizzling and spitting she rinsed her hands. Then she dared let herself look at him, her lover, about to leave her.

"I wish my life had been different," he said. "I wish I was different."

But she was past wishes. Her future was life without him. She turned away to see to the fish.

"When you come home again," she said, "you'll be able to cook some. For the five of us."

She opened the window. The wind cut in, cooled the smell of cooking.

"You never complain," he said. "You just get on and make the best of it."

She loosened the herring with the fish slice, gave the pan a shake to distribute the fat.

"Best?" she said. "There's one thing needed before it's the *best*. And that can't happen. Not in this world."

She turned the fish with the slice, the white flesh bulging at the slits in the backs.

"This job of yours," she said. "Are you taking it because of Raymond? So you can pay him some wages?"

It was quietly asked. But it was too vague a question to answer, too open to womanly interpretations.

"The firm needs me," he said.

Miriam took the kettle off the stove, poured hot water into the bowl. Then put a couple of plates in to warm.

"The fish won't be long now, Major" she said. "If you'd like to tell Mrs Dawson?"

Nothing in the way she spoke suggested she was anything but Mrs Whatling, cook and housekeeper at St Matthew's Hall, a sensible soul who knew her place and kept her thoughts to herself.

# CHAPTER 20

A few gas lamps shed dull light along the Beckthorp main street. And when Joseph and Muriel got out on to the country roads there were no lights at all. It had been raining, the road was greasy in places, Joseph slowed the pony to a walk for fear of slipping. Not that Muriel minded. She didn't want to get there early. Visiting time at the hospital was from seven till eight, and much as she wanted to see her sister and worried about her hand, she didn't look forward to spending a whole hour with Maudie. She felt bad about it, wished she did want to spend time with her – but she'd wintered and summered Maudie. Maudie was best in small doses.

"*Would* have to be her," she said. "If there's a silly way of doing anything, Maudie'll find it."

Muriel was used to him not answering. He was slumped in thought, the reins loose in his hand. She guessed what was on his mind. It was on all their minds. Stanley had heard the story last night in the pub. She hoped her father hadn't heard it, but it was all round the parish: *Maudie Stelfox had been seen going into Henry Henman's cabin.*

"People will talk!"

He hadn't meant to say it. He coughed as if clearing his throat.

"Who'll talk, Pa?"

It was what she had feared. She, Barbara, and now her Pa, all tormented with it. *Maudie had been with Henry Henman.* Of *all* the men the little fool could have picked!

Joseph straightened a little, cleared his throat.

Muriel felt sorry for him. To have such a fool of a daughter to have to bring up and look after. And now to have this worry on his poor old head!

"What talk, Pa?"

He sighed. Something he'd overheard at market. Was meant to overhear, no doubt.

"In the cabin with Henry Henman," he said. "If you ever heard such nonsense! All round Beckthorp, no doubt."

All round St Matthew's as well, Muriel thought. All round every farmhouse, every cottage in the parish.

"Can't think the girl would disgrace herself!"

Muriel was glad it was dark. She wouldn't have wanted to see him upset.

"What her poor mother would have thought!" He absent-mindedly let the whip dangle across Dapple's rump, had to rein him back when he started to trot. "She don't mean it, you know."

"Don't you think so, Pa?"

"Oh, no! The girl don't mean it."

*Doesn't mean what?* she thought. *Exactly what stupid thing doesn't the girl mean?*

All too soon they saw the street lights of Elmsfield. She was uneasy about facing a sister who brought so much trouble to herself and the family. She wished the girl could stay in hospital for months. At least she would be out of the way, and what she did would be someone else's responsibility.

The streets had begun to dry. Joseph touched the pony into a trot, and with half the visiting time already gone they drew into the hospital driveway.

Maudie looked well. She was sitting up in bed, chatting away to the woman in the next bed. When she saw Muriel and her Pa she seemed quite surprised to see them.

"That old woman at the end," she pointed to a bed near the door. "They put her there this morning. So if she dies they can wheel her out quick!"

The woman was a Mrs Long from Beckthorp. She'd had her voice cut out, had to hiss what she wanted to say, mostly wanted a fag to cheer herself up.

Maudie laughed, brushed her hair back off her face, told them about Peggy, a woman the other side of the ward, telling the nurse she wanted her bottom wiped.

Muriel had made the girl a cake, had shaped an M on the top in marzipan. She put it on a cupboard beside the bed.

"She's always telling the nurses to shut them *bloody winders*," Maudie laughed. "'Damn draught on my back! I feel wuss now than I did when they brought me in.'"

She pointed to a couple of nurses at the end of the ward. "See that? Pulling the curtains round that bed!" She twisted over, asked the woman in the next bed, "Think she's going to die?"

Muriel and her father stayed till nearly eight, said good bye. At the doorway they looked back to wave. Maudie was smiling, but whether at them or at something her friend was telling her they couldn't decide.

"Evening, Mr Stelfox. Miss Stelfox."

Major Richard Dawson was pulling his greatcoat on as he went past on his way out. He'd been in the men's ward to see Dibby Dobson, blacksmith from Beckthorp, now getting over an operation for appendix.

They told him about Maudie. He hadn't heard about the accident, was sorry to hear it. He'd pop in now for a minute and say hello.

"Someone said you'd chopped your hand off." It was the following evening. Eva Briggs had come to see how she was. "And someone else said you were pregnant."

The girls giggled, heads touching, voices in whispers.

"Pregnant? Who by?"

"Henry Henman!"

"Eeugh!"

"Everyone says it's true!"

"Who's everyone?"

Eva couldn't say. People who came in the shop. "Someone said they'd seen you go in his hut."

"Me?"

Eva studied her face, detected no trace of a lie.

"Did you?"

"Course I did!"

Wide-eyed, Eva waited for the secret, the juicy whisper, to hear what happened, what it was like!

Her sister Babs had noticed some cheese had gone missing. Maudie was suspicious of Walter Leggett, believed he was stealing from the farm, been stealing for weeks. She'd noticed how close he and Henry were, so she took her chance and went into Henry's hut. And there was Babs's cheese!

"That's why he's saying all this. Trying to get his own back. Cause Pa sacked him."

Eva didn't see.

"Pa sacked him on the spot. Gave him two weeks' money, told him to get off the farm."

"So – what about Henry?"

"Henry?" Maudie was puzzled. "Don't remember mentioning *Henry!* I saw Walter Leggett talking to him, so I guessed that's where the cheese went. And when I looked in that's where it was. On that shelf at the back!"

Maudie lay back on her pillows, her bandaged hand getting more comfortable by the day.

"There's *something!*" Eva studied her face. "I can tell *something's* happened."

Maudie sighed, smiled, sighed again.

"Something nice?"

"Nice?" Maudie turned away, closed her eyes with the niceness of it.

"Tell us!"

"You wouldn't believe it!"

Eva was close, eager.

"Who is it?"

Maudie shook her head. People in beds either side had ears like gramophone horns.

"Someone," she whispered. "Can't tell you in here."

She was reliving the moment she had relived a hundred times, the Major coming in like that, smiling with his deep brown eyes.

*So this is the invalid!*

He didn't say much because it was time to leave. But his voice! The way he'd looked at her!

She closed her eyes. This stay in hospital had been the happiest time of her life.

"Not Henry?"

Maudie sat up, wide awake.

"Henry?" she jeered. "You must be daft about the bloke! I thought you'd got more sense! *Henry Henman!* Good God, Eva!"

Eva left, annoyed at being jeered at, annoyed at the taletellers who'd spread such stupid rumours about Henry and stopped her hearing the real news.

A few days later Maudie was in the trap with her Pa on the way home. Life was different. She was in love, she knew she was loved, life was sweet at last. Elmsfield Hospital was a shrine, the place where it began. Her injured hand was a sign. Even when it had healed she'd look at the scar and say *I wear it for him!*

"You're looking better," Joseph told her. "Didn't think you'd get over it so quick!"

"Oh, I'm feeling better, Pa!" She was glad her happiness showed. "I can move my fingers better now. Look."

The trap bowled along easily, the wheel rims sang on the road, father and daughter smiled, glad to be in each other's company. But the question in Joseph's mind cried to be asked: *Is it true about you and Henry Henman?* He knew it wasn't true. She was little more than a child, younger for her age than the other two. It was wrong even to think such a thing! Yet it wouldn't go away.

"Is it true?" he blurted out. Saw her pretty little face, her mother's eyes. "Truly better? Your hand?"

She held it up, showed him the undamaged fingers, the fresh dressing to come home with.

"Course it is."

At the foot of St Matthew's hill Joseph got out and led Dapple by the bridle to make it easier for the pony up the hill, but half way up she got out and made her father ride instead.

"Turn and turn about," she laughed, echoing one of his sayings to them as children. At the top when she rejoined him she showed no hint of tiredness. And so soon out of hospital!

At the fork by the post box the road to the right went towards Beck Farm, that to the left led to Church Lane in which were St Matthew's church, the Hall and the barn.

She felt pulled, had to grip the rail with her good hand to stop herself jumping out of the trap, to stop herself running towards her future, the man she loved.

The moment passed, the trap rattled away towards home. For the present she must live in hopes, sit back and wait till the time was right.

"Oh, I *love* that little red post box, Pa!"

"Thought you'd lost your tongue, you were so quiet."

"But I *love* it! That's where it starts!"

"What starts?"

"Oh – everything, Pa!"

The post box was more than a place for letters! It was the boundary between where she lived and where he lived. Its shiny red post office paint would be something she could look at when things went wrong.

"I shall have to start writing letters!" she sighed.

Joseph chuckled, shook the reins across Dainty's back. "You can always write me one."

"That I will, Pa. One of these days I'll write it all down and send it to you!"

She leaned across, gave him a kiss on the cheek.

# CHAPTER 21

Herbert locked up Bumford's shop at closing time as usual, cycled home to the mill workers' area of Hadale as usual, opened the little iron gate to Ann and Jimmy Thwaites's terrace house and let himself in the front door. He got the usual friendly welcome from them, smelt the appetizing smell of the evening meal. He took his jacket off, had his wash, and Ann brought his dinner in.

And reached him down the letter she had put beside the clock.

Addressed in a young woman's hand. On a lavender envelope. He guessed by the postmark, but daren't believe it. He ate half his dinner with it propped against his cup, looking at it, hoping it was from Kate, afraid to open it in case it wasn't. And afraid that it was.

"It's a bill," Jimmy murmured. "What he owes the landlord. Hadale Arms."

Ann put a finger to her lips, took Jimmy's empty plate and her own into the kitchen and came back with the pudding. Herbert carried on eating, his attention on the shape of the writing and the young-womanly way of writing his name. He thought of the hand that had held the pen, the spit of her mouth that had wetted the stamp. And then, his dinner still unfinished, he tore the envelope open.

*Werndby House*
*Werndby*
*Hadale*
*Yorks*

*13th December 1919*

*Dear Herbert,*

*Unless you're too busy reading Keats we're having a party the Saturday evening after Christmas and would like you to come. Let me know that you will, and please*

*Your cousin*

*Kate*

He read it again. And again.

"Summat wrong wi't dinner?" Ann asked.

He cleared his plate, handed it up to her to take through to the kitchen.

"Note from a customer."

"Oh, ah!" she said, and gave the lavender envelope a certain look.

He was fond of Ann and Jimmy. They weren't old enough to be his parents but were easier to get on with.

"Inviting me to her party," he said when Ann came back with his pudding. "After Christmas."

"Shall you go?"

He hadn't decided. Thought not. Couldn't be sure.

"Her up at Werndby?"

His face confirmed it.

"Fancy her, do you?"

"What makes you think that?"

"Good looking one, that. Shall you go?"

He knew Kate wouldn't be breaking her heart for him to accept. She'd got a mind of her own, an eye to the future.

"I'll tell you what, young Herbert," Ann said. "There'll be no dinner for you here that night if you don't."

She took off her specs, looked across at Jimmy, now settled by the fire with his paper. "Hear that, Jimmy Thwaites? Invited up to the Stelfoxes at Werndby House." She jerked her thumb at Herbert. "'Im!"

Herbert Stelfox he might be, but it was a standing wonder to the Thwaites's that their lodger should actually be related to Arthur Stelfox, owner of the mill where both of them worked. Came from a hundred acre farm in Suffolk yet worked as a butcher's apprentice up here in Hadale. And more than content to lodge in their little terraced house!

From Herbert's point of view there was little to wonder at. Farming was continuous toil. The only prospect in it nowadays was more toil. Farmhouses were comfortless places where you could slog your guts out and still be bankrupt come quarter day, whereas this was a cosy, warm little house, and butchering was a job you could cycle home from at the end of the day and leave your work at the shop. And every Friday you got your wages in cash..

"Shouldn't mind seeing Kate," he conceded.

"Then go," Ann told him.

He shook his head. He wasn't up to Kate. It wasn't just that she was well-to-do. Or found life less of a burden than he did, able to be on top of things and make a joke of it all. Half-crazed by the war, shellbursts still roaring inside his skull of a night-time – yet it was more than that that made him want to stay away.

Ann was fierce for him. "You're as good as any of them!"

Jimmy, his legs stretched out to warm in front of the fire, folded his paper down.

"Be some nobs there, son," he said. "A do at Werndby House! Bound to be nobs there."

"Don't tell him that!" Ann said. "It's Kate he wants to see! Not the nobs."

"Saw enough of them in the war," Herbert said. "Useless beggars!" His face reddened at the thought. They'd be Kate's sort, she'd be their sort. Them nobs who found life as easy as she did!

"Know what we got called when we came back, Jimmy? Clowns in khaki! *Clowns!* People didn't want us when we got back home!"

He banged the table, confused, too red behind the eyes to think straight.

"Now look what you've done, Jimmy Thwaites! You go all the same, Herbert. You're as good as any of that lot!"

It calmed him, her opinion of him.

"Any road, she'd think you'd let her down if you didn't go."

It hadn't occurred to him, Kate wanting him there *because* of the nobs!

The lavender envelope lay on the cloth in front of him, his name in her handwriting, every loop, every upright stroked down by *her* fingers, but a voice not saying what he wanted to hear.

"And don't forget your pudding," she added.

He loved her, this mother-come-back of a woman. Many a time he had blessed the day he'd got lodgings with the Thwaites's.

"Nay, I'll not," he said, imitating her.

She smacked his arm.

He grinned across at Jimmy, grateful to the pair of them for being what they were.

"She the one who got you to give up the booze, son?" He sounded suspicious of a woman with that amount of influence.

"Said I'd ruin what little brain I'd got."

He remembered the roller they'd sat on that Sunday morning, the lichen-covered cowshed behind them, and Kate saying it, her voice part of the purple distance of the moors. And because of that, in spite of Jimmy telling him that for a man who'd spent as long a time in France as Herbert had, a skinful a week was only right and proper, he knew he wouldn't over-indulge again.

"I'd better say I'll go, then."

"You better had," Ann said. "'Stead of sittin' there feeling sorry for theselves."

She felt her hand gripped by two strong butcher's hands, saw him looking at her as if at the mother she'd never been.

"I'll write now, then," he said.

"Fool if you don't," she told him.

# CHAPTER 22

December was cold, the days raw. Muriel was taking Stanley's jacket back to him. It had got torn on a hinge while he was lifting a stable door off. The thought of the look on his face when she gave him the jacket all nice and mended gave her a glow. Maudie noted her healthy look, the way she stepped it out in her rubber boots along by the headlands, the way she swung over stiles. in and out of ditches. Seemed years younger since going out with Stanley. Not a nice person, but at least she had a smile on her face. Whether Muriel *deserved* to be happy Maudie doubted. Happiness didn't go where it was deserved. Seemed to go where it was undeserved.

Holly Farm lay in the direction of St Matthew's Hall, which meant nothing to Muriel. She merely noted that her invalid sister was making a remarkable recovery, was looking better for being out and about, even though she was for ever looking about, over hedges, lingering at gateways to study the countryside, everywhere bar where she was going.

"Looking for someone?"

"Someone?"

"You seem to keep looking over towards the Hall, that's all."

"Interested in what's going on, Muriel. When you've been cooped up in a hospital it's a treat to look around for a change."

To prove how interested she was she spent several minutes studying a couple of rooks wheeling above a harrow working in a field nowhere near St Matthew's Hall.

Muriel watched her, wondered what other weird notions the girl had. "Soon be dark. You'll have to come and look at them tomorrow."

Maudie watched the birds, too interested to move.

"I think I will."

Behind Muriel's back she darted a look at the cluster of trees that hid the Hall, at the smoke that hung above a far-off chimney, smudging itself into the afternoon mist. She knew whose chimney it was, knew he was thinking of her.

"Bless him," she whispered. "Bless him, O God and make him mine soon!"

All trace of interest in those damned old rooks dismissed, she hurried to catch her sister up.

Stanley was adzing an ash bough into the shape of a doorpost for a stable. A timber knocked deep in the ground served as a stop for the bough to rest against, a couple more timbers angled into the earth either side prevented any sideways movement. He leaned over his work, feet astride, swung the adze blade towards him, slivered off chip after chip till the side he was trimming was flat and at right angles to the one he'd already done. He hadn't heard Muriel and Maudie approach, was unaware of them watching. Because he was bending, a gobbet of phlegm slid into his throat. He coughed, spat it out, cleared his throat. "Get out and walk, y'bugger," he muttered, and swung the adze back for the next stroke.

The snort was Maudie trying not to laugh; his smile as he straightened his back was for Muriel.

"Brought you your jacket."

He opened the bag, took the jacket out.

"You've made it like new!" He ran his knuckles across the thick brown material, the rent all but invisible. "Wonderful job!"

He made it an excuse to kiss her. Muriel laughed, turned away, pleased in spite of herself. Maudie wondered if she'd have been so reluctant if there'd only been the two of them there. It irritated her how girlish her sister could be, that hard, square face all soft and loving, pretending to be young and charming just because she was with Stanley. And the way they looked at each other -hardly seemed like that bitch Muriel!

"Glad you like it," Muriel said.

"That I do!" Stanley held the jacket up, studied the repair. "I do like it, Muriel. Don't you?"

The pair of them turned away, laughing, murmuring close together, eyes only for each other.

Maudie coughed. Sighed. Tried to yawn.

"What's this you've brought with you?" Stanley asked. "Looks like young Maudie!"

He asked her how she was, asked after her hand.

"Made wonderful progress," Muriel said. "Thought she'd like to come for a walk, being a decent sort of day."

"Someone else'll be pleased it's a decent sort of day," Stanley said. "Whatlings move into the Hall today."

"Whatlings? You mean that *Miriam* Whatling? Moving in with the Major?"

"Don't know about moving in with the Major," he said. "Mrs Dawson, more likely."

Maudie couldn't believe it! Moving into the Hall!

Anyone but Miriam Whatling. And all Stanley Chatham could do was to grin about it!

"*Don't know about moving in with the Major!*" she jeered. "I should think everyone in Suffolk knows the Major lives at the Hall!"

"Well, the Major do live at the Hall. Then again, Maudie, he *don't*."

"Fat lot you know!"

"Funny thing is," Stanley said, "he's leaving in a few weeks. For good."

The moment burnt into her mind: Stanley's humorous face, the muscles at the back of his jaw, his blue-striped shirt open at the neck, hairs from his chest curling over it.

"Leaving?"

"Going to London. Shan't be seeing no more of the Major after Christmas."

"Don't know about seeing the Major," Muriel murmured, glancing around at the strands of mist beginning to float above the furrows. "If *we* don't make a move soon, Maudie, we shan't see much of anything by the time we get back."

She was numb. Followed where Muriel walked. Neither saw nor cared where her feet went, how her hand was, whether it hurt. Saw Stanley's mouth, his lips as he came out withit.

*Shan't be seeing the Major no more!*

Beating into her mind.

*Shan't be seeing the Major no more!*

That was the pain. Not getting your hand crushed in the chaff cutter. She'd do it again, crush her other hand and welcome, if it would make the Major keep at St Matthews.

She swung the injured hand against a gatepost. Pain shot up to her shoulder, made her sway with dizziness.

*Shan't be seeing the Major much more!*

With the pain, and the news that Miriam moving into the Hall, that the Major was leaving, she stood still and howled. Like a heartbroken child, a wounded animal, she howled.

"Maudie! Whatever – !"

Across the fields, over bare hedges. Didn't care who heard.

The pain pealed out.

Her Major was leaving, comfort of her world was leaving.

"Maudie! Sshh, Maudie! Everyone'll hear you!"

Muriel's arm was round her, trying to soften the noise, trying to soothe the pain.

"What is it, girl? Whatever is it!"

Maudie wanted to say it, wanted to tell her her love was leaving, wanted to curse the Whatlings for moving into the Hall, making the Major go away. And under it all the pain in her hand shrieked into her.

"*May* – !" she shrieked. Wanted to his name. "*May – May – May!*" Like an animal. "*May – May – May!*"

Muriel held her, tried to shake the nonsense out of her,

"Maudie! What are you trying to say!"

It burst out of her, unstoppable as vomit, his name, her dearest sound.

Then two thoughts came together: *Whatling woman moving in. Major Dawson moving out.*

Made a different sense. The Major was leaving *because* she was moving in. Couldn't stand her!

She stopped crying, shuddered, a child sobbing for breath. Then she laughed. It was obvious! He couldn't stand her!

Peal after peal of laughter, loud in the twilight, bursting out of pain.

Muriel shook her arm.

"What is it, girl? What's come over you?"

Couldn't explain, only feel relief. What she ought to have known all the time. The Major loved her, *was leaving the Hall because he loved her.*

She couldn't stop laughing. Out over the fields, the laugh, the comfort, knowing what it meant, he couldn't stand them, daft old Mrs Dawson, that dreadful Whatling woman. Leaving the pair of them. Because of his love for her!

"Oh, Muriel!" She laughed and cried; he'd left them both for the love of her!

When she was calmer she said, "Muriel, dear. I hope Stanley and you get married. I know how much you love each other." Feeling calmer, she forgave him for what he had told her. "Poor Stanley! I want you to be happy, dear Muriel."

The howling, the laughing, the girl suddenly talking about Stanley was too much for her sister. She turned away, wanted to get home, get away from the little fool she'd been silly enough to go for a walk with.

But for Maudie, a certain matter – needed to be settled.

"They say old Mrs Dawson is a witch."

"Who says!"

"Everybody. Eva Briggs says so."

"What does Eva Briggs know, living in Beckthorp?"

"Well, what do you know, stuck out here on the farm?"

Twilight had given way to dusk. The hedges deepened the dusk on the headlands, the path ran barely distinguishable from the grass under the bushes.

"How can Mrs Dawson be a witch!"

"Goes about on a broomstick."

Muriel didn't answer.

"There was a broomstick in her garden if you don't believe me. Stuck into the ground."

Muriel felt the skin prickle on her face. Being with Maudie was like being with a stranger. "You don't believe that squit, do you?"

"It's not squit. Look what she did to that baby she found."

"It died in childbirth. The coroner said so."

"Ah, Muriel! But *why* did it die in childbirth?"

"It was strangled by the cord."

Maudie had to laugh at her. "But who *caused* it to be strangled by the cord?"

A blackbird started up almost under their feet, its warning shrieks sharp, angry. Muriel felt uneasy. The Parks weren't the sort to believe in such nonsense. She remembered her mother, how she used to listen to Maudie as a child, the little mind gabbling away so intently about what she'd had seen or thought she'd seen. Muriel recalled how her mother would smooth the child's forehead and say, "There, there! Never mind, little one!" It was always a puzzle to know what was true and what the child had made up.

"*Caused* it?"

She didn't pursue it. It was too foolish to argue about. Mrs Dawson a witch! Caused a baby in Beckthorp to be strangled by its cord! But it was her own sister, her own flesh and blood, daft enough to talk about witchcraft! The darkness they were having to find their way home through was one thing; the darkness in her sister's mind was another.

"Why he's leaving," Maudie insisted. "The Major. Can't stand living with a witch!"

Muriel plodded on, didn't answer. The thought of setting up home with Stanley seemed nicer than ever.

# CHAPTER 23

He turned off the road into the deeper darkness of the driveway. After a yard or two he had to get off his bike and push it. His uncle had had the driveway covered with shingle, yet another change Werndby House had been afflicted with since the war. While millions of blokes were being blown to bits in France, some men in England had managed to dig themselves a gold mine. Uncle Arthur Stelfox, mill owner, clothing manufacturer, maker of uniforms to the army, had dug himself one of the richest.

Herbert pushed on. Hard work, cycle wheels sliding and grinding about on a surface more suited to Arthur's well-to-do friends with carriages and cars to ride over than to a butcher's assistant with a bike But this was the driveway to Kate.

Suddenly he shaded his eyes.

Werndby was a house made of light. As if its walls were trying to enclose a vast luminous block, windows and open doors leaking brightness that streaked the lawn, gleamed on the roofs of parked cars, shone on the varnished sides of traps, even on the chromium-plated handlebars of his bike. He guessed there must be scores of people here, maybe more than a hundred.

He pulled off his cycle clips, hung them on the crossbar, wished he hadn't said he'd come.

Fashionably dressed young men and women were chatting and laughing at the doorway, their voices loud, careless. A young man came out to his car, held a white fur wrap up into the light for a girl at a bedroom window to see.

"That'll do," she called.

Herbert made his way over the lawn to the entrance hall. Loops of coloured electric light bulbs glowed over door frames, around windows, across the mantelpiece. Candles flowered from Christmas trees, tubs sprouted fountains of colour, ropes of rainbow decoration swung from beam to picture frame, others hung in swags from the sides of the room to a device on the ceiling. Not so much a room, more a tent shaped by lights. He left his scarf and gloves on an antique chest, went into the next room. It was a house he used to know, had stayed there as a child with his family, had gone there once or twice when he'd first come up to Hadale after the war, but now with its extensions, redecorations and expensive furnishings it was unfamiliar, a no-man's land between himself and Kate. It wasn't only the house that was the barrier; her father rubbed shoulders with the well-to-do, Kate's friends would be monied friends. Her fancy would be on someone better off, one of the articulate modern set.

A dog bounded in, thrust its nose sharply up under his crotch and bounded away.

"Gypsy! Oh, that dog!"

It was Aunt May, Kate's mother.

"Herbert!"

Her sad long face was suddenly pleased.

"That blessed dog of hers! Herbert, I'm sent down to tell you she's with a friend upstairs. She hopes she won't be long." She lowered her voice. "Being ill in the bathroom, the friend is. I ask you! At this time in the evening!"

She didn't sound puritanical about it. He liked his aunt, her mournful face. It made him smile just to look at her. She had aged since he had last seen her, her hair greyer, the wrinkles more furrowed, but she was still his favourite aunt. It was a comfort the way she could look on the black side of anything and make it humorous.

She kissed him, said wasn't it good about Muriel and Stanley.

"Stanley?" he asked. "Stanley Chatham?"

"Going out together," she explained.

It hadn't occurred to him anyone would be rash enough to want to go out with one of his sisters. Least of all Stanley. He was such an amiable chap. Didn't seem fair.

"Poor old Stanley! Think they'll make a go of it, Aunt?"

"As long as it doesn't lead to the altar, dear. That's the main thing."

"For Stanley's sake, you mean?"

"For both their sakes." And seeing he was puzzled she added, "It's love *or* marriage, Herbert. You can't have both."

Herbert smiled, changed the subject by looking around at the alterations and improvements. He noticed a photograph on the mantelpiece, Kate a year or two before the modern fashion for female shapelessness had come in. The portrait caught the girl exactly, the droll way she looked at him, weighing him up, making allowances for deficiencies. He wished he could have been the photographer, arranging how she stood, telling her to hold her head so.

"Like it?" his aunt asked, watching him.

*Like* didn't convey the half of it. It was the most charming thing he had seen in his life – except for the girl herself.

"Charles likes that one."

"Charles?"

Charles Maye, she explained, whose father owned Maye's Engineering in Harrogate.

*Charles likes that one.* He knew what she meant. Kate was spoken for.

"Big concern, Maye's. Nice young chap. Arthur likes him."

The seal of approval. It was inevitable, two wealthy families and two nice offspring. And the match blessed by the parents. He didn't blame Kate. He studied the photo again, guessed she was telling him, "I hope you understand."

He determined to stay for his aunt's sake, at least for a while. He wanted to see him, this Charles Maye, the luckiest man in the world. Conceited, like as not. And Kate probably thinking she was the luckiest of women to have him.

A wave of dance music raged out from one of the elegant new rooms nearby. Red, blue and green electric bulbs were strung across the ceiling, young men and women danced to music from saxophone and piano, girls in short low-waisted dresses and coloured stockings, everyone singing, *"Hold that tiger! Hold that tiger!"*

A young man in a fashionable check suit came towards them with a tray of drinks.

"Thought you'd gone to join the girls in the bathroom, Mrs Stelfox," he joked, offering her and Herbert a glass of something with ice. "Haven't seen Kate for hours."

"Charles, I've just been telling Herbert about you," Aunt May said. "Herbert was in France. How many years, Herbert?"

Herbert didn't answer, hated any talk of his years in France. Charles took his hand warmly enough. Seemed genuine enough.

"Expect you're glad to be back in England," he said. "Bit of a mess out there, by all accounts."

Already, Herbert realised, there were those for whom the war was over and done with, something that had happened far away to another generation.

"Charlie's got some!"

A couple of large young men had spotted the drinks tray, were pushing their way through the crowd towards them.

"Hugh's father is in some commission to do with the Armistice," May said. Hugh the taller of the two, dark haired, with noticeably red lips, Stephen, fairer, his eyebrows and eyelashes auburn like his hair. In keeping with the latest fashion neither man wore a moustache.

"Reparations," Hugh said. "For losses sustained."

"Herbert'll be interested," May told them. "He was in the war."

"Talking of which, Hugh," Charles said, "has your old man worked out what the Germans have got to pay us? Going to squeeze till the pips squeak, is he?"

"Trouble is," Hugh said, "the French want their cut too."

"Should've carried on to Berlin," Stephen said. "Whatever the cost. Not let them off with an armistice."

"Always assuming we get rid of Lloyd George," Charles said. "All these strikes! Guv'nor reckons wages are sky high."

"Your guv'nor can't be doing too badly," Stephen joked. "Government spending thirty million on roads. Be motor cars everywhere!"

"So long as they come to Harrogate," Charles laughed. "And buy them at Maye's Engineering."

"I daresay you'd like to see the Germans stung,"

Hugh asked, turning to Herbert. "After what you've been through?"

"Rather see our top brass stung," Herbert said. "Them and the warmongers back in England."

"Warmongers! Who are you calling warmongers?"

"Them who talk about *going on to Berlin*. No-one out there wanted to *go on to Berlin*. All we wanted was to come home. So would you have done!"

"Had to be crushed, didn't they? They'd have invaded us if they'd had the chance."

Their argumentativeness surprised him. Talk in the trenches wasn't about *crushing* anybody. All the troops wanted was to get out of it.

"So what would you have done," Hugh asked, "if you'd seen a German about to rape your sister? Let him get on with it?"

Same old question, bandied about at the start of the war by old men who knew they'd never have to join up, and now by youngsters who'd never see a Jerry even through a telescope.

Herbert gripped the man by the elbow. His hands, always strong, had been strengthened by butchering.

"Never mind about him being a *German*," he said quietly. "I'd shove my bayonet into his guts, and I'd lean on it till it broke his spine and I saw his eyes stare as if he didn't believe me!"

The music stopped as he spoke. For one or two it was like hearing the voice of another age, an eyewitness from faraway trenches.

"Jesus," Charles said.

Kate came up, a young blonde girl holding on to her arm.

"You're all very quiet," she said.

"I think we've just been hearing something I'm rather glad I missed," Charles said.

"It's Herbert!" Her voice made a fuss of him.

"Not a little tiddly, are we, Jane?" Charles asked.

Jane ignored him. "Introduce us, Kate. This wouldn't be your long lost cousin Herbert, would it?"

"Who's left his Suffolk farm and come up here to Hadale," Kate said.

"Specially to see Kate?" Jane asked him.

"Hadale?" Stephen was interested. "So what do you do in Hadale?"

"Work at Bumford the butcher's."

"Rather kill things than rear them, would you?"

After all the killing these last four years it was a clever point. He knew they hated him, these quick-thinking, quick-talking young men, Kate's friends, with their money and smart clothes. He guessed they looked down on him, outsider that he was, back from the war, fit only to be a butcher's assistant. Yet they were the sort Kate was used to, was going to marry into.

"Specially to see Kate, Herbert?" Jane insisted, hanging on to Kate's arm for support. "Gave up farm and everything for her?"

"Shh, Jane!" Kate said. "You know you're tiddly!"

"Least you can do, Kate," Jane giggled, "is have a dance with him!" She managed to push Kate towards him, swayed, had to be helped to a chair.

Kate was wearing a black dress with an orange sash. This dress, this scent of make-up, this shape, this Kate herself – in his arms, moving where he moved, content to be taken with the music! Yet she wasn't in his arms. He and she were close together, dancing, his hand was spread against her back. But it was only the shell of her, lent to him till the dance ended, till she was wanted by Charles. But just for the moment, here she was, in his arms and pleased to see him. He squeezed her a little to convince himself.

"Lost your tongue, young man?"

He could feel the ripple of her back through her dress as she danced.

"Lost more than that. If you can lose what you never had."

They circled past the white-jacketed musicians, professional players, the time crisp, witty. He wished he could dance better, knew she was comparing him to Charles.

"Lost? What have you lost?" She leaned away, amused.

"Someone I've dreamed about. In a black dress."

"Someone you didn't recognise when you saw her?"

He loved her quickness, knew he couldn't match her.

"Thinking about beer, I expect."

She was glad he could laugh at himself. "You mustn't dream, Herbert." Her voice was low, under the sound of the music. "Not that sort of dream. I don't want you to be hurt."

"A dream is all there is. I don't expect it to come true."

They stopped dancing. He walked her to the side, pulled a small package from his jacket pocket. "A bit belated, I'm afraid."

She unwrapped it. *The Rubaiyyat*, bound in green leather.

"Herbert!" She held the book unopened, looked at it as though it emitted radiance.

"You've already got it, I expect?"

She read what he'd written on the flyleaf.

*Ah, love! Could you and I with time conspire*
*To grasp this sorry scheme of things entire,*
*Would we not shatter it to bits, and then*
*Rebuild it nearer to our heart's desire!*

"Not one like this, I haven't."

She closed the book, wrapped the paper round it again. He knew what the gesture meant. More than the book was closed.

She took his arm. "It *is* a sorry scheme of things. As you know better than most."

She saw the disappointment in him. Out of place, and in a none too well-cut suit, he was older than her friends, lifetimes older. She could only guess what his eyes had seen.

"I think it's worth trying to rebuild. Don't you?"

"If you were there I'd rebuild anything. But if you weren't -" He opened his hands as if letting something fall.

She released his arm. "You've done your share of trying to put things right. I haven't, you see."

Tables had been arranged endways to form long benches covered with white tablecloths, though as people remarked, there was so much food you couldn't see much of the cloths anyway. From cold meats, tongues and hams, to jellies, blancmanges and cream, by way of half cheeses, breads and cakes and sponges, with excursions on this side to crab and lobster and smaller seafood, on that to puddings of lemon or chocolate or orange or pear, there was more food than could possibly be eaten by those present. Arthur Stelfox had set out small tables for the older guests, was calling them over.

"Get theself sat down, Robbie, with thee missus. I'll see you don't miss owt. And Cliff and Mabel, if thee'd like to sit over there -"

He called helpers over to look after them.

Kate joined Jane and a couple of friends. Her mother, with Gypsy on a lead, was talking to a friend near the drinks table when the dog suddenly took it into its head to pull away and bound over to Kate. It leapt up, pushed her backwards to the floor. The fall dragged the cloth off, the book dropped out of her hand, fruit salad and lemonade shot all over her. A moment later the dog was licking food off her dress, her face. And they laughed all the more when Jane unsteadily tried to help Kate to her feet, staggered, and Kate fell back, and the cream that had been on her hair poured down over her face.

Kate, Jane, Arthur, everyone doubled up laughing.

Except Herbert. That the dog was in the room annoyed him. That Kate should be subjected to such treatment annoyed him. And what hurt more was that she loved it as much as anyone, the chaos, everything topsy-turvy. He couldn't bear it, couldn't bear a world so disorderly.

He went over to look at a framed photograph, Kate, as a girl in school skirt and blouse, school hat and jacket. Young, her features rounder, she was already attractive, had an eye that knew something of what it was looking at. A different world when that picture was taken.

"So this is where you've got to, young man." Arthur Stelfox had come up behind him. "We had that one taken in Harrogate. On her birthday. Cost a penny, I'll tell ye. And worth every penny, bless her!"

It was unbearable that the man knew Kate better than he did, had had her on his knee as a child, had watched her grow up.

"Were going to 'ave the party on her birthday. Wouldn't 'ave been fitting, of course. So I suggested after Christmas. They thought it a good idea."

"Why not on her birthday?"

"Why not?" He sounded shocked that anyone could have forgotten. "Eleventh of November! Anniversary of the armistice! Couldn't have a do then!"

"We had a bit of a drink Armistice Day," Herbert remembered. "Not enough booze to make a job of it, though."

"Oh, we had a real good party that day I can tell thee! We pushed the boat out proper. Food and drink galore!" He said it as he said most things, as though to an audience. "Real good time!"

Several guests, in the act of pushing the boat out proper again, agreed.

"Wouldn't have been fitting to have one on the *anniversary*," he insisted. "Not this year. Wouldn't have shown respect to the dead."

"Blokes I was with," Herbert said, "didn't care about respect to the dead. They'd rather have had a booze up."

Arthur leaned closer, his paunch making room for itself.

"You wait till you're older, young man. Then you might be able to imagine what it's like being a parent, having a son lying dead out there. You wouldn't talk about boozing on Armistice Day!"

"What do you know about sons lying dead out there?" Herbert asked. "Most people back in England, stuffing themselves and making money -"

"I'm talking about a day of *respect* – something some people don't seem to know much about," his uncle insisted. "There's a time and place for everythin'. And the armistice anniversary's neither the time or the place for a party. So that's why we're holdin' party today, if you want to know!"

"All we had armistice day," Herbert said, aware of the paunch in front of him, "was bully beef and biscuits.

Wasn't much of a shortage in some places by the looks of it!"

The room had gone quiet. People had come to the doorway to listen, those at the buffet tables helped themselves quietly, handled their cutlery quietly.

"I'll not argue with such as you." Arthur Stelfox, mill owner, councillor, employer of hundreds, flushed with a toast or two. "It's easy-goin' ways were nearly the ruin of England."

"I'll tell you what nearly ruined England," Herbert heard himself telling him. "It was them at the top, didn't care what they were at. It was sending all them blokes to slaughter was the ruin of England."

The words burst out of him, for the poor sods in the mud and shell holes, all those thousands, broken, finished with.

Arthur's face reddened.

"Talk is cheap," he jeered. "I get dozens of people like you round my mill every week looking for a job. Most don't last three months. Why? Because all they can do is *talk*. Good day's work would kill 'em."

Murmurs of support from the cold meat tables, from those choosing between stilton and cheshire or having some of both, all agreed: *a good day's work would kill 'em!*

"Fifty per cent don't last three months!" Arthur insisted. "And why? Because all they can do is argue the hind leg off a donkey!"

He knew whose side they were on, these well-off people, closing ranks against the men they had done without these four or five years and could do without now. He knew what they were thinking, butcher's boy, come here on a bike, trying to tell the biggest employer in the neighbourhood the rights and wrongs of the war.

"I expect *you* all sleep of a night! You don't -"

A volcano of mud and fire and metal burst in his mind. Deafened him. Part of a torso. Barbed wire, big and long as hedges –

Words died. He couldn't shape it, what he'd been through, what he'd seen, what he'd –

"You don't -"

"No, we don't," Arthur jeered. "We damn well don't! Nor the likes of you, either!"

The door opened, Aunt May came back in. The dog chased across, bounded up to Herbert, snuffed its nose into his crotch. Everyone laughed, Arthur the loudest.

"That's what the dog thinks of him!"

His uncle's waistcoat was large, sported a gold chain across its middle. One of thousands, tailored uniforms of the well-clothed and well-shod. And he? In his cheap suit? He was one of the silly damn fools who'd been in France and didn't count, who there was no room for now they'd come back.

He turned away, walked out of the room.

"Thank you for asking me, Aunt May," he said.

"You're not leaving already?"

Her poor anxious face. He couldn't explain. He picked up his scarf and gloves from the chest, went out to his bike, made his way back down the drive. He liked the darkness. It was old and welcoming, the trees like an arch overhead, the night a blanket to hide under.

Presently he reached Hadale. Glad to be back in the dim streets, the rows of terraced houses, their doors opening on to the pavement, into small iron-railinged yards. He felt easier amongst them, these people who lived in small houses, who took you in and made you welcome.

He wheeled his bike round the back, parked it in Jimmy's shed and went indoors.

# CHAPTER 24

Christmas over, Richard Dawson was impatient for the old year to go, the new to take its place. Come January he was impatient for the days to drop away and the 20th to arrive. He liked the house and its grounds, liked Suffolk and the countryside, even liked its secretiveness that regarded him as a stranger to be smiled at, deferred to, yet always kept away from the heart of things. But what he really cherished was the prospect of leaving it, the pony trap to clip-clop him out of the drive away from his wife, his house, the woman bearing his child, away to a brand new future, free from so much as a sniff of St Matthews.

He knew he was being wished away, that Rose was counting the days as eagerly as he was. There were no arguments, nor even conversation. It was as though both were holding their breath in case they might lose this chance of freedom, be trapped into living with each other for ever.

Miriam marvelled at the luggage piling up in the hall, the cases, the trunks, baggage that betokened the Major's station in life, and marvelled at the child in her belly, that someone who owned enough to fill so many cases should have thought her, a woman who owned almost nothing, fit to have his baby. And she wondered how she would be able to provide, and whether the little one might one day puzzle at the poor thing he knew as his daddy.

A few days before the 20th she happened to see Richard passing the woodshed. Raymond was inside chopping wood for kindling.

"Go and look in the barn, Raymond," she said. "There's a chopper by the door. It'll cut better than that one."

"As I shan't see you any more," she said to Richard when her husband had gone, "there's something I want you to know."

She pointed to a besom broom in the corner of the shed.

" You remember that morning?"

He remembered it all too well, the violence, the pointed end of the broom pushed deep into the earth.

"I chopped these off to sharpen the point." She showed him some wood shavings chipped off a witch's broom. "I made sure you saw it next morning."

She tossed the chips away. "I felt the only thing between me and having you was your wife. I wanted her dead. When I pushed that point into the ground it was like killing her!"

She enjoyed the look on his face.

"All I'd got was Raymond. Your wife didn't want you. Nor wants you now. When I think how she treats you! And how I could!"

She went to embrace him. A woman he was seeing for the first time. He moved away.

"You hate her that much?"

"I feel sorry for her. I'll have your absence. Here." She touched her belly. "She won't miss you. I'll be the one who'll wake up in the night and know you're not here – missing you – feeling your boy growing!"

Her face reddened, the countrywoman he had told himself she was not.

"All she thinks about is herself! When I think how she treats you! And how I could!"

"You still hate her?"

"Because of you. I shan't when you've gone."

Raymond was coming towards them with the axe.

It was the nearest she'd been to tears.

"We'll be happy, won't we, Raymond. You, me and the Missus."

Raymond grinned. "Huh? Course we will."

"By the way, Raymond," Richard told him. "Mrs Dawson'll be the boss while I'm away."

He didn't want Miriam to have any misunderstanding in the matter of her and her husband's status. The contract the Whatlings had signed had been carefully drawn up.

"Missus'll be the boss, Raymond."

"Women generally are," Raymond said.

In the days before he went Rose seemed more attentive, asked from time to time if he had packed this or that item he might need when he was away, so he didn't have to come back to get it. One evening she showed him a wedding portrait of themselves outside the church porch, the happy pair, apparently looking forward to happy years together.

"How little we knew," he murmured. He went to put his arm round her, but she moved away. There was something upstairs, she said, she wanted to bring down and show him. But it never appeared.

Sometimes she pottered about in the garden to be out of his way, then remembered that in so many days' time she'd be free to potter to her heart's content for the rest of her life, and she'd go in and ask if he'd remembered to pack his socks, his spare shoes.

He would only write occasionally, he said. She would know no news was good news.

"Very true," she said.

The day before he left he gave her a legal-looking envelope. He explained what it was and what he wanted her to do. All the documents were inside. Everything was properly drawn up. It would be the last thing she would ever have to do for him.

As for money, he confirmed, she need never be short of money. Nineteen nineteen had been an excellent year for the company. And the house, garden, contents, everything had been properly made over to her, which she already knew, having heard the solicitor read certain documents through to her, and signing where he told her to sign.

Stanley arrived with the pony trap. The larger cases had been sent luggage in advance, the two smaller cases went in the back of the trap.

Rose offered her cheek. Richard shook hands with Miriam and Raymond, then he was up on board and they were clattering into the lane and out on the road to Beckthorp.

The grass was pale in the winter wind, the hedges nipped clean of leaves. Here and there through a gateway a field showed frost on the sides of the furrows. In the distance, winter trees no longer obscuring it, the church steeple ignored him, as it ignored all who left their parish to catch the train for life in London.

At the bridge a young girl stood by the road, waving. Stanley reined in.

"Maudie? What's got you up?"

"Goodbye, Major," she called. "Goodbye."

"Goodbye, my dear."

"You going to London now?"

"Just off to Beckthorp station."

"Come back soon."

Stanley flicked the reins.

"Goodbye! Come back soon!"

She called and waved till they turned away down Beckthorp hill, her voice obliterated by the wind, the rattle of wheels and hooves.

# CHAPTER 25

"Can't make out where they've got to! Maurice knows what time we have tea."

Mrs Briggs came away from her best-room window, adjusted the lace curtains.

"Not a sign of them. Maurice knows what time we have tea! Look at that clock!" Which meant the hands were pointing to a time they'd no right to point to. "Knows what time we have tea!"

It was a few Sundays after Christmas at the grocery shop in Beckthorp. Maudie's friend Eva had asked her to tea, and Maudie had been glad to accept and get away from her sisters. Having a shop, Mrs Briggs put a plateful of fancy cakes out, which made a change from that home-made muck Muriel always dished up.

"And what your father can be up to I can't imagine!"

A door opened and closed. Footsteps came uncertainly closer. Mr Briggs huffed and puffed into the room, stinking of beer. He had receding hair, round eyes, a narrow grey-rabbit moustache under his nose.

Mrs Briggs sniffed.

"I know what you've been up to!"

"Meeting went on a long time, Alice."

"Meetings wouldn't go on if you didn't hold them in the George and Dragon!"

"I've told you before. George and Dragon's the easiest place for folk to get to."

"Easiest! Asleep till nearly teatime! Easy for some!" She turned to the window, lifted a net curtain. "Maurice *knows* what time we have tea on a Sunday! What he and Phyllis can be doing!"

Eva gave Maudie a nudge.

"Look at 'em! Dawdling along as if they've got all the time in the world!"

Maurice and his young lady came in, the boy thin, the girl fat, both of them pale as a pair of sheets. His mother's attention was on their shoes, walking over her best carpet.

"Phyllis didn't feel too good," Maurice told them. "Had to sit down a few minutes."

"You look washed out!" Mrs Briggs studied the girl's full moon of a face. "Can't think what you've been up to!"

"Haven't quite got my strength back yet, Mrs Briggs."

"Yet?" Mrs Briggs queried. "You been ill?" She shot a look at her son. "Didn't tell *me* she's been ill."

"Had a bit of an upset. Didn't you, Phyllis. Bit of an upset tummy."

"All right now, though." But sat down gladly enough when Maurice got her a chair.

"I've opened the tin of salmon," Eva said.

"Might as well start then." Mrs Briggs made a point of looking at the clock. "You'll have to sort out between yourselves where you're all going to sit."

Mr Briggs pulled out the chair next to him. "Here y'are, Maudie. Then Maurice can sit next to Phyllis over there."

Maudie watched Phyllis's smooth little face munching away like a child, bread and butter and strawberry jam, tinned fruit and jelly Wondered how she could have done it – letting Maurice get on top of her – letting him put it in

– the pair of them – time after time – till she got pregnant! Then the baby – all unexpected – and dying like that a few minutes later – having to be got rid of. Phyllis, no more than a child herself, munching into jam tarts and sponge cake – knowing all about doing it with a man – getting herself full of a baby.

"Oh! Oh! A mouse!"

She brushed her knee with her hand, sat back, startled.

"Was that your leg?" Mr Briggs asked, all surprised.

Maudie looked under the table.

"I thought it was a mouse!" she said, laughed a little, as if the shock had stopped her breath. "Thought it must be a mouse on my knee!"

Everyone had gone quiet. Mr Briggs coloured a little, said their damned cat was too damned fat to bother about catching mice nowadays and they'd have to get another.

Mrs Briggs said it wasn't her fault the cat was fat. *She* wasn't the one who fed it bits at the table, she said, and looked at Briggs as if she could kill him.

"Mouse?" Maurice was surprised. "Never seen a mouse here! Did you feel it on your foot, Maudie?"

"Only up my leg."

"Couldn't have been a mouse, then," he told her. "You'd a' been sure to feel it on your foot to start with."

His father glared at him. "What do you know about mice! You're never here! Always gadding about!"

"Only been round at Phyllis's. Be different when we're married."

His thin face had gone red, as if he wasn't used to having words with his father.

"Married! I should say so!" Mr Briggs's buck rabbit eyes stared at him. "Can't support yourself, let alone a wife! You'll get no permission off me till you've got yourself a job!"

"Not for want of looking. Town's full of people out of the army."

"Army!" Mr Briggs snorted. "Never mind the army! Robinson's didn't give you the shove for nothing." He turned to his wife. "Never did hear the ins and outs of him getting the sack, did we?"

Mrs Briggs looked past him, asked Maudie if she'd like a piece of cake. And cut her a bigger piece than she otherwise would have done. That was the way to treat a guest! Not what her husband had been up to!

They were in Eva's bedroom. Maudie said how much she had enjoyed the tea, said how kind of Eva's mother to have her. "How pale Phyllis looked!" she said. "Think she's got over it?"

Didn't know she was pregnant till a week or two before she had it, Eva said. "Then one day, there it was, in the bedroom!"

Easier to talk about Phyllis, a way of not talking about her father.

"Seemed all right when it was born!"

The two lay close together on the bed, speaking in whispers, afraid of who might be listening. "Her mother sounded a bit dubious. Said the baby might have something wrong with it. 'You go and get into my bed and have a rest,' she told Phyllis. 'I'll see to him.' When Phyllis went back the little mite was dead. 'Never mind, m'dear,' her mother told her, 'there'll be plenty more. Used to happen to some of mine sometimes.'"

The two lay quiet.

"Do you think – ?"

Eva nodded.

"Her mother – ?"

"Poor little thing. And poor little Maurice!"

"Poor Maurice?"

Surely if anyone was to blame it was Maurice!

But the thought wouldn't leave her, the young chap taking the tiny mite, his own son, wrapped in a newspaper under his overcoat, his own little son and leaving him, alone and cold under the hedge.

"He really cried, Maurice did."

"Does your mother know about the baby?"

Eva put a finger to her lips, glanced at the door. "Nor Father. He'd kick Maurice out if he knew. Might affect trade! Thinks more about trade than anything. Isn't very nice, Father."

Their young eyes met, their tears for the little mite under the hedge, and because it could so easily have happened to them.

Maudie cycled away from the shop, away from the lit streets. With Beckthorp behind her and the darkness ahead, she reached the hill towards St Matthew's, her mind in a whirl, what with old Briggs's hand on her knee, and the baby wrapped round with newspaper, and Maurice carrying him away because he daren't be seen digging about in the garden.

It was a cold night, her breath white and momentary as she biked up the hill. She reached the black tarred stable, ivy growing over it. Then the postbox. She gazed at it as if it was holy.

To the right the road led home, to her sisters and the life she was sick of.

To the left lay Church Lane.

That lane! That night! The moon through the branches! The path round the pond, the drooping willow fingers!

Those knots in the great barn doors! She wanted to ride down the lane, breathe the air he'd breathed, walk on the ground he'd walked on. But like an everlasting ache that thought: *Miriam Whatling lives there now.*

Because of her he'd gone to London.

She gripped the mouth of the letter box.

He'd be expecting her to write. All she needed was the address!

Yet he'd know she couldn't write, didn't know his address, couldn't ask, couldn't ever find out.

As if out of the mouth of the postbox the thought came: *Richard was in London!* Out of the postbox itself – *And you must go to London and find him!*

She kissed the cold metal lips in blessing.

She pedalled home, back to the bitches, the farm where she wouldn't be living much longer!

# CHAPTER 26

He went over the plan again. He'd use a couple of cartridges, the red ones with brass ends everyone used hereabouts. He'd bike up Hill Lane to the tradesman's entrance to Werndby House, the gun in pieces in a bag, he'd hide the bike under the hedge, put the gun together, wait in the plantation till the dog got let out for its late night run. Then he'd whistle it. When it came he'd cock the gun and – goodbye dog!

"Few nice bones for a stew, please?"

Herbert laid the steel down he'd been putting an edge on the knife with, gave the old lady a bit more meat with the bones than was Mr Bumford's custom.

"Oh! They'll make – "

"There we are, Mrs Curtis."

Herbert wrapped her purchase up, put it in the bag for her, opened the till and gave her her change.

"Oh, thank you! Thank you very much!"

She turned away, her old feet careful across the sawdust, relieved when she got to the door and someone outside opened it for her.

"Oh, thank you! Thank you very much!"

The person who came in was the gardener from Werndby House. He'd brought the order from Mrs Norman, the Stelfox's housekeeper.

Well-to-do customers were served by Mr Bumford. Herbert saw to the others. When he realised who it was, Walter Bumford put the liver aside he was about to cut up for old Mrs Hammond, took the order and read it through.

"Tomorrow afternoon all right?" he asked.

"Mrs Norman said must be mornin'."

The butcher twitched the paper round with his bloodstained fingers, considered it, put it on a spike.

"She'll have it before twelve. Anything for now?"

He had an unusual voice, like the shriek of a pig, but distant, as though obstructed by phlegm.

The man wanting nothing for now, Bumford turned back to Mrs Hammond.

"Three quarters of liver, ma'am? Three quarters of lovely liver."

He gripped the dark slippery meat, gave it a slice or two through with his knife, dropped a handful on the scales.

"Three quarters of lovely – "

The pans came level, the metal finger pointed almost vertical, the meat was whipped off, was wrapped in a moment.

"Near as dammit, missus. Blind man'd be glad to see it. Anything else?"

He gave her her change, was already looking at the next customer.

He'd got a little job to do round the back of the shop, he told Ann and Jimmy. Something he'd been meaning to do for ages. A shame he'd got to go out again so late, but he'd been too busy during the day.

They understood. Where Herbert was concerned they always understood.

He tied the bag to his crossbar, wheeled his bike to the gate, pushed away up the street. It was a clear night, cold, the moon on the wane. He was glad it was cold because eyes would be watching and it wouldn't look strange to wear gloves.

He cycled down Chapel Lane, past the slaughterhouse, round into Market Place. Like the war, he thought, the exercise planned beforehand, little left to chance. It was when things weren't planned properly that they went wrong. He pictured putting the cartridges into the breech, snapping the gun shut, waiting for the dog to come out for its run. He'd whistle it, wait for it to come up to the hedge, its tail still, head up, nose tasting the scent, and when it was close enough, squeeze the trigger. Then it'd be a case of biking casually up Hill Lane to that place where he could hide the bag with the gun in it. And because of the gloves there wouldn't be a trace of a fingerprint.

The shop was in sight. He rode down the back lane, felt for the yard key in his pocket.

"Herbert! That you, Herbert?"

Someone lurched towards him. The pig-squeal voice sounded strange.

"Mr Bumford?"

"Thank God! Had to find someone -" The striped shirt was undone at the neck, no white collar, no tie. "It's Doris!"

He was almost in tears.

Herbert jumped off his bike, Bumford grabbed his arm, hurried him towards the house, the front door wide open. Herbert followed him upstairs into the front bedroom.

"What's up?"

Bumford pointed to his wife, unconscious, half covered on the bed. The lamplight caught eyes that were neither closed nor open, showed her grey-black hair tangled across the pillow, the face pallid except for a patch of burning on the cheek. The noise was her breath, rattling like shingle.

"Had the doctor?"

"Couldn't leave her." The man was panting, his face shiny with sweat.

"Who's your doctor?"

Bumford didn't know. The Bumfords had never been ill. All they knew about doctors was what their orders were for meat.

"I'll go and get MacDonald."

Herbert ran back to his bike, hurried away. The doctor's house was up the hill in the posher part of the town. He cycled hard, arrived.

He rang the bell. Waited. Rang again. Rang till the front door opened.

Dr MacDonald, in slippers, jacketless, his spectacles low on his nose, viewed the disturber.

"Surgery's closed." He tried to push the door shut.

Herbert put his boot against it.

"This is urgent."

"Open at nine in the morning."

"It's Mrs Bumford. Butcher's wife. She's collapsed."

Maybe the novelty of attending the Bumfords and the prospect of a butcherly reward changed his mind. He asked who Herbert was, checked where the Bumfords lived.

"Right. Wait there."

He closed the door, soon emerged round the back of the house, his black case strapped to his cycle carrier.

The wave of influenza which at the end of the Great War washed over Europe had left puddles of infection across the continent. One such had appeared at Hadale. There was little a doctor could do beyond taking soundings with stethoscope and thermometer, examining the tongue and the drawn-back eyelid, and giving instruction as to warmth, rest, comfort and liquid intake. It was up to the patients whether they survived or not.

"How is she, doctor? Is she bad?"

Doctor MacDonald shook the thermometer down, washed it in a tumbler of water on the washstand, wiped it on the towel on the side rail, all the time viewing Bumford as he might a specimen, detached.

He slid the thermometer into its container, put the tube back in the case.

"May last the night." His eyes were hard blue, pitiless. "Or she may not."

It was the other side of doctoring, seeing the effect of death when it walked into a family. Bumford's mouth hung open, his eyes empty.

"One thing you can do," the doctor told him. "Warm flannel, wipe her face and hands, dry them with a towel. Might as well keep her fairly comfortable."

Herbert let him out.

Mr Bumford sat by the bed. Except for their honeymoon they had slept every sleep of their married life on this bed, surrounded by this same pink flowered wallpaper, these bits of furniture that had belonged to his parents. Doris used to say one day they'd have the room redecorated, get some new furniture. The years had passed, they'd sold meat over the counter, they'd taken meat round the parishes, the wallpaper and furniture had stayed the same. She never complained. She ran the house and half the business. Walter had never wanted for a clean shirt, a hot meal or a tidy bed, had never had to say please, never bothered to say thank you. Now here she was, near death!

Doris had always been strong. He'd never bothered about a holiday, or a servant to help her out. Plenty of people with less to rub together than he'd got had a servant, but he'd never given Doris much. Except his name.

"Be round first thing in the morning," Herbert told him.

Bumford roused himself, remembered who Herbert was.

"What about tomorrow?" Herbert asked him.

"Tomorrow?"

"The shop. And the round. Shall I do it?"

"That's it."

No more than a mumble. He couldn't take his eyes off the shape in the bed, couldn't hear beyond her throat rasping at the air, rasping at it.

"See to the shop in the morning, shall I?"

"Flannel! Where's she keep the flannel?"

There was one on the washstand. There was no fire. No warm water. No bowl that Herbert could see.

He took charge, asked where things were. Presently the fire was laid and lit in the bedroom, the kettle was on the hob, the lamp turned up to brighten the room. The butcher sat like a man paralysed, watching what was left of his wife.

"Give me the keys," Herbert told him. "I'll open the shop up tomorrow. See about the round."

Bumford tried to fish out the keys from the front pocket of his trousers. His leg was too fat, the pocket too tight.

"You'll have to stand up."

The butcher did as he was told, fetched the keys out, handed them over. Never took his eyes off her. It was the first time the keys had been handled by anyone other than Walter or Doris Bumford – and he was scarcely aware of it.

Herbert left them, a man and his wife, at the moment that comes to all.

Went back to the shop, unlocked the door at the back, hid the bag with the gun in it under a bench in the stable.

It hadn't worked out. Things had gone wrong tonight. One of these nights they'd go right.

# CHAPTER 27

A little after four in the morning Herbert wheeled his bike out, set off for Hadale. The remains of a moon lit the frost, cold air caught the throat. Here and there an owl shrieked, occasionally a white shape dipped out of the darkness, and with a beat of its wing lifted back into the night. Presently, along the bigger streets, gas lamps lit the mist, a halo of whiteness either side, the glow inseparable from fog.

He let himself into the shop. He lit a lantern, went through to the back to the stable, gave the pony a feed and told him they'd be setting out on the round about eleven o'clock.

"Werndby House. Be a treat, won't it?"

The last visit had been a fiasco, last night's effort had come to nothing, he knew the sort of woman Mrs Norman the housekeeper was. But it was a case of unfinished business. He'd probably come off worst, but with Kate in London that would be one complication the less.

He lit the gas lamps in the shop, set to work on the display, sawing, cutting, chopping on the salt-scrubbed bench, taking cuts and joints through on trays to the white-tiled window shelf. There were sausages to make and hang, hearts, liver and other offal to put in the three white enamel trays, rabbits, pheasants and wood pigeons to arrange down the sides at the front door. He checked the order book, got the orders up into the wicker baskets ready for the round, each order with its blue and white bill, got the bucket of sawdust and shovelled a covering over the floor.

Outdoors it was starting to get light. He wiped his hands, ate the sandwiches Ann had made him the night before. Then he raised the blinds. Everywhere wet with fog. People were cycling into work, vans, lorries, horses and carts were moving about their business. He opened the shop and waited for business.

All went well enough, considering there was only one person to serve behind the counter instead of three.

"Never known the Bumfords miss a day," people said. "Not in all these years!"

He got on well with them, as if they appreciated a normal voice instead of Bumford's cattle-market rasp.

Come mid morning when custom slackened he took the opportunity to close the shop. He put a notice up to say the closure was because of illness and tomorrow would be business as usual, then harnessed Dainty up ready for the round.

Then realized the snag.

The order book was a living thing, had a past stretching back many years. Doris had added customer after customer, she knew the families, their range of meat, knew where everyone lived, knew whether you drove up or took the basket and walked up. And knowing all this she hadn't found it necessary to write it down. She had talked about these things. She had talked about her meat round more than she had talked about anything else. Everything worth knowing about the round had come off Doris's tongue, the house with the rhododendron where the newcomers lived, the cottage where only Widow Spencer lived, who bought mutton enough to feed a man as well, which was more than likely knowing Widow Spencer. She talked of the row of houses where the Hunters used to live till they moved down into Werndford, who still hadn't paid for that half of liver and two chops must be two years ago now. She talked about Mrs Bloomfield and that daughter of hers – but it was only now, with the orders loaded and ready to be taken round, that Herbert realized what he ought to have realized earlier, that the addresses were in Mrs Bumford's head. Delivery was going to take a lot longer than he'd thought.

One name he did know. It was the cottage where Jack Longbotham lived who used to come into the Hadale Arms of a Sunday. He drew to a stop outside, tethered the pony and went to the door with his basket. After a while he heard someone approaching from within. The locks were drawn, the door opened.

"Only butcher," Mrs Longbotham called out, relieved. "Why ever didn't thee come round back, lad? Missus always comes round back! Wherever has she got to?"

Herbert told her what little he knew. Mrs Longbotham and Mrs Bumford went back years, and the little he could tell them had to be retold, the astonishment lived through again, the questions answered again, his scrap of news repeated again.

"I never would have – never dreamt – thee's fair –!"

But they were helpful telling him where many of his customers lived and how to find them.

Werndby House was on five or six acres, bounded in front by the road that led to Werndby and on one side by Hill Lane, a narrow road leading up to High Moor. Dainty knew Hill Lane, knew the way into the paddock at the back of the house, the way to the tradesmen's entrance. In the moments before the pony came to a stop, Herbert's mind relived what he had planned for the previous evening, hiding in the hazel thicket, waiting on one knee, shotgun cocked ready, the dog out for its last run of the evening. It heard his whistle, bounded towards the thicket – closer – came to the hedge –

Didn't even yelp. Half its head blown away, its brains across the grass.

What ought to have happened.

The pony stopped at the yard. Herbert jumped down, carried the basket up to the door. The bell push was a brass button set in a white porcelain surround. In this, in black lettering, the word TRADESMEN.

He rang, glad Kate was away in London, wouldn't have wanted her to be embarrassed by a tradesman. He rang again.

The original building of Werndby House was of stone block cut so well that little mortar had been needed for pointing. The construction was solid, the stone natural to the area, grey, with here and there blocks of green-grey or purple-grey, a good-looking old house. Spreading away from the main building were modern yellow brick extensions, the chimney bricks bright red. And a concrete path all round. The sort of thing Arthur Stelfox would build.

He rang again, heard it echo deep indoors.

The door opened.

Mrs Norman was a lean-faced woman, hair swept tight back, her eyes cold. She looked at him, seemed not know who this individual on the doorstep with a butcher's basket could be.

"Well?"

The meat, he told her.

"The meat! At this time of day!"

She had made it clear, she said, the meat was wanted this morning. She wanted no excuses. Had the gardener said what time the order was required? Had he said it was wanted in the morning? Had the order been accepted by the shop? In that case, if Bumford's couldn't supply what was needed when it was needed there were plenty of butchers who could.

She spoke calmly. She had right on her side. It was useless to argue.

"Do you go without, then, missus!"

He lifted the basket, swung it round – only to see Kate, mounted on Beauty, sitting listening to what had been going on.

"Thought you were in London!"

"I came back yesterday."

Herbert carried on past her, put the basket back in the cart.

"I only hope, Kate, I never have the misfortune to have to come to this house again."

He climbed in, shook the reins.

"Miss Stelfox!" the housekeeper called. "Tell that young man to leave the meat!"

"Miss Stelfox," Herbert called. "Tell that ugly old woman to go to hell."

He shook the reins, Dainty started forward.

"Miss Stelfox! Tell him to leave the meat!"

Herbert clicked his tongue at the pony. "Gee up!"

Kate wheeled her horse round, rode beside him.

"Aren't you going to leave the meat?"

"I'd rather chuck it in the ditch."

Angry with her. Elated that she was near.

"Won't you get into trouble?"

"Trouble?"

"If Pa has to tell Mr Bumford – ?"

"If Pa has to tell!"

He knew whose side she was on! Why can't you be loyal to me? he asked in his mind. Whether I'm right or wrong, be loyal to me!

The cart rumbled out on to the road up towards High Moor.

"Thank Christ to be away from there!"

To his surprise Kate had followed him. He urged Dainty into a trot.

"You don't have to come too! I can find my own way."

"I'm upset we've made you angry."

"You haven't. I know you're not on my side – but I've known that long time."

Ahead was a house, its front wall almost abutting the roadside. Herbert checked his addresses, asked her if Mr Perry lived at the place.

"He does. But why are you doing the round?"

He climbed down off the cart, took the basket.

"Someone's got to."

He knocked at the door, delivered the order. Mr Perry was all questions about Mrs Bumford, amazed at this upset in routine. He settled the bill, got away as soon as he could.

Kate had tied Beauty's bridle to the back of the cart, was sitting in the passenger's seat.

"I hope you don't mind. I couldn't talk back there."

"I'd rather sit next to you than anyone in the world! You know that!"

He wanted to talk to her, wanted to explain all sorts of things, wanted things to go right, and they wouldn't go right.

He completed his deliveries to the isolated houses on the moor, then started the descent to the hamlets where the rest were to be delivered.

"Is Mrs Bumford ill?"

Whether Doris Bumford was alive or dead, he had no idea. From what he'd seen last night it could have gone either way.

"And Walter Bumford?"

From what he'd seen last night, Herbert said, all Bumford cared about now was that little old woman under the bedclothes. So far as Bumford was concerned the business would have to look after itself.

"So you've been seeing to it? Alone? The shop and the round?"

She pieced together something of his day, the half past four start, the preparation, serving the customers and taking the money, doing the round – and finding out details that were mainly in Doris's head. And he'd still got the rest of the round to do, then feed the pony and put the cart away, get the meat out for tomorrow, and then bike home to his lodgings.

"Have you had anything to eat?"

He was over the worst part, he told her, working out who he'd got to visit. Might not be so hard tomorrow. He'd be all right till he ran out of meat. Then he'd have to slaughter. He'd have to go to a sale and buy a steer first. Next week some time. Maybe Bumford would be back by then.

"Worst part is meeting someone like your housekeeper. Thinks tradesman are dirt. Who she can keep waiting!"

Too many like her about in England, men as well as women. They couldn't slaughter a beast and cut the hide off and butcher the carcass and lift the sides on to hooks and cut the joints for someone's table. And work out how much to charge and not overcharge or undercharge. A tradesman could! Nothing to be sneered at in being a tradesman –

The fog that all day had been high and hazy began to thicken. Either side of the lane the treetops and then the hedges became shrouded in mist. They were travelling alone through a grey-white world on a road that appeared a yard or two in front and disappeared a yard or two behind.

"If I came in tomorrow, could I take the money while you served?"

"What would your friends Charles and Hugh say if they heard you'd been helping a tradesman?"

There was no reply, only the sound of iron-shod hooves, the roll of iron tyres.

He wished she would answer, wished she would give him more cause for bitterness.

But she was sitting beside him. Had bothered to be with him ever since the row with the housekeeper.

Ahead he made out the opening to the tradesman's entrance at Werndby House. He stopped, jumped down, undid the rope to Beauty's bridle.

"I thought you weren't going to stop here any more!"

He lifted out a basket, put the Stelfox's meat in it.

"Or leave us any meat."

"I wouldn't want you to go without. You know that."

He carried the basket with the meat. She walked with him, leading the horse.

"I must have made you very angry."

He felt able to look at her.

"Sometimes I wish I hadn't come back."

"Herbert!"

"England's no place for people like me to come back home to."

They were at the edge of the yard. Light came from a window, the rays solidifying against the fog.

"Is that how you feel you've been treated?"

"Isn't just me, Kate." He handed her the basket. "And tell that ugly old woman I hope it chokes her."

He said she could return the basket any time. "As for you and Charles, I wish you well. No -" when she went to interrupt. "I mean it. He's not a bad bloke."

He gave Beauty a stroke on the nose. "And you tell your mistress she's the last person in the world I'd want to be unkind to."

"Your shop," she asked, "did you say you open at half past eight? And by the way – not that it makes any difference – there isn't any Charles. Or any anybody."

He finished the round, finished what he had to do in the shop. He gave Dainty a rub down, a good feed and a reassuring talking-to.

He cycled home, put his bike away and went indoors. Ann and Jimmy asked him how his day had gone.

He loved them, this caring couple. He told them about the customers, the trouble with the round, the awful housekeeper at Werndby House.

"Leave the meat!" he mimicked. "Tell him to leave the meat!"

Jimmy laughed. "Sounds just like the old bitch!"

"Went pretty well, I suppose," Herbert said. "All in all."

# CHAPTER 28

He was used to seeing in the dark, even at four o'clock of a winter morning. And when the gas was lit the tiled walls, the bench, the sawdusted floor, glowed with cheerfulness. *There isn't any Charles,* she'd said. *There isn't any anybody.* He felt like singing.

There were fewer orders for the round, the shop not having been open so long the previous day. What orders there were he got up and put in the baskets along with the bills. Then it was a matter of bringing in a side of pork or a forequarter of beef and sliding them round on the rails to be sawn, jointed, displayed.

Time passed. Work the day depended on was complete. He went through to the stable, fed and watered Dainty, sat and ate his sandwiches with her. At the shop door someone knocked.

"Knock away," he said. Ate another sandwich. The knocking continued. He finished his breakfast, went through, opened the door.

"Kate!"

She had Beauty on a rein, was in her riding habit and hat for warmth.

"Get me a saw, Herbert. I'm here to help."

He looked at his watch. It was eight o'clock. *There isn't any Charles,"* rang in his head.

He showed her how the till worked, how to do the bills and carbons, was surprised how quick she was.

Time to do the rabbits. The chopper thudded against the bench four times. Then a fifth time. A furry head joined four furry feet in the pail. He slit the skin, dragged it off the pinky-grey body. Then prepared three more, arranged the pale-thighed, narrow-hipped creatures on metal trays in the shop window.

"What we have to do to animals!"

She was a farmer's daughter. It wasn't a reproach.

Herbert opened on time, and with him calling the amount and Kate handling the bills and giving change, service was speedy. He noticed the attention she gave the customers, her pleasantness to the children, the interest she took in what was said. These who were mouths and purses to Bumford.

He'd saved a few bones, bits of meat.

"For that dog of yours, when you go."

"He'll love his Uncle Herbert."

He said he'd go and get Beauty for her.

"I'm coming on the round. If you'll have me."

"If! Never an *if* with you, Kate. Or ever will be."

He carried the morning's unsold meat through to the cool room, he scrubbed the benches with salt and cold water, he wiped them dry, he loaded the baskets with meat to be delivered.

The words sang.

*I'm coming on the rounds – if you'll have me.*

Outside the fog had melted away, the sky looked threatening but the air had turned warmer. He harnessed Dainty into the cart.

"Ready?"

She rolled Gypsy's scraps tighter, he locked the shop behind them. They went to the yard, he loaded the baskets on to the cart, covered them with the tilt.

A crack of thunder, the heavens opened.

"Quick!"

They ran back through the rain, Herbert unlocked the yard door for her, they raced across to the stables.

"How absolutely – !"

She laughed, took off her riding hat, shook her hair. They sat side by side in the gloom, clothes, faces streaming, the downpour hammered on the roof, slashed down the timbers, rattled out of the gutters.

"I could sit with you like this for ever."

"Thee'd not get that round done, lad!" she laughed.

The rain eased. He looked out to check what the prospects were, disappointed to see the sky brightening.

"Herbert!"

She wondered if she could borrow a bag she'd seen under the bench to put the meat and bones in for Gypsy. The newspaper they were in was soaked through. "I'll bring it back in the morning."

He took it to her, took out the sections of shotgun.

She put her soggy package in it, smiled her thanks. "Your gun?"

"I was going to shoot your dog."

He thought how beautiful she was, how fine her eyes, how they changed as his remark sank in.

"Gypsy?"

She looked from him to the gun, the grey steel barrels narrowing towards the killing end, the ears of the hammers ready for cocking, the twin triggers ready within the guard.

"*Shoot* him!"

She studied his face, couldn't believe, wanted the fiction dispelled.

"*Gypsy?*"

But he wanted her to know him. It was no good if she didn't know him.

177

"You weren't!"

She wanted to smile, as if it was a joke, the kind of unfunny joke people make sometimes.

Then knew it wasn't a joke.

"Going to kill him?"

She seemed to withdraw. Even her voice pulled back.

But she'd got to know him for what he was. He couldn't bear falseness between them.

"But why?" She sounded sorry, as if he'd become something incomplete.

He heard the distance in her, the separation from something repellent.

"I can't believe it, Herbert! Say it isn't true!"

His words weren't ready. He was back in Werndby House, Kate upstairs, laughing with her friends. The dog burst in, ran up to him, straight to his crotch. And Arthur laughing *That's what the dog thinks of him!*

Well-to-do friends of hers with easy lives, all of them laughing. He in scuffed shoes, a butcher's boy who had gone on a bike, and Kate, who'd invited him, upstairs with her friends, oblivious of him.

"Where you were going to do it?"

"On your back meadow."

She pictured it, saw the way in from the road, the cover from the hedge, the road to get away on. It was believable. The gun in pieces, the bag to carry it in, transportable on a bike. It was all believable.

"But you don't say *why!*"

"Because I couldn't nicely shoot your father!"

She could only stare at him. This man, angry enough to think he had right on his side.

"If I'd had a gun that night I'd have shot him. Yes, in his own house! That sneering, jeering – you can look shocked!

If you'd been invited to a party you didn't particularly want to go to except to see the only girl in the world, and been looked down on and made a fool of by people who'd had it easy in the war and made money out of it! If you'd been -"

He was too angry to carry on, knew it was the end of them.

"And that dog – bursting in, straight at your crotch and everyone laughing, your father the loudest of the lot – so I told myself, when I got the chance -"

She'd get her horse and ride away. It would be the last he'd see of her.

"I'd got it all planned."

"You'd actually have shot my dog?"

"Dog!" he jeered. "Shot a *dog*! I've been four years – killing *men!* You don't know! None of you! Hundreds of men. I've seen all my friends -"

He saw her for the person she was, one of those who didn't know, couldn't know.

"Every night – I see it! Shells bursting, men cut to pieces. Every night! I've seen all my friends -"

He seized the gun barrel, threw it across the floor.

"Don't you think I saw enough of guns?"

His great strong hands gripped the gun stock as if it was something living, something that could be killed.

"Then they send us home!"

He turned and faced her.

"And when we get home no-one wants us. We're in the way! You can feel it all round you. All your fatgut father can do is jeer at us, tell us we don't know how to work. But if they'd been through what we've been through -!"

He seemed to see them, almost smiled to see them in the same predicament.

"Them who had it cushy at home – wonder how hard they'd work!"

Outside the rain had stopped, the din on the roof silent.

"I could have shot your dog, Kate. I wouldn't have turned a hair."

He spoke quietly, the heat of his anger over. He knew he had said too much, too much to be unsaid. He picked the gun barrel up, put it on the shelf with the other parts.

"So now you know what I'm like. Not that it matters."

He opened the door and peered out. Patches of blue showed here and there amongst the clouds.

"I'd better get started."

He lifted Beauty's saddle down for her, laid it on the horse.

"You'll be wanting to get home. I'll open the gate."

Kate led Beauty out, hitched her to the back of the cart.

"You don't have to come." he said. "After that."

"I think I do have to."

She was quiet, unsmiling. He hoped he wasn't in for a session of the sulks.

"I don't intend to shoot the bloody thing now," he said.

He led the pony and cart out, closed the gate and climbed in. Kate climbed in beside him.

"I didn't thank you for the meat for Gypsy," she said. "I'll tell him it's a present from his Uncle Herbert."

But what he'd said stung him like a cut.

Gradually they found out who was who on the round, where they lived, what was wanted for the following delivery. Kate wrote the list of addresses appropriate to the names. After a while Herbert asked if he could have a look at the list. He looked at it so long she asked if she'd spelt something wrong.

It was her handwriting, he said. It reminded him of the invitation she'd sent him about the party.

"The times I read it. I pictured you writing it. The way you held the pen. Pictured you licking the envelope."

He had a readable face. Reading her writing lit it up.

She said she was sorry the way the party had turned out for him. "I didn't realise what I was inviting you to."

"San fairy ann, Kate."

The round took them to isolated homesteads on the edge of the moor. They had to sort out where customers lived, the new orders, the standing orders. Gradually the shock of what he had thought of doing lifted, his anger at her father eased.

"What you were saying about the soldiers who came back from the war," she said. "I'm glad you told me."

He didn't respond, wished she'd leave it alone.

"What you feel about them," she said, "is what I feel about women."

"Women?"

Women, like soldiers, were also thought of as second-class, she said.

"Think of the trouble women have had just to be allowed to vote."

But the suffrage battle was being won. What was important now was the battle for contraception.

"This is nineteen-twenty. If a man has intercourse, that's fine. If a woman has intercourse, that's awful. Why? Because it's the woman who bears the child. If a young man fathers a child he's sowing his wild oats. If a young woman has a baby she's immoral, she's lost her reputation. Where's the fairness in that? So the battle I want to fight is the battle for women's contraception."

It startled him, hearing such talk, especially from a woman. It was like an attack on society, on standards he had been brought up with. Not that he cared much about society. Society had no time for him, and he didn't see why he should bother what happened to society. What she said made sense, he supposed.

"So what can you do? Geld all the men?"

"I was looking at those mothers and children in your shop this morning. Mrs Meakins, was it? And all her little ones. The poorer the society, generally speaking, the higher the birth-rate, because those women have a lower status, and less control over their fertility."

She hadn't said anything he disagreed with, but it sounded wrong. Or if not wrong, disturbing. Yet he would back Kate against the world.

"So what can you do?"

She asked him if he'd heard of Marie Stopes. "Published that notorious *Married Love* a year or two ago."

Wasn't that the book the newspapers said was outrageous? He hadn't read it, had heard it was dreadful. Especially for a woman to write. Didn't know anything about Marie Stopes, though.

It was Marie Stopes, Kate told him, that she'd like to help.

"You agree with her?"

"Very much so. From what I've heard of her. But I'm not medically qualified. That's why I'm hoping to train as a nurse."

"A nurse! Where?"

"London."

They had reached Hadale. A little later Herbert unlocked the gate to the yard and drove in. He dismounted, handed Kate down. For a moment he held her hand.

"I can't help what I feel about you. I'll see even less of you in London."

She stroked Beauty's nose.

"It's not that I don't like you, Herbert. In spite of what you were going to do. But I must get qualified. And London's the place to do it."

She'd written to two or three hospitals, and was waiting to hear. It would be a three-year course.

"I daresay we'll get a few days off sometimes. But it's a long way to come home."

For Herbert, the shop, Hadale, the very idea of butchering suddenly seemed pointless.

"If I'd known you were going away," he said, "I wouldn't have -"

"Wouldn't have thought of shooting the dog?"

"Wouldn't have told you about it."

He thought it decent of her to laugh.

He took the baskets inside, unharnessed Dainty and put him in his stable.

"Have this." He gave her some money. "It's what I get for a days work. You've earnt the shop a lot more than this. I'll let Mr Bumford know.'

When she demurred he said, "It's no more than you deserve. It's a day's work, after all."

"And women should be equal to men," she agreed, taking it. "It's more than I'll earn this next three years."

She remembered she'd brought a bag of sandwiches for their lunch. Had left it on a shelf in the cool room.

"If it isn't too late?"

He remembered it for years, the wooden walls of the stable, the day closing in outside, and he and Kate sitting on a pile of straw sharing her sandwiches, their light the light from a paraffin lantern high up over the horseshoes nailed to the timbers.

"Where did you get the idea of Charles from?" she asked. "I mean me and Charles?"

He supposed it was from Aunt May. She'd said something to that effect when he was looking at her photograph.

"Poor Mum." Kate smiled. "It's Mum all over. Pairing people off."

"I got the impression she wasn't very keen on marriage."

"She loathes the very idea of marriage. She knows what a poor deal it is for women. But she likes the idea of pairs."

Were her parents unhappy, Herbert asked. He knew what a loud personality her father was.

Which, Kate said, wasn't his fault any more than being a quiet personality was another person's fault. Her mother had all the material things she wanted, a nice home, nice clothes, nice things.

"But she doesn't have her own life, you see."

Herbert did see. He couldn't imagine how any woman could live five minutes with Arthur Stelfox, let alone a woman like poor Aunt May.

That was the point, Kate said. Her mother had had an illegitimate baby.

"You?"

Yet he knew lots of couples who'd married when the girl was pregnant. "Happens to thousands," he said. "Your Pa was doing no more than his duty, marrying her."

"It wasn't his duty at all."

They couldn't have been said more calmly, those half dozen words that changed everything.

"Wasn't? So he – ! So you're not – my cousin?"

"I hope I'll be as much your cousin as ever."

He shook his head. The idea was so new, so big!

*It wasn't his duty at all!*

"Pa's been nothing but a loving father to me," she said. "Nothing he's ever said or done would have led me to think he wasn't my own loving Pa."

He could only watch her, listen to her. Her looks, the things she said – the girl was suddenly brand new!

"Does your Pa know you know?"

"I hope he never knows, Herbert. I know he's a hard man in business, but he's never been hard to me. And if you really want to know, I wish he was my father."

They sat and finished their sandwiches.

"And what about Aunt May?" he asked. "She told you, did she?"

Kate got to her feet, brushed the straw from her clothes.

"A year or two ago. As if she wanted me to forgive her. Poor Mum. As if it was any of my business how I was brought into the world!"

She undid Beauty's tether, stroked her ears.

"But now partly it is my business. This business of fertility and contraception I told you about. If Mum hadn't fallen for me – by someone I don't enquire after – she wouldn't have felt she had to marry someone she didn't love. Which thousands of women have to every year. So that's why I want to join the Marie Stopes movement. It's what I must do."

"Everything else," she added, "comes second."

He knew it was unintended. She had helped him all day, she had told him a secret – and now she was as good as gone.

"I'm used to coming second."

"Never think that."

She held his hand, face to face with him.

"You made me ashamed earlier, the way you were spoken to at the party. A man who's been through what you've been through – Werndby House didn't know who its guest was."

He held the bridle, she was up in the saddle.

"You do understand? What I want to do? It's like you volunteering for the war. You couldn't *not* do it. It's me that's volunteering this time."

He opened the gate for her. He liked being in the darkness with her, the two of them bonded by shadow.

"Shall I come again tomorrow?" she asked.

"Kate!"

He asked her how long it was before she went to London.

It depended when the hospital started its courses, she said. Now that she'd made up her mind, the sooner she started the better.

She told Beauty to walk on. He watched her till she was part of the night.

He went across to the saddler and bought a braided leather dog lead. Waited till the man had attached a disc with GYPSY stamped across it.

On his way home he dropped in to see the Bumfords.

The room was as disappointing as ever, the furniture poor, the carpet worn. Despite their money the couple had never won their battle with poverty. It was their habit to live poorly.

"We'll need a carcass come Thursday," Herbert told him.

"Tha's shifted some meat, then!"

But it was only professional interest. And when Herbert gave him the bags of money from the till Bumford poured it out on to the table, made a few cylinders of coins, then lost interest.

"And Mrs Bumford?"

He had hoped not to have to ask.

"Out of danger, lad. Out of danger."

But there was no enthusiasm, no relief in the voice.

"She's up and about?"

The woman had been such a *doer*, it was what one could expect of her.

"Now and then," Bumford said. "She's up now and then."

"Miss Stelfox has been in to help," Herbert told him. "Couldn't have managed without her."

He showed him the bills with Kate's writing on, the list of addresses of the round.

"Neat hand!" Bumford commented. "Very neat!"

Herbert told him what he'd paid her.

"Taken your own wages?" Bumford asked.

"Not yet. Not till Friday."

"Don't forget then, Friday."

Herbert asked him if he wanted him to slaughter or whether he wanted to do it himself.

"You can manage it," Bumford said. "I'd as well you managed it."

His face hung with weight where it used to be buoyant with flesh.

"Mrs Bumford'll be back on the round soon, will she?" Herbert asked, putting his cycle clips on.

Bumford gripped his arm. "Between me and thee, lad, if tha wants to be lookin' round," he murmured. "I'm sayin' nowt yet. But if tha wants to be lookin' about -" He indicated upstairs. "I think we're about to shut up shop. If tha sees what I mean."

Herbert cycled home slowly, his mind vivid with what had come, what had gone, what he'd been told in confidence.

# CHAPTER 29

*My beloved spake and said unto me, Rise up, my love, my fair one, and come away. For lo, the winter is past, the rain is over and gone.*

*The flowers appear on the earth, the time of the singing of birds is come, and the voice of the turtle is heard in our land.*

As soon as she heard it in church she knew it was his message. Richard had been calling her in secret ways, and now spring had come. Once or twice in Beckthorp lately she'd caught murmurs, people whispering "That Major Dawson!" Sometimes a bird's chirrup would repeat "Major Dawson! Major Dawson!" over and over. Then again – that evening at the barn, the way they'd danced, the way he'd looked at her! The dream had been so vivid – felt she'd danced with him all night.

*Rise up, my love, my fair one, and come away!*

"Oh, I did enjoy the service this morning!" she said at dinner. "I think I'll go again this evening."

Muriel and her father looked at each other. Barbara muttered, "Let her go. Anything to get her out of the way!"

It was the walk home Maudie enjoyed. Sometimes she'd see a star like the star in the east – guiding her. Primroses in the ditches waved as she passed, small yellow bouquets waving farewell. And down the lane from the church was St Matthew's Hall. This time of year she could see the Hall from her house, less than a mile as the crow flew, the leaves on the trees not yet thick enough to hide it.

She made a point of using her hand so people could see it was better, began to talk of getting a job away from home; and when they'd got used to that she mentioned London.

Her Pa was against it immediately. London was no place for a young girl, he said. Never knew who you might meet. She'd do better to get a job in Beckthorp. But Barbara said one town was much like another. She couldn't see that London was much worse than Beckthorp. After all, Muriel couldn't *stand* Beckthorp. In any case, Maudie could get in touch with the Stewards before she went.

"Who are the Stewards?" Maudie asked. "Never heard of them."

Barbara hesitated, waited for Muriel.

Malcolm Steward was a relation of their mother's, Muriel told her. Might still work in London. Hadn't heard from him or Nancy for years. She'd ask Pa if he'd got their address. Used to work on a newspaper, she thought.

"They might even let you stay there for a while."

Muriel hadn't got time to keep answering questions. Wasn't like some people, idling their time away dreaming.

A week of sunshine and showers. On the Sunday it rained hard all morning, the sun appeared, the roads dried, and Maudie said she must go to evening service if it was the last thing she did.

"Keep to the road," they said, "and you should be all right. And take your umbrella."

She looked quite nice, they told her, with her Sunday clothes, her new shoes and white handbag.

The service dragged on, the sermon and prayers never-ending. As soon as one prayer finished another one started, as if nobody could ever do enough or say enough to satisfy God. Soon the service will end, she told herself, soon I'll be out of here and free.

Eventually the praying dragged to an end. People walked out slowly, as if they couldn't get enough of the damned old place, stacked their hymn books slowly, stacked the prayer books. Then she was out, breathing the evening air, sniffing the new flowers, the bursting leaves.

It was almost dark. The moon was full. Now she could walk along the field paths to where she could see the Hall without being seen.

"*My* holy place," she thought. "Where I can think of *him*!"

She knew she'd find him one day, knew she'd soon go to London and look for the him. How it would happen, what she'd say, what he'd say, all was in the future. But it would come to pass. She had faith, and knew it would come to pass.

"That's what *my* faith is," she told herself. "Faith in Richard."

She pushed on to where two paths joined, the place from which she had often gazed at the Hall. These last few days the hedges had thickened, brambles had opened their leaves, were starting to obscure the view. But the group of trees round the place was still visible, and looking up to the darkness above she knew she could send her thoughts directly to him now, in London.

"By the mystery of love," she whispered, "I send you my love."

She set off for home, didn't want to retrace her way back to the road. She knew the path, and when she slipped on the mud and had to clutch hold of a bough with her glove, and then slipped again and dropped her handbag she thought, "I don't care! I shan't be here much longer! Don't care what they say!"

The moon had risen, perfectly round, its silver softness touching fields and trees and hedgerows. To the south the land stretched away in moonlight. To the north clouds lingered, heavy with rain. And exactly in the place where one might expect a rainbow to form, a glow of light arched the sky, a moonbow, its yellow merging to green.

"You heard me," she whispered. "You've sent me your sign!"

She watched it hanging under the rain clouds, a yellow-white arc smaller than a rainbow, the yellow tinged with green. It was in no hurry to fade, and to the south the moon was brilliant. She knew what it was. It was his signal to her. He wanted her to find him, to come to London and find him. Like the star in the east to the wise men, love had sent a wonder, and she'd seen it.

She continued her way home, stumbling sometimes, grabbing into the hedge to steady herself, sliding into puddles on the clayey stretches, on one occasion felt a jab of pain from her hand. When she looked again the moonbow had gone. Richard had heard her message, had sent his sign.

She heard the separator going in the dairy. Babs was still working. Babs worked from dawn till after dusk. There were no wonders in Babs's life. Her life was work. If she went on like that all the wonders and moonbows would pass her by.

"Oh, Babs," she said as she burst into the dairy. "I wish you could have seen it! I really wish you'd been there!"

The whine of the separator subsided. Stopped. The coil of cream narrowed, died.

"Where have – where *have* you been!"

"Her new shoes were split right across the welt," she told Muriel later. "That white handbag of hers is ruined – and them stockings she had new at Christmas – well, you never saw! And between you and me I think she's hurt that hand again! '*You've never been to no church service,*' I told her. I think she's going crackers, Muriel. I really do!"

It wasn't often she got worked up.

"Do you think she's fit to go and live away from home?"

"Might be the making of her, Muriel. She's daft enough here, living with us!"

# CHAPTER 30

Richard's card for Rose arrived on her birthday. Rose was just as prompt: it was in the bin by the time Miriam brought her breakfast.

Miriam noted the one or two cards on the mantelpiece, wished her a happy birthday.

"Tell me, Miriam. How do you like living here?"

Rose still had her meals in the dining-room, insisted her place be properly laid.

"Very much, ma'am. I hope my work is satisfactory?"

"I thought it must be agreeing with you. I believe you're putting on weight."

Miriam put the tray down. She'd wondered when the remark would come.

"I'm expecting, ma'am."

Rose's knife and fork came to a pause.

"I thought you were here to look after me."

"And so I will, ma'am. Have no fear. The babe won't make any difference, what with me and Raymond to look after it. You won't know it's in the house."

Rose's face seemed to close slightly.

"What did the Major think – you being pregnant?"

"The Major? He doesn't know, ma'am."

"You ought to have told him, Miriam. Then he'd have told me. There are no secrets between us, you know."

She was a cat, toying with a mouse.

"As I'm sure there are none between you and Raymond, Miriam."

"No indeed, ma'am."

Rose took a sip of tea. She had the art of being able to swallow without being seen to do so.

"No secrets means no complications, don't you agree?"

Miriam would rather have been grumbled at than have this – this scratching! It was beyond her, too clever, too old-womanish.

"I'm sure Raymond must be delighted?"

"Oh, he is, ma'am."

"After all this time, too."

Rose resumed her breakfast, took a small mouthful, seemed scarcely to chew.

"I'd thought of a name," she said, her mind apparently elsewhere.

Miriam hoped it was a name she could accept. Sometimes the woman frightened her down to her womb.

"But it's gone. Isn't that a pity?"

Miriam knew she was being played with, was out of her depth with her.

"Stanley!" Rose said. "There! That's the name, Miriam."

"Stanley, ma'am?" She felt numb, not knowing where this was leading.

"Stanley. I'm quite definite about it, Miriam. That was the name in my mind. If you see him today, ask him to come and see me, will you?"

She sat back, almost smiling, her body loose in her untied dressing-gown.

"He'll be pleased to see me, don't you think?"

"Of course, ma'am. As soon as I can."

Miriam went out. Rose's amusement followed her.

# CHAPTER 31

The newspapers of 1920 were full of it, discontent in Germany, revolution in Russia, disturbances in Ireland. What excited less comment was the trouble in England. Two thirds of Britain's wealth was owned by three per cent of the population. In the countryside one and a half million acres of land changed hands in those post-war years. Farm incomes fell. Women who had begun to breathe the air of emancipation found themselves obliged to seek posts as servants to the better-off. The message to the men back from the war was, "You who came back uninjured should count yourselves lucky, and help those who didn't!"

In the parish of St Matthews in Suffolk, Aubrey Knight felt he could no longer carry on against competition from nearby Beckthorp, his little butcher's shop having been hit by the meat restrictions imposed during the wartime and post-war years. The shop was put up for sale, Knight waited for a buyer. He had no regrets. He was getting old, had done well in his time.

"The fall of Knight," he would say cheerfully. "Time for me to put me feet up."

Stanley heard about it first. Stanley was a sort of relation to Knight; Stanley was a sort of relation to most people hereabouts, was usually the first to hear about things.

"Get your dad to let Herbert know," he told Muriel. "He might like to take it."

He told her quietly, almost in her ear. There was no need to be confidential: the two of them were in the hay meadow at the bottom of Holly Farm where the Chatham's land abutted Beck Farm, at least a mile from any road.

It had been a hot day, warmth lingered amongst the high hedges. A light breeze washed across the grass, stirred the seed heads into waves that hissed like feathers.

They'd cut it tomorrow, Stanley said.

He and Muriel lay in the sun. From time to time his lips were warm on her, shivering her skin.

" Don't!" she laughed. "I can't bear it!"

And when he tried to see what she couldn't bear she sat up away from him, rubbed the touch of his lips off her neck.

"Bought you this, Muriel," he said. "Don't know if you'd have much use for it."

He felt in his pocket, brought out an engagement ring.

"How do you know my size?"

"Just have to try it on, shan't we?"

He slid it on the appropriate finger. It fitted a treat.

"So how do y'feel about that, then?"

"Stanley!"

She said it softly, allowed him to kiss her.

Talk of the best time for a wedding, what with haysel and harvest coming on, or whether she ought to get married at all, with her Pa getting on and times not good.

"As to that," Stanley said, "we'll only be down the lane if we take that cottage of ours. You can give him a shout out of the bedroom window if you want to."

Muriel turned her hand about, let the evening sun sparkle its rainbows off the diamonds.

"Isn't it pretty!"

"As to that, are you going to keep it or do I take it back?"

"What do you mean, take it back!"

"You know what it is?"

"Engagement ring."

"Engagement to be married. You haven't said you're going to marry me yet."

"Don't be so daft! Haven't we talked about the cottage and everything!"

"Still haven't said you'll marry me."

"Course I'm going to marry you. You knew that years ago!"

Stanley lay back in the headland grass, his head on his cap.

After a while he said, "Funny thing happened today."

"Who to?"

"Me."

"Always funny things happening to you."

"Ah," he said, "not funny like this."

"Go on, then."

"Secret, you see."

"Aren't supposed to be secrets between man and wife."

"Had to go and see old Mrs Dawson."

"Rose Dawson? Whatever did she want?"

"Ah, that's the secret."

"Stanley Chatham – !" She tried to kick him. Her shoe came off and disappeared into the grass by the ditch.

"That's what old Rose Dawson said. 'Are you Mr Stanley Chatham?' She handed me this great old envelope. I didn't know what it was. I just stood there. She said, 'That's all there is. There isn't anything else!' All hoity-toity. So I said, 'Thank y' ma'am.' An' come away."

"So what was it?"

"What d'you think?"

"How should I know! Birthday card?"

"Better than a birthday card." He leaned closer, murmured, "Title deeds to that Barn field we rent off the Major. He's given it to me!"

"Given it!"

"Lovely bit o' land. Give me the lot! Must have had it drawn up afore he went to London."

"Gave it to you?"

"Every clod."

Muriel retrieved her shoe, pushed her foot into it.

"What would he do that for?"

She watched him, guessed there was more to be explained.

The day was fading. They made their way back towards the farmhouse. The air sang with the evening warbling of birds, the sky was tinted with sunset.

"That Major must have thought a lot of you," Muriel said after a while. "Making that land over to you like that."

"Dunno what the man thought."

Muriel let the matter drop. Or allowed him to believe she had let it drop. She'd find out one day, she promised herself. If Stanley Chatham thought he could keep it secret from her, Stanley Chatham had another think coming!

"Another one going to leave home, Babs. Soon be only you left!"

Joseph paused outside the open half-door. In the twilit dairy his daughter was busy cleaning the churn, busy making the butter, busy washing the separator. Barbara was the worker, the one prepared to wait and see it through. More than the others, she was the one who took after him. Yet she'd never been his favourite.

Muriel wasn't going far, Barbara pointed out. Hardly out of sight, in fact. There'd be nothing to stop her coming in and doing a bit of baking during the week. And with Stanley as his son-in-law he'd have a good man to call on sometimes. If Stanley got that tractor and cutter he'd talked about getting, with farm-workers' wages due to go up in August, maybe he'd cut a field or two at Beck Farm when he was doing his own. And seeing how well Holly Farm had done over the years, Barbara thought Muriel had made a jolly good match! The Stelfoxes ought to thank their lucky stars things had turned out as well as they had!

Joseph preferred it when things didn't change. He'd had all the change he wanted when Sarah died.

"Nothing so nice as normal, Babs."

As to that, Barbara thought there'd be less chance of Maudie doing something silly if she was where she wanted to be.

"Never know what she's going to do next here, Pa. She's getting dafter by the day!"

She worked away at the butter, straining, squeezing, shaping, getting it ready for Beckthorp market. What she had said wasn't what he wanted to hear, but he knew it was true. Once Maudie got some notion in her head there was no getting it out again. The girl was like her mother. Too like her mother.

The reply came sooner than expected. Maudie tore the envelope open.

*4a, Hunters Hill*
*Upper Southwood*
*LONDON*

*20th June 1920*

*Dear Maudie*

*Nice surprise to hear from you.*

*There is a vacancy for a chambermaid at the King James hotel in central London not far from the Strand. Mr Perkins could interview you there this coming Friday at 9 a.m. If you're suitable you may be able to start straight away. I see a train leaves Beckthorp station at 11.46 Thursday morning. You should arrive at Liverpool Street at about 4 o'clock. As soon as you get this letter let me know if you are coming so that I can arrange to meet you. Nancy suggests you stay with us overnight and go up to town with me Friday morning.*

*Please give our best wishes to your father and Muriel and Barbara. I still remember you all from before the war. We look forward to seeing you.*

*Malcolm Steward*

*PS On <u>no account</u> mention my name to Mr Perkins or anyone to do with the hotel. Can't explain now. It's essential you bring this letter and give it to me on Thursday!*

Instead of all that dancing about and waving the letter, Barbara said, she'd do better to be thinking what she ought to pack. She wouldn't be able to ask others what to do in future, so she might as well start getting her thoughts together now.

"So I will, Babs," Maudie said. "I'll make a start right now."

She met her Pa at the door with the news. Joseph carried on washing his boots with the hand brush in the bowl beside the step. When they were clean he stood them on the grass to dry.

He asked her when she intended going. She was going to write that afternoon, she said, and tell Malcolm she'd arrive when he said, on the Thursday.

"And this is what you want, Maudie?"

She knew he was going to let her go.

"Oh, Pa!"

It was so much what she wanted she felt like crying.

"I'll write to you, Pa," she promised. "I'll write often."

"That's something I shall look forward to, my dear," he said. "I'll be pleased to hear how you're getting on."

Muriel told him she'd pack the girl some writing paper and envelopes and a few stamps. "Perhaps you won't feel so bad about it then, Pa," she said. "When you get a letter."

Next day a reply came from Herbert. By the look on Joseph's face it was as if the sun had come out.

"Says he'll give that shop of Knight's a look," he said. "Depends how things turn out where he is."

"Be a risk if he takes it," Barbara warned. "If Aubrey Knights can't make it pay I don't know that Herbert'll do any better."

"He hopes to come for a day or two as soon as he can," Joseph said. "If anyone can make it pay, Herbert can."

"No good throwing good money after bad," Barbara said.

Joseph didn't argue. He'd heard his good news. Nothing Barbara said could spoil that.

It was her last day in Suffolk. The bitches had such weird ideas about what she ought to take with her she left them to it and went and visited her mother's grave.

The churchyard was unmown, the grass as high as the gravestones. Maudie sheared the grass on the grave, cleaned the stone, put lupins in the container. She breathed their peppery summer smell, and told her mother about the sign in the sky and why she was off to London tomorrow.

"I'm following the moonbow, my dear," she whispered. "To the man I love."

She knew her mother would approve. She might find him quickly, or it might take ages, but one day they would meet, one day they'd marry and live happily ever after.

And Muriel was going to marry Stanley, and Herbert was coming home for a visit, so Pa was pleased, and Barbara looked as if she'd soon have the place to herself so she'd be pleased.

"And you sleep in peace, dear mother," she said. "You loved me most of all."

To keep thoughts of the funeral away she noted the rooks in the elms, the wild wallflowers in bloom on the steeple, the dog-roses in the hedges. If she thought about them hard enough her mother would get to know about them too.

She gathered up the dead flowers and shearings from the grave, put them on the heap.

At the churchyard gate she looked back. In amongst the tall grass were the tops of gravestones, weather-stained, lichen-covered. They said: *My name was such and such. I was born on this date and I died on that.* They were graves of people she could call back to life. She knew they could reassemble themselves with their funny old smiles and funny old ways and wearing their ordinary clothes.

She didn't want them to. She loved them where they were, quiet, on their own, glad of a visit sometimes.

# CHAPTER 32

The whistle blew, the engine coughed out spurts of steam and smoke, the carriages lurched forward. She was on her way to London. She leaned out of the window, waved to her Pa till he was too far back to call to her any more, came away and sat down. She had waved enough. It was time to sit back and enjoy herself.

She lay back in the sunshine, thankful to be on her way, not have to wave or argue or have anything to do with her family again.

Her body rocked to the movement of the train. Through half closed eyes she noticed the young man opposite admiring her. She stretched a little as if almost asleep, knowing it would emphasise her bosom and show the shape of her legs. It would have infuriated the bitches, and to spite them she stretched her foot, accidentally brushing the man's leg.

"Oh, sorry," she said.

She knew she had a good colour and her hair had only been washed a couple of days. She supposed she might get lots of admiring looks in London.

The train picked up speed, then slowed. Telegraph wires rose more slowly to the top of the carriage window, were snatched down by the telegraph poles less frequently. The young man stood up to get his luggage, and she wondered if she couldn't still see the shape of his admiration. The train stopped. He got off, and looked at her with such longing she felt sorry for him and wished she'd got to know him.

People got in, the train started again, one of a dozen or more starts and stops on the journey. The motion of the train quivered through her, the countryside rolled past, fields and farms appeared and receded, and disappearing with them were the years of living with the bitches. She was free of them, free of them, free of them - -

When she awoke the countryside had gone. The train was passing through a gloom of smoke-grimed walls, was travelling slowly, gliding from one rail to the next, click, clack, as though descending invisible steps down to London. Yet it didn't descend, but slid gently along, preparing her for her first view of the capital of England, the biggest city in the world. Then it picked up speed a little, the walls came to an end, and the sky was full of a glorious light, not blue as it had been in Beckthorp, but golden, full of promise. This was London, the place for her!

The train shuddered, stopped. She got her case down with her good hand, was on the platform, was hurrying where everyone else was hurrying. Her skin prickled. This crowded cavern echoing with voices, whistles, shrieks of locomotives, how huge it was, how loud! How different from anything she was used to!

She reached the barrier, gave up her ticket. People scanned the faces of those passing through.

She stood, waited. Wondered what to do if he didn't turn up.

Passengers streamed away out of the exits, more streamed in, knew where to go, where to stand and wait. She scanned their faces, hoped to see someone with ginger hair, a big man, wearing spectacles.

"You can't mistake Malcolm," Barbara had told her.

Sometimes a man would watch her, thought she was looking at him specially. She looked away, debated whether to go to one of the exits or stay where she was.

"Maudie Stelfox?"

Good-looking, blonde, her coat and hat pale blue, the hat with a dark blue band.

"I'm Nancy," the lady said. "Malcolm couldn't get here. As usual!"

Over a cup of tea in the station buffet Nancy said Malcolm was delayed by work. Malcolm was always delayed by work. It didn't make sense to her, spending all that time on a newspaper.

"We'd better wait," she said. "He'll turn up sooner or later, if only to show you the sights. Don't know about you, I've got better things to do than look at buildings."

Her neat, pretty eyes were full of life. Maudie was glad she had such an elegant relation.

"By the way," Nancy said. "If you've got Malcolm's letter I might as well take it." She folded it small, put it in her handbag. "Must perform my wifely duties."

Maudie asked if she was proud of having a reporter for a husband.

"Once you start washing their shirts," Nancy said, "you're not proud of any man for long."

Her eyes followed a foreign-looking man in a dark suit making his way to the counter.

"Though they can be quite nice, if someone else is washing their shirts."

"I suppose Malcolm can be quite nice at times?" Maudie joked.

The neat eyes regarded her, made her feel the rough young girl from the country she knew she was.

"Tell me, Maudie. Isn't there someone special waiting for you somewhere?"

She felt found out, off guard.

"What's his name?" Nancy asked.

His name was in her heart, not in her mouth. But it was exciting to say it to a stranger.

"Richard. Richard Dawson." She said it softly. She didn't want to part with it, merely say it over and over. "Major Richard Dawson."

She hadn't told it, just let it brush her tongue and lips.

"He's not married, is he!"

A crazy woman wasn't a wife, Maudie said. Especially for a gentleman like the Major. And because Nancy's question had been rather sharp, she added that if going about the parish with a pair of secateurs tidying up hedgerows and snipping bits off haystacks wasn't crazy, then people didn't know what crazy meant.

"So why have you come to London?"

Maudie recalled the evening, how the grass had sparkled in the moonlight, how she had seen amongst the rain clouds this rim of yellowy-green mist that didn't come and go but hung there for minutes, its edges like coloured cloud.

"How unusual," Nancy said.

"But no-one believed me."

"How strange."

Maudie began to feel she was being examined, her account of the moonbow considered instead of being marvelled at.

"So that's why I'm in London," she repeated.

"This Major Dawson has given you his address?"

The question was disappointing. She wondered if she ought to have told Nancy anything.

"Not yet -"

"Has he been in touch with you?"

"Of course not -"

"Does he know you're in London?"

"Oh, no. It's the test, you see. If I can find him."

Nancy was sorry to insist, but she had to know if Maudie was all right. It was essential if she and Malcolm were to try to get her fixed up in a job. "What I mean, Maudie, is, have you and this Major been alone together?"

Oh, yes, Maudie said, in hospital when she'd ripped her hand in the chaff-cutter and had to have it stitched up. She'd woken up, and there he was beside her bed.

And inwardly laughed to see Nancy's face. Served her right, she thought. Asking all those questions!

But Nancy was looking at someone else.

"I know!" she said. "Don't tell me! Something cropped up."

The freckled face was large, the gingery hair turning white. Eyes gleamed at her through thick lenses.

Malcolm took her hand in his moist paw.

"Our Maudie Stelfox?"

"Why ever you said you'd be here!" Nancy flared. "I've managed often enough on my own in the past!"

"You're looking at an orphan," Malcolm was saying, still holding her hand. "You Stelfoxes and Nancy are the only relations I've got."

She still had the feeling of being examined.

"I hope you get that job," he murmured. "I want you to get it."

He looked across at Nancy, as though she could confirm he wanted her to get the job.

"By the way, Nancy," he said. "Something came up at the desk."

Nancy placed her hands flat on the table, exasperated.

"If I was an accident," she said to Maudie. "If I was an item of bad news I'd be on his front page."

Please, not a quarrel, Maudie thought. Not a quarrel here!

"But I'm not bad news. And I'm not good news. Am I, Malcolm? I haven't been news to Malcolm for years." She opened her handbag, gave him the letter. "There's only one thing on Malcolm's mind nowadays."

Malcolm shot her a look.

"I shan't say a word," she mocked. "Your secret's safe with me!"

Malcolm glanced at the letter, tore it up, put the pieces in his pocket.

"You understand not to mention my name?" he said to Maudie. "I don't exist. You understand?"

What Maudie understood was that he was a shapeless lump married to an attractive intelligent woman, a lump that behaved in a way she didn't understand.

"Understand what?"

He took it as a joke.

"That's what we like to hear, Nancy!"

Nancy said, "On your own head be it, duckie!"

The air was rich with exhaust fumes. Cabs, vans, knife-box buses passed by everlastingly. She loved the shouts of street-callers, the foreign faces, the fashionable clothes, the drunk who staggered and sang, bottle in hand. People here were free, the sun was golden on buildings, on people, on everything. She wished she had always lived in London. "Oh, I love it," she sighed. "No wonder you're both so happy."

She knew she was being mischievous. But she wanted to believe they were happy together. Nancy and Malcolm smiled, perhaps embarrassed. Nancy looked up at him, her eyes hurt.

She squeezed his arm to her.

"You!" she said.

They were walking over London Bridge to a bus-stop on the south side. It was safer to travel by Company bus, Malcolm said. You never knew where those pirate buses would take you. Sometimes they changed their destination according to where most of the passengers wanted to go, whereas Company buses kept to a timetable.

Half way across Malcolm pointed back to St Paul's.

"That's the mark of greatness! When a cathedral gets burnt down - and gets built even better than before!" That was the spirit that had made London the heart of the Empire. "Once the heart decays. Or goes rotten -"

At the edge of the river a group of people were looking at something on the mud. It seemed someone might have been swimming, hadn't had the strength to reach the shore.

"Ignore it!" Nancy warned.

But Malcolm was leaning over the edge to see better. Someone bent down, turned the swimmer over.

"I shall have to -"

"For God's sake, Malcolm!"

"It could be what -"

Her hands snatched at him. "Malcolm!"

He pulled away. "Could be what I've -"

More people were on the foreshore. Whatever it was they were looking at lay unmoving on the mud.

"See you back at Norwood," Malcolm said.

"Please yourself!" Nancy called after him. "You'll find out whether you see me there!"

But Malcolm had already disappeared among the pedestrians on the bridge.

Nancy turned away.

"You be warned," she said. "Don't throw yourself at this Major. Or any of them!"

They walked back over the bridge the way they had come. People crowded the side, looking down at the foreshore.

"Why should we go home like good little girls?" She sounded almost amused. Maudie could tell she was livid. "I know where we can go. *He's* doing what *he* wants!"

They reached a Lyons Corner House. Half London was already there, but Nancy managed to find a place for two, ordered a pot of tea and something on toast.

The other half of London was streaming past outside. The road was so crowded, the crowds passing so vast, Maudie was amazed. It was what they called the rush hour, Nancy said. When you lived in London you got used to little things like the rush hour. There were more important things in life than the rush hour.

Maudie was disappointed to hear such an elegant-looking woman sounding so sharp. She wished she hadn't been so reckless as to tell her her secret.

"You won't tell Malcolm? What I told you - why I'm here?"

Nancy sniffed. "You see what chance I get to talk to Malcolm."

The couple opposite at the table moved away. Nancy took off her hat, put it on one of the chairs, her pale gold hair lovely against the blue coat.

Maudie asked what paper Malcolm worked for.

"You don't read the *Daily Brief?*"

Malcolm was apparently well respected. He was running a campaign to help the common man, as he called it.

"I tell him, what about the common woman?" Nancy

said. "They're the ones who need the help. Now more than ever."

The rush hour was easing. People were leaving, there were empty chairs. But the man who had just come in was looking for someone.

Nancy waved the tips of her fingers, removed her hat from the chair.

The man's face lit as though he had seen good news.

"I thought I'd drop in. On the off-chance."

He was smartly dressed in dark suit and tie. He had dark brown eyes, his greying hair had once been black. Nancy introduced him as Mr Vincy, her employer.

"The young lady who's come to London to make her fortune?" He took Maudie's hand. "I wish you good luck at the King James." To Nancy he murmured, "If she is unsuccessful she must let me know."

But Nancy was watching his face for something else, awaited some other message.

"Monty got it?" she murmured.

The dark eyes softened, the blue-black lower face broadened.

"I've just heard. He's delighted."

"James!"

It seemed only natural in the circumstances that employer and employee should clasp hands.

The two of them, the one blonde, the other dark, shared their news. It seemed Mr Vincy's cousin had just been promoted to a post in the newly established Ministry of Health. Maudie settled down to what she hoped would be an interesting eavesdrop, but when they noticed her listening they spoke in a kind of code, with references to our Lloyd George merchant and Ebenezer Scrooge, and half a remark was sufficient to cause Nancy's eyes to widen as if she understood perfectly. It was the sort of secretive language she had had to endure at home, the bitches excluding her as if she was too much of a dunce to grasp what adults were talking about. She yawned, stretched herself, closed her eyes and let her head drop.

Mr Vincy said, "Your young friend is tired."

Maudie looked up at once. "No, not tired!"

Then she heard it, a silence that seemed like a decision.

"I tell you what," Mr Vincy said. "Why don't you and Nancy go along to the King James now, and see if Mr Perkins can have a look at you? He might even be able to take you on tonight."

Nancy thought it an excellent idea. The hotel couldn't be more than a twenty minute walk.

"And if he does take you on you'll miss that awful journey in the morning."

They left Mr Vincy to order his meal. He'd be in the restaurant for some time yet, he said. He'd had nothing to eat all day.

Nancy gave him the slightest of waves with her fingertips but didn't glance at him again, though his eyes were on her all the way to the door.

# CHAPTER 33

"Mr Perkins isn't seeing anyone this evening," the receptionist said. "Except guests."

A superior young woman with pale eyes, pale hair, and every hair in its place. Yet there was something comical about the nasty little face, the crease down beside the nose and curving under the cheek as knowing as an old woman's.

Did they have an appointment? In that case, she suggested they came in the morning, at the appointed time.

Like a little owl, Maudie thought, guarding the proprietor's door, enjoying being unhelpful.

It was about a job for the young lady, Nancy said, indicating Maudie. Since Mr Perkins knew she was coming he might like to see her this evening.

The receptionist was icy. Mr Perkins had given instructions he was not to be disturbed. It would be to no-one's advantage to disturb him. But Nancy was not to be put off. Sometimes, she said, someone in Mr Perkins' position was only too thankful to get an interview done of an evening rather than waste time on it in the morning.

The owl stared. Maudie wanted to smile, icy as the little bitch was.

"Some might," the owl said. But her employer was Mr Perkins. And Mr Perkins did things his way. And this evening he didn't want to be disturbed.

Maudie almost saw herself in the little bitch's place, glorying in being awkward.

"I know who Mr Perkins is," Nancy told her. "And what I know and you don't know is that we've come straight here from seeing Mr Vincy. And if you don't tell Mr Perkins that, I shouldn't like to be in your shoes when he finds out."

The receptionist lifted her chin to disclaim responsibility for the consequences, tapped on the office door and went in.

A fleshy-limbed man appeared.

"Mr Vincy?"

His eyes darted round the reception area. Saw no Mr Vincy.

"I said they'd come from seeing Mr Vincy," the owl said.

Mr Perkins stared at the visitors, gestured them into his office.

The receptionist raised her eyes. She'd done her noble best to protect the man.

The office was strong with the smell of tobacco. A single window, closed in spite of the warmth, looked out on to the main road through a framework of scaffolding where the front of the hotel was being renovated.

Mr Perkins indicated a couple of seats, seemed to crouch at his desk as if about to spring.

"This young lady is Maudie Stelfox," Nancy said. "Mr Vincy would regard it as a favour if you would see her now rather than in the morning"

"See?"

"She's got an appointment in the morning for a chambermaid's job. Or anything suitable. She could start immediately."

Mr Perkins leaned back, seemed suddenly to understand. "And you are?"

"Nancy Stelfox. We've just come from Mr Vincy."

"So that's what -"

He indicated the door behind which the receptionist worked.

He took out a desk diary. Maudie sat up to show herself to advantage. He looked her over, she faced him back as she thought Nancy would, woman to man. She wondered whether she should correct Nancy's slip regarding her name.

She looked a strong young girl, Mr Perkins said. Was she used to hard work? And getting up early? And doing as she was told?

He remembered Mr Vincy mentioning her now, he said.

His attention faded, or switched to somewhere beyond the window, his mind on another problem.

He looked at the clock, at Maudie. There was one main rule for staff at the King James hotel, he said. The hotel came first. What was good for the hotel was good for the staff, because as the hotel prospered, so would the staff. If the hotel failed they would all lose their jobs. A lot of money was being spent on renovations so it was essential for the hotel to prosper. Maudie must always remember: if it was good for the hotel, it was good for her, whatever it was she might be asked to do. That was the way to get on in the hotel trade.

"And in the event of pregnancy -" His gesture seemed to sever more than the link with the hotel.

"I'm sure that's not Maudie's style, Mr Perkins," Nancy said.

But his gesture was quite definite.

"She'd better see Mrs Critoph now," he said. There was a vacancy, as it happened, so everything was satisfactory. "Perhaps Mr Vincy can be told everything is satisfactory?"

He smiled them uneasily to the door, told the receptionist to take the young lady to see Mrs Critoph.

Nancy widened her eyes in warning to say nothing.

"Let us know how you get on," she said.

Mr Perkins was back behind his desk, the engagement of the latest member of staff already forgotten.

# CHAPTER 34

Mrs Critoph had her own views about the appointment of staff.

"Mr Perkins may want you taken on," she told Maudie on their way upstairs to the service wing, "and I shall take you on. But if your face don't fit you won't want to stay. You can get that into your head as quick as you like."

She was a short, thick-built little body with soft grey hair and hard grey eyes. She leaned a little to one side, left arm held out for balance. She climbed the stairs with surprising energy, and at the top led the way along a green-distempered corridor, the air stale with the smell of bedrooms and chamber-pots.

She stopped outside one of a row of doors.

"You're in here. With Rosie Durrell."

It was a long narrow room with a window in the far wall. The two single beds were separated by a chest of drawers. On the bed nearest the window a young woman sat brushing her hair.

"Rosie'll show you where the rooms are and everything. Be sure you're up and ready by six."

Mrs Critoph waddled off.

Rosie's cupid-bow lips were unsmiling. She tossed the hairbrush on the bed, went over to the window.

"Whatever you've turned up for! Properly mucked things up!"

She was a solid little person, a year or two older than Maudie.

"I was supposed to see Mr Perkins in the morning," Maudie explained. "But I was brought here tonight. Not much I could do about it."

Rosie sniffed. "Soon took you on! Just looked you up and down, I suppose. I thought he wasn't seeing anyone tonight."

She seemed ill at ease. Once or twice Maudie tried to start a conversation but Rosie didn't reply. She stood at the window, stared out into the yard below, gripping the window sill, her breasts pressed between her upper arms.

The summer light was leaving the sky. From nearby came the comforting sound of traffic. Maudie ignored the girl. In her opinion a dose of bitches' tongues would have done that young woman no harm at all.

She lifted her suitcase up on to the bed, undid the strap.

Lying on top of her things was a photograph of her mother. Her father must have wanted her to have it now she was away from home. The face looked at her, kindly, caring. She loved her mother. But lately she'd realised what a limited life that generation had had. Young people were nearer the thrill of life, nearer its problems. It wasn't fair to have been brought up in the country, hidden away, knowing only old-fashioned country people and country ways. No-one in London looked up at the clouds or bothered which way the wind blew, and as for the way they dressed, country people knew no more than the cows in the meadow. Even this photograph was old-fashioned, the glass secured by a border of passepartout instead of being properly framed.

She looked at the clothes her sisters had made her bring, the skirt Barbara said would be useful, the jumper Muriel insisted she looked nice in. There they were, every garment reminding her of some quarrel or other. It was like looking at a caseful of her childhood, her life pressed and ironed by the bitches.

She lifted the case up, shot the contents out across the bed and over the floor. She seized garments and tossed them into the air up and up again, then grabbed the photo of her mother and scudded it into the door.

She was panting, her arms felt trembly. But she had shaken her sisters out of her clothes.

She picked up the photograph. The glass was splintered across the eyes. She laid it down on the chest of drawers, stroked the face where it was cracked. Her mother had seen violence enough.

Rosie was staring at her.

"I can put up with a certain amount," Maudie said. "Then I fly."

But she felt better.

"You hadn't better let Mrs Critoph see all this. She'll think you're barmy."

She made as if to fold a skirt for her but Maudie snatched it away, opened a drawer and dropped it in.

"All my life," she said, "I've wanted to do that."

"Please yourself."

"And that!" She threw the clothes into the drawers at random. "And that!"

She pushed the clothes down, forced the drawers shut. Then lay down on the bed with her shoes on.

Rosie sat beside her.

"You all right?"

She stared up at the girl, her tawny hair, her rough red

cheeks and cupid-bow lips. She reached out, touched her hand. No-one had sat on her bed since her mother died.

Rosie asked what she had done to her hand.

"Only an accident."

But it was nice to be asked.

"Do me a favour?" Rosie said. "If you'd sleep in another room tonight? You can guess why."

Rosie knew of a room. No-one need know. It was only the one night. If Maudie would like to get what things she needed?

"I'll call you in good time in the morning."

She'd do the same for Maudie when she liked.

She took the key out of the door without locking it behind her, led the way down to a room at the bottom of the first flight of stairs, let herself and Maudie in.

"They all fit," she whispered, meaning the key.

They were in a nicely furnished little room, separate from the staff bedrooms.

"Doesn't this belong to someone?"

Rosie shook her head. "Lock yourself in," she whispered. "And keep the light off. No-one need know."

Maudie turned the key, left it in the lock. She undressed, lay on the bed. It was too warm to get under the bedclothes.

Traffic droned in the distance, comforting, like bees. Only that morning she had fed the fowls at Beck Farm. By now the evening milking would be finished, Muriel would be wandering home from the hay meadows with Stanley, over at St Matthews Hall the mad woman would be at her madness. It was like remembering pictures in a book.

But she was free of the bitches now. Free to search for her love.

She realized what she had seen. She was out of bed in a flash. Closed the curtain. Switched on the light.

Shoes under the bed! Fashionable clothes in the wardrobe! She was in someone's bedroom!

She noticed a covered trunk at the foot of the bed. She took the cover off, raised the lid. An oyster chiffon scarf; a wide-brimmed oyster hat with a deep red ribbon; a book; a cushion in the art nouveau style...

She rummaged deeper, felt entitled to after the trick Rosie had played on her.

The title of the book took her eye. *Married Love.* By someone called Marie Stopes. She turned a page or two. Sentences, passages – her eye raced down page after page. Never had she dreamed of reading such words! Here, in print in a book, out in the open and in grown-up language, a woman was talking about sex, things she had heard about in whispers as a child, had come to regard as rude, had heard about in dirty jokes or from people like Eva Briggs, yet here it was, waiting to be read. And she'd hardly been in the hotel an hour!

*Welling up in her,* she read, *are the wonderful tides, scented and enriched by the myriad experiences of the human race from its ancient days of leisure and flower-wreathed love-making, urging her to transports and self-expressions, were the man but ready to take the first step in the initiative or to recognise it and welcome it in her. To the initiate she will be able to reveal that the tide is up by a hundred subtle signs, upon which he will seize with delight. But if her husband is blind to them there is for her nothing but silence, self-suppression, and their inevitable consequence of self-scorn . . . He was so ignorant that he did not know that her husband's lips upon her breast melt a wife to tenderness, and are one of the husband's first and surest ways to make her physically ready for complete union . . .*

She laid the book aside. Her body pulsed, tingled with images.

*Her husband's lips upon her breast . . .*

She imagined her fingers were a man's fingers, wished her nipples could be caressed...

Someone outside the door! Trying to push a key into the lock.

She was out of bed, on her knees. Scooped the contents back into the trunk.

"Someone's in there."

The man knocked, rattled the door.

She pulled the cover over the trunk, slid into bed.

"The light's on!"

A quieter voice. "Open up! Police!"

She lay, paralysed.

"Who's in there? Open this door!"

The knocking sharper, angrier. She couldn't speak.

"If you don't open up NOW I shall break the door in and place you under arrest."

She tried to say, "Coming." It was a croak. Like someone waking up.

She was out of bed, yawning. Was at the door, yawning.

"Who is it?" she yawned.

Realised she hadn't put the book away.

"Police! Unlock the door!"

She hid the book under her skirt on the chair. Sleepily unlocked the door. Mr Perkins pushed past her.

The policeman closed the door. "This the woman's room?"

Mr Perkins said it was. He glanced at Maudie, recognised her from earlier that evening.

"What are you doing here?"

She stared about her, stared at the key in her hand.

"I must have -"

The policeman took the key, tried it in the door, then tried the one he had with him. Both fitted.

"Rim locks, Mr Perkins!"

"I haven't had the place long." He sounded nettled by the criticism. "I've already changed the locks in the guest rooms."

"I only started here tonight," Maudie said. "I must have lost my way."

"She's nothing to do with it," Mr Perkins muttered. "She wouldn't know one room from another."

He told her how to get back up to the servant's quarters.

"Unless the officer -?"

The policeman asked her her name, where she came from. Then dismissed her.

"I've only been here an hour or two," Maudie said.

She hugged her clothes to her. The policeman waited for her to leave, waited till she had gone upstairs before closing the door.

She found her bedroom, could hear what was going on inside. Someone was going to go through the bedsprings, she thought, the way they were going at it, the man sounding as if he was fighting for breath. It was all very well for Rosie, enjoying herself while others were being frightened to death on her behalf.

She let herself in, closed the door, then rapped from the inside to interrupt them.

The motion became a convulsion. Then ceased.

"It's only me," she said.

A whisper, "Pull the clothes up!"

"Hope I'm not interrupting."

A silence, then, "It's that new little cow! What the hell are you doing back here!"

Maudie's eyes adjusted to the darkness. She made out the bed, the two in it together.

"Cows can't answer."

"Do you want me to knock an answer out of you?"

Maudie put her clothes on a chair, slid the book under them. "And cows can't hurry."

Rosie hissed, "I'll make such a mess of your face -"

"Oh, dear!" Maudie said. "And you'll make a mess of that policeman's face, too, will you?"

"Police?"

Rosie sat up on the bed, pulled her nightie on.

"The police didn't go into that room, did they?"

"Didn't he?" She could hear the girl was worried. "Not if you say so."

"Was there a policeman there or not, for God's sake?"

"I shouldn't squawk too loud. He's still there."

"Did he say what he wanted?"

"I don't know what he wants. Cows can't understand things like that."

Rosie sighed. "Oh, for God's sake, girl! Did he say what he was there for?" She sounded desperate.

"He tried to open the door," Maudie said. "I let him in. I told him I'd had to go to the bathroom and got lost on the way back."

"Did he believe you?"

Believe! Maudie thought. Did he believe you? She, who'd had years of deceiving the bitches!

"I'll put the light on," she said.

A man was sitting up on the bed, buttoning his trousers. He was wearing a striped shirt, socks and a cap.

"Sorry I had to come in," Maudie said.

"That's Peter."

He grinned. "That's all right. We'd had it by then, hadn't we, Rosie?"

He was small-faced and skinny. Wouldn't have been much of a weight on Rosie, by the look of it. Active, but not heavy. He seemed more amused than embarrassed.

Rosie put a skirt on over her nightie. Despite the warmth of the night she was shivering. "Haven't heard him leave, have you?"

"I expect he and Mr Perkins are still having a nose round," Maudie said.

"Perkins! He's not there too, is he?" Her face sagged with worry. "Whatever does Perkins want there?"

"You'll have to ask him," Maudie said. She didn't like to see anyone quite so lost.

Peter draped a white scarf round his shoulders. He stood up, put his foot on the bed to do his shoe up and winked at Maudie about Rosie.

"Always got things on her mind, Rosie has," he said, as though it was one of his burdens. "I often come up here," he joked. "Don't I, Rosie? I often come up here."

His face was rodent-like, unshaven.

"I'm glad you didn't tell them anything," Rosie said.

"Rosie should know," Peter joked. "She comes too."

Rosie went to the window, peered round the edge of the curtain.

"There they go," she whispered, drawing back. "Perkins and the copper. I wonder where they're going this time of night!"

"Heard a good one today," Peter said. "About these two prostitutes. One of 'em worked in a top floor flat, five storeys up and the lift had broke. She said to her friend, 'Oh, I have had a busy night,' she said. 'On the go all the time. Up and down these stairs all night long, one after another, up and down all night long.' The other prostitute said, 'Oh, your poor feet!'"

Maudie laughed. Peter laughed too, watching her.

"They've gone." Rosie came away from the window. "Too dark to see where they went."

"All Rosie bothers about," Peter said, "is what's going on somewhere else." He blew her a kiss on his way out. "Don't let it worry you, my treasure."

But his grin was for Maudie.

"You needn't worry about Perkins," Maudie told her, closing the door. "He doesn't know it was your idea. I didn't mention you."

Rosie sighed, her face heavy.

"Don't think me ungrateful," she said. "But that's the least of my worries."

Maudie dreamed she was on the train, rattling through a long green tunnel. From nearby came the sound of sobbing. An inspector was approaching, asking in compartment after compartment if any passenger had found a missing book. It was called *Married Love*.

# CHAPTER 35

The staff were full of it at breakfast.

Found her in the river. Like a piece of rubbish washed up.

With so many rumours flying about they hardly realised Maudie was new.

Throat cut, they say. Nicest person you could wish to meet, Maggie Hines was.

This Maggie Hines, Maudie asked, who was she?

Maggie was the receptionist, June said. Or was, till yesterday. Marvellous head on her shoulders. How Perkins was going to manage without her, she didn't know. Always asking Maggie's opinion, what she thought of this or that. Put old Mrs Critoph's nose out a treat.

"I thought I spoke to the receptionist yesterday evening."

"Oh no, that would have been Beryl. Funny little cow, Beryl. Perky's niece. Not that she's any good at the job. Maggie was the receptionist. This Beryl you spoke to was orphaned or something. So Perky was landed with her."

He put the girl with Maggie Hines to learn receptioneering but she was hopeless. And now, here was poor Maggie, done for.

"So shall we be," Rosie said, "if we don't get them bedrooms done."

Rosie was senior chambermaid. She took Maudie upstairs to show her what to do, starting with the chamber-pot and slop pail routine. For God's sake, she told her, handle things carefully or cleaning up could take ages. Then there was the bed-making. No need to change the linen till the end of the week unless the guest was leaving – or unless it was necessary!

Doing the second bed they found a case where it was necessary.

"And you see them in their posh clothes, looking at you as if you was dirt. Ain't much posh about what happens in bed, what I can see of it!"

"Awful about that Maggie Hines," Maudie said.

Rosie straightened up from mopping the lino.

"More than awful. And I should watch what you say to that June Trick, if I were you!"

She wouldn't explain. She'd got her all her own bedrooms to do as yet. And if Maudie wanted to keep her job she hadn't better get on the wrong side of Mrs Critoph. Or waste time gossiping.

There was the furniture to be dusted, the washstand jug and bowl to be cleaned, the drinking water carafe to be refilled and the tumbler inverted over it, and fresh towels to be hung on the rail.

"Here's your kitchen."

Rosie showed her into a small room at the end of the corridor. It was the chambermaid's kitchen for that floor. Maudie would be responsible for everything in it, the sink, gas rings, the shelves stacked with stuff needed for bedroom service. This was where you prepared early morning tea for guests who had ordered it. Hot water for washing had to be delivered in jugs to each room by eight o'clock at the latest, and shaving water for the men, and woe betide you if the gas-rings, teapots, crockery, cutlery, trays and trolleys, as well as the kitchen itself, weren't spotless when Mrs Critoph inspected them.

"One good thing. Some rooms are out of use because of the alterations. So you've only got fifteen more to do!"

Maudie was amazed at the girl's energy, how she could put her back into the work and bustle on and on.

"And always knock on a bedroom door and make sure they hear you before you go in. Round here it's called good manners. Otherwise you never know what might be going on."

Maudie guessed she was referring to what had happened last night. She said she was sorry she'd burst in.

"Can't be helped," Rosie said. "People like us can't afford privacy."

But she'd be private one day, she added, or know the reason why.

The way she flashed it out, young girl that she was, sounded more than a promise.

A small, middle-aged woman wandered towards them.

"Ah, Mrs Gibbs," Rosie said, "I've just been telling Maudie here, 'I hope we see Mrs Gibbs so I can introduce you to her. Special people first,' I told her."

Mrs Gibbs's laugh was vague. Her face had sagged, as though a sausage had been inserted each side of her jaw. And she had a strange little laugh, as if she wasn't sure what she was laughing at.

"Wouldn't have seen a cut-throat razor on your travels, would you?" she asked. "Poor old Bernard can't find his anywhere."

No, they hadn't, Rosie said. Had Bernard had a good look in his room?

"I doubt it'" Mrs Gibbs tittered. "You know what men are."

A missing razor, when someone had had her throat cut, didn't seem of the slightest consequence to her.

"Little old hen!" Maudie said as Mrs Gibbs wandered off. Privately she wondered how Rosie could tell such lies, telling the old gal she was special and wonderful.

"Pay you to keep in with her," Rosie muttered. "Ain't such a fool as she looks."

Mrs Gibbs was the linen-maid. In charge of the linen-room and responsible for bed linen and table linen, towels, stuff like that. She kept a tally of what she issued and what was returned.

"So don't try to – you know," Rosie warned.

But if Mrs Gibbs took a fancy to you the occasional item might come your way to help with your bottom drawer.

"So you can get married?"

"Married!" Rosie scoffed. "So I can get out of this place, you mean!"

Everything you touched in a place like this belonged to someone else. The room, the furniture. Even in bed you felt like a servant.

"You can't have anything but what other people breathe over it. Even your body don't feel like it's your own."

All Rosie wanted was her own place. Nothing big or special. Just a few rooms she could call her own. She didn't blame the hotel. It was no worse than others she'd worked in.

"But I know how I ought to feel. And I know how I do feel. And I don't want to feel like it any longer than I have to. I just want a little place I can go home to at the end of the day and feel it's mine."

She seemed uneasy, kept looking at the row of doors along the corridor. Outside the door to Room 39 she hesitated, seemed to want to go in. It looked like any other bedroom door in that block of bedrooms, solid deal, panelled and stained after the modern fashion, nothing special. But Rosie was tense, had to press her palms to her apron to dry them. Suddenly she took a key, and let herself in.

After a look round she came out.

"What's in there?" Maudie asked.

Nothing much, Rosie said. Out of use because of the decorators.

"Want to have a look?"

She was suddenly easier. She opened the door, let Maudie in.

Apart from the scaffolding outside the window it was a bedroom like all the others. It had the usual decor, the usual furniture, similarly arranged. Nothing else.

Rosie shut the door, locked it.

"Now we both know," she said.

"Wake up!"

Iris gave her a flick with soapsuds to keep her mind on her work. As they were short-staffed in the kitchen Mrs Critoph had asked Maudie to help out with the washing-up. She could finish her rooms after lunch, she said. Maudie was pleased to help, it made her feel part of the company.

She marvelled at the speed at which Londoners worked. Waiters and waitresses bobbed in through the entrance door, left their orders, collected dishes and bobbed out through the exit door to the dining-room. No pleases, no thank yous, no bad temper. She was surprised how quickly they moved about in the kitchen, among busy colleagues, out through doors with an armful of dishes, never seemed to tire. She loved the noise – baking tins, crockery, cutlery, serving dishes, voices calling, ordering, joking. Life here was a million times better than that damned old countryside she had left behind.

The chef, Mr Took, seemed to be doing six things at once, carving joints, straining potatoes, getting Yorkshire puddings out of gas stoves that stood in a row down the middle of the kitchen. His assistants were as busy as bees, and what they didn't have time for, Mr Took helped out with. He was never flustered, always had time for a joke with Mr Lexford the head waiter, always had time to shout, listen, and serve as if he had six hands. When it was time for the pudding course and the lids were taken off the great black saucepans, and roomfuls of steam rose up and curled across under the ceiling, Mr Took would be calling for dishes, testing a custard, warming sauces, staff would be moving as quick as light, scurrying here, carrying there, calling everywhere.

And then it was over. Oven doors were slammed less frantically, food served up less feverishly, more crockery came back than went out.

Iris Carter shook the suds from her hands.

"Time to fill our guts now!"

She leaned her tray against her fat stomach, calves bulging out behind her.

"Old Critoph didn't send anyone to relieve you," she reminded Maudie. "You want to make out you're busy when that old sod's about."

"I don't mind helping out."

Iris sniffed. "Don't want to get too helpful. Look what's happened to Maggie Hines."

"What makes you think it was Maggie?" Rosie asked.

She sounded back to her irritable self.

"Everyone says so. You ask June." Iris put her tray down, bawled, "June, you said it was Maggie in the river, didn't you? Rosie don't believe it."

"I don't care what Rosie think," June called back. "Course it was Maggie."

Of course it was Maggie!

Maudie knew it now! That thing on the shore yesterday. Which Malcolm had to leave them so suddenly for! That was Maggie Hines!

The staff had their meals at a long composite table, at which staff had recognised places.

Maudie found herself seated next to Eileen, was reminded of a little white hen she had back at Beck Farm. It too had red-rimmed eyes.

"Two and two don't make five," Mrs Critoph was saying. " Nothing about Maggie in my newspaper."

She helped herself from the tureens, passed them along the table.

"Come to think of it," June said, "ain't in mine either."

"Ain't in mine, neither," someone else said.

"Nothing but idle gossip!" Mrs Critoph was impatient with such talk.

"But gossip or not, Elsie," Mr Took said, passing the gravy to Mr Lexford, "being dead would explain why Maggie isn't here."

"All her things are still here," Mr Lexford said, passing a tureen to Mr Took. "So wherever she is, she don't seem to need them."

"Good as one of your jigsaw puzzles, Victor." Mr Lexford closed and opened one eye as if he'd already started putting certain pieces together.

"Someone said there weren't a drop of blood left in her body," Mrs Gibbs said, as though remarking there wasn't a drop of milk left in the jug.

"Eileen was the one who said that," Pamela said.

Maudie felt her stomach tighten. An image from childhood came into her mind: she was on the beach, at a Punch and Judy show. The tiny stage was empty. Something frightening was about to appear.

"It mustn't!" she whispered. "Mustn't!"

"Well," Eileen was saying, "if I said it, it was because it was in my newspaper!"

She unfolded a copy of the Daily Brief, read a piece out.

*The body of a young female person was found at about teatime yesterday. There were deep gashes down the side of the throat. The deceased was buxom, dark-haired and in her twenties. She was fully clothed.*

"There you are," Mrs Gibbs said happily. "I knew I'd heard it somewhere."

*Mr Leon Hipperson, an unemployed waterman from Walworth, described how he had noticed something underwater near London Bridge. "When I realised it was a body I dragged it ashore," he said. "There was a dreadful slash across the throat. The current near the Embankment would have swung the body towards the shore."*

*Subsequent enquiries have revealed that a young woman of similar description to the deceased had been working at a hotel near the Strand for the last couple of years. She had not been seen there during the twenty-four hours prior to the finding of the body.*

*A copy of the controversial book "Married Love" by Dr Marie Stopes was later found amongst her belongings.*

"I thought you said there wasn't a drop of blood left in her body," Iris said.

"Nor there wasn't."

"It don't say that, not in what you read out."

Eileen studied the account, failed to find the proof. Her hen-eyes flicked round at her listeners.

"Stands to reason. Throat cut like that!"

Iris grinned round at Pamela. "I'd like to get hold of that *Married Love* book, wouldn't you? Get a few ideas"

The pain in Maudie's stomach worsened. If she could sit quiet, she thought. If only she could let the thing that was about to show itself slither away.

*Married Love* came out a couple of years ago." Beryl's ice-voice splintered across the room. "Not that I've read it. Couldnae get ma hands on ut!"

People laughed, recognising the take-off of her uncle.

"It's about this contra-ception," she added. "Whatever that may mean!"

Maudie loved her Scottish drawl, her comical owl face. Contra-ception!

The cramp across her belly tightened. She gripped the edge of the table, afraid of the red-gaping shape about to slither into her mind.

"When women talk about things like that," Mrs Gibbs said, "you don't know what the world is coming to!"

She laughed a little, as if it didn't matter in the slightest what the world was coming to.

"That sort of book never ought to have been published!" Mrs Critoph declared.

"Read it, have you, Elsie?" Mr Took asked.

"I should think not! Give the hotel a bad name if people thought we went in for that sort of thing here."

"Talking about a bad name," Mr Lexford said. "Just as well there weren't any reporters here last night."

"Marvellous what you can see from a window," Mr Took agreed.

He framed his hands as if at such a window.

He'd had his bedroom window open last night, he said. Because of the heat. He woke up and heard voices. And when he looked out of the window, lo and behold! Mr Perkins and a policeman were leaving the premises. This would be about two in the morning.

"So if that news item of yours is correct," he said to Eileen, "we can only guess why Mr Perkins was called out by the police at that hour."

"So he wouldn't be seen and give the place a bad name!" Mr Lexford joked.

"Hour or two later," Mr Took said, "I heard a car door slam. And when I looked out, there was our Mr Perkins coming back. On his own!"

He looked round at the staff, let them draw their own conclusions.

"What a blessing these alterations are!" Mr Lexford said. "Otherwise people would have been able to slip in and out the front way, and none of us any the wiser."

Mrs Critoph struggled to her feet. "If you must know, Mr Perkins did go to the police station last night."

A body had been recovered from the Thames in the afternoon. That of a young woman – whose throat had been cut. It wasn't till the early hours that the police had got in touch with the hotel. Mr Perkins had had to go to the hospital and identify it. It was Maggie Hines. He'd been too upset to tell the staff himself.

Mrs Critoph waddled off, her left arm sideways away from her body, warding off lesser beings.

But why, Maudie wondered to herself, did Malcolm decide he'd got to go and look at that body in the river?

"All very well Perky pretending to be so upset," Mr Took remarked. "He kept very quiet about her being missing all day yesterday and all the previous night."

"What I can't understand," Mrs Gibbs said in her sing-song little voice, "is how the *Daily Brief* knew about *Married Love* being in Maggie's room."

She sat hugging her knees, staring into space.

Mr Lexford grinned round at his friend.

"That's the last thing to worry about, Irene," Mr Took remarked. "The police would have told them. They'd have found it when they searched her room."

Maudie did her best not to look at Rosie. It was Rosie who had asked her to sleep in Maggie's room, so Rosie must have known Maggie wasn't going to be there. Rosie had told her to lock the door and not to put the light on. And if Rosie knew all that, it made you wonder what else Rosie knew.

And tonight she'd got to share a room with Rosie!

"An – y n – ews?"

The man who'd come in looked as if his face had been struck by lightning. Maudie marvelled how he could go about like it. Like unwrapping a wound in public. But the staff were pleased to see Bernard, made room for him at the table, told him where Maggie's body had been found, told him what had happened to her, and about Perkins identifying the body.

He put his face in his hands.

"P – oor k – id!"

He was more upset than any of them, was sorry for the girl herself, whereas the others were just intrigued. He was the nicest of the lot, Maudie thought.

And then remembered it was Bernard's razor that was missing.

She watched him rub his face, noted the way one side of it was distorted, as if a gale of wind had caught it and torn it out of shape.

"They didn't, you know." Mrs Gibbs' quavery little voice drifted out towards anyone who might want to hear.

"Didn't what, Irene?" Mr Lexford said.

"Tell the *Daily Brief*. Couldn't have done, if you think about it."

Mr Lexford shaded his eyes as if to view the peculiar little woman more clearly.

"They do it by telephone, Irene," he explained. "There's a wire, comes out of the speaking tube, goes all the way from the police station to the newspaper office."

Mrs Gibbs's face wrinkled into a laugh. "Yes, Victor. But the police didn't know she was Maggie. Let alone that the book was hers."

Victor Lexford turned to his friend. "Didn't you tell us, Martin, you saw Perky leave with a policeman? Man in a blue suit? Helmet?" He spoke patiently, wanting to help a person of limited intelligence. "Maybe," he said, "the policeman had lost his way? Just popped into the hotel to find out where he was."

Mrs Gibbs tittered again. "But if the police knew earlier why didn't they come here earlier? Why wait till two in the morning?"

"You don't know the police," Mr Took said. "It's their favourite time."

"But even if they did know the dead girl was Maggie," Mrs Gibbs said, "and even if they did know the book belonged to Maggie, which I don't see how they could till they looked in her room, they still couldn't have been the ones to tell the newspaper."

Mr Took tried not to look amused. "Go on then, Irene. Give us a surprise."

"Well, you say they left here about two o'clock? Mrs Critoph says Mr Perkins and the police went to the hospital and identified the body. The police would be sure to ask Mr Perkins a few questions and maybe sign something. It'd be gone three o'clock by that time, and the papers'd already be printed and on the train."

Mr Took didn't reply, merely wagged a finger very slowly as if what he'd got to say was too deep to go into. Mr Lexford shook his head, looked wiser than ever.

Mrs Critoph came back into the room. Closed the door behind her.

"Before anybody goes," she said. She kept her voice low. "I've just been to Maggie Hines' room. There's no sign of that Stopes' book. I've had a thorough search. If she did have such a book, someone here knows more about this affair than they're saying."

Maudie refused to catch her eye. She knew the woman was waiting for her to raise her head, waiting for her acknowledge her like everyone else. But she didn't want an eye to eye challenge. She had had enough of hostility, of justifying herself.

Someone pressed her foot to look up at the woman. But she refused to look at the woman, refused to behave like a child listening to a horrible adult.

*You don't want to get too helpful,* Iris had said. *Look what's happened to Maggie Hines.*

The silence had caught her. She was caught in the silence like a fly in a web. Knew everyone was looking at her.

"Somebody here knows more than they ought," Mrs Critoph repeated.

Maudie knew who the *somebody* was. Everyone did, and when Mrs Critoph went out there was a burst of sympathy for her. "That's how she is!" they told her. "Always picks on someone who can't answer back!"

They told her not to worry about the old bitch. Perkins was the boss, not Mrs Critoph.

But as they left the staffroom to get back to work the message came. Maudie Stelfox was to go and see Mrs Critoph in her room straight away.

Maudie knocked.

Mrs Critoph seemed to loom over her.

"Ah, you! Your rooms aren't finished. Doesn't look as if you're up to the job." The outburst took her by surprise. "This is where you work, young lady! Not where you just turn up for meals!"

Maudie put on the uncomplaining pose she usually wore against unfairness. "I quite enjoyed helping out in the kitchen before lunch. They said there was more to do there than usual."

"Never mind what you enjoyed. You aren't here to enjoy anything. You're here to do what you're told to do."

"I only meant -" she hesitated, looked down at the floor, "I meant I enjoyed doing what you told me to do, Mrs Critoph."

"I don't care what you enjoy. I don't think you're suited to working here. I don't know what made you come here in the first place."

Maudie had nothing to say.

"I said," Mrs Critoph repeated, "I don't know what made you come here in the first place."

The eyes bit into her. Maudie had seen a stoat about to kill a rabbit, intent, almost loving the creature whose blood it was about to drink.

She was from the country, she said, from a farm. There wasn't any money in farming now. "We're poor. I had to find somewhere to work."

Mrs Critoph hardly listened.

"I'm going to watch you, my girl. I shall watch you like a hawk. I'll make sure you work every minute you're supposed to work."

Her voice was as cruel as her face, Maudie thought, yet her hair was as soft and grey as a grandmother's.

"I'll try not to disappoint you, Mrs Critoph," she said. "I'll do everything I can to please you."

"Time you were at work, then," Mrs Critoph said. "Standing there, idling!"

Later, before going to sleep, Maudie whispered the day's happenings to her mother's photo.

"But don't worry about me, dear. I'll put up with anything to find him."

# CHAPTER 36

She worked hard, faster than she had worked in her life in spite of the pain inside her. She cleaned her quota of rooms, cleaned up the chambermaid's kitchen, and finished late.

Back in the bedroom the girl in the washstand mirror was pale. It was the time of the month, she was exhausted by all her new work, but it was the usual Maudie Stelfox, the usual face, the usual shape. But behind that face in the mirror there was no terrible thing to escape, no nightmare that could never be hidden again.

And that girl in the mirror wasn't a girl who'd come all the way to London only to find herself face to face with someone as bad as the bitches. Or worse. Yet it was a comfort to know that face wasn't frightened. She didn't want that young girl to live the life she was having to live, bullied by day, scared by night, living where the girl had lived whose throat had been cut. Nor want her to know her journey from country to town had been a journey from one kind of madness to another.

"Get yourself to sleep," she whispered to her.

The girl smiled too, blew a kiss back.

There was nowhere to hide the book. It was only small, might go undetected a day or two under her clothes in the drawer. But she'd soon have to find somewhere better.

She got into bed. Rosie hadn't come in yet. She couldn't bother about Rosie. Since coming to London she'd lived in a world she hadn't dreamed of, and underneath was the nightmare she thought she'd buried years ago. But the Major had sent her his sign in the sky and she didn't care what she'd have to suffer. If suffering was the price she had to pay she would pay it, because one day she'd find him, and all she had had to put up with would be worthwhile.

She fell asleep, too deep to hear Rosie come up in the early hours, or hear her count the takings for her evening's work.

She was up and ready to start before six. She prepared the tea, took jugs of hot water round, she made beds, swept and dusted, and when in the early afternoon June Trick came with a message from Mrs Critoph she wasn't altogether surprised.

Would Maudie Stelfox stop what she was doing and go and give Peter a hand in the public bar for an hour.

"I shouldn't fly down quite yet," June said, amused at her starting to rush off. "You're a different kettle of fish to that Beryl. I reckon you'd do that reception job ten times better than she's doing it!"

"What do you think of the old place, then?"

The bar was closed, the customers had gone. Peter was washing the rows of used mugs and glasses. He gave the impression of owning the place, turning his little body this way and that, surveying the room, considering how it could be improved to deal with more customers. He worked fast. Maudie tried to keep pace, drying the glasses and putting them back on the shelves. She wanted to please, wanted to work as fast as a Londoner. After a while Peter remarked,

"You're picking it up a treat." So she tried to work faster still, and tried looking about the room like him – till she almost dropped a glass and was told to watch what she was doing.

What he'd really like, Peter said, was for him and Rosie to work in a bar somewhere, he as potman and cellarman, Rosie serving. The customers would take to a girl like Rosie. Trade would be that brisk they'd be able to take a pub themselves.

"But she ain't interested. Ain't what she wants."

When the glasses were washed and stacked away he gave Maudie the polish box, told her to polish the counter. She remembered how the bitches used to complain: *Never puts her back into her work! Never makes a good job of anything!* She wished they could see her now, putting her back into it enough to make herself sweat. Imagined the look on their faces, seeing the mahogany surface of the counter shine like a river. She moved her hand to and fro over it to show them how it shone.

Saw the reflection of her hand in the wood.

A drowned hand.

Her stomach tightened, sick with what was forming inside her. The girl in the river. She felt sick with what was starting to form inside her.

She asked Peter where the beer came from.

"This particular brew," he said, indicating a pump, "comes from Burton-on-Trent."

"How does it get into the pumps?"

She didn't care what she asked or what he answered. She wanted him to keep talking, wanted to forget what was trying to form in her mind.

Peter was only too pleased to talk about keeping and dispensing beer. Under the bar was the cellar where the beer barrels were kept. Pipes were attached to the barrels, so when the pumps were pulled in the bar, ale or beer or stout was drawn up and out of the tap into the customer's glass.

"Come and look down here."

He unbolted a door at the back of the bar. Just outside, a couple of trap doors to the cellar lay open. A ladder led down into the darkness below. He was expecting a delivery any minute from the brewers.

She asked what was down there, apart from the barrels.

"Just the racks what the barrels rest on, an' the tools for when Bernard cleans the pipes out." Which he or Bernard had to do every week to keep them clean, otherwise the pipes would get blocked and the pumps wouldn't draw.

He told her how the cleaning was done, told her about the bath and the jug – on and on, the way men will talk about *things*. She didn't care. She loved him, little buck rabbit that he was, because what she had seen was a place to hide *Married Love*.

They came away. Peter closed the bar door. It was a change to talk to someone who showed interest, he said. Rosie never bothered. He couldn't make Rosie out. All she thought about was getting a place of her own.

"Don't know why she worries about it so much. Must want jam on it! She's got a bed here, not like me. I have to walk three miles here and three miles back every day!"

He asked Maudie if she'd like to try and pull some beer. He told her which pump handle to pull, gave her a glass to hold in her other hand. She gripped the pump handle, pulled it towards her. The pressure on her injury was more than she'd bargained for. The pain shot through her hand and up her arm.

She winced, nursed the hand to her.

"War wound?" he joked. But he held it gently, seeing the scar.

Rosie let the door slam behind her.

"Soon as I turn my back!" She sounded weary rather than cross.

"See this scar, Rosie?"

Rosie glanced at it, slumped down in one of the armchairs and put her feet up.

"You sound done up," Maudie said. "Anything up?"

She immersed her hand in the rinsing water to ease the pain.

"The only thing up with Rosie," Peter said, "is she imagines things." He was fitting a new bottle of whisky into the nip dispenser. "You tell Maudie. See what she thinks." He finished with the dispenser, came across to the counter. "Rosie reckons she saw the bloke what done it."

Rosie glanced at the door.

"Course I saw him. I let him in."

Maudie forgot her hand enough to rest it on her newly polished counter.

"That bedroom I let you see into," Rosie said. "That was where."

She'd gone to check if the window was fastened because the decorators were going to paint it. And while she was there this man came along the scaffolding and tapped on the window.

"And the silly little sod let him."

"You'd never do anything, would you?" Rosie rounded on him. "You'd stay in this dump and never want anything better!"

"What's that got to do with it?"

"Would you turn down ten bob?"

"You never said nothin' about ten bob."

"I take what I can get, mister. I shan't stay here for the rest of my life, even if you do."

"See what I mean?" Peter asked. "That's all she's on about. A place of her own!"

Maudie asked her what made her think the man was anything to do with Maggie.

"He asked me if he could pop into her room a moment. Had this ten shilling note in his hand. I couldn't see no harm. I knew Maggie had gone out. I thought he was a friend of hers. We didn't know but what she'd soon be back. So I let him in. He wasn't in there long. That's how I knew her room wasn't going to be used that night."

"How did you know?"

"Because she was dead."

"Did he say she was dead?"

"On his way out he said, 'That was Maggie Hines, then.' I said, '*Was?*' 'Oh, you won't see her no more,' he said. Drew his hand across his throat. Before I could get my breath, he'd gone."

"Now she reckons she's mixed up in it," Peter jeered. "Just because she let him in."

"That's why I daren't say anything," Rosie explained. "Not after I've took his money."

Dust flecks floated across a shaft of sunlight through the front window. The instant they left the light they vanished as though they had never existed.

Maudie dried the counter where her hand had dripped. The scar still ached, but the sharpness had eased. She asked Peter if he wanted any more help. She was glad he didn't, was glad to get back to cleaning her kitchen.

# CHAPTER 37

She practised moving about like a Londoner, briskly, upstairs and down, found it easier than the slow old country way of walking, found she got through her work quicker. You didn't get tired if you worked at it, put a bit of go into it. And ringing a cheerful little bell at the back of her mind was June saying: *you'd make a better job of reception than that Beryl!* And Peter saying: *you're picking it up a treat!*

Mrs Critoph didn't spare her, sent her off to help people, making the day longer. But she was determined to please. She knew her belongings had been gone through because one day she noticed a jumper was further back in the drawer than a petticoat she had matched it with. She was as polite as ever to Mrs Critoph, helpful whatever extra she was asked to do, preferred to think of the woman's kindly hair rather than her callous eyes, but if she really was a callous old bitch, a bit of helpfulness would undermine her, just as it had the bitches.

It was the end of the week. She lay in bed, had drifted into sleep. The image of the door to Room 39 appeared, vivid as if she was standing in front of it, the wood a reddish brown, the lower panels longer than the upper panels, the number 39 burning like flames. She was in the shadows of the corridor, the room and its secrets were calling her in. She was in the room, was standing at the window. He spoke. She knew the voice, the way he breathed, the sounds of his mouth. His hand invited her to step out to him. She took it, her hand in his, stepping out on to the scaffold, she and the Major.

*Come away! The time of the singing of birds has come! Come away!*

"Away!"

She woke up. The shout echoed in her head. Away!

It was no dream. Richard had called her, had called her name in the night. As soon as she could she'd look for him. One day she'd find him.

She fell asleep, slept deeply. By the time she awoke she had made up her mind.

She would find out about Room 39.

She worked quickly, was quicker at seeing to the needs of the guests, quicker at doing the rooms, and had almost finished when the usual order came from Mrs Critoph, this time to help with preparing the vegetables in the kitchen for the evening meal.

"She's got her knife into you!" June laughed. "Proper favourite, you are!"

"I don't mind. Anything to help."

And knowing about vegetables she worked with a will and got the job done.

"Don't you go and leave us," Julie Moores said. "Don't get many like you."

But the joy for Maudie was the thought of her sisters' faces if they could see her now, young lazybones they couldn't wait to see the back of!

Come late afternoon, her work done, she went past Room 39. Went to the end of the corridor, checked the stairs up and down. Stopped, stamped her foot as if she'd remembered something and had to go back for it. Walked quickly. Paused. Was outside the room. Glanced about her. Quick as light she had the key in the lock, was inside.

She leaned against the door, caught her breath.

This was the room! The window! She went over to it, looked out. Beyond the scaffolding across the front of the hotel was the roof of London. It lay in the summer sun as in a vast bowl, its millions of roofs, its houses and factories, its spires and towers and the Thames itself, as far as the blue-grey mists in the distance.

And somewhere amongst it all was Richard.

She imagined him at his desk, straightening his back after helping the men unload a vessel, busy with his day-to-day affairs, but knowing she had started her search, that sooner or later they'd meet and their future would begin.

She leaned out into the afternoon as Rosie had leaned out that first evening, her arms pressing against the breasts she hoped one day his lips would kiss. She closed her eyes, imagined his face....

"You got the job, then?"

A disembodied voice.

Immediately below her on the scaffolding. A slim young man, leaning back against a rail, paint kettle in one hand, brush in the other.

"You got fixed up?" he asked.

"Fixed up?"

"I saw you come in the other night. You and the other lady. I guessed you might have come about a job."

He smiled, seemed pleasant enough. She noticed his eyes, how intense they were, searching her, waiting for answers.

"I'm on a month's trial."

She wondered if he'd noticed her bosom.

"I hoped you'd be lucky. I've been keeping my eye open for you."

He had a nice face, friendly, open, but his eyes were what she noticed, as if he'd got a hundred ideas behind them.

"I've never seen London before." She waved an arm at the city spread out below them. "It's so big!"

He pointed out the dome of St Paul's, the sparkle of the sun on the Crystal Palace out at Sydenham, the pinnacles and turrets of Westminster.

"I'll take you round one day and show you."

"I'm not sure how long I'm going to be here."

"You'll still be here. After I've gone." He waved his brush vaguely. "Like all this."

He could have been indicating the paintwork, or the spread of London below them.

She asked him what his name was. It was Tony Abbington.

There was something in the way he was obliged to look up at her that was rather pleasing. She was able to toss her curls back and let the sun play on her cheek.

"I can't stay," she smiled, knowing the risks of being overheard.

"Your name can."

She could tell he found her attractive.

"Maudie," she said, waving her fingertips at him ever so slightly as she withdrew.

The trapdoors to the cellar lay open, the ladder led down into darkness. Some time soon a delivery of barrels was expected.

She had the book in her laundry bag. She twitched a handkerchief out, watched it fall into the shadows.

"Excuse me," she called down.

There was no reply.

She gripped the top of the ladder, got her feet on the rungs, climbed down into the darkness to the floor. The cellar was damp, cool enough on her bare arms to give her goose pimples. Daylight and safety were a long way above.

When her eyes had adjusted she retrieved her handkerchief. At the back of the cellar the row of barrels tilted forward on a timber rack; to the left, on cobwebby shelves were tools and barrel taps; to the right she noticed a brass water tap, an enamel jug, a tin bath.

Little else.

She tried moving a floor brick with her foot. It was set firm. She tried others, tried the wall. Nothing moved.

Somewhere above footsteps approached.

She pulled the book out of her bag, flew to the end of the barrel rack, squeezed herself between the end barrel and the wall. The wall was slimy as though covered in grey snow, but she forced herself to the rear corner, hid the book between the wall and the rack.

Someone was at the trapdoor, had his foot on the rung. She wriggled herself out from beside the barrel, her clothes and hands filthy.

He came down, switched the light on. His face, as if a gale had torn at it!

"Miss Stelfox?"

"I dropped my hanky." She held it up. "When I came down I tripped over."

"I 'ust have left the 'ath in the way."

He pushed the bath with his foot. Then noticed her dress.

"'Etter not let Elsie Critoph see you like that."

It was like watching some cartoon trying to talk.

"You 'ow what she is"

He gave her some water in the jug and a piece of soap. Then pulled his neckerchief off for her to dry herself on. She didn't like not to use it.

A veil of cobweb softened the light from the bare bulb. His undeformed cheek curved down to his jaw, the facial hair manly over his chin. One side of him was quite good-looking.

He asked how she liked being at the hotel.

Loved it, she said, even though the day she started was the day Maggie's body had been found. Was it true that Mr Perkins had known about it without saying anything to the staff?

Bernard didn't know, couldn't say. But in his opinion Mr Perkins was all right, had always treated him all right. He wasn't full-time, he explained, but there weren't many jobs to choose from nowadays, especially for a bloke whose face wasn't up to standard.

She realised she was understanding him more easily. And that he had changed the subject away from Maggie.

What sort of girl was she, in his opinion?

"Too willing to please. That was Maggie's trouble."

"Trouble?"

Bernard put his finger to his lips, pointed to the trapdoor.

"Draymen!" he whispered.

She hurried her way up the ladder. Noticed he was nice enough to move away rather than stand underneath while she climbed.

Her dress looked worse than ever in daylight. She crossed through the guests' wing, got to her own corridor of rooms without trouble, had only to get up a couple of flights of stairs to be safe in the service wing.

"Ah, Maudie! I wondered if I should see you!"

Little old Mrs Gibbs wandered out of the laundry room, half laughing at a recollection she wanted Maudie to hear.

"I never told you what happened last November, did I. It was these children."

"Oh Mrs Gibbs -"

"Collecting pennies for the guy. They'd got this old pram. I'd seen them getting it ready. They only live next door to where I live..."

The little curved face smiled, the eyes dreamy.

"They'd got this old sack, stuffed straw into it and this old pair of gloves on the youngest, Michael I think his name was. About four. They'd drawn this face on a brown paper bag and put it over his head. He did look funny!"

She laughed her faint faraway laugh. Maudie tried to pretend she was interested, tried to get away.

"The things children get up to!" Mrs Gibbs said. "They put him in this pram, and away they went. They got as far as the butcher's, asked for a penny for the guy."

There were voices on the stair. Mrs Critoph and two or three of the chambermaids were at the end of the corridor, coming towards them, Mrs Critoph laying the law down about hotel rules.

"Butcher boy – only a young lad," Mrs Gibbs was saying. "About fifteen or sixteen. He came out and had a look. He laughed when he saw their guy, and gave them a penny. Eldest girl said, 'That's my little brother, that is.' The butcher boy said, 'I bet it ain't.' So the girl said, 'I bet it is.' So the boy said, 'You can't kid me,' and jabbed his butcher's knife right into the sack."

"What these children get up to!" Mrs Gibbs tittered. "There's no out-thinking them."

"What happened to the child?"

"Took him to the hospital, I suppose." She spoke as if that wasn't the point of the story at all.

"Maudie Stelfox!"

Maudie closed her eyes.

"What do you look like!" The woman was red with anger. "You are the most disgraceful looking urchin I ever – !"

She pulled Maudie round to face her, stared up and down at her clothes. "And you think you're fit to work in a hotel?"

It wasn't Mrs Critoph's face. It was her mother's.

So much she wanted to tell her mother.

"Don't stare at me, girl! Look at those clothes!"

It wasn't her mother. It was a mask. Maudie turned away, hid her face.

Mrs Critoph seized her arm, flung her round like a child. "I will NOT have staff look like this!"

The mask splintered. Snapshots of faces surrounded her, Rosie, her hand to her mouth, June, Pamela, staring, wanting to help.

Jigsaw pieces whirled in her mind, out of her mind, formed what must never be seen.

A face rose out of the river, grew, erected itself out of the mud, its hair matted with river rubbish.

Changed to a corpse, its throat grinning with red lips.

There were wreaths on the grave. The word was in her mouth, wanting to burst out.

A voice was saying, "You're a disgrace to the hotel! We can do without such as you!"

The word boiled over inside her, the scream-word she could hold no longer.

"Mummee! Mummee!"

The scream broke, over and over. The wreaths became flowers, petals, falling, turning and falling.

"Have you gone crazy!"

Her mother was going through petals to her grave. As she passed, Maudie gave her the gentlest little wave with her fingertips, but Mrs Critoph didn't know it was a wave good-bye and cracked her a blow across the face with her extended arm, and the figure vanished and the screaming stopped.

Rosie was beside her, her arm round her.

"Young people nowadays," Mrs Gibbs laughed to Mrs Critoph as they went, "you never know what they'll do next!"

"Don't let her know she hurt you, Maudie," Rosie whispered. "Or she'll try and sack you on the spot."

Her cheek and mouth felt numb, but the storm in her head had cleared.

Old Critoph could do what she liked.

"What a cat!" the others said. "Vicious old cow!"

The muddle had been in her head for years. Now it had gone. She was clear about her mother now.

"Isn't the first time," Maudie meant the blow across her face. "Be all right with some cold water."

She'd seen the crowd round Maggie's body, she explained. She'd been on London Bridge and seen the body.

"Never mind that now," Rosie said. "Go and get a clean dress on before the old sod comes back. And mind you keep busy."

But she had to get it out of her mind. She had wanted to comfort the body. Had wanted to comfort the body! Because of that other death Maggie's had got muddled up with.

"For God's sake, girl!" Rosie urged. "Get a move on! She's gone to see Perkins about you!"

She'd been in a muddle, she said, and what she'd seen at the river had made it worse. But it was clear in her head now.

Rosie pushed her along, pointed the way. "Tell me later!"

Maudie hurried away, got to the bedrooms.

She pulled her soiled dress off, put a clean one on. Wished she could do the same with the years, pull them off over her head and wash the terrible ones away.

Yet she felt grateful. She had received a kind of blessing. No good blaming the dead. They'd got their reasons for being dead. No good being afraid of them, or blaming them, however it happened.

She knew she no longer blamed her dear mother for killing herself.

# CHAPTER 38

"Lucky little cow!"

Rosie sat herself on Maudie's bed, resumed brushing her hair.

"There's me awake nearly all night, and here's you sleeping like a baby!"

Maudie liked her sitting on her bed. And being called a lucky little cow the way Rosie said it.

"Aren't you worried?" Rosie asked. "After all that, yesterday?"

Maudie wasn't, hadn't given it another thought.

"If I do get the sack," she said, "I'll get a job somewhere else."

But she liked the hotel. A lot better than home. She'd be sorry if Critoph sacked her now she was starting to get the knack of chambermaiding. If only she could do it twice as quick, she joked, she'd be as good as Rosie.

"I'd leave here like a shot," Rosie said, "if I'd got somewhere decent to go. You don't really like it here, do you?"

"Love it." And she liked it even more knowing Rosie didn't like it.

"I'll believe you." The girl was nervous, didn't look well. "That bloke I let in. I keep seeing him, in my mind."

"He could hardly have been the killer," Maudie said. "A murderer would hardly want to be seen, let alone ask someone to show him to the bedroom where his victim used to sleep."

"You may be right," Rosie sighed. "What we do for money, us women!"

Maudie got out of bed. Normally if anyone was in the room she covered herself up, but this morning she felt different. She felt confident, full of health, so she pulled her nightie off and washed naked.

"If Peter could see you now," Rosie said, "he'd lose what little hair he has got."

Maudie looked round to laugh, saw that Rosie had turned her back.

"What about when he sees you?" Maudie asked.

"Me! I make sure he never sees me undressed. I shouldn't like to show myself off to any of them!" She shuddered. "And as for seeing a man! Seeing animals is bad enough!"

Maudie had been seeing animals all her life on the farm. It was over in a minute. The male had his jump and got off, the female kept on chewing. There was no relationship between them, no tenderness. A few months later the female gave birth, and the cycle started again.

She looked at the reflection of her body in the mirror, its curves, its shadows in the early morning light. She felt the towel move across her skin, and thought of the words of Marie Stopes: Her husband's lips upon her breast... She would want to look at her lover's body, see him as he really was under his clothes, would want Richard and herself to be tender together. She thought of the country women she knew, hardy as pigs some of them, all tenderness gone, even from their voices. She had lived all her life in the country and never found tenderness. She would find it in the town.

She was washed, dressed and ready in a quarter of the time it used to take her, and having a minute or two to spare, and feeling more open about things she took out the photo of her mother and showed it to Rosie.

"My dear mum," she explained. "She committed suicide."

Her mother's face was as loving as ever, unmoved by the disclosure.

"Didn't you, my darling."

It was the first time she had admitted as much to anyone, even to herself. She was glad she had brought it into the open. She felt free of something, as if the layers of curtain she had hidden behind for years had lifted. It made her feel lighter, more carefree, not having to hide any more, like washing with no clothes on. And catching herself in the mirror a little later she thought the excitement in her cheeks quite suited her.

The window of her chambermaid's kitchen was glazed with frosted glass, the small shellshapes of which were patterns of dark edges and brightness. The brighter they were the better her day was likely to be. Sometimes shadow fingered its way across the shapes, other times the window glowed like a sheet of pearls. This morning, knowing she had an appointment to see Mr Perkins later on, she was comforted to see the window studded with sunshine.

She dealt the hot water and early morning tea out to bedroom after bedroom promptly enough, got on well with the guests, was pleased she could remember who wanted what without having to check the guest-list all the time. But seeing the postmark on the letter, the word *Beckthorp* across the stamp like a threat, her heart sank. She took it up to her kitchen, filled a kettle and put it on the gas-ring to be heating while she read it.

*Dear Maudie,*

*All this time and still never a word Pa is worried sick not hearing, says he never ought to have let you go, I enclose a stamped envelope in case you're short and am sending this to the hotel in case you got the job there I've already written to Malcolm as I know the intention was for you to stay a few days with them first.*

*Cousin Kate has started nursing in London you may bump into her one of these days she cant be far away can she we are all fairly well though will feel better when we know you're safe though as I said to Pa what did he expect. Muriel and Pa send their love I hope you think of those you left behind.*

*Your affectionate sister*

*Barbara Stelfox*

Maudie finished reading it, tore it up, stamped envelope and all. She would write when she wanted to, not when Bossy Barbara thought she should. And as for thinking she'd bump into Kate in a place the size of London, the silly bitch probably thought London was the size of Beckthorp.

"You can carry on with your work," Mrs Critoph said.

The woman advanced into the kitchen, threatening as ever.

"I'm sorry about my dress," Maudie said. "I tripped over."

"Dress! I see more than a dress! It's what I hear!" There was something brilliant about the woman's eyes.

"I didn't mean to scream." She spoke quietly, hoped to pacify the old woman. "I'm sorry."

Mrs Critoph drew her stocky figure back a shade as if preparing to strike. Maudie kept herself within reach of the kettle for self defence.

"I didn't mean to call you -"

She wasn't going to apologise any more, wouldn't honour the old woman with that word. If she wanted to dismiss her she'd have to come out with it and dismiss her.

"You didn't mean what!"

She knew what Mrs Critoph was at: she wanted Maudie to say she was leaving so she could tell Mr Perkins it wasn't her fault. She didn't sack the girl, she'd say; the girl didn't want to stay any longer.

The kettle banged a couple of times as the water heated up. And still Mrs Critoph waited, as if willing her to say the word Maudie had called her yesterday.

Maudie looked away, reliving the moment when her mind had exploded and that dear name screamed out of her mouth, the moment when she could acknowledge what her mother had done and love her just the same.

"I was out of my mind."

"So it's ridiculous, what you called me?"

Maudie didn't want to argue. She wanted to forget.

"Oh, you don't have to answer," the woman sneered. "But don't imagine you can make a fool out of me!"

Maudie stared at her. A grey-haired old woman, old enough to be her grandmother, annoyed over a word said in distress.

"I was there when the body was found," she said.

She began to see her own side of the affair. She had needed help, and all she had got was to be hit about.

"I look like your mother, I suppose!"

"My mother's dead."

A succession of small explosions rang within the kettle, a jet of vapour formed, streamed its way out of the spout.

The woman stared at her, cold as a lizard. The arm jerked. The little body swung away.

"I see." Mrs Critoph stopped at the doorway, seemed to view the corridor. "I see, Maudie."

Her voice seemed less sharp. "Don't forget. Mr Perkins wants you to see him at four-thirty."

The kettle on the gas-ring boiled too furiously, boiled itself over. The flame spluttered, turned yellow and amber. Maudie turned the gas flame off, the volleys of bangs and rattles softened, died away.

Mrs Critoph waddled off. By the time Maudie had wiped the bench dry the corridor was empty.

"Mr Perkins is engaged."

Beryl's icicle voice was of a piece with her blonde hair and pale blue eyes. She seemed to have little to do. Maudie could well believe such a competent-looking person would have completed her work early.

The clock said almost four-thirty.

Maudie sat down to wait. Despite the heat she hugged her black dress tight across her knees.

"No need to worry," the icicle scratched. "He's like that."

"Like what?"

"Making appointments to see two people at the same time, so he can keep the least important one waiting."

Beryl's ice-blue eyes glittered a moment, then drifted down to Maudie's knees. Maudie took the hint, smoothed her dress and sat up. She wasn't particularly nervous, was sure she could get another job. Old Critoph might not have sacked her after all. Maudie half wished she had because she felt she was starting to work like a Londoner, felt she could do a Londoner's job at any hotel.

Twenty to five.

She willed the door to open. What she was nervous of wasn't of being sacked or being given notice; she was just nervous of waiting.

"Whatever made you choose to work at the King James?" Beryl asked. "Of all places!"

"Someone I know knows someone who knows the owner," Maudie explained. "She knows someone who knows Mr Perkins."

Beryl's eyes sparkled.

"Owner? If Uncle Perky owns this I own Buckingham Palace."

"Who does own it, then?"

Beryl pulled a face.

"Who cares? Uncle Perky might own ten per cent. He's the manager."

She resumed her work, which appeared to consist of copying items from a wad of rough notes into an account book. Every now and then she paused to rearrange objects on her desk, such as lining up book, pen and pad so that they were parallel to each other or parallel to the side of the desk. Sometimes it seemed a certain matter was amusing her, then she'd sigh, copy more notes, and rearrange her desk again.

She sat back, put her pen down.

"You've made a hit with Mrs Critoph, I hear."

Maudie had thought as much. The incident was all round the hotel.

"I don't know what came over me. It was when I realised I'd seen the body. I think I'm going to get the sack."

Beryl nodded, absent-mindedly arranging the items on the desk to radiate out like the spokes of a wheel. Yet something was amusing her.

"You'll have heard about a razor." She placed a paperweight to form the hub. "Belonged to a certain gentleman?"

Maudie had.

"'orning, Mr Perkins."

The heartless little bitch girl had got Bernard to a T.

"'orning, Maudie."

Maudie laughed out loud, tried to smother it back. Beryl, her pale blue eyes gentle, almost pitying, watched her.

"'ome and see what I've 'ot in my cellar, Maudie."

She turned to her notes, studied their transcription to the book and let the remark bite its way in.

"Oh, you mean -"

But Beryl was putting in a burst of concentration, managed to copy half a dozen words without stopping.

"I dropped my hanky down there," Maudie explained. "I had to climb down there to get it."

Beryl continued her work, too engrossed to reply.

"It was a handkerchief my mother gave me when I was a child. Just before she died."

Beryl put her pen down, looked at her in relief.

"There! I knew it, Maudie! I knew there must be an innocent explanation. In spite of what everybody's saying!"

"Saying? What are they saying?"

"Oh," Beryl waved vaguely, as if dispelling something unpleasant in the air. "Filthy talk. You know the sort of thing. I couldn't listen to such rumours – you and him."

Maudie felt like cracking the little torment across the face, yet daren't because of what else she might know.

"I knew there was nothing in it," Beryl said. "In spite of -"

"In spite of what?"

"Such details, Maudie! All exaggeration."

"Details?"

"I couldn't repeat them. And all because there was a speck of dust on your clothes, I believe."

"Speck!" Maudie was amused at the word. "My dress was covered!"

"You and Bernard up against the wall. On the floor, others said. I couldn't listen!"

She shuddered, waved the air as if by referring to such matters she had contaminated it.

"Made me sick to hear such lies about you, Maudie!"

She turned away, too upset to work or even rearrange her patterning.

"What else did they tell you?" Maudie demanded.

" Tell me! Nobody tells Mr Perkins' niece anything. It's like being a leper. I had to piece it together in dribs and drabs."

She sounded as if she had done Maudie a kindness, even managed to look sincere.

Maudie asked her if her uncle knew of the rumours.

"My dear! Uncle Perky doesn't confide in me! He doesn't even want me here, I can't understand why. I was supposed to be learning how to be a receptionist till Maggie went and got herself done in. Now I'm even more unwanted."

Not that she sounded unwanted. She had the sort of face and voice that could make anything sound humorous. Maudie wanted to laugh, much as she hated the girl.

"Who?" she asked. "Who's saying all this?"

"I don't know who. They all look alike, that class of person, don't you think? That's why I'm glad there's someone like you on the staff."

For a moment she gave another impression of being sincere.

The office door opened. Mr Perkins smiled his visitor out. The smile had gone by the time he asked Maudie in.

"Now, young woman. About time I took down your particulars."

She sat facing his desk, her black dress hot on her body. Mr Perkins found the piece of paper he was looking for, leaned back in his chair to look at her. His eyes lingered on her throat, her bosom. She was reminded of the ferret they kept at Beck Farm, its nose snuffing around.

He needed some answers, he said. Life nowadays was nothing but finding things out for other people.

She told him her name was Maudie Stelfox, of Beck Farm, St Matthew's, Beckthorp, Suffolk, she was nineteen and this was her first job away from home.

"Not married, I take it? Engaged?"

He scarcely looked up, nor when he had to explain what was meant by next of kin. Eventually, the questions finished, he put his pen down, looked her over again.

"Had a turn the other day, I hear."

She had wondered when he would get round to it. When he'd got the details down she would be dismissed.

She didn't actually see the corpse, she explained, she saw the people round it, but it wasn't till next day she was told whose body it was. She couldn't say, she said, why she'd had that funny turn when she realised exactly what she'd seen, but she'd got it out of her system now and it wouldn't happen again.

"I suppose you were on the bridge with that lady who came into the office with you?"

And was that lady her relation? Who worked for Mr Vincy? And did the lady know Mr Vincy well?

As to how well she knew Mr Vincy Maudie couldn't say.

"But I've got over the shock now," she assured him. "It made me wonder what could be behind such a terrible thing."

Mr Perkins' reaction was immediate.

"Sin was behind it!"

He snapped it out, his voice rougher, more Scottish. It was as if he'd been waiting for a chance to say it.

"Sin drags us all down. Even those who haven't sinned."

He sounded utterly sure of himself, as though he'd read God's mind and knew it by heart. When someone stumbled in filth other people got splashed, he said. Filth dragged everything down, the staff, the hotel, even himself.

"You know where Maggie Hines is now?"

She wasn't given the chance to say.

"She's in the mortuary at the Charles Lamb hospital. With her throat cut."

His hands pressed white against the desk. "Some might call it divine punishment."

She watched him, unsure of him. But she wanted him to be clear, wanted to know if she had a job or not. She turned away because of the sun on her back, sensed he admired her figure.

"Bernard says how grateful he is to you," she said. "Giving him a job."

He took his pipe out of his pocket, examined the empty bowl. He seemed to relax, filled the bowl with straggly tobacco and lit a match.

"I was with him when he was blown up."

He indicated the side of his face where Bernard's was disfigured, and sucked the flame into the tobacco until it glowed.

"He was in my patrol. Could have been any of us."

Cellaring wasn't much of a job, he said, but it was something.

Maudie liked the smell of lit tobacco. She sensed she might hear more about her coming dismissal when he'd got a bank of smoke to shelter behind.

"So you know Mr Vincy?" he asked.

She gave the impression that Mr Vincy was more than a name she'd heard.

"Known him long?"

He asked casually, and as casually as she could said, "Quite long."

He rested his pipe on an ashtray, seemed to study it.

"Like working here, do you?"

She liked it very much, she said. Then found herself saying she hoped her work was up to standard because she wanted the hotel to do well.

He shot a look at her, sharp as glass. That was the sort of talk he liked to hear, he said. He wished all the staff thought like that. "You think of staying long?"

She watched him, wondered if he was mocking her.

Because, he said, a time might come when she'd be glad she'd stayed. He couldn't say anything at the moment, but Mrs Critoph had been to see him, had spoken highly of her. But on no account whatever was Maudie to mention a breath of this to anyone, especially not to Mrs Critoph. Like that affair of Maggie Hines, he said. The less that came out about that the better for everybody.

He stood up, let his eyes linger on her shape as though something pleased him. The interview was over.

At the door he said, "If you see Mr Vincy you can tell him you're getting on well."

Rosie didn't go out that evening. Maudie noted the pale face and heavy eyes, made no comment.

"I'm glad he didn't sack you," Rosie said. "Maybe he's taken a fancy to you."

Maudie shuddered. The idea had crossed her mind. She felt she had been snuffed over by a ferret.

In the lull before drifting off to sleep she recalled the sunlit shellshapes in the window that morning, how truly their brightness had foretold her luck. Even though it was hidden at the moment she knew her way ahead would be sunny.

# CHAPTER 39

June, her grey eyes sympathetic as ever, gave her the message first thing next morning.

"The old cow said you're to go to her office at one o'clock!"

Maudie thanked her for telling her, set about her work briskly to get it completed before she got dismissed. It pleased her that Mrs Critoph wouldn't be able to find fault with what she had done, wouldn't be able to point to a room not dusted or dishes not properly washed up. She wanted the woman to be pleased with her. Yet she hated her. The very thought of her was a worry.

"Come in."

Mrs Critoph's face was like thunder, yet her soft grey hair had been newly set and showed well against her dark green two-piece. She told Maudie to close the door, didn't ask her to sit down.

"About time you got some fresh air, my girl!"

And said it as though she was saying, "About time you put some fresh sheets on that bed, my girl!"

"All work and no play will put anyone in the dumps."

"All work!" Maudie thought. "Who's been landing me with two or three extra hours a day!"

But she remained silent, waited for her dismissal. So much for what Mr Perkins said, she thought, telling me the old cow likes the way I work!

"I shall expect you to get your work finished early tomorrow and get yourself out for the evening."

She made it sound like a threat.

"Out?"

"Out in the fresh air, enjoying yourself!"

"Oh," Maudie said, a smile breaking through. "Oh, thank you very much!"

The woman's eyes froze, scrub-brushed away any sign of pleasantness.

"You remember where you are, young lady, and who you're talking to!"

Maudie supposed she had been too familiar. She curtsied, remained silent. Even when the old cow was trying to be nice she made it sound like an order.

"Get back to your work! And make sure you're back by ten-thirty tomorrow night, or it'll be the last time you go!"

"Very kind of you, Mrs Critoph. I'm so grateful."

She recalled a saying of her Pa's: *there's more than one way to kill a cat!*

The air was scented with traffic. Wonderful to see so many people, hear their voices. London voices were louder than Suffolk voices, had more to say, didn't go in for those long silences you got from country folk.

She walked away from the hotel, hadn't the slightest idea where the road led. But the roads themselves were exciting, full of roaring rattling vehicles, the pavements loud with people, the air all rose and gold as if it came down from the golden-pink clouds.

She noticed a particularly colourful cloud, wondered if Richard was watching it too, whether it was a sign to show where he was.

"Won't find heaven up there, you know."

It was Tony Abbington, the painter who had asked her her name at the window a few days earlier. He was waiting at a bus-stop a few feet away, looking smart in his grey suit, grey cap and white silk scarf.

"Where will I find it, then?"

The question amused him.

"They've just started building it."

She asked him where that could be, at which he grinned, said he hoped to get a job helping to build it.

"Maybe I'll take you there one day. If you're still interested."

But tonight he was off to a meeting. The borough council organised meetings so people could come and hear speakers at first hand whose views might interest them, rather than having to depend on what newspapers said they'd said. Sometimes speakers with opposing points of view were invited to the same platform. That was where the fun was, Tony said, in the controversy. Maudie could come too, if she liked.

She saw how lit up he was, as if he could already hear the arguments. She wouldn't mind going, she said, so long as she could get back to the King James by ten-thirty.

The bus drew up, the queue moved forward, began boarding it. He'd get her back in time, he said. Mostly it was people like him who went to meetings, so meetings didn't go on late as a rule. He'd got to be up early himself.

They were on the top deck of a knife-box bus. London opened out in front of them, rows and yet more rows of houses, terraces, crescents, vistas from hillsides covered in houses, tarmacked valleys, canyons of houses; then office blocks, tall buildings, larger shops and wider pavements of a town centre, then away to the endlessly unfolding views of roofs and walls of yet more dwellings. Maudie kept thinking they would soon be through the city and out the other side, but the road led on past streets and side-streets with narrow or non-existent pavements, children playing or hanging about or pushing something in a pram, youths and girls lounging outside corner-shops, grown-ups queuing for fish and chips or making their way to a pub; and all the time the bus shook and rattled along, delayed by traffic and its own stops for passengers, then it would pull out again into the stream of traffic. This, she realized, this was the city she had dreamed of living in, the capital of England, the greatest city in the world. Now, travelling through it wide awake on a summer's evening, it took some believing that this really was where Dick Whittington had lived, the London of St Paul's and the Houses of Parliament, the London where the King of England lived in Buckingham Palace. She'd never imagined it looked like this.

"Heard of who?" she asked.

"Marie Stopes."

"Oh, didn't she write *Married Love?*" she said. "Haven't been listening, I'm afraid."

Which was another thing she liked about Londoners. They laughed more than country people.

"She's going to be there."

He said he thought *Married Love* a marvellous book. It offended most men's way of thinking of course, especially those who reckoned women were inferior to men and shouldn't enjoy love and sex.

"Upsets the boss-brigade, who think treating women like slaves is their right. They can't bear the thought of women enjoying what men enjoy. Men have the pleasure and women have the kids, but if there was more contraception women could have some pleasure too."

Maudie listened astonished, her cheeks burning at hearing a man, a stranger, talk about such things, and on top of a bus at that! She wished he would change the subject, and when he didn't she turned away, hoped people would think he wasn't with her. She agreed with what he said but couldn't bear to hear him say it.

It was their stop. This London was like a foreign land!

The hall had been built just before the war, Tony told her. The brickwork looked new, the interior was light and airy, the furniture was of pale polished wood, and the windows let the warmth of the evening sun into the auditorium. Tony found a couple of seats in front of a group of four or five nurses in scarlet capes. The hall was abuzz with talk about Marie Stopes, where she worked, what she'd done and said and what people thought of her, until Maudie wondered how she'd lived all these years and never heard of the woman until now. To add to her sense of wonder she realized that the large bespectacled man standing at the side of the hall, notebook in hand, was none other than Malcolm Steward! Marie Stopes, she realised, must be famous!

"See the chairs?"

The sight of seven empty chairs on the platform was apparently of interest. It meant that in addition to the chairman of the Society, the treasurer and the secretary, there were to be four speakers. Tony settled back on his chair, as excited at the prospect of four speakers as a schoolboy at a pantomime.

The hall went quiet. Officials and speakers walked on to the platform. Everyone's eyes were on Marie Stopes, an attractive woman with chestnut hair and alert eyes, though she couldn't be described as good-looking. She sat one side of the chairman. On the other was a tall man with something of a brooding air, and next to him a rotund man in the robes of a prelate. The remaining chair was unoccupied.

"Ladies and gentlemen."

The chairman expressed pleasure at having secured such eminent speakers on the controversial subject of birth control which was causing such interest up and down the land. He hoped the audience would allow the speakers to say what they had come to say without interruption. All three had indicated that if time allowed at the end they would answer questions from the audience.

Almost everyone, he believed, had heard of Dr Marie Stopes, double honours graduate of University College London and later the youngest doctor of science in Britain. More recently Dr Stopes had become known for her book *Married Love*, first published a couple of years ago, and for her advocacy of birth control. Dr Stopes was, he had no hesitation in saying, the most controversial figure in Britain, a person who could inspire tremendous support and, it had to be said, equally fierce opposition.

Regarding that opposition the chairman turned first to Dr Halliday Sutherland, secretary of the League of National Life, and author of *Birth Control: A Statement of Christian Doctrine Against the Neo-Malthusians*. Dr Sutherland was directly opposed to the teachings of Dr Stopes, as he would undoubtedly make clear when occasion arose.

The chairman then introduced Monsignor Canon Brown who, while he had not come officially to express the views of the Roman Catholic Church, would make clear the grounds on which Dr Stopes' teaching was in opposition to the wisdom of Rome.

As to the empty chair, invitations had been sent to all the main political parties but all had declined to declare themselves either for or against birth control. No doubt, the chairman said, when they saw which way the votes lay, the politicians would claim that they had made their position on the matter very clear ages ago.

"But for the moment," he indicated the empty chair and cupped his hand to his ear, "ladies and gentlemen – the voice of the politician!"

He then invited Dr Stopes to address the meeting.

Though Marie Stopes spoke quietly Maudie heard every syllable – and to her surprise every syllable struck her as true.

For generations, she said, women had carried too much of the burden of the world. As children, girls were considered inferior to boys, often scarcely worthy to be educated. As workers, women had only recently been tolerated in the workplace and were invariably paid lower wages than their male counterparts. As citizens, they had only within the last eighteen months achieved the right to vote, and then only for those over thirty. As partners in marriage, a woman's needs were as nothing to the marital rights of the man. It was of the institution of marriage that she wished to speak tonight.

It was marriage alone, she said, that sanctified the sexual act. Outside marriage sexual intercourse was immoral and, for the woman, demeaning. Within marriage, sex ought to be thought of not as a gratification of lust, nor as an exercise of the prerogative of the husband, nor even as the prelude to the conception of a child, but as an awakening of the love of the partners for each other, a delight akin to a sacrament. Tonight, she said, she intended to try to convince her listeners that few women fearful of conceiving could enter wholeheartedly into the act of sex.

Women were moral creatures. They refrained from sex, not from fear of the consequences of sin but because they were moral. They did not wish to bring more and more little ones into the world because they knew the horror of famine, disease and deformity that waited wherever poverty trailed its miserable carcase. Women had a right to a knowledge of birth control, not because they wanted a life of unbridled pleasure but because they were moral enough to foresee the consequences of too many mouths and too few crusts. It was this sense of morality that obliged many wives, even loving wives with a need for their own fulfilment, to deny themselves to their husbands. They were not unloving or unheedful of the sexual need of their partner; they were concerned that their resources for the proper upbringing of the children they already had were too meagre.

Dr Stopes quoted Lord Dawson, personal physician to King George Vth, almost the first doctor to be given a peerage: has not sexual union over and over again been the physical expression of our love without thought or intention of procreation?

"Alas for the medical profession," Dr Stopes said. "They have, as a body, completely failed to speak out as Lord Dawson has spoken out." Many women, she said, had told her that their doctors had advised them not to have any more children because the consequences of further childbearing would be dangerous. "'But they don't tell us how to avoid having them!' is the women's constant cry. If we knew how many women were married to selfish, lustful, drunken husbands who demand their rights without a thought for their responsibilities we should weep as we weep for the martyrs."

There were a few doctors, she said, who did give their patients details of birth control, but the vast majority, supported by the British Medical Association, not only didn't give advice but were actively hostile to giving any information on the subject whatsoever. "The reason," Dr Stopes declared, "is to do with money. A woman having her seventh delivery, her umpteenth miscarriage, may be forced to send for the doctor. The desperation of childbirth provides the medical profession with one of its most regular sources of income. This is the reason for the suffering of most women."

There was agreement with this. One or two shouted "Good old Marie!" Others cheered, stamped their feet.

"The curious thing is," Dr Stopes continued, "that although doctors tell their patients – as no doubt you will be told later this evening, that contraception causes women all kind of disabilities, the medical profession as a whole practises birth control all the time."

Dr Sutherland leaned round to glare at her, his pale face burning paler, and a voice from the crowd shouted "Prove it!"

Dr Stopes, her pleasant voice reaching quietly across the hall, said she would be happy to do so. In 1911 a Census had been taken in England and Wales. An analysis of births per thousand of every section of the population revealed that the medical profession had the lowest birth rate of any. "In that statistic," she said, "is your evidence. We are in the hands of a profession which refuses to preach by day what it practises by night."

There was another outburst of applause. Malcolm Steward, Maudie noticed, was busy with his notebook, his nose close to the page.

It was not only, however, in the medical profession, Dr Stopes said, that the birth rate was falling. It was falling, though less fast, in the middle classes as a whole. Was it fair, she asked, to deny the working classes such beneficial knowledge? In any case there was, to her mind, another and serious aspect to whole question of the birth rate. In the Census of 1881, she said, in both middle-class Hampstead and working-class Shoreditch there were about thirty births per thousand of the population. By 1914, while the birth rate in Shoreditch had risen to thirty-one births per thousand, that in Hampstead had fallen to fifteen per thousand.

What, she asked, would be the effect of continually preventing the spread of contraception to the lower classes?

"We shall have set about the destruction of the British race as we know it," she said. "We are allowing the feeble-minded, the most diseased members of society to breed at a rate that will impoverish the nation."

During the Great War, she said, the Medical Officer for Health for Leicester, Dr Killick Millard, had put on record his opinion that those who opposed birth control did so because they wanted a plentiful supply of cannon fodder. What would he say now, she asked, now that there were no more cannon? We were seeing the lower classes fill institutions, hospitals and prisons. It was an inevitable process if the lower orders bred and the middle classes did not. There was already a strata of society which was only partly self-supporting and which cost enormous sums to maintain, warped and stunted in their minds, feckless and potentially rebellious.

"Those who oppose birth control," Dr Stopes declared, "must lay to their hearts and consciences the dilution of the British race, the fading of our native genius, and ultimately the loss of Empire."

Dr Stopes sat down to a deafening response of mixed cheering and booing. An egg struck the wall behind the speakers. Moments later stewards escorted a young man from the hall. Tony, Maudie noticed, was less enthusiastic than he had been.

"She makes me uneasy," he said. "I don't know whether it's because her logic is faulty, or because I'm afraid of it."

Maudie said nothing. She had nothing to say, hadn't an opinion on anything Dr Stopes had said except that she agreed that women always got the rough end of the stick. But the atmosphere in the hall was full of opinions. Everybody had a point of view, some had several points of view, and all were being aired, exchanged, argued over. It was like being in a henhouse, the poultry clucking and scratching about to find something to squabble over – yet at least, she thought, they were all alive, which was more than she could say for her own mind, without a thought or an opinion in it.

The chairman was on his feet. He thanked Dr Stopes for her lively and thought-provoking speech which had given everyone a great deal to think about. She hadn't pulled any punches and had certainly enlivened the audience. He now invited Dr Halliday Sutherland to put his side of the argument.

Dr Sutherland, a tall stooping figure stood awhile without speaking, meeting his audience eye to eye, particularly that section which had been loudest in their support of Dr Stopes.

"I do not see," he said in his soft Scottish drawl, "why it must always be the poor that are picked on."

The remark was greeted with a few hear hears

"It could equally well be argued," he said, "by those of us who have the interests of the poor at heart that this whole birth control campaign is little more than a conspiracy against the working class. The conspiracy runs like this: if we can keep the numbers of the poor to a minimum we won't have to give them a pay rise or better conditions, because the fewer there are, the fewer votes they have. You see, ladies and gentlemen, the poor have no power except as they combine in, say, a union, or some other organisation. The law does not favour the poor; society does not favour the poor; Dr Stopes does not favour the poor. She does not even favour them having families. But then, from Dr Stopes this would be quite natural; as she has just told you, she does not consider the poor good enough to have families.

"Now, Dr Stopes has said that doctors deliberately withhold advice on birth control because they want the income from attending childbirth. If Dr Stopes had been a medical practitioner, indeed, if she had had any medical training at all, she would know that a doctor takes the Hippocratic oath in which he swears absolute integrity to his patients' welfare."

Dr Sutherland studied the faces in front of him. He wished, he said, to take a moment to explain the significance of what he had said. He would quote from what Dr Anne Louise McIlroy, professor of Obstetrics and Gynaecology at the Royal Free Hospital, had said about the use of contraceptives. *The most harmful method of which I have had experience is the use of the pessary.* That was her professional judgement. What conclusion would the audience draw, he asked, if they were told that the method of contraception favoured by Dr Stopes, nay, insisted upon by Dr Stopes to the exclusion of every other method, was the rubber check pessary? They would, Dr Sutherland imagined, wish to ask a question, and the question would be this: on which species of animal had the necessary experimentation been done to ensure the safety, never mind the efficaciousness, of the method? And the answer, he assured the audience, would be this: the animals which were bearing the brunt of the experimentation were the wives and mothers of the working classes.

Dr Sutherland raised his hand for quiet.

"That is the significance of the Hippocratic oath, ladies and gentlemen. That is why doctors are reluctant to prescribe. Because there is every possibility that the prescription will not be in the best interests of the patient."

Maudie wasn't sure that she liked public meetings. There were undercurrents, points to be scored on matters she didn't understand. She didn't mind point-scoring against her sisters. She had enjoyed that for years. But these people did their scratching with ideas. They hated each other, but they did it with long words and complicated ideas which made it difficult to decide whose side to be on, because when Dr Stopes was speaking she agreed with her, and when Dr Sutherland was speaking she agreed with him.

She crab-stalked her eyes round. Everyone else seemed to know what they thought, even the young nurses behind her. It made her feel hard done by, brought up in the depths of the country where such matters were hardly mentioned let alone discussed. Even Tony, she realized, even a young man like him knew what he thought about women's affairs. She watched him. He was alive with it, nodding or shaking his head as the arguments flowed. It was all very well for him, she thought, brought up in a city, used to arguing the ins and outs.

Dr Sutherland said he was going to conclude by referring to expert opinion, an element that was lacking in Dr Stopes's argument. Dr Amand Routh, Consulting

Obstetric Physician at Charing Cross Hospital, had put it on record that artificial methods of birth control were harmful and could lead to nervous exhaustion and an inability to concentrate. The Eugenics Review, a publication that even Dr Stopes might pay attention to, had pointed out to its readers only the previous year the danger of laceration and probable cancer which the cap might cause. Would it be wise, he asked, in view of the opinion of these authorities, to subject the wives and mothers of the poorest classes in our society to a practice that could do irreparable damage?

"Let me remind you," he said, "of the years of study every doctor has to undergo to become qualified, and the extra years of study needed for specialist training. And let me contrast it with the training Dr Stopes has received. Dr Stopes studied botany, and did extremely well. She studied zoology, and did extremely well. She studied geology, and did extremely well. Indeed she did extremely well in all her studies. But, ladies and gentlemen, the lady who aspires to give you information on healthy motherhood not only has no family herself, she has had no medical training at all! Dr Stopes is not a medical doctor. She is an expert on coal. Part of Dr Stopes' studies were pursued in a German university. Yet here she is, telling British men and women not to have British children."

Dr Stopes' opinions did not affect him personally, Dr Sutherland said, because he was able to see them for what they were. But he believed it was his duty to point out to those most at risk from Dr Stopes' opinions that they were nothing more than her opinions. The members of the audience were as entitled their opinions as Dr Stopes was to hers.

He sat down to applause which, Maudie thought, was almost as enthusiastic as it had been for Dr Stopes. A wave of voices filled the hall, people comparing opinions, disagreeing, conceding, all with a point of view and all able to express it. If only she hadn't been brought up in the country, she thought, she'd have as much to say as anybody – and know how to say it!

"Made a good case," Tony said. "He's cut her down a bit."

Someone to his left agreed, and the two were soon chatting away about the speeches and which of the speakers had got the better ideas, which the better delivery. Maudie happened to look across the hall. Malcolm Steward was still making notes -

Malcolm Steward!

Malcolm Steward had been at the window offering money to Rosie to be let in! He'd seen the dead girl on the foreshore, must somehow have recognised her, and that was why he had left Nancy and herself half way across the bridge! Because he wanted to get to the hotel and look in the girl's room. Which was why the news about her was in the Daily Brief and not in the other papers!

Before she had drawn two breaths the thought had turned into a conviction. The mystery man was Malcolm Steward!

Maudie studied the man, his large shape, his thick brown-rimmed spectacles, his grey-white hair thick at the back and bald at the front, the tall forehead freckled like the rest of his face. And then there was that notebook with the red mottled cover. She would describe him to Rosie, see if the description rang a bell. And if it did?

She didn't know what she'd do if it did.

She felt a touch on her shoulder.

"Excuse me, but you wouldn't be Maudie Stelfox, would you?"

She turned, knew in an instant. The good-looking child had become the good-looking young woman.

"Cousin Kate!"

"Fancy seeing you here!"

Not only good-looking, Maudie saw, but even more so with her colour set off by that scarlet cape.

Kate squeezed her arm, pleased as punch to see her.

"We'll have a chat afterwards," she whispered.

The chairman was introducing the final speaker.

Monsignor Canon Brown's pink complexion contrasted pleasantly with his silvering hair, his face smooth, his voice inoffensive. He began by making it clear that he was not there to speak officially on behalf of the Catholic church, merely to give an indication from a personal point of view of what impact, if any, the controversy over contraception might have on Catholic thought. As for what practical impact it would have on Roman Catholics he thought he could clarify that matter immediately. It would have no impact whatsoever.

Maudie liked the look of the old man. She decided that whatever he said she was going to agree with it.

"I wonder," he was saying, "whether sufficient consideration has been given to what the situation in society will be in two or three generations' time if Protestants practice contraception and Catholics don't. Not that it's a prospect that fills me with alarm."

He allowed himself a smile.

"There will be a larger and larger Catholic proportion of the population. More and more Catholic members of parliament. And eventually a Catholic majority in parliament. Catholic lawmakers. Catholic laws! I look forward to that future. I am merely a little surprised that a Protestant population can so easily contemplate parliamentary suicide."

There was amusement at this, and Maudie flashed Tony a smile, aware that it showed off her best profile to the nurses.

But the reference to suicide, Canon Brown explained, led a thinking person to consider sin in a wider context. The first reason for marriage in the Church of England service was, as they had already heard, the procreation of children. All down the centuries the people of Britain had accepted the duty that common sense and the Church laid upon them. The memory of the recent war was too fresh for anyone to contemplate what the outcome would have been had not the previous generation heeded the first duty of matrimony. Heaven help Britain in a future war, he said, if it was obliged to fight with a depleted population.

"And what of the question of morality?" he asked. Dr Mary Scharlieb, a gynaecologist of many years' experience, was on record as saying that discussion of contraception lowered the moral sense and damaged the reserve and purity of decently brought-up young people. The use of contraceptives, she maintained, would lead to too much sexual enjoyment. "What becomes gradually acceptable to the present generation will, for the next generation, be merely a springboard for further licentiousness."

There was a further matter, Canon Brown continued, which he hoped would not be too disturbing to women in the audience. It had to do with the dangers inherent in contraception itself. Father F M Zulueta had been assured by a doctor that the cervical cap could lead to neurasthenia, neuralgia, and dysmenorrhoea. The Roman Catholic Archbishop of New York had stated that contraception was worse than abortion. "To prevent human life that the Creator is about to bring into being is Satanic." And Professor Leonard Hill, in a publication edited by the secretary of the National Birth Rate Commission had argued that the woman who uses preventatives tends to lose her beauty early, and becomes thin and neurotic.

In view of the opinion of those authorities, Canon Brown asked, did it not follow that the woman who used contraception was putting her own selfish pleasure above her duty to her husband, above her duty to her country, above the law of the Church, even above the soul of her unconceived child? Was this the traditional attitude of women, he asked. He was sure it was not. Women, he declared, had always had a high sense of duty. And, in his opinion, the vast majority always would have.

He sat down to a mixture of applause and catcalls. Dr Sutherland leaned across and shook his hand. The chairman then said there would be a short break, after which the speakers would be glad to answer questions raised by the audience. But Maudie had had enough of argument for one night, especially of a matter she had never heard discussed by women, let alone by men, and when Kate and her colleagues started getting to their feet she did so as well.

"What a coincidence, seeing you at a meeting like this! I didn't even know you were in London."

Kate took her hands, overjoyed to see her.

"I came with Tony," Maudie said. "He's painting the hotel I work at."

They shuffled their way to the gangway. Kate and her friends pulled their capes on properly, brushed the creases out, helped each other to look tidy.

"Must look spick and span for Matron," one said.

"Bless her cotton socks," said another, a private joke at which they all laughed. They seemed to Maudie a group of well-dressed, well-off, good-looking young women with nothing else to do but laugh and make jokes and enjoy life. Very different, she thought, from the lives most people had to live.

"The thing about Marie Stopes," Tony mused, "is she's a bit like God. An extremist."

But otherwise he thought she had put the better case. The nurses agreed she had probably made the strongest impression on the audience, and long before they had chatted their way to the outside door they and Tony were joking and arguing as if they had known one another years. Maudie pretended to be amused, but she hated people who could talk about such matters so openly. Like maggots in a cowpat, she thought, crawling their ideas over each other. She hated herself for being brought up as quiet as a cow, and hated Tony for saying their names so easily as if he'd got more in common with them than he had with her. Georgina, he'd say, Jean and Erika he'd say as if he'd got something special with them, and Kate he'd say, as if Kate was his cousin rather then hers. Kate's life, of course, had been a bowl of roses! Always had been! Her parents had plenty of money and she'd never had a care in the world, different from being brought up by a pair of bitches after your own poor mother had killed herself.

"I shall remember tonight, my dear," Kate said, taking her hand, "meeting you like this. I'm training at the Charles Lamb. It's not all that far from the Strand."

She kissed her cheek, the other nurses shook her hand.

"We must meet again when we can, Maudie," she called. Then they were crossing the road, laughing, taking their high spirits with them, and Maudie and Tony were left on their own, waiting at the bus-stop.

When they got off the bus it was Tony's idea to walk part of the way back beside the river. He liked the view down-river, he said, the smoky-purple haze in which ship and crane merged. Maudie preferred the view to the west with the river smooth in the last of the sunset, and the buildings and trees sharp black against the sky.

"I like things to be definite," she said.

He asked her when she next got time off. She wasn't sure. In about a fortnight, she supposed.

"I expect I'll be gone by then," he said. "The hotel job'll be finished."

She was disappointed. She hadn't envisaged a time when the scaffolding would come down and the decorators would leave.

"Where will you go?"

"To that heaven I was telling you about – if I'm lucky." Then seeing her glance skywards he added, "There's only stars up there. I shall be over that way."

He pointed away from the river, over to their right.

"Place called Welwyn. A new city. Where we can start all over again."

She asked him why he kept calling it heaven.

"Because it'll be as near as we shall get. If we don't build it soon, we'll lose the chance – then there'll never be a heaven."

It seemed a stupid thing to say, calling a building site heaven.

"Where will you get the angels?" she asked. "You can't have heaven without angels."

"Depends if you'll come and live there," he laughed.

It was a novel idea. Her sisters would be furious, which made it even better. She was amazed at herself, the way her thoughts flew. She wouldn't want to be in his company long, let alone marry him. Yet he was pleasant to talk to, alive, as if there was some huge entertainment in his mind, and when he talked of building a city in a far-off place she pictured a great plain with a forest nearby and a castle in the distance, its flag flying and the city white and shining behind its walls, a place where people could go and start life again.

"Will you live there?"

One day, he hoped. The first houses would probably be for workmen, so he'd heard.

"What about your parents?"

He was less interested in talking about his family. He preferred the future. But she gathered his father had been lost at sea in the war, his sister and her baby lived with his mother in Bermondsey, he was twenty-four years old and he was lodging about half a mile from the hotel. And at that stage he appeared to go deaf to such questions, whereas to Maudie family affairs were a hundred times more interesting than public meetings.

The silence lengthened. It was as if he had gone away. It was maddening. A little earlier his eyes had been alive with the ideas in him, as if he wasn't so much talking as spreading ideas over her. Now it was as though a butterfly with glowing wings had suddenly lost its colour and was about to fly away.

They reached an alleyway near the hotel. The stars overhead reminded her of his remark about heaven.

"That's where heaven is," she said. "The other side of the stars."

Seeing her upturned chin he kissed her throat.

"Or there," he said.

"Don't you really believe in heaven?"

"I believe in this," he said, kissing her cheek.

He stood close, his arm round her. There was something awkward about him. He squeezed her waist but there was no comfort in the pressure. It was as though it was a gesture he felt he ought to make rather than what he wanted to do.

She asked how he could believe in God if he didn't believe in heaven.

"What if I told you I don't believe in Beck Farm?" he asked. "I still believe in you."

"But there is a Beck Farm," she insisted. "I could take you there."

"But if I don't believe it," he said, "it doesn't make you disappear, does it?"

He stroked her shoulders, let his fingers travel down her spine. She softened towards him.

Behind them, on the road at the end of the alleyway, traffic passed continually, the beams of the headlamps yellow as pounds of butter, all moving past as though half London had got to get somewhere else.

She eased towards him, wanted a nice long kiss to complete the evening. But his hand was idle on her back, repetitive.

"It's an astonishing thought."

"Now what's up?"

"The soft bodies of young women bear the whole human race."

For some reason he found the idea startling. He held her hand, looked her up and down.

"The whole race," he repeated. "Held in arms like these. Fed at that breast!"

It took the comfort out of being with him, his finding so much to marvel at. He didn't seem to be able to take anything for granted.

He asked her if she would like to go on a bus ride with him on her day off. He wanted to go over to Welwyn to see about a job there.

She said she'd like to. It would be nice to see his idea of heaven. She watched him go, head down, dreaming away. He didn't so much as turn back or wave.

The light was on the bedroom when she got back.
"Oh, Maudie," Rosie said, "there's been such rumours!"
A customer in the bar had told them he'd seen the police looking over an old boat up river past Millbank and taking things away in bags. This evening they'd come to the hotel for Bernard.
"Our Bernard? Did you see him go?"
Rosie said he didn't make any trouble.
"He looked – well, almost relieved."

# CHAPTER 40

The voices had been in her head all night, still raged as she got ready for work. It was what Marie Stopes had said she remembered most – women got the rough end of the stick. Always had done. If a couple had a baby it was the woman's fault! But contraception meant a woman needn't have a baby if she didn't want to.

She thought of poor Maurice and Phyllis. Their baby, put down like a puppy because of the shame. Maurice, carrying his little dead son out all alone into the cold. That was what the rough end of the stick meant.

Rosie asked what the meeting had been about last night.

"All about birth control. Them rubber stop pessaries."

Rosie shook her hair in the mirror to see how it fell round her face.

"They tell you where you can get them?"

That was the trouble, Maudie said. Women couldn't nicely buy them.

"As if a woman chooses to get pregnant! The man's the one who ought to get the blame!"

Rosie shot her a look, leaned close to the mirror to apply her lipstick.

"You're right there, duckie!"

At breakfast Bernard was still not back. A post-mortem had shown that Maggie Hines was pregnant.

Mrs Critoph was triumphant. "No more than I thought! Do they know how many months?"

"Read that bit out again," Irene Gibbs said, "about her death wasn't due to drowning."

Eileen read it again, that death was due to loss of blood following an injury to the throat, not to drowning.

"If she was dead before she went in the water," Mrs Gibbs pondered, "why was she in the water? How did she get in the river if she was already dead?"

Her sausage-jowls hung mournful as ever, but there was no mocking from Mr Lexford or Mr Took

The morning was already hot, the air heavy as sweat. Maudie washed up her guests' pre-breakfast things in her kitchen, set about her work, was one of the last to hear that Mr Perkins had been called to the police station and still hadn't come back.

The day grew hotter. Scarcely a breath of air came in the opened windows. Maudie's black dress and stockings clung to her as she did the daily cleaning and dusting, but her feelings of heaviness and breathlessness she put down to thinking about Bernard. He was almost certainly at the police station because of Maggie Hines. Perhaps suspected of murder.

"Afraid I do too," she thought.

Yet it was unthinkable.

But it was thinkable. Everything was thinkable now. If he was hanged she would be miserable for him. And as her sisters had often told her, she would have to put up with being miserable.

She emptied a wastepaper basket in one of her rooms, noticed a copy of the morning's Daily Brief. She folded it up, hid it in her apron.

"Heard the latest?" June was in the corridor with Iris and Mr Lexford. "Perky's back! And Bernard's with him!"

"Charged?" Mr Lexford scoffed when Iris asked. "Nobody gets charged with anything nowadays. Perky's to have a word with the staff this afternoon. Bet he don't tell us much."

She got a chance to skim the Daily Brief. Not so much as a mention of last night's meeting. Yet Malcolm Steward had been watching like a hawk, scribbling away in his notebook. One item she couldn't make head or tail of. A Mr Maundy Gregory, who had recently become the owner of the Ambassador Club, had lately been seen in the company of Sir William Vesty, owner of the Union Cold Storage company, the firm which in 1915 had moved to Buenos Aires to avoid paying income tax in Britain.

*Readers may recall,* the article said, *that last year Mr Maundy Gregory was to be seen in the company of Dundee whisky distiller Sir John Stewart who was rumoured to have paid Mr Gregory £50,000 to arrange his baronetcy. Gossip has it that it may not be long before the Honours List shows Sir William to have received a barony, the going rate for which is currently put at £100,000!*

"Don't often see you reading the paper," Mr Took said. "Anything good?"

Was reading about someone called Maundy Gregory, she said.

"What's he been up to this time?"

Maudie showed him the article, surprised he'd heard of the man.

"In with Lloyd George – old Maundy." He closed an eye at Mr Lexford.

"In with anyone who wants a handle," Mr Lexford agreed, and rubbed the side of his nose at Mr Took. The couple understood each other perfectly.

The door closed, the room went quiet. Mr Perkins glanced at his notes. He said he wanted the staff to hear the facts of Maggie Hines' death. Anyone not prepared to keep what he said confidential should leave the room now.

No-one stirred.

The mystery of Maggie Hines was solved, he said. Early the previous morning a waterman had boarded a disused lighter moored up at Millbank. What he found caused him to get in touch with the police.

The gunwale on the after-part of the vessel was heavily bloodstained. Nearby was an open cut-throat razor similarly stained. This razor was subsequently identified by Bernard as being his, one that had been missing a few days. A handbag had been pushed between a bulwark and a broken deck timber. Letters retrieved from the bag enabled the police to state that they were not looking for anyone else in connection with the incident.

Mr Perkins hadn't been allowed to read the letters, though he understood that in one of them Maggie apologised to Bernard for taking his razor. Apparently some of the handwriting was unclear, and one of the officers had been of the opinion that the letters might be fakes.

"Especially," Mr Perkins said, "as you will have heard, the girl was pregnant."

He was happy to say that the police were now satisfied that the hotel was not involved in any way with the girl's unfortunate death.

"As you make your bed," Mr Perkins added, looking round at the staff, "so you must lie in it!" In his opinion, he said, Maggie Hines had come to believe she was wicked. And she used Bernard's razor to let the wickedness out.

"The other item found on the lighter," he added, "was a bag of baby clothes she was knitting."

Mr Perkins eyed the staff, folded his notes and turned to go. Iris asked what colour the baby clothes were.

"Colour!" He glared at the girl. "What does it matter what colour? You don't think they're still needed, do you?"

"This man you let in through that window," Maudie said. "Remember what he looked like?"

She and Rosie were alone. It was evening. The sun still coloured the sky, the air outside was warm.

"Biggish bloke," Rosie said. "Wore specs. Going a bit bald at the front. Why, think you've seen him?"

"Did he have any freckles?"

Rosie wasn't sure. Might have had a few on his forehead, she thought.

Maudie was sure of it. Malcolm had known Maggie worked here! Must have known the hotel pretty well.

"I can tell you when your next afternoon off is," Rosie said.

The new time-off rota was on the staffroom board. Maudie was due for a half day in a little over a week's time. The thing was, Rosie wanted to go and see someone, so would Maudie do a swap for tomorrow afternoon?

"I'd be ever so grateful. I'll clear it with Mrs Critoph."

Maudie didn't mind. She could start her search for the Major.

"Needn't mention this to Peter," Rosie said. "Ain't his business."

What Rosie's other business was, Maudie thought it best not to enquire into.

# CHAPTER 41

Someone on the bus said it was London Bridge.
Steps led down to the river. Stones, rubbish, putrefying mud – little else. The smell took her by the throat, things festering, too long in water. Here Maggie had drifted out of the river. Only last week she had worn her wide-brimmed hat with its crimson ribbon, her oyster chiffon scarf, had looked as gay and alive as anyone. And this week, her face in that stench, lifting away on the tide, floating to the shore, her mouth settling back into the slime, this girl, crimson ribbon and delicate fashion shoes, a splash of what she used to be!

A man wandered along the drying foreshore, turned over with his boot debris exposed by the falling tide. Behind him the road was noisy with traffic, in front a string of barges passed unheeded. The river itself was smooth, slid smoothly under the bridge. Maudie liked its smoothness, its thinness at the edge where it brushed the shore like a fin. Could believe Maggie's spirit hovered hereabouts, somewhere between the shore and London Bridge. Hoped she was at peace.

She asked the way to the docks. So many faces, hundreds of faces, none resembling his. Strange, amongst so many not one the face she looked for, as if they were deliberately not being the Major. London was a thousand streams, every stream a road full of houses, every house full of rooms full of faces. But she knew she would find him.

Masts, cranes, the sound of ships. The air was spicy, then tainted with fish, then sweet with the smell of timber. Seamen passed with navy blue jerseys and coloured neckerchiefs, dockers with great necks and red hands. They reminded her of the farm labourers at home, eccentric, dressing to please themselves.

She went in a shop where people sat at oilcloth covered tables eating eel pie and green liquor sauce. No-one had heard of Richard Dawson. She tried a shop that sold saveloys and pease-pudding in basins. The man was helpful, brushed the grains from his mouth before answering. No-one had heard of *Richard* Dawson. Used to be a firm called Dawson, one said, before the war. Was it the Surrey, he wondered. Or the West India? No, you're thinking of Dorlings, his friend said.

An alleyway between tall buildings gave a view of masts and funnels. Iron railings prevented access to the wharf, but on one ship she could see men unloading netfuls of sacks, hoisting them up to a warehouse gantry. Knew she was getting close, felt if she watched and waited long enough she'd see him.

She waited. The hoist received its sacks, was hauled up by the engine in the warehouse, was swung through into an unloading bay, appeared again, was lowered down into the hold, the sacks like the coomb sacks her Pa and the labourers heaved aboard the waggon after threshing. Time after time the filled hoist was raised, time after time was lowered empty back into the hold.

A breeze freshened off the river, the ship was no longer in full sun. Maudie loosened her grip on the railings, aware of the rust, the flakes of metal digging into her hand.

Perhaps it wouldn't be today she'd find him, perhaps next time. The moonbow hadn't been an order for her to look for him, more a promise that one day she would find him.

She wandered back along the alleyway towards the street. She was enjoying the afternoon, felt easier than she had for a long while. And then, as she had always known she would, she saw him.

Two other men and the Major were crossing the road a little ahead of her. She held her skirt, ran to where they'd crossed.

"Major! Major Dawson!"

The men glanced back, saw her stop, her hand to her mouth. Understanding the mistake, they laughed.

She leaned against a wall, breathless with the pain of not seeing him.

The weather was on the change. Cloud had come up, enclosing the heat. Back in Suffolk the air would be called sultry, there would be talk of a tempest on the way. By the time she had caught the bus and got back to the hotel the sky had a greenish tinge, thunder stumbled about in the distance.

She knew something was wrong as soon as she went in the bedroom. Peter was on Rosie's bed, Rosie lay on Maudie's, the silence between them edgy, smelling of alcohol.

"What was Perkins hinting at the other day?" Maudie asked for the sake of something to say. "When he said Maggie's trouble was men?"

"Most people's is," Rosie muttered.

Maudie took her shoes off, sat on the bed with her.

"It was all wrong what Perkins said about her," Rosie said. "She could have had dozens of men but she only had the one. I know that for a fact."

Peter blew a jet of cigarette smoke at the ceiling. "Them other letters Perkins talked about. He didn't say much about them, did he?"

Rosie didn't answer.

Maudie said, "Perhaps the police didn't tell him what was in them."

"And Perkins knew she only had the one boy friend," Rosie added. "So what did he want to be so nasty about her for?"

"Did you know her boy friend?" Maudie asked.

"He knew one of them letters was to her parents," Peter said. "He knew she blamed herself for what went wrong. So if he knew that, what else did he know?"

Maudie didn't answer, wanted to hear about Maggie's young man.

"I knew of him," Rosie said.

"That's why he didn't want no questions," Peter said. "There's something in them letters he's afraid of. Or that's what I think."

"What was he like?" Maudie asked her.

"Course, it don't matter a bugger what I think," Peter sneered. "I'm only a man!"

"You're right there!" A murmur, meant for Maudie.

"All Perkins cares about is this hotel!" Peter declared. "He don't care about his niece here. Didn't care about Maggie. You know what he did when he heard she'd gone missing? Went and locked her door. Didn't tell the police. Didn't want anyone to know in case it hurt the hotel! Just wanted to keep it hushed up!"

"Some sort of business man," Rosie told her. "Maggie thought the world of him. I bet he's worried sick. Of course, whether he's a married man -!"

"That's what I've been telling you!"

Rosie jerked her thumb towards him. "Always telling somebody something, he is. Proper little know-all!"

"What I'm saying," Peter insisted, "is Perkins don't want anything to come out about Maggie!"

"Oh, are you!" Rosie retorted. "I thought you were saying all Perkins cares about is the hotel."

"Same thing," he insisted. "What I've been trying to tell you!"

"There's no need for you to try and tell me anything!" Rosie said. "I've heard all I want to hear from you!"

The air outside had darkened to purple. A few spots of rain, large as bird droppings, splashed across the window. Maudie let her head droop, let the pair of them argue on, neither very clear what the point of the argument was. She got into bed, was soon asleep.

Rain sheeted against the window. Now and then lightning flickered across her eyelids, the thunder an intrusion as inexplicable as a quarrel in a neighbouring room. She saw the boat where Maggie cut her throat, the bloodstained deck, rain falling, falling. Then it stopped. The boat had been cleansed, blood gone, rain water running clear along the wooden deck.

The dream deepened, deep as memory. When she woke she had heard a voice, desperate, telling the man, "You shouldn't have come! You know you shouldn't have come!"

Her mother's voice.

# CHAPTER 42

"So this is your bus to heaven?"

She and Tony were on their way to the site of the new town of Welwyn Garden City.

"No good heaven being in the stars. Here's where it's needed."

They were taken through dilapidated neighbourhoods, mile after mile of run-down housing, windows mended with cardboard, walls scarred with crumbling brickwork, litter and debris in gutters and on pavements. Men without work eyed the traffic, stood around in groups, lounged against area railings. Children in ragged adult clothing played, watched others play, big-sistered little ones. Here and there men with banners and placards stood in groups outside their place of work. They were on strike, Tony said. Everyone had been on strike lately, railwaymen, dockers, cotton spinners, weavers, wireless telegraphists, electricians, even clerks from Pearl Assurance. The war had solved nothing. Thousands had no work. Thousands had to work too long for what they were paid. This was a landscape without hope.

It was only temporary, Tony said. When people saw the Garden City and saw what life could be like they'd pull all this down, roll it flat and start again. They'd build houses the new way, families would live in comfort in houses with gardens, there'd be trees in the street, green leaves outside the window.

For Maudie it was a ride through a land she'd never imagined. These dreary miles were *London*. Hard to believe that the shabbily dressed inhabitants who lived and died here, these dirty streets and unpainted railings, these miles of rotting brickwork, that it all part of the greatest city on earth. Easier to believe that as soon as the bus had passed the whole miserable scene would be rolled up and put away.

"They fought for England," Tony said, pointing to a group of placard-waving men outside a factory. "Their fathers and brothers died for a decent land with a decent future – look what they've got!"

His indignation didn't last. "It's all temporary," he said. "Ten years from now there won't be a slum house or a mean street left in London."

Builders weren't fools, he said. Once they'd seen the new Welwyn they'd change their ways. No-one would build the bad when they'd seen how to build the good.

Further out, nearer the suburbs, he pointed out the occasional new piece of architecture, an Underground station here, a cinema or garage there, constructed of concrete or faced with stone, with a horizontal line about it, sometimes with a curve instead of a corner, as though streamlined for progress into the future. Further out still the roads were lined with a few new houses, piles of new bricks and newly sawn wood, awaiting workmen, and immediately behind the building line was open farmland, newly-made haystacks and men trimming back hedges around cornfields in preparation for harvest.

What was this place called, she asked. Was it the edge of London?

Neither London nor Finchley nor anywhere else, Tony said. This was No-man's Land.

"If these speculative builders aren't stopped they'll cover all England with this ribbon development."

It was Tony's belief that new roads were being built, not to take people from A to B, because there were as yet no people at A to travel to B, but so that houses could be built alongside the roads. He reckoned hundreds of miles of new roads had been constructed in the last ten years solely for that purpose. It was only the spec builder who profited from that sort of development, he said. They provided a certain amount of employment during the period of construction.

"It's the least they can do in return for destroying the face of England."

At the next stop Tony and Maudie had to get off and wait for a Company bus to take them to the Garden City site. Behind them a couple of workmen were tending a milky-white pond a yard or so in diameter contained within a circular bank of sand. Now and then the substance bubbled, as though it had come to the boil.

"Lime being slaked," Tony explained. "They'll make it into mortar."

But that circle of sand enclosing the lime, he said, was a model to explain Ebenezer Howard's idea of a garden city. There would be an urban centre surrounded by a rural outer ring, two separate but related parts of the same city, the centre, represented by the lime, being where the citizens lived, worked and played, and the outer agricultural zone, represented by the sand, producing food for the town within. The outer zone was to be thought of as much a part of the city as the inner, not as a ring of spare land to be built on when builders ran out of other land. It would be the garden of the Garden City, providing fresh vegetables, eggs and milk and other produce right on the doorstep of the city, without need for transport or delay.

The Company bus drew up. On its side was painted Welwyn Garden City Ltd, a couple of posters advertised London's First Satellite Town.

A gaunt man in his thirties made room for them on the seat beside him.

"Going to try your luck?" he asked Tony "I hear they're short of tradesman."

By the time the bus moved away the workmen at the roadside site were folding the sand shovelful by shovelful into the lime, one man each side, the pair of them circling round turning the mixture over till it became mortar, deep cheese coloured, moist.

The gaunt man was a carpenter by trade. He wore a white scarf inside his jacket, a necktie with the tips of his shirt collar pinned underneath. Maudie liked the way his eyes twinkled, the way his mouth turned down when he smiled. He said his name was George.

The road went on for miles, became more countrified. It was the Great North Road, George told her, the one Dick Turpin had galloped along on his way to York. The story reminded Maudie of her dream city, with stone walls, a white castle and a flag flying over noble buildings. When the bus passed Hatfield House he told her it was under a tree in its grounds that the young Elizabeth heard she was Queen of England.

After a while the bus slowed, turned off into a wooded lane. This was Brock's Wood, George said. This was the place.

No sign of a city, or even a castle wall.

"I might have guessed." She smiled her turndown smile.

The bus parked beside a row of other buses. Behind them to the north were great trees and extensive woodlands, to the south the land was open. Under the summer sun it stretched away into the distance, with scattered farmsteads and stackyards, a copse or two, hay meadows, yellowing fields and the distant chimneys of a brickworks. The lane along which they had come continued eastward towards a north-south railway line which emerged here and there among folds of farmland. That was the Great Northern Line, Tony explained, which would be the link between the Garden City and London, and also the route along which material for the building would come.

"Coming to put your name down?" George asked. "Looks as if there's a queue."

Tony said he'd join him in a minute. He wanted to show Maudie what the town would eventually look like. What she could see of the so-called new town was unpromising enough: large wooden accommodation huts, a canteen, an office, smaller huts for storage and on-site use. And innumerable stacks of bricks, sewer pipes, manhole covers, paving stones, sand and tiles. Tony pointed out a diagram of the proposed town plan on a window of one of the huts. It showed they were in the hamlet of Handside, the lane they had come in on was Brockswood Lane, and a farm roadway running south past a couple of farmhouses was known as Handside Lane. He seemed able to visualize the network of streets that would lead to the industrial area the other side of the railway line, the civic square in the centre, the residential area in the meadows where he and she were standing.

"Imagine what it'll be like what it's finished!"

But Maudie was looking for a place for Rosie's little house of her own. She pictured it down Handside Lane, there, where a gate hung away from its post. Maybe Rosie could persuade Peter to put his name down for a job here so the management could make a house available for them.

The queue to sign on had lengthened. A ginger-haired heavily built man said waiting was typical of the place.

"Management must think we're dirt, keeping us hanging about. Be different when we get a union here. Only one way ahead for England."

"What is?"

"Do what the Russians do! Give power to the people. Mines, land, stock exchange – all of it! In the hands of the workers. So we have decent houses, plenty of food, good income for everyone!"

"What the Labour Party wants."

"Can't trust your Labour Party! They aren't proper socialist."

He took out a packet of sandwiches, unwrapped them, let the paper drift away across the grass.

"One hopeful development," the man said.

"What's that?" Tony asked.

Support was growing in the party for a Council of Action. "Come the autumn we'll have one."

"Action for what?" Tony asked.

"For what?" The man's tone was one of ridicule. "General strike, of course."

The managers of this Garden City were no good. Workers didn't know where they stood with them. Terms of employment were vague, jobs weren't secure. Things would be different when they got a union going here.

The queue moved forward.

Unions by themselves wouldn't solve anything, Tony said. He sounded as definite as the other man. This project was a leap of faith. It was work and cooperation that were needed, everybody pulling together to build a city where people could lead full lives, where children could grow up in better conditions than the present generation –

"Faith!" the man jeered. "Faith won't pay the bills. You can't take a packet of faith home to the wife and tell her to feed the children on that! What the workers deserve is a fair deal! And that's what we intend to get!"

But if the project didn't succeed, Tony said, there wouldn't be a deal of any sort, either for the workmen, the management or anyone else. Refusing to work wouldn't get the houses built! And decent housing was what people needed most.

"What the workers want," the man replied, "is their rights. Not the bosses getting everything and the workers working long hours in rotten conditions and getting a pittance at the end of the week. When we get a union here, we'll show you!"

"That's the sort of attitude kills everything. Everyone out for their own ends." Tony was starting to get steamed up. "What we want here is co-operation – not confrontation!"

Raised voices, angry faces. Bad as being with the bitches, Maudie thought. And gave him and the union man a toss of her head.

"See you when you've signed up," she told Tony.

She walked away, glad to get the sound of dispute out of her ears.

She went over to the shade of trees. A car was parked there, a couple were setting out chairs for a picnic.

"Maudie Stelfox?"

Elegant from her blonde hair down to her little city shoes, and in an up-to-the-minute dress of peach edged with black, Nancy looked as attractive a woman as one could wish to see. And not overjoyed to see Maudie, by the sound of her voice.

She was spreading a small white tablecloth over a table which Mr Vincy had set up on the grass beside the car.

"What on earth are you doing in a place like this?"

"Tony's signing on to work at Welwyn Garden City," Maudie told them. "I came to see what the place was like."

"Someone's going to work here?" Mr Vincy sounded concerned. "Anywhere but *here*."

He unwrapped a bottle of something. Nancy brought out sandwiches and cakes. Mr Vincy looked at his watch.

"I suppose he'll turn up?" he murmured.

"Don't worry, old bean," Nancy said. "He knows it's worth his while."

The crockery was white porcelain with gold edging. The wine glasses glowed with sunlight from the unshaded grass all around. Mr Vincy spread open a map like the plan of the proposed town in the hut window. Maudie, having only just met them, didn't nicely know how to leave.

"Digswell Lodge farm must be over there," he said, pointing to a distant group of buildings. He sounded less than happy at the discovery. "And Sherrardspark Wood's back there."

He indicated the trees behind them.

"Must stretch nearly a mile! And all to remain agricultural! Agricultural! And none of us can get a sniff at it! All wrong, you know!"

He had a way of looking at Maudie as he spoke, not engaging her, his eye pausing at her as at a stopping-place before going to Nancy. Being included Maudie felt she ought to stay, almost that she ought to agree with him, though she hadn't the faintest idea what he was talking about.

"If Ebenezer Howard thinks he can develop this lot!" He swept his arm in an arc suggesting swathes of land.

"And still pretend he doesn't want to make money out of it."

Nancy touched his arm. "Don't forget, old bean. There's always Monty!"

He gripped her hand, grateful for being reminded.

"Of course! If he's able to help!"

"He will, my dear. You'll see."

Mr Vincy's dark eyes, Nancy's blue eyes, Maudie knew what it meant, their lingering look.

"In the meantime," his attention was back in the direction of Digswell Park, "can you imagine?" He indicated another arc of land. "How they'd sell? If we could put houses – ? How they'd sell? And none of us can get a sniff at it!"

"Could all change, my dear – in the long term!"

She knew how to plant them, her little remarks. Maudie saw how he depended on her, understood why Nancy liked him. She thought it nice, the way their eyes wandered over the other's face, lingering.

"As for your young man," he said to Maudie, "why doesn't he try my firm, Rural Developments? They sometimes have a vacancy for a skilled man."

She'd make a point of telling him, Maudie said. She was about to remark that Tony wasn't at all her young man when a limousine turned towards them and rocked to a halt alongside Mr Vincy's car. The chauffeur got out, opened the passenger door. A strange-looking man, arm extended, came towards them.

"My dear James Vincy! Found you at last!"

"Mr Maundy Gregory?"

A seedy, run-down sort of a man, Maudie thought, though whether it was because of his sallow skin or the fact that he was wearing a bow-tie she couldn't decide.

"Or shall I call you Sir James?" he joked.

Nancy asked if he would care to take a little refreshment with them.

"Well, I will," he said.

He sounded as though he could easily be persuaded to anything pleasurable. And when Mr Vincy commented on an expensive-looking scarab ring he was wearing Maundy Gregory laid one hand across the other to show it off. It had been Oscar Wilde's, he said. It was his joy, one of the few things he hadn't let slip through his fingers.

"Reminds me of a dinner I was at with Lloyd George -"

At which point Nancy, a finger to her lips, took Maudie's arm, walked her away across the meadow. "Mr Vincy wants you know he's had good reports of you from Mr Perkins," she murmured.

Maudie said she was glad to be at the King James. It was nice to be away from home.

"I'm glad you're more settled now. It's nice to have seen you. Would that be your friend?"

Tony was beckoning Maudie to go and join him.

Nancy left her, went back to her employer.

Maudie didn't hurry. She wondered if Tony wasn't rather misguided. So enthusiastic about things, desperate to listen to that Marie Stopes, bursting to work at this Welwyn Garden City – and here he was now, urgent for her to join him – as if a building site like this was a place where dreams came true! She felt sorry he was so innocent as to believe such stuff. She'd got the impression, listening to Mr Vincy, that clouds were gathering over this Garden City dream.

Tony came across, took her arm.

"He's just about to start!"

"Who is?"

"Ebenezer Howard!"

He'd agreed to say a few words. The man whose idea all this was. The inspiration behind the Garden City. In the canteen! Wasn't it marvellous!

"You don't get the chance to hear a man like Ebenezer Howard every day!"

He was so pleased, found it all wonderful. She hurried along to the canteen with him, but wanted to warn him – yet all the warning amounted to was that Mr Vincy didn't seem to like Ebenezer Howard's idea.

"Did they take you on?"

He nodded, eyes as bright as a child's. "Hope we can get a seat!"

"We will, my dear," she said. "You'll see."

# CHAPTER 43

Ebenezer Howard was elderly, kindly-looking, with white hair and a long white moustache, reminded Maudie of Father Christmas. The canteen was crowded, people sitting on the floor, couldn't have been more in the place if the old boy had been handing out presents. The place was silent as a church.

The idea of creating a garden city, Mr Howard said, of which Welwyn was not the first example, came to him when he realised what was happening to Britain.

"Thousands of people have no homes, tens of thousands live in poor and inadequate housing, thousands of building workers have no work, and there are thousands of acres of unused land, the value of which is declining because of the failure of agriculture."

In Britain almost all new building was either along the sides of roads, giving rise to ribbon development which ruined the countryside, or around the edges of existing towns, creating endless urban sprawl and causing people to work further and further from where they lived. Night and morning, time and money were wasted in travelling to and from work, the worker had little time for his family and less for leisure, the employer had difficulty attracting the people he wanted because of the housing situation.

"Our plan," Mr Howard said, "is to build a city to live in, a city to work in, to relax in, to enjoy family life in. Part of Welwyn Garden City will be residential, with well-planned housing; part will be industrial and commercial, which is why land has been bought to include the Great North Road and the Great Northern line; part will be public, with schools, hospitals, sports fields and park land; and part will be agricultural. This agricultural land, stretching in a band around the perimeter of the urban area, is to be regarded as much a part of the city as the residential and industrial part. It will be a lung for the citizens, a provider of pure clean air. It will also produce fresh fruit and vegetables, eggs and dairy produce for the citizens on its doorstep."

Industry, Mr Howard said, would be in modern well-lit, well-planned factories to the east of the railway line. The residential areas would be to the west, separate but within easy reach so that the worker would not have to spend time and energy battling his or her way to work of a morning and battling back again at night. In the Garden City there would be time for leisure, for sport, and for the family.

As to the ownership of the city, Mr Howard explained that it would be owned by its citizens through the Welwyn Garden City Association. While most houses would be for rent, some would be for sale on a long lease, and all profits made by the Association, after repaying interest and an annual proportion of the capital debt, would be put into a fund for the benefit of the city, not for private profit. And since this aspect would be uppermost in some people's minds he would take a moment to deal with the question of the value of land. Without people, he explained, land was virtually valueless. When no-one wanted it a hundred acres of land cost very little. It was the advent of people that gave land its value, yet it was not those who caused the rise in its value, the would-be buyers, who benefited from its rise in value. Indeed it was they who were the losers, because they had to pay more for it, yet if they went away the value of land would fall. Therefore, he said, it would be right for the Association to ensure that any increase in the value of land under its control should benefit the people whose presence had contributed to that increase.

"You might have thought," he said, "that such a scheme as ours would be welcomed by politicians, seeing that they are forever bemoaning the conditions people live in. But the opposite is the case. The Right are critical of this project because they want all the profit to go to the speculator. We wish to benefit the inhabitants, they wish to benefit the builder. We want the town to be planned at least in part by those who will live there, they want it to be planned by an office in the pay of those who build for maximum profit. The Left, I fear, are equally sceptical. The Garden City does not fit into Socialist ideology. They believe the State has the best designs, the State plants the most colourful gardens, the State builds the most efficient factories and cultivates the greenest parks. Those with an ear to the ground have already heard that if they get the chance the Socialists will take this enterprise over and put it in the hands of those who have not had the least apprenticeship for the tasks to be faced."

The Garden City, Mr Howard explained, would try to take account of human nature. All animals, including the human animal, needed private territory. One had only to observe the behaviour of birds, or the attitude of road users, or to see the great estates with which the rich surrounded themselves, to realise the strength of the instinct for territory. The invasion of territory, even when there was only a nominal ownership of that territory, was one of the major causes of aggression in society.

"That is why," he said, "we shall include many cul-de-sacs, closes, courts, small groupings, so that there is a sense of neighbourhood as well as a right to privacy."

There was one respect, he conceded, where his critics might well be right: the Garden City as at present planned might be too small.

"We look on this venture as an experiment. Experience will help us see what we've done right and what we've got wrong. We've got learn the right way. We simply must learn to get it right. The building of a neighbourhood is far too important to leave to the builders.

"Isn't it obvious," he asked his listeners, "when we look at the squalor of our cities, with their rivers running with filth, their factories that debilitate those who work in them or live around them, when we see their acres of ugly, inadequate dwellings, their suburbs spreading like mould around a dying core, their charms neglected, their vistas destroyed, that we have got to find a better way?

"After the battle of Trafalgar," he reminded his audience, "our predecessors showed their gratitude by laying out Trafalgar Square. Britain has just come through four years of the most terrible war in history. Let us show our gratitude by building cities worthy of the memory of those who died to save us."

The applause when he finished was so loud and heartfelt that Maudie began to think that maybe Rosie's wish for a place of her own was not so unusual a wish after all.

Mr Howard said he could spend a little while answering any questions his listeners might have.

A resident of nearby Digswell Water made the point that its inhabitants were opposed to the Garden City being built so close to a small and traditional village because of their quite natural objection to becoming merged into the new town.

Howard's response was to point out that that objection exactly made the point he had been trying to emphasise.

"Welwyn Garden City will not ooze outwards, because that is the very type of development the Association wishes to avoid."

There was no threat to Digswell Water from the Garden City, but when one looked at the map it was clear that London was spreading at an alarming rate in every direction because of ribbon development.

"The most vulnerable areas are the very villages and picturesque valleys you wish to preserve, because there the speculative builder can most easily sell his houses. My advice to Digswell Water is to support us if only to save yourselves."

What about the railway service? someone asked. Will it improve?

As soon as the Railway Company saw the profits to be made from serving the new town, Mr Howard replied, a new station would speedily be approved. A good rail link was essential for the building of the town.

"I've every confidence it will soon be provided."

There was some amusement at this. "You don't know the Great Northern Railway," someone remarked.

"Regarding education," a woman asked. "What provision will be made for the children?"

The Association, Mr Howard told her, had already been in touch with the education authority, Hertfordshire County Council, who were sympathetic to the needs of children coming into the new town. Plans were already under way for a new school, to be known as Handside

School, to be built as soon as possible. A second school, possibly in the Sherrards Park area, would be considered later. He believed the schools would be among the best of their type, and it was also the intention to provide a number of boys' clubs for indoor and outdoor sports, as well as a craft-room and a library.

"And if Welwyn Garden City doesn't make a name for itself on the football field," he declared, "I'll take up refereeing myself!"

Another questioner asked where the millions of pounds were to come from to build the new town.

Mr Howard explained that the Welwyn Garden City Association would issue a share flotation of £25,000 in shares of £1 each. Also it was hoped that the various local authorities and district councils would be as supportive of services as Hertfordshire had been in the matter of education. In addition, the 1919 Housing Act laid an obligation on government to provide funds for the provision of housing.

"This means," he said, "grants should be forthcoming from the recently established Ministry of Health by means of a Public Works Loans Board. All we need is a little good will. We don't ask for special treatment, but if we can obtain the backing other projects receive, then the Garden City may become the first small step in making England a land fit for its people to live in."

Whether it was the old man's vision of what a city could be, or merely his kindly face and flowing hair, something of the occasion appealed to Maudie, so much so that when she and Tony took a walk after the meeting she felt part of the bold new experiment. She'd been wrong about Tony. He wasn't the silly little enthusiastic fool she had thought him. She liked Nancy, she liked Mr Vincy, and she was grateful to them for helping her get her job in London, but compared to Mr Howard's vision of what England ought to be like, the criticisms she'd heard Mr Vincy make about the new town seemed mean and small-minded.

The hillside path climbed until it skirted the grounds of Digswell Lodge. The day was clear, the countryside viewable for miles. Nearby she could see farms, a mill, a tree-covered valley; and further off the patterning of field, hedgerow and meadow; further away still only the sweep of the land itself remained, its features indistinct in the encircling haze of smoke and mist.

She and Tony sat on the grass, the woodland behind them, in front of them the slope from hilltop down to the plain below. Tony identified the old village of Welwyn and, more to the east and half hidden in a valley of willows, Digswell Water.

Maudie asked him the name of a small river visible here and there amongst the folds of countryside.

He told her. She asked him to repeat it.

"Mimram."

She watched his mouth.

"Mimram," she laughed. "Mimram."

It was an Alice-in-Wonderland name.

"Mimram."

She sighed, happy with him, easy with herself. "So this is where you'll build your brand new town?" She pictured it across the landscape in front of them, the castle with towers and flags, a ring of white wall encircling it, a huddle of a town within. And hoped the blue sky and sunshine and the green hill where they sat would always be part of that city. "And this is where you'll build your heaven?"

He lay beside her, watching her. "Not only my heaven, I hope."

He traced the curve of her eyebrow with his fingertip, the line of her nose. "If I was a sculptor, I'd make copies of your face in stone, and put them up in public places. And I'd say to visitors 'This is a girl who lives in Welwyn Garden City.'"

His touch was gentle. Her mother had been gentle when years ago she used to do her curls of a night.

At this very moment her mother would be looking down at her from the mist at the end of the earth, would see how well things were turning out for her. And feeling blessed she let her sight climb upwards mile upon mile into the sky, felt she was actually climbing so that there was blueness all around her and if she looked down it would be blue beneath her feet, a dome of blue over the world. She felt she had the power to look higher still, but something stopped her. She was afraid that suddenly the blueness might thin and she'd see what no person from earth ought to see – a moment later she was back on earth and the chance had gone.

She was aware of Tony watching her, lying close, his head propped up on his hand, looking at her face, her forehead, her hair. She closed her eyes, expecting his lips to caress her lips, his arm to reach over, his hand on her back. She felt his breath on her face.

Only his breath.

She wondered if he liked her as a person or only as a shape that pleased him. Or if she was even a shape that pleased him.

They lay side by side, the breeze from the woodland drifting over them, the summer grass brushing her arm. Lying like that with a young man, almost touching, she could believe there were only the two of them in the world.

She felt him take her hand, felt him take it to his lips.

But when he went to uncurl her fingers she resisted a little, embarrassed that he should see the scar. But she let him touch his lips along it, her arm limp, her fingers curling over loosely so that he had to ease them straight. It was a form of sacrifice, letting him examine the scar, like being naked in front of him. And having allowed it she felt closer to him, as if what she had permitted had become a bond.

Then he was kneeling beside her, his arms open as if she was something to be adored. She was glad no-one was near. She didn't mind being adored if no-one was watching, though she was afraid she was rather solidly built.

"You really are -"

He seemed to survey her from head to foot. It made her tingle, being admired, made her think she was special. But that was the trouble. So many things were special with Tony.

He leaned over her, leaned close. And being so close, he looked cross-eyed.

She raised her head close to his to keep him cross-eyed, then fell back laughing.

"Mimram!"

She wished he'd put his arm round her, wished he'd kissed her, but he seemed surrounded by thoughts, as if everything had to be *thought* about first.

Something on the hillside took his interest. He went over to it, came back with one of the bits of twig that had blown down. He pushed the end into the ground beside them.

"To mark the spot."

It was time for them to be getting back to the bus. She stretched her hand out for him to pull her up. "What spot?"

The twig stood precariously, its few leaves limp and yellowing.

"When all this is houses and streets," he said, indicating the scene around them, "and all round here becomes part of the new city, I'll remember this afternoon. And this spot especially."

"What for?"

"Because it's the place where I told you."

She didn't like to ask what he'd told her in case he'd mentioned something she'd forgotten. But so far as she could recall there had been nothing significant.

# CHAPTER 44

Mrs Critoph had called her dear!
"Mr Perkins wants to see you," she'd said. "Now, my dear! Now means now! Just take your apron off and go as you are!"

But it didn't stop her worrying she was going to get the sack, didn't stop her hands sweating and her mouth going dry, even if the old woman had called her dear. She couldn't think of anything she'd done wrong, anything she'd forgotten to do.

She hurried along to his office. Beryl was at her desk, studying her fingernails.

"He wants to see me," Maudie whispered. "What's he want?"

Beryl couldn't be bothered to look up at her, merely lapsed into broad Scots.

"Knock and see."

"Has he said – have you heard – anything?"

Beryl spread her hands to examine her nails, gave one or two a touch with the nail file.

"Beryl?"

"Dinna fash yeself!" she murmured. "He's not going ta eat ye!" Then added, just loud enough to hear, "At least, not yet!"

Maudie swung away from the little tease, went towards his door. But Beryl calmly wandered over and knocked for her.

"It's Miss Stelfox to see you," she said.

The room smelt bossy.

Mr Perkins indicated the same chair as last time. He lit his pipe, watched her through the smoke. Again it reminded her of her Pa. She was glad she had at last written to her father. This evening she'd definitely make a point of posting it.

Mr Perkins asked her if she liked her job.

She liked it very much.

And hotel life generally?

Very much.

He looked her up and down, sucked on his pipe, studying her.

What would she say to doing a different job, he asked.

She didn't know, she said. She wouldn't mind a change. She'd do her best.

There were going to be changes, he told her. The old ways would have to go. People would have to go. Staff might have to do different things.

"Somebody recommended you," he said. "And I agree."

She had to let the idea sink in. Her! Receptionist!

It was June. June had said weeks ago she could do the job better than Beryl.

She'd love to, she said. If he thought she could do it.

"I'll have to train you myself," Mr Perkins said.

He didn't want her picking up Beryl's ways. She'd soon get the feel of it if he showed her.

"You knew?"

Beryl gave her a smile. The little bitch could be charming if she wanted to.

"I told him I wanted to leave," she said. "He said who on earth could he get with my capabilities. I thought of you."

She'd been wanting to leave. Uncle Perky wasn't too pleased with her work, she couldn't think why.

"A friend of mine suggested I try the music-hall. As an impressionist. So I asked Uncle P. if he'd mind if I left. He said he thought my talent was in a class of its own."

He'd agreed to let her go at the end of the week if she had a job to go to.

"Of course, he didna want ta lose me. 'The hotel willna be the same without ye,' he said. He thought I'd probably be as good on the stage as I am here. So next week, if you're a good girl, all this'll be yours."

She lay back in the chair, offered chair, desk, the piles of paperwork all to Maudie. Then laughed, "It'll break ma heart to part wi'it."

The news spread, was round the hotel before Maudie had got to the staffroom. She heard the comments through the half-open door: Mr Took asking who they thought the new receptionist was going to be, someone saying it was going to be that country bumpkin, someone else working out how many minutes she'd been employed there. Then they saw her. The room went quiet. The look on their faces said what they thought.

June came in. Had she heard, someone asked.

"Heard? I'll say I've heard!"

She went straight over to Maudie, eyes like stones.

"Too much like hard work, being a chambermaid, was it? Always in and out of Perkins' office! Now we know why!"

Rosie was the kindest.

"Now you know why I don't want to stick here all my life. Not that I could do that reception job if he'd asked me. Nor could June or them others."

They were in the bedroom. Rosie looked fed up, sounded fed up.

"Peter's been given notice. Along with several more. Why he's been so ratty lately. He don't know what he'll do. There's nothing about. Everywhere's cutting back and cutting down."

"So I earn where I can," she said.

Maudie couldn't help but admire her. It was the only thing left to the girl, and she had quietly made up her mind to do it. Maudie thought of the little house to be built one day down Handside Lane where the gate hung off its post. Thought of the hundreds of little houses that were going to be built or were already built, and wondered how many other women who had got themselves out of the gutter had had to pay as high a price as Rosie, selling her pretty body in the street.

With the renovations finished, even the staff had to concede that the hotel was no worse than it had been. Total waste of money, of course, money that could have been spent on the wages of those who kept the hotel going. Maudie rather liked the new colour. Biscuit-brown walls and white sash windows – reminded her of houses in Suffolk.

Most of the workmen had left, the scaffolding had been taken down, the last load was being driven away. Tony was putting a final coat on the white pillars either side of the main entrance. He was to start at Welwyn the following day. He hoped he'd be there years. Yes, he said, he'd see if there was a job for Peter. Wouldn't surprise him if there was. He'd let her know. And Maudie would have to come over sometime and see how the town was growing.

She didn't remind him of their walk on the hillside, or of the twig that marked where something memorable was supposed to have happened. She might not understand all his ideas and arguments but she understood him. In his mind Tony had already left her for Welwyn.

The inquest verdict was that Maggie Hines had committed suicide while the balance of her mind was disturbed. Letters in her handwriting written shortly before her death put the matter beyond dispute. What was in dispute, at least by the staff of the King James hotel, was the evidence given by Mr Perkins. He had told the coroner that he had always done his best to advise the girl as to respectable conduct. He was distressed, of course, by what had happened but he had to say he hadn't been altogether surprised.

Mr Perkins, the staff said, was a hypocritical humbug. His contribution to Maggie's respectable conduct had been to lock her door when it was certain she was missing and then to say nothing to anyone for as long as possible.

Not that Maudie could complain of him. He worked her hard, but the work was to her liking. It was a new feeling for her, wanting to do things right. She liked dealing with the guests, explaining where rooms were, issuing keys, summoning the porter, getting them to sign the visitors' book. And she liked being compared favourably to Beryl – though anyone would have compared favourably to Beryl. She liked getting to work early, liked hearing Mr Perkins say, "Here already, Maudie?" when he arrived.

One job she liked was seeing to the incoming mail. It was a chance to see who on the staff got letters. Before long she began to recognise handwriting on an envelope as being similar to handwriting the person had received before, and a squeeze of the envelope would tell her whether the letter inside was brief or lengthy.

One day she recognised Barbara's handwriting. Her heart sank. She put the envelope aside, laid it at the back of the desk, decided not to open it. But every now and then she found herself gazing at it, wondering what it was about, and eventually turned it face down so she shouldn't keep seeing her name calling her to open it. She was grown up now, was hundreds of miles away from the bitches, could work as hard as them if not harder. Let them write, she said to herself. Let them scream their heads off. She wasn't going to take any notice of them any more!

Then suddenly she'd torn the envelope open, was racing through the contents.

*Dear Maudie,*

*Thank goodness to hear from you at last glad you like London so much better than the country I'm not surprised, you never took to hard work did you we all keep pretty fair Pa is hoping Herbert will come back home and buy that butcher's shop I can't see much sense in the idea still Herbert's old enough to know what he's doing.*

*Muriel is getting married to Stanley on Saturday the 16th October at St Matthews and hopes you can get the time off she wants as many of the family there as possible.*

*That housekeeper at Major Dawson's place has had a little girl Julia because of the month funny how she fell for a baby so soon after moving to the Major's Mrs Dawson is bad again with her head they say she can't be let out of the house nobody has seen hair or hide of the Major since the day he left.*

*Muriel hopes you can spare the time to let her know whether you can come to her wedding or not.*

*Your affectionate sister*

*Barbara Stelfox*

She thought she'd probably go. It would be nice to see Stanley again. And her Pa. One of these days she'd have to write and tell Muriel she'd go if she could get the time off.

# CHAPTER 45

In the eighteen months since the war most of the stables at the back of the King James had been pulled down and the space given over to car parking. Half a dozen stables were still in regular use, and now Bernard's duties included those of ostler as well as cellarman and caretaker. Occasionally well-to-do guests arrived by carriage, but for the most part the horses were those of hauliers and market traders who found it convenient to stable at the hotel.

Maudie liked the look of town horses, their groomed coats, their tack smelling of saddle soap. She liked the look of Bernard as well, shovelling straw and horse droppings into a barrow, his braided leather belt creaking with the strength of his body, his trousers tightening as he bent. He had his jacket off, his shirt sleeves rolled up, a green neckerchief inside a collarless shirt.

"You look as if you're enjoying your work, Bernard."

He was forking wet straw and dung off the stable floor, a smell he and Maudie were used to. "I do," he said. "You've had a change too, I hear."

It wasn't a popular change, she said. She liked the job very much, but she hardly went into the staffroom now because of the remarks she got. Sometimes she wished she hadn't taken the job.

"They'd have taken it," Bernard told her. "They wouldn't have cared if you'd been jealous."

But she was afraid that if people made a fuss about it Mr Perkins might want to get rid of her.

"He won't get rid of you. One or two of the others he might. But he knows a good'un when he sees one."

It was Mr Took and Mr Lexford, she said. They seemed to rule the staff, the way they could make a fool of anybody.

Bernard straightened his back, pushed the fork into the mound on the barrow.

"You don't want to worry about them two. They wouldn't want to get on the wrong side of the boss, not them two. If he slung them out they'd be done for."

He wheeled the barrowload up a plank out the doorway, emptied it on a heap behind the stables, then came back and forked fresh straw over the floor.

"What do you mean, them two?"

Bernard took a cloth and a jar of saddle soap and started attending to a saddle.

"You don't want to know nothin' about that."

"Ah, but I do want to know about it."

"You go and look after them guests," he said. "That's what you want to keep your mind on."

She watched him at work, the way his strong hands worked the leather, brought a gleam where a few minutes earlier had been grime and dullness.

"Come on, old bean. You can tell me."

Bernard put a dab of soap on the cloth, made a point of cleaning the crevices in a piece of strapwork. "You're too young to know about that sort of thing."

"I'm a woman, not a child."

"You're a woman all right." He looked her up and down. "That's why I shan't tell you."

She wanted him to tell her. She didn't care what that sort of thing meant. She began to guess what it meant, but wanted to hear him say it. She could smell horses and straw and Bernard's body, and she wanted him to say it.

"Someone'll tell you more than you want, one of these days," he said.

She didn't have time to argue the point if he was going to be awkward.

"Some young bloke will," he called as she went. "If you aren't careful."

She had hidden it away to look at later.

She thought about it on and off, hoped she'd get some time to herself before bedtime.

Then at last she could slide the envelope out. Addressed to Miss Margaret Hines.

She tore it open, read the letter. Read it several times.

Heartless. The more she thought about the way the girl died the more she realized how heartless it was.

It was from Dr Marie Stopes, in reply to a letter from Maggie.

Poor girl! At her wits' end, desperate to know what to do for the best, no-one to ask, no-one to turn to! And then to get a reply from that Marie Stopes like that!

It upset her. Enough to want to talk about it to someone. There and then she wrote to Malcolm Steward, asked if she could see him.

# CHAPTER 46

He was pleased she'd got in touch. He'd been looking forward to seeing her again. Nancy was sorry she couldn't come as well. She was too busy to get away.

Maudie didn't mind, could guess where Nancy was spending her time.

Malcolm seemed older, the freckles on his face more like age spots, his spectacles more to hide his eyes than to see through. But he was still the big energetic riddle of a man she remembered from childhood.

Seated, waiting for their mixed grills to arrive, she was aware of being observed. It wasn't unpleasant, any more than being looked at by an animal was unpleasant.

"Anyone would think you were going to draw me," she joked.

The waitress brought the tray, served them their meal and drinks.

"I wish I could draw you. You're the only family I've got," he said. "You Stelfoxes. And Nancy. You'll have to let me have a photograph one day."

If she had one done, she promised, she'd have one for him as well.

"I'd like that."

She showed him the letter from Dr Stopes.

How anyone could be so cold-hearted, she said, to write such a letter! Especially someone supposedly on the side of women!

He read it through.

*Dear Miss Hines,*

*Thank you for your letter. Dr Stopes is sorry she was unable to reply sooner. She is unable to advise on the matter of abortion.*

*It is to obviate the need for abortion that Dr Stopes so strenuously fights for the right of women to understand and to have at their disposal the means of contraception. It is Dr Stopes' view that sexual union should take place only within marriage, and that the engendering of life should be undertaken only when the child-to-be will have the love and dedicated care of both its parents.*

The letter was over the signature of a secretary.

Malcolm folded it, handed it back without comment.

"You were at the meeting," she said. "What did you think of her?"

"She's like me. Up against the powers-that-be."

"Don't you think it's a cruel way to write to someone so desperate about being pregnant? Forced to think about an abortion!"

She'd read the article in the Daily Brief, she said. It sounded as if Malcolm didn't like Marie Stopes, didn't agree with her ideas about women having a bit more freedom, yet seemed to agree with her when she said she didn't approve of abortion for a woman who was pregnant and didn't want to be.

Perhaps the way he pressed his lips together so hard together meant he didn't care to have the contradiction pointed out, or merely that he was bored with the subject.

"I suppose I didn't agree with abortion, Maudie -"

"But don't you think the way she replied to poor Maggie was cruel?

He conceded it probably was cruel. "But what if I were to tell you -" He leaned close, close enough for her to smell the warmth of his body. "What if I were to tell you there are people in public life in England – people alive and thriving – a hundred times more cruel than Dr Stopes?"

His eyes burned at her through their lenses.

"Your brother was in France in the war. Risking his life for his country."

"Over three years there."

"So what would you say if I told you that while your brother and thousands of our young men were fighting Germany, a certain Englishman was supplying Germany with war material?"

She remembered Malcolm had been a war correspondent.

"And what if I told you this same man is at this moment being recommended by people in high places for a peerage?"

He seemed calm enough. Didn't seem to have been drinking. But an Englishman, selling war materials to the very country England was at war with!

"What if I were to tell you," Malcolm said, "that Sir Archibald Williamson is accused in the House of Commons of having traded with the enemy! And that Lloyd George wants to include Sir Archibald in the honours list!"

It sounded too extraordinary to be anything but gossip!

"And what if I were to tell you," Malcolm asked, "that the king of England has actually written to Lloyd George complaining that advice to the king to honour people like that is little less that an insult to the Crown? What would you say to that?"

"I'd say the king was right. I'd say the man was a traitor, helping the enemy."

"Well, my dear, there are powers in England this very minute who are betraying the people of England! What do you say to that?"

She didn't know what to say. It was an extraordinary allegation. Here was this man, her mother's cousin, whispering secrets about people she'd never heard of!

"By the way," she said, "they've taken the scaffolding down at the hotel."

Malcolm sat back away from her. Seemed to be waiting.

"So I was able to take a look at that window you got in by that afternoon."

He waited.

"The funny thing was," she said, "I was in Maggie Hines's room when the police came that night – the day she was found. I was actually reading that very book – *Married Love* – when they banged on the door."

His spectacles were like mirrors, glittering the restaurant lights back at her.

"So I guessed you must have already known Maggie, which was why you were able to recognise her –"

The waitress came for their plates, asked if they'd like anything else. Malcolm ordered an ice-cream sundae for her and a selection of cakes. And some tea.

"I'd seen her before."

He'd stayed a night at the King James. He'd got a good memory for faces – and some faces were easy to remember.

"So I knew – when I saw the poor soul in the river – I went straight to the King James. Workmen were knocking off for tea. I climbed up a ladder, saw one of the chambermaids at a window, showed her a ten shilling note – window opened like magic. She showed me Maggie's room. I had a look round. Saw the Stopes book. Wasn't what I was after, but I was anti-Stopes at the time, wondered if it might come in useful – easy for newspapers to add two and two and make five. I made my own way out. Maid daren't say anything – after the bribe. I wrote my account for the paper, didn't let on to the police who the girl was till I knew we'd got an exclusive."

The waitress brought ice-cream, tea and cakes.

Why did he want to look round Maggie's room, Maudie asked. What did he mean, the book might have come in useful?

"Because if it turned out the girl had been murdered, I might have run a campaign against Stopes. Or if the suicide was linked to someone famous – or if there'd been a bit of scandal – I could easily have run an anti-Stopes campaign –"

"But not now?"

"Not now. Not after hearing her talk. I know she's on the side of England."

Maudie was out of her depth. "You'd have used her? To get something you wanted!"

Malcolm gripped her arm. His eyes seemed to bore into her, pupils intense as bradawls.

"Maggie's death was a pity. It was a pity she felt she had to kill herself, a pity she got pregnant, a pity the man didn't marry her. England is full of pities like this. One day my death will be a pity. So will yours. But they're one-at-a-time pities, luck of the draw misfortunes."

He lowered his head almost to the tablecloth, his face like the face of a stranger.

"But now and then we come across a person with the – I can only call it talent – to cause suffering on a scale you know nothing about. The damage they do is terrible."

The freckles, the lines and hairs of his face ran damp with sweat.

"What I'm concerned about is what's happening to Britain. Men like your brother – hundreds and thousands of men like your brother – went out and fought for Britain. And when they come back – those who did come back – they find the rich who stayed at home are richer, and the powerful men more powerful, than before the war started. And the men who went away and fought – they come home and find they've got no work and no homes and no prospects!"

Maudie started her ice-cream in case it was bad manners to let it melt. Malcolm scarcely noticed.

"The war's been over nearly two years. For most people things are getting worse. I ask myself who this war was fought for. And the answer I keep coming to is this, that if the people of Britain are what Britain is, then this war wasn't fought for Britain. If the people who won the war are worse off, which they are, and the hard-faced men who did well out of it are richer and more powerful than before, which they are, then all that killing and all that suffering can't have been for Britain. Therefore it must have been for the enemies of Britain."

It was like being in that lecture hall with Tony: when she heard this speaker she agreed with her, and when she heard that speaker she agreed with him. What Malcolm had said regarding her brother was true. Poor old Herbert had been away all the war – and there'd been precious little for him to come home to.

Malcolm was watching her.

"Enemies of Britain?"

It was his eyes! The rest of his face, the brown splashes of age-spots, the great lined cheeks, the nose that had lost its shape, these could have belonged to any ageing man. But the eyes were the eyes of a watcher. She'd seen one or two old women back in Suffolk with eyes like that. Saw everything, remembered everything, were forever putting two and two together and frightening you.

"What I need, Maudie," he said, "are eyes and ears."

She hoped she was wrong, what she thought he was driving at.

What did he have in mind?

"An ear to the ground, shall we say?"

Not for the first time she wondered if he was mad.

She quite liked Mr Perkins, she said. He'd always treated her pretty well.

"Oh, congratulations on your promotion."

Her skin tightened. "I didn't think I'd mentioned it?"

"We thought you'd be – competent."

She liked being at the King James, she said. Liked Mr Perkins.

"Not Perkins. Perkins is only peripheral. He'd been worth a look once. Hence my visit to that bedroom."

He removed his spectacles, huffed on them, polished them on a clean handkerchief. He reminded her of mole that had accidentally pushed its way up into daylight, unsure of itself away from its darkness. She felt easier with him, seeing this helplessness. She wondered whether Nancy hadn't been too impatient with him, hadn't appreciated him, or given him the support he deserved, a man brave enough to campaign for men like her brother.

"But some need a rather closer look." He settled his spectacles back on, as if there was someone he was already looking closely at.

"You mean the man who got Maggie into trouble?"

"Ever hear of a Mr Vincy?"

Her heart sank. She couldn't make head or tail of him.

"Who Nancy works for?"

"I hear you went to see the new Garden City."

I also saw Nancy, she thought. And I could mention a certain someone who was there with her.

"You do understand?"

That Nancy was Vincy's mistress? she thought. She had understood that in the first few minutes. It was Malcolm who needed to understand a few things now.

"About Nancy and Vincy," he persisted. "You do understand?"

"That she's his secretary?"

She didn't blame Nancy. She remembered her begging him not to leave her that day on London Bridge. If they split up she'd know whose fault it was.

"I mean why she's his secretary."

She felt like telling him. Because she's in love with him. And who's to blame her, with you for a husband?

She caught the look on his face. Willing her to realise what he meant.

But it couldn't be what he meant!

"So now you know."

That a husband should ask – could even think of asking his wife! It was like hiring her out as a prostitute!

"Another eye, you see."

So all that – the loving looks, the wave of the fingers in the tea-room – only a web?

"I thought -"

But perhaps she'd only imagined it, that Nancy had told her she'd got her own flat, glad to be away from Malcolm.

"It's only temporary," he said.

All it amounted to, a couple of spiders? Waiting to catch their fly?

"But what can you do? Even if you find out that what Vincy is doing is wrong?"

"What can I do?" A touch of satisfaction lit his face. "You've asked it at last! The key to it is, it isn't only Vincy."

She wanted to go back to the hotel. She had had enough of intrigues. Nothing justified him sacrificing Nancy.

"What I'll do, Maudie, is publish. When I know enough. It'll be the ruin of them all. Or me."

She didn't pursue it. Didn't want to hear any more.

"Your friend like the look of the New Town?" he asked.

All Tony lived for, she said. According to him, garden cities were what the country needed most.

"Sounds a sensible chap. Tony Fraser, is it?"

"Tony Abbington." She was glad there was something she could put him right about.

"He hopes it's a fruit the maggots won't get into, no doubt."

She supposed he did. Maggots weren't things she and Tony discussed much.

"Trouble is," he said, "wherever there's fruit there's maggots."

She'd do her best about the hotel, she said. If she noticed anything strange she'd get in touch.

She picked up her handbag, ready to leave.

"Don't forget. I'd be glad of a photo." His attention floated across her face, seemed to want her to stay. "Your mother will never be dead while you're alive."

"I'm afraid she is dead."

"More's the pity!"

There was something in his voice, as if a door had opened.

"Were you there?"

"Where?"

"I know she killed herself – But I don't know – you see?"

"You want to know?"

"I don't know why! I don't know how, I don't even know where!"

Malcolm turned away.

"You really want to know?"

She touched his arm. "Please."

"Seen the knife they kill the pigs with?"

"Throat?" She could only whisper. She felt sick. She saw the blade, the curve that knew where to dig for blood. "Where they kill the pigs?"

Malcolm didn't answer, didn't deny it.

She didn't want to picture it, the sunless room, her mother's blood running along that trough across the floor, out through the wall at the side –

She tried not to think of it. But her thoughts had no mercy – her mother kneeling in that terrible place, out of her mind with misery, leaning over that indentation across the floor so as not to make a mess –

She wouldn't cry for her. She put her hands to her head, slapped her head to stop the pictures coming. "Mum! My poor mum!"

And here, his face turned away, the man who knew.

"Why? Tell me why!"

She hated him. All these years with the horror inside him, living his life! Yet he had been kind enough to tell her. She had to come to London to hear the truth, and now it was out!

"I was at the farm on holiday. We got on well, her and me. Cousins. Whether she thought she loved me -"

He opened his hands, as if something had been let go. "Nothing – so far as I was concerned. I was going home next day. I suppose I represented the life she was used to."

He held Maudie's hand.

"She tried to like it, the farm. Whether she ever settled – we were from London, you see, her family and mine. She tried though. She tried to like it."

The past was falling into place, began to make sense. Malcolm was her family, her mother's people. She had never settled to farm life either.

She felt closer to her mother. Both of them had hated farm life. She had left it in her way, her mother in hers.

Malcolm released her hand, looked at his watch. It was time to leave. He settled the bill. They went out into the evening. A few sparrows chirruped in nearby trees. Cars went past with sidelights on.

"As I say," he said. "It's a cruel world."

He showed her to the bus-stop, waited with her till the bus came.

"If you see Nancy, give her my kind regards."

"I hear from Nancy all right," he said. He sounded confident. "She keeps me in touch, Nancy does."

The bus approached, drew up at the stop.

"She's the one I can rely on," Malcolm assured her.

Maudie boarded the bus, thankful to leave him, sorry to lose a window into the past. When she turned to wave he was already part of the night, the most visible part of him the glint of street light on his spectacles.

# CHAPTER 47

She could have the time off, he told her. Could go early on the Saturday morning, come back early on the Sunday morning.

She replied promptly, told Muriel she would be coming to the wedding. She liked to answer letters promptly, she said, couldn't bear it when guests were slow confirming their bookings.

The train slackened speed. She lifted her case down, realised how little the hand hurt now. On the platform a man took the case for her.

"Nice day for a wedding, Maudie!"

Herbert looked older, worn, but as pleased to see her as ever. The two had always got on well. If she didn't mind, he said, he'd like to go and have a look at a shop he'd heard was for sale.

"We shall only be in the way at home if we're there too soon."

They both knew whose way they'd be in. She took his arm, glad there was someone on her side at last.

Beckthorp seemed pleased to see her. The gold lettering in a pub window still called out the name of the brewers Youngs Crawshay and Youngs, the carved angel was still singing at the corner of the half-timbered stationer's shop, the brown metal dog still begged for alms in the doorway at the baker's. The sash windows, the plaster frontages, the coloured blinds of the shops, it was friendly of them to be so unchanged. Yet everything had changed. Looking at Beckthorp now was like looking at snapshots that belonged to someone else.

When they reached the other side of Beckthorp Herbert reined in, drew up beside a small wooden building. "What do you think of it?"

Maudie hesitated to say what she thought of it. She remembered Aubrey Knights's butcher's shop when the window wasn't cracked, the guttering hadn't come adrift and the woodwork and fence had been freshly painted white.

"I could do it up, I suppose."

She heard the reservation in his voice.

"You don't sound very keen."

"Barbara's against the idea, for one thing."

"Barbara's against everything except Barbara."

She found it easy to talk to Herbert. "She wants you back in Yorkshire, she wants me in London, she wants Muriel married off to Stanley. Then she'll have the place to herself. That's what Barbara wants."

So what did she honestly think of him buying the shop?

"Is coming back here what you really want?"

He rubbed at the window, peered in at the distemper peeling off the walls, the floor that needed seeing to.

"Not much chance of what I really want," he muttered. He told her about the Bumfords, the wife poorly. "He's going to give up."

"Couldn't you try for his shop?"

"Not in Hadale. Not now."

The way he spoke reminded her of Tony back in London. As soon as you ask them what they feel, or mention anything about the family they dry up!

"Because of Uncle Arthur?" she asked. "It'd be Pa's dearest wish – if you did come back. You're the apple of his eye."

He handed her up into the trap, climbed in beside her.

"I think of him when I'm in London," she said. "His wife dead, us children leaving, the farming not doing well. And him getting old."

As if he hadn't heard, Herbert shook the reins, the pony's mane rose and fell to the rhythm of the trot, the trap wheels rang on the narrow road. It was mid October, the time of St Luke's little summer, the day of their sister's wedding. The sun shone, the sky was hazy blue, and beyond the hedgerows were steep-pitched corn stacks and fields of stubble. It was the countryside of their childhood, these red-tiled, black-walled barns, these flint and brick cottages, the open landscape, the Suffolk sky.

"You've grown up, Maudie. Look more like Mother than ever."

That she was like her dear mother! The words almost made her cry. In spite of his silences she loved him. He was nicer than twenty sisters. But it worried her that he looked so much older. Like Bernard, another old-young man. Even like Mr Perkins. She supposed they had brought the war back in their heads.

The pony trap had arrived at the fork in the road. To the right was the way to Beck Farm, to the left lay Church Lane.

Church Lane!

Ghosts stirred. The little black-tarred stable, the ivy growing across it – the letterbox! That narrow red mouth she had gripped the evening she heard the Major was leaving.

She reached across for the rein, drew the pony to a stop. "How are we for time?"

"Nearly twelve." He caught sight of her face. "You all right, Maudie?"

If he didn't mind, she said, she'd like to take a look down Church Lane.

"Suits me. Wedding's not till three."

She had a shivery, holy feeling.

This was where she had seen the moonbow, seen the sign across the rain clouds that she should join him. Right at this minute he was close by! Her soul and his were whirling like birds in springtime. One day, one wonderful day, she and the Major would be as one.

The church was smaller than she remembered it. The grass had been trimmed, there were flowers in the porch for the wedding. It was nice. But on the night of the dance there was moonlight on the windows, the shadows were full of magic, Richard Dawson was in the lane.

Herbert walked the pony on towards the Hall. The very door she had seen in dream after dream!

"Oh, I don't know!"

They were nonsense words. She bent over, pretended to scratch her ankle.

"What don't you know, Maudie?"

She shook her head. She had wished huge things. His eyes, his dark moustache, his smile, these were real! Everything else was nonsense.

The surface of the pond showed green in the autumn sunshine, there were paths through the trees where village boys came with their rods and lines and jam jars, some youngsters were having a roadside picnic – but the willows had trailed their fingers in the moonlight, the leafless branches of the hazels had reached into darkness.

"Old barn don't change much," Herbert remarked.

It stood as it had stood all her life, with its flint and brick walls, its great roof, its doors through which a stacked waggon could pass. Its unchangingness made her feel there was something heroic about it, as if it was setting her an example.

Herbert lit his pipe. "Nice old place."

Nice he called it!

"Funny thing about that bit of land," he said.

"Do they know why he gave it to Stanley?"

Maybe something to do with the war, Herbert wondered. The Major and Stanley were in the same regiment for a time. Stanley would know the truth of the matter. "And you know Stanley."

She knew Stanley all right. In her opinion Muriel was marrying the most popular man in the neighbourhood.

"How's Mrs Dawson?" she asked.

Herbert got down, attracted by noises in the barn. "About to peg out, so they say."

"Oh, God," Maudie prayed, "please let her live till Christmas, or till I get some time off. Then take her to your everlasting arms!"

"Major never comes near nor by, they say." Herbert said. "I suppose he'll turn up for the funeral."

She jumped down, too agitated to sit still.

Herbert pushed open the small door let into one of the waggon doors. Inside, in the half light, thirty or forty Norfolk turkeys scratched about for scraps. At the sight of Herbert they fluttered round him, squawking to be fed.

"These look well." He eyed them like a butcher. "Should make a bob or two at Christmas."

No musicians on the platform now, no lamps hanging from the tie-beams. No ladies with drinks and sandwiches, no guests in pretty dresses and best suits. And the floor once smooth enough for dancing was now a litter of straw and turkey mess.

"I wonder if Mrs Dawson knows that dreadful woman has got these here?"

"Oh, excuse me, Miss Stelfox, I thought I saw you go past."

Poorly dressed as ever except for a well-cut town coat thrown over her shoulders.

"Miriam! You're as quiet as a witch!"

"Sorry, Miss Stelfox. I wondered if you could tell Miss Muriel I won't be at the church this afternoon. I'd love to see her married but Mrs Dawson is so poorly I daren't leave her."

"Is she going to die?"

"Oh, Miss Stelfox!" Her hand was to her chest. "I'd give anything to think she could pull through, I really would."

Herbert waved his pipe at the turkeys. "These look well, Miriam."

"I have to do something, Mr Herbert, Raymond the way he is."

Maudie said she supposed the Major could come home any day now, Mrs Dawson being so bad.

"Well there, Miss Stelfox, your guess is as good as mine about that."

A turkey stepped near them, paused, stepped again, its wattles quivering like long purple ears. It stopped, quivered its wattles at them.

"All spoken for, Miriam?"

"I wish they were, Mr Herbert. And I only hope we're here long enough to make a price."

"Bad as that?"

"The Hall's the only home we've got, me and Raymond. And now we've got the babe! If the Missus doesn't pull through -"

Maudie tried to appear sympathetic, clucked at the turkey.

"What you need," Herbert said, "is a butcher to take the lot off your hands."

"Oh, it'd be like a miracle. They cost the earth to fatten."

Maudie scratched a poultry flea off her hand. She didn't want to hear about turkey miracles. If Mrs Dawson died, that would be the miracle she wanted.

"Time we made a move," she said. "Wouldn't do to be late for the wedding."

She said she was sure people would understand why Miriam couldn't come.

"What about you?" Maudie asked him as they left. "Will there be wedding bells for Herbert soon?"

Herbert let the whip end dangle against the pony's rump.

Not soon, he told her, nor late either.

"Never seen anyone you fancied?" she asked.

The trap was making short work of the journey home and she knew no more about her brother now than when he'd met her at the station.

Best to put it out of mind, he said. No good chasing after what you couldn't have.

"Oh, yes it is. Don't chase, don't catch."

He was surprised at his young sister. "You sound pretty sure of yourself."

"I am sure."

She wanted to tell him about the moonbow, knew she couldn't.

"So who have you caught then?" seeing how she had coloured up.

"Maybe one day," she said. "Maybe I'll tell you one day."

She knew he wouldn't pry. "What about you?" she asked. "Sounds as if there's someone."

Herbert slowed the pony, turned into the driveway to Beck Farm.

"Never be anyone for me, Maudie."

# CHAPTER 48

There were pony traps and carriages, there were cars and motor bikes and sidecars, there were people standing about drinking and chatting in the Top Meadow enjoying themselves in the sunshine. When they saw her they waved, called out to her, pleased to see her.

She waved back. "More like London!" she told Herbert. "All these people!"

Home again. The same iron foot scraper on the doorstep, the same back door, its green paint blistered where it had always been blistered, the same scents of box and lavender in the garden. Indoors, the same homey smell of polish and cushions and old wood – but never so many people!

"Here's young Maudie!"

"Look who's here!"

"You remember Maudie, Bertie! Don't she look well!"

People kissed her, shook her hand, asked how she was, said they'd missed her.

She'd thought of them, she said. Was glad to get back and see them. Wouldn't have missed the wedding for the world.

"I knew you'd come."

Quiet as ever.

His face a little older, what hair he had left a little greyer, his attention only on her. You're the one, his face seemed to say, the one I'm longing to see.

She wished she'd got here earlier, wished she hadn't had to listen to Muriel and them damned turkeys. Never mind the room full of family and guests, she knew who made her Pa's eyes light up.

She was aware of the din, one voice in particular.

"I were just tellin' th' Pa we thought rail strike had 'appened this Saturday instead of next, weren't I, Joseph?"

Her Uncle Arthur, a big loud Yorkshire version of her father, the men round him almost as loud as he was.

"Nay, it's miners on strike today," he laughed. "We thought train 'ad run out of coal and thee 'ad 'ad to push it!"

He pushed his glass into a stomach or two to inspire more laughter.

"Whole country'll be on strike soon," he boomed. "Bar Stanley. He'll not be on strike tonight, eh, Joseph?"

Her Pa smiled, saw to his guests. She was glad she had him for a father, glad she had remembered the sovereigns.

"Y'can make th'self useful now you're here, lass, and get me and John here another one."

He handed her some glasses.

"Come to that, young Maudie, if thee'd bring us the bottle – !"

His shout of merriment brought three or four little girls getting dressed as bridesmaids to the middle-room door. They looked up, round-eyed, then dodged back inside again, except one little one who stayed to gaze, till a plump young woman came out to collect her.

"You'll have plenty of time to look at the men when you're older, Janet," she told her.

"Takes after her ma, Oona!" a man told her.

Oona's eyes were dark, the voice slow.

"Hope so, Joe!"

The child laughed too, ran back to her mother.

"You've turned up at last, then."

Nothing soft or yielding about this voice. Barbara handed her a teacloth.

"Perhaps you can spare a minute to help poor Aunt May in the kitchen. I haven't washed the dairy things up yet, let alone had time to change. Muriel's been upstairs hours with her blessed dress."

"Got to get people a drink first," Maudie told her. "I can't help it if the train was late."

But Barbara had gone.

"I'll see to the drinks, Maudie." It was Edna Graves, family friend, she of the motherly widow's hump and solid shoulders. "Your aunt will be so pleased to see you."

"Didn't expect to see that one here!"

"Oona Pegsby?" She raised her eyes to heaven. "Her and that Joe Bryant!" Edna leaned close, breathed titbits into Maudie's ear. Oona had been seen in his car. Time and again. "And you know how many girls Joe Bryant's been out with!"

Oona hadn't been in parish long. Friendly enough. Too friendly, some thought. Bit of a needlewoman too. Had made all the bridesmaids' clothes for the wedding.

"Isn't she the one whose husband's in the Navy?"

"Navy! I don't believe he's in no navy!"

Didn't believe Oona had a husband anywhere.

"That Oona Pegsby and Joe Bryant make a fine pair, if you ask me! And he's Stanley's best man."

Neither did she think Muriel was best pleased with someone like him as best man! In charge of the ring and everything!

Maudie felt Joe couldn't be all bad if Muriel disliked him. Must have something good about him.

Because by now it wouldn't look as though she was doing what Barbara told her, she made her way to the kitchen.

Aunt May threw the cloth down. "Oh, my lovely!"

She dried her hands, gave her a kiss, stood and gazed at the girl. Maudie loved her long comical face, her children-kindly ways.

"Oh, it's lovely to see you, my Maudie!"

They washed and wiped up together. But despite being so pleased to see her, Aunt May seemed to have something on her mind.

It was the wedding, May admitted. She couldn't help it. She always felt sorry for a bride and groom.

"If only they knew what they were letting themselves in for!"

Yet even if they did know, Maudie said, she didn't suppose a couple would chose not to get married.

"That's the sad part," May agreed.

She loved to see young people getting together.

"Then they go and spoil it, getting married."

Surely, Maudie said, all marriages couldn't be bad. There must be some that worked out all right?

May rinsed a batch of glasses. "You may be right, dear," she conceded. "I can but hope Muriel's is one of them."

"Mother! You know it's a match made in heaven!"

It was cousin Kate. She had got permission for a day off, had travelled down first thing.

"Mother's enjoying herself, I see. At the kitchen sink, talking about marriage!"

May looked at the pair of them, young women on the brink of life.

"You were two happy little girls last time I saw you together," she said. "Now here you both are, grown up, and can't wait to throw yourselves away, I don't doubt."

"Last time I met Maudie," Kate told her, "we were at a contraception meeting. The young man Maudie was with seemed to know all about such matters, so I'm sure Maudie won't have to get married. As for me, I only have eyes for the matron."

"Take no notice, Maudie," May said. "She always did say outrageous things. Can't think where she gets it from!"

Even as a child it was easy to be jealous of Kate – the girl was so damned nice, so helpful, the sort of person always able to make the best of things. And now she'd turned out to be good-looking as well! Maudie wasn't heartbroken that her hands looked as if they'd been in a lot of cold water.

Kate put her arm round her mother.

"I'll ask Pa to stay here another week. The change will do you good. I'm sure Uncle Joseph and Barbara will be only too pleased."

They seemed such a happy mother and daughter. Maudie would have given anything to have had her own mother giving her such a favourite-person look.

"Pity you can't stay too, dear," May said.

But Kate had to be back by midnight, and even then it was by special favour of the matron. Maudie realised how good Mr Perkins had been to give her till the following midday.

Getting ready to go to the church was the familiar muddle: whether these gloves would go with that scarf, whether the bridesmaids were to come back in this or that vehicle, whether anyone had seen Barbara's prayer-book she'd laid on the window sill specially. In the kitchen Uncle Arthur was cleaning his dentures at the sink with a dishcloth and Vim.

She left the house before the others, went by the footpath over the fields to go in the churchyard the back way. She wanted to see her mother's grave, wanted to tell her she understood now, knew her better now, loved her more than ever.

The sun shone through an autumn haze, a few wallflowers coloured the church tower, a single bell called the wedding over the countryside. Someone had put chrysanthemums in the vase. She loved the smell of chrysanthemums. They smelt of earth and autumn and things resting.

She blessed her mother, asked her blessing. But she wouldn't ask for that great secret wish to come true because it would seem like plaguing. Her mother would watch over her without being plagued.

The church was full. Barbara had kept a place for her. "Thought you were never coming. People will think you're a fine one!"

Wilfred Jackson, rector of St Matthew's, was unwell. His health had worsened during the year and the Reverend Henry Griffin, vicar of the next parish, was standing in for him.

"Look at him," she muttered to Barbara. "Glaring and glowering just because Muriel's a bit late!"

She hated him standing there on the chancel steps just in front of them, his angry-pig eyes watching the door, irritable at being kept waiting. And when a dreadful smell came from behind them and Arthur shifted in his pew and muttered "By – !" and the parson moved away and stood by the altar, she knew it was God's way of striking those puffed up with pride.

The music signified. Her father, Muriel and the bridesmaids were proceeding up the aisle.

"Such a shame!" Aunt May murmured.

Muriel's face had lost its everyday look. She was nervous, she was pleased, she looked as if she couldn't believe it was she who was about to be married, but to Maudie during that short walk she looked quite beautiful.

The age-old ritual proceeded. The vows of constancy, the ring, the declaration, Muriel herself and Stanley, all were given and taken in matrimony. Stanley and Muriel were man and wife.

Aunt May wiped her eyes.

The Reverend Griffin said in his address that a marriage contract was not a guarantee of happiness. In his experience, it was a common mistake to believe that marriage was a contract between equals. That it most certainly was not. Marriage was a contract between a man and a woman who had promised to obey her husband. Anyone who had seen a spoilt dog, had heard it yapping and snarling at the master it was supposed to obey knew that happiness did not come from a sense of equality. A spoilt dog was not a happy dog. It was the same with mankind. A country whose people questioned the authority of God was a miserable country. Could anyone doubt, he asked, but that the Russia of recent years, since atheism had replaced Christianity, was the most miserable country on earth? And take the case of Judas Iscariot. There was a man whose lack of respect for the Master had stunk down the ages. Did such a man enjoy a day's happiness? Or command the respect of others? Never. Judas Iscariot died by his own hand in self-disgust. As God cherishes those who love Him in obedience, so are subjects blessed in obedience to their king – and a wife in obedience to her husband.

On her way out afterwards Maudie noted the parson's wife, but those manly features gave no clue to Mrs Griffin's view of marriage.

Back at Beck Farm everyone said how well it had gone, how lovely the bride looked, how hard people must have worked to make it go so well. They remarked how willing young Kate was, taking tea round and everything, yet having to get ready soon to go back to London. How wonderful our nurses were!

Young Kate, Maudie thought to herself, hadn't had to put up with years of being bossed about by bitches! Even saintly Kate might have been inclined to be missing when there were chores to be done if she'd had to live with them. Running about for others could be taken a bit too far!

She realised how little she'd seen of Herbert. Not that she blamed him for keeping out of the way of Uncle Arthur, who was the centre of attention with his stories.

"Bride said, 'No, sorry, Jim, I can't tonight!' 'Why not?' Jim asks. 'It's our wedding night.' 'Well,' bride replies, 'it's Lent!' 'Lent?' Jim says. 'Well, thee wants to get it back. Thee'd no business to part wi'it!'"

Oona Pegsby's little girl laughed with everyone else, Joe caught Oona's eye, even Stanley's dog Kruger raised his head and beat his tail on the floor. Arthur emptied his glass, thought of his next joke.

"Oh, Maudie, wasn't she lovely!"

Aunt May came to sit with her. It was a relief to see that comical long face.

"If only they knew what they were letting themselves in for, poor dears!"

"Is marriage so bad?"

"It's the living together, my dear. Never knowing what time's your own. Such a muddle."

"What does Kate think of marriage?"

"Seeing all those pink little nuisances on the maternity ward, I should think it's put her off for life. One can but hope."

"But what if you fall in love?"

May patted her niece's hand.

"It doesn't last, thank God."

A disagreeable smell drifted across the room.

Arthur Stelfox stood up to get himself another drink, coughed, glared round.

"Who the 'ell -?"

Kruger thumped his tail on the floor, got up, crossed the room and thrust his nose into Arthur's bottom.

May shaded her face.

"Marriage!" she sighed.

As in many Suffolk farmhouses the rooms at Beck Farm had a single, south-facing window, which was why her Pa's writing bureau was on that side of the room. From what Maudie could see by the failing light no-one was in the garden, no-one on the staircase opposite. She moved the chair, knelt in the recess under the bureau, found the key and unlocked the lid. She unwrapped each sovereign separately, replaced all four, lowered the lid.

Someone came in from the next room, a moment later someone else came down the stairs.

"Scarlet cloak already?"

Hidden by the bureau Maudie recognised her brother's voice. He sounded disappointed.

"It goes at six forty-five, I'm afraid." It was her cousin Kate! "You're sure you don't mind taking me to the station?"

"Mind?" Herbert pushed the parlour door shut, reducing the noise from the next room. "The only thing I mind is you going away."

"I've hardly seen you. You've scarcely been near all day."

"I thought it best. People would have noticed. I couldn't have kept my eyes off you."

In the darkening room Maudie crouched low, strained to hear every word.

"That shop," Kate said. "Is it any good?"

"In the right hands, maybe. If it was done up."

"No hands better than yours, Herbert. Perhaps you ought to buy it."

"If you think so."

He sounded non-committal, as if the go had been taken out of him.

"Herbert," Kate said, "*If looking well won't win her, Will looking ill prevail?* Remember?"

"Only too well."

There was a comparative lull in the noise from the next room, as if someone was making a speech or telling a story. Maudie hoped her stomach wouldn't make noises.

"Still read poetry?" Herbert asked.

"Not on horseback."

A memory seemed to amuse them both.

"You must have thought me dull."

"Oh, I did," Kate agreed. "About what, particularly?"

Outside, the sky was clear, the garden almost dark. Suddenly from the next room laughter, applause, the noise as loud as ever.

"We'd better be going," Herbert said. "I'll bring the trap round. At least we can have a chat on the way to the station."

"That'll be nice. I don't want us to separate, you know."

When they had gone Maudie locked the lid, replaced the key. The prospect of anything more than friendship between her brother and her cousin appalled her.

*Couldn't have kept my eyes off you!*

She felt betrayed. The pair of them, thinking of the other as someone special! She hated it. Hated them!

Oona brought a couple of slices of cream sponge back for herself and Janet. Joe came and sat on the arm of her chair.

"Like a little bit?" she murmured, offering him some.

"Soon as you like."

Muriel came downstairs. She was in her going-away clothes. Maudie had to admit she still had a vaguely enchanted air about her.

"Muriel," she asked, "why don't you and Stanley go to the station with Herbert when he goes? I expect he'll be taking Kate soon."

"Good idea," Oona said. "Then Joe'll be able to take me and Janet home. It's past her bedtime."

Stanley cottoned on at once. Didn't mind in the least, he said.

He winked at Joe. "Mustn't miss bedtime."

"We'll see what Herbert thinks." Muriel had had a lifetime of Maudie's bright ideas.

"Oh, I'm sure Herbert won't mind," Maudie said.

Kate came in, a picture in her nurse's hat and scarlet cape.

"Kate," Maudie said, "if you're going with Herbert, you wouldn't mind if Stanley and Muriel came with you, would you?"

"Joe's car broken down?" Kate asked.

"Only we thought -"

"One of Maudie's bright ideas," Muriel said. "I didn't think there'd be room. Then there's the cases."

"You see, Maudie," Kate said, "Herbert and I have got one or two things to talk over. We've hardly seen each other all day."

"Better keep things as they were, Stanley," Muriel said. "It's all arranged with Joe."

"Just as you wish, m'dear," Stanley said. "Just as you wish."

"I do wish," she said.

Herbert came in.

"If you're ready, cousin Kate?"

"Ready when you are, cousin Herbert," she smiled.

She said her goodbyes, the two of them left.

"We shan't need to leave for a few minutes, shall we, Joe?" Muriel said, "if we're going by car?"

Whatever, Maudie thought, whatever Stanley had to go and marry Muriel for! His life would never be his own any more.

The guests drifted back indoors from seeing them off. Maudie stayed out with her Pa.

The night air was warm, sweet with countryside smells. Behind them, shapes she had known all her life loomed, indistinct, friendly, the waggon shed, the barn, the house itself. While she had been away she had thought of the farm with fondness. Except that, with the bitches, the farm had been the place where she didn't grow up.

She clutched her Pa's arm, more alone now, his wife dead, his children leaving.

"Oh, Pa."

His hair had silvered since she had been away.

"Still no rain," he said. "I don't think Stanley would've been able to plough if he was here. Not that he'll bother about that yet."

She loved his quiet way of talking. She wanted to listen to him, wanted to get to know him.

"Poverty Farm's still for sale," he said. "Didn't go at Michaelmas. Not that it' ll make much, lock, stock and barrel."

"Can't they make it pay?"

"No money in farming now. A lot of farms can't stand it. They say it's the best crop round here now – the for-sale boards."

"Can this farm stand it, Pa?"

The farm she had known as home all her life seemed suddenly precarious.

"Have to stand it."

If any man would hold to the last it would be her Pa.

"I expect you'll miss Muriel."

"Spect so. I miss you. Sometimes I catch a shape in the fire. Brings your face back."

She squeezed his arm. "Oh, Pa! I wish it could bring Mother back."

He patted her hand. "Well, there. Won't do to wish too much."

All these years he'd known, and never so much as a word.

"That she's – gone!"

He patted her hand again, glanced up at the sky. He turned to go indoors. "Be no rain again tonight. By the look of things."

Her train drew in at Liverpool Street station. She remembered her first arrival there, the magic, the din, the crowds that drew her along. No Nancy this time to meet her, but she wasn't nervous, threading her way across the concourse against the incoming crowds. She was glad to be back in London, away from home and its complications.

"If it isn't little Maudie Stelfox!"

His brown eyes twinkled. He raised his hat, paused on the way to his train.

"Oh, hello," she said. "Hello, Major."

She didn't stop walking, didn't know what to say to him.

His face was bronzed, his moustache as lovely as ever.

He stood for a moment, replaced his hat. And then they had gone their ways.

She tried to run back after him. But the concourse was so full, people with cases, people standing about studying timetables, people in groups meeting people. Crowds were going through this gate, through that gate to the platforms. She ran where she could, scanning men's faces.

Let him be here, she prayed. Oh, let him be here!

She found herself at the barrier where she had got off her train. The man asked to see her ticket. She shook her head, watched the people on the platform, not knowing whether he'd gone through.

An engine shrieked, buffer clanked against buffer, wheels shuddered.

She gripped the railings as if caged. Fewer people were boarding the train. The guard was slamming carriage doors. A young man raced up, showed his ticket, dashed to the nearest carriage.

The guard checked the door, blew his whistle, waved his green flag. The train jolted, started its journey.

# CHAPTER 49

She worked.
She started early, left off late, allowed details of bookings, cancellations and correspondence to fill her mind. Nothing was too trivial. She designated space for the bookings ledger, the accounts ledger, the letter tray, so the least request by Mr Perkins could be met immediately. She made a point of seeing there was sufficient ink, the pens were clean, the blotting-paper renewed.

When the days were full they were bearable, but at night! To have walked away from him! When he'd called her name, had wanted to see her – to have walked on, away from the one she worshipped!

Her solace was work. She recalled conversations she had had with guests, imitated to herself the way they spoke, the way they asked things, made inquiries. She began to understand what it was that made one way of speaking more effective than another, what made her more urgent to please some people than others, why she might favour one guest as opposed to another. She found she could imitate their accents, could hear what was countrified in her own voice.

But there were nights when nothing could hide what she had done. He would appear, sun-tanned, his moustache dark, waiting for her to stop and talk.

"Oh, hello," she would say. "Hello, Major."

He would be smiling, his eyes twinkling because he'd seen her. She would talk easily, use her hotel voice, her shyness gone, and after the small talk they would talk intimately, heart to heart. "I knew you would come," he would say. "Now we can start our life together."

Other times she would see his puzzled look, see him raise his hat as she walked away. Then she would find herself gripping the bedclothes, holding her breath at what she had done. She cursed herself for the chance she had thrown away, would lie awake and long for morning.

After a certain vivid dream she wrote a letter. For days she scanned the incoming mail but no reply came. She wished she hadn't written.

Christmas was still some way off but bookings were increasing, the hotel was doing well.

One day Mr Perkins stopped as he was going past, took a good look at her. Time she had a break, he said. She said there was a possibility she'd want to go to a funeral in due course, but Mr Perkins told her he'd like her to get outdoors and get some air. It was his policy to look after those who looked after the hotel, he said. In that case, she said, she'd go to the East End and try some of that sarsaparilla Londoners were always telling her about.

There was a stall selling antiques, another footwear, another pets. Green birds with letterbox red heads; kittens with bright empty eyes; puppies whimpering, their box soaked with urine; fish with exaggerated fins, now large, now small, drinking with padded lips, swimming endlessly round in their glass globe. There was a stall of children's toys with dolls asleep in their boxes, teddy bears propped up against other teddy bears, guns that fired rubber bands at cardboard gangsters. A little boy was being lifted up to look at a toy blue delivery van with doors that opened. Was lifted closer. Money changed hands. The van was boxed but not wrapped. The child pulled the flap open, took the vehicle out, looked up at his father, his face a joy.

The man was Bernard. He was as delighted as the youngster.

A woman ran forward, grabbed the boy, pulled him away.

"That's all you do! Spoil him!" She snatched the toy, put it back in the box. "You don't have the looking after him day in and day out!"

"Mum!"

"Let him enjoy himself!" Bernard looked as upset as the child.

"Enjoy yourself, you mean!"

"Mum!"

"Pity you come and see him at all. Always makes him worse!" Her face was blotchy with anger, her coat open over a bulging belly.

The boy was trying to get the toy away from his mother.

"Not till you get home. And me not knowin' where he'd got to!" She appealed to the group of people watching. "Now what am I supposed to get him for Christmas!"

She pulled the child away into the crowd, the boy crying for his toy.

The afternoon sun had gone. The air was cold, thickening with mist.

Bernard leaned against a stall post, gazing at where his son had disappeared. Maudie touched his arm. His misery looked through her.

"I want Paddy!"

He roused himself, looked all around, bent down to child level as if it would help him to see better. "Paddy! Paddy!" He rushed into the crowd, dashed about amongst the shoppers, calling, shouting. Maudie rushed after him, pushed past people. "Paddy! Come back to your dad!"

People stared at her, some mocked "Paddy! Paddy!" Most ignored her. She turned back, unsure which way she'd come, almost bumped into him. He was alone, his face in his hands. She stood beside him, waited.

The street lamps were smudged with fog.

"Was that your son?"

"She has him all the time."

Smuts from the iron chimney of a fish and chip stall hung in the air, became part of the smell of frying.

He kept his face covered. She touched his arm, hoped he wasn't crying.

"You'll get him back. I know you will."

"How will I?"

She put her hand to her heart. "Because you deserve him."

Around them the air was slanted by light from the stalls.

"You don't know what it's like."

"That's where you're wrong."

He looked at her without interest.

"I live it in my mind."

"Live what?"

"Looking for someone. Like you look for Paddy."

"Someone?" He sounded bitter. "Who's someone?"

"What do you think I'm doing in London? I come from a farm in Suffolk. What do you think I'm in London for?" She heard herself, sounding off like one of her sisters. "I got a job here so I could look for him. I searched for months and never saw a sign of him. And one day when I wasn't expecting it I met him. Face to face. What do you think I did? I walked away! I walked away! After searching for months I found him – and I walked away! Too tongue-tied. He raised his hat to me as I went. So don't you tell me I don't know what it's like to lose someone! I know better than most. I see his face day and night – nearly drives me crazy. I had my chance and messed it up. You keep looking – you'll get your chance. And don't mess it up like I did!"

She felt better for telling him.

"Poor old Maudie."

"Never mind about poor old Maudie! Or poor old Bernard! You be sure you take your chance when it comes."

The fog had thickened. They were in a private world. Traffic noise, the calls of traders, the bargaining, such sounds came through a wall of greyness from a world beyond.

"I didn't know you had a son," she said.

"Why we got married – Paddy on the way."

"Maybe when she has the next one you'll be able to see more of Paddy."

He shot her a look.

"When she's got the new baby, she'll be glad if you can take Paddy off her hands for the afternoon. She can't look after both."

"True!" He searched her face. "That's true! She won't be able to look after both."

"Not when she's had the baby," Maudie said. "Not for a while."

"Not when she's had the baby."

"She might get into the habit -"

"Me seeing him!"

Little enough, she thought. But Bernard was revived enough to follow his nose towards the chip stall. He bought two lots, salted and vinegared them, gave a bag to her.

"Might see more of him! Little old Paddy!"

She was glad she had cheered him up, felt better herself.

The afternoon had thickened into night. Cold hung round their faces, whitened the breath into more mist.

They found themselves passing the pet stall. Bernard asked the man to hold up one of the pups. It whimpered, hung limp, its belly smooth and pale.

"There y'are, Maudie," he said. "Something to keep you company."

"Not in the hotel, Bernard."

"Look at him. Little old dear!"

She took his arm, walked him away. She had seen too many sacks of unwanted pups and kittens thrown in the pond. "I know, old bean," she said. "I know how you feel."

Horse-drawn traffic went by at a walk through the fog, cars had their windscreens open for better visibility.

They might as well walk back to the hotel, Bernard said. He doubted if there'd be any buses, night like this. "Won't take more than an hour or two to walk. Proper old pea-souper!"

She squeezed herself against his arm. Being with a married man was a kind of comfort. She hoped he liked to have her close.

The fog thickened. Bernard could tell they were by the river because of the breeze and the foghorns. Knew the docks fairly well, he said. He'd worked on the docks years ago, used to have a docker's card. How he'd met Moira. Most of the foremen were Irish so it was best to wear a green scarf and make out you were Irish too. He'd got friendly with a chap by the name of Murphy, somehow got friendly with his daughter.

"Man who pleases Moira," Murphy told him, "he'll be a man in a million."

That was 1914, the year they got married, and Paddy on the way. He soon found he wasn't a man in a million. Then he got called up.

"She got friendly with someone else. So when I got blown up that was good enough for her."

He didn't altogether blame her. Not many women would want to live with a man with a face like his. So he found himself invalided out of the army with no face, no job and no wife, except in name. Then one day he bumped into Mr Perkins who he'd been in the army with for a while. Mr Perkins was able to give him a few hours' work a week, cellaring and that, and as Perkins prospered so he gave Bernard more work.

"Turned out to be the best friend I ever had."

"If Paddy hadn't been on the way," Maudie asked, "would you have married her?"

Bernard sighed. "Should have listened to Murphy."

The fog stank of smoke and filth, began to sting her eyes. Seeing her rub them Bernard took his handkerchief out, asked if she'd like to borrow it to breathe through.

"Yours being a bit on the small side, I remember."

She was glad to take it, told him she'd wash it for him when they got back. Yet she couldn't help feeling what a long time it was taking them to get back. She had no idea where they were, whether they were even going in the right direction. It was like being in a tunnel with no sides and no end, with a man she knew little about. But she knew she could trust him. He wouldn't harm a fly.

There seemed fewer people about, street noises were muffled, she seemed to hear only the sound of their own footsteps and the echo of their footsteps

"Like working as a cellarman?"

He didn't mind the work, he said. There were worse jobs.

She said she supposed all sorts of rubbish could blow into a cellar. Must be difficult to keep the place tidy. Did he give it a spring-clean very often?

He tidied it when it needed it, he said. Mr Perkins liked the place to be clean.

"Ever find anything down there?" she asked.

Underfoot the pavement sounded watery. Windows and walls ran with dampness. She trailed her hand across a door, found it edged with grime.

"I mean, anything could find its way into a cellar," she said. "Old clothes, papers, books, anything."

His step faltered.

There was a book there once, he said.

She asked him what it was called. But he was intent on staring into the fog. If only he could see a street sign, he said.

The book must have had a title, she insisted. What was it called, for goodness' sake?

She could tell he was edgy. Served him right for reminding her of the cellar.

"How many words in the title, then? Two? Twenty-two?"

He stopped walking. Under the halo of a gas lamp he looked pale.

"It is all over, isn't it?"

"What's all over?" She was suddenly chilled from the fog.

"Maggie's inquest. Was suicide, wasn't it?"

He looked dreadful, his eyes searching her. She wondered what she was hearing.

"Any reason why it shouldn't have been suicide?"

He had to lean against the post, rubbed his throat, sweating.

"If someone had found it!"

"The book?"

"I might have hung!"

She could almost see his corpse hanging from the lamp post, his feet swaying as people walked past.

"What made you think – you might hang?"

He seemed unable to settle, his mind on the street, the fog.

"Why you? Why not someone else?"

"After my razor –" He ran his hand over his face. His skin was wet. "That book – what they were talking about in the paper. Then the police came."

He shook his head. It put her in mind of a horse trying to shake off something that was stinging it.

"If they'd found it there – with my razor gone – they wouldn't have looked for anybody else. I might have hung!"

She saw what he meant. It was only too likely.

She found herself looking up at the crosspiece on the lamp post where the rope might have swung.

"I'd have hung all right." His voice was a murmur, sounded tired out.

"Didn't Maggie write a note about taking the razor?" she asked.

"One of the coppers reckoned it was a fake. So they had to check my writing. I had to wait till they were sure. If they'd found that book before –"

"I'd have told them I put it there."

"You're a good girl."

"But I did put it there!"

If she'd been his wife she wouldn't have deserted him just because his face was damaged.

"You don't have to bother now, Maudie. It's over and done with."

"Think it was suicide?" She had to know, had to test him.

"Letters point that way, they say. Did it for the best, they say."

They started walking, from one dim lamplit glow to the next. Occasionally a motor vehicle passed at a crawl, its lights a blur of cloud.

"Though how that blessed book got there!" he mused.

"I tell you I put it there. That time I dropped my hanky."

"You mean – in the staffroom – when they were talking about -" She felt him stare at her. "You mean you knew it was in the cellar?"

"That's what I've been trying to tell you."

"You've known – all this time?"

She explained how she had done someone a favour, had slept in a spare room which turned out to be Maggie's, had found the book and started reading it. She told him how the police had almost caught her with it, how she hadn't known what to do with it.

"And you never said a word?"

"I'm sorry it worried you. I wouldn't have wanted to worry you for the world."

Criticism, she thought, when the whole affair wasn't her fault in the first place, was something she could do without.

One good thing about it, she said, her hiding the book had stopped it coming out at the inquest what sort of stuff Maggie read.

"You did right, Maudie," he agreed. "No-one could fault what you did."

He was so innocent. Easy to throw a net over him and catch him with words. Not that she wanted him, she thought, not with his past. Didn't want to catch that kind of pain.

Night had set in. Apart from the occasional street lamp, the occasional horse-drawn vehicle, it was like being in a tomb, a couple of ghosts in a world they wanted to escape from.

"You'll find him one day," she said.

He looked at her, didn't answer. She wondered if he had the remotest idea how to keep in touch with his son, any more than he had about how to get back to the hotel.

"I daresay."

She heard the way he breathed, knew what was in his heart.

"Look," she said, "you know things are going to get better. You know you'll see more of Paddy when she has the baby. So you might as well cheer up. Paddy wouldn't like to see his dad like this."

They came to a crossroads, had no idea which road to take. She felt she was in a grey world that grazed the face, chafed the throat, tightened the chest. The street lamps barely lit the pavement beneath, showed nothing they could recognize.

"You sure you're going the right way?"

She couldn't help sounding a bit tart, began to doubt whether Bernard had any more notion how to get them back to the hotel than he had in managing his affairs.

"Not too sure," he said.

He plodded on. Suddenly she wondered if he might be deliberately be going the wrong way, if he might know where they were and was taking her further and further from the hotel. The police didn't believe him about the razor. His wife didn't trust him to with their son. And she remembered what she'd felt the first time she saw him. She hung back, not enough for him to vanish into the fog but enough to give herself a chance –

She told herself not to be a fool. He was only a chap unlucky enough to have lost his son and his wife and his face. He trudged on ahead of her, head sunk forward.

She asked him where that book *Married Love* was now.

Hidden it in the boiler-room, he said. He supposed he ought to burn it.

She asked him if he'd read it. "Though I suppose you know all about married love."

"Don't look like it!"

He wasn't sorry for himself, almost made a joke of it. She caught up with him, wanted to help him.

"Can't do any harm to have a look at it before you burn it. Get an idea of the woman's point of view."

Maybe he would, he said. Maybe. One day.

"I can show you which bits."

He stopped at a shop window.

"I know this place!"

It sold saveloys, pies, pease pudding.

"Like something to eat?"

They ate as they walked. He knew where they were now. Knew where the main road was.

"See it?"

It ought to have been the blaze of a hundred lights. The hotel was a twilight, a few lights struggling out.

"You've done it, old bean." She hugged his arm, grateful. "Don't forget about that book." They crossed over to the hotel. "Even if you only read bits of it."

She felt closer to him, as if they had shared something, felt sorry to have to leave him when they got indoors.

"That Moira," she told him. "Doesn't know what she's thrown away!"

# CHAPTER 50

One morning she received two letters. One was in a hand she knew.

*Dear Maudie,*

*I told Pa you'd write if you wanted anything he was upset poor old boy when Aunt May and Uncle Arthur left but as I told him he can't expect people to stay at Beck Farm for ever just to keep him company anyway Herbert's bought that blessed shop so that cheered Pa up but it hasn't cheered me up I told Herbert straight expecting me to wash and cook and look after him there's too much to do on the farm as it is.*

*As for your letter I didn't know you cared anything about that Mrs Dawson I didn't think you cared about anyone round here wasn't that why you went to London Mrs Dawson is a bit better they say so you won't have to come to her funeral but what her old mind is like goodness knows the Major came home for a couple of days when she was bad they say that Miriam's little girl Julia is the Major's not Raymond's but there's some wicked tongues about as you well know Maudie I don't know why you say you're losing sleep over the old woman it's not like you as for Christmas it's a long way to come home as you say.*

*Your affectionate sister*

*Barbara Stelfox*

Maudie read it through twice, then tore it up, especially through the signature.

The other letter was from Tony.

*Dear Maudie,*

*I often picture you as you were on our visit to Welwyn, your blue eyes and your black hair and nice complexion. If I'd had any sense I'd have told you how attractive you were but I didn't so that's why I'm writing now. I'd love a snapshot of you to put beside my bed to look at before I go to sleep.*

*You'd laugh if you saw the way we live. There's a dormitory full of hard little beds, and other huts for the canteen and recreation. Most of the men play cards or darts or ping-pong and suchlike. I don't know what the company would have done if it hadn't been for the contractors, Trollope and Colls, because they've supplied the huts and everything during these early months. The first couple of houses should be ready next month for the first workers and their families to move into.*

*I've managed to get on the management/workers committee which decides who goes on the housing list and who gets a high or low priority. I've got my name down, but being single I shall have a long wait. Not that I mind. One day when the town is finished and everyone has moved in and the gardens are planted and the trees are green I wonder if the citizens will give a thought to those who believed such a place was possible. I dream of that time. The troubles we're putting up with now will be worth it when the people of Welwyn see their children's healthy faces.*

*Of course not everyone is optimistic. I enclose an article which talks about the opposition to the town behind the scenes – though I don't believe everything I read in the papers.*

*All best wishes*

*Tony*

She unfolded the newspaper cutting. It was no surprise to see it was from the *Daily Brief* and by Malcolm Steward.

*The silence surrounding the building of Welwyn Garden City is deafening. Almost suspicious. On the one hand we have tens of thousands of people with no work and nowhere to live, and on the other we have a project that will provide housing and employment for thousands in a clean environment and with excellent amenities. The land has been acquired. The architecture has been designed. A reputable firm has started building. The first residents are about to move in. So the reader might be forgiven for believing that all is well. Nothing could be further from the truth. The Garden City Company has no money. It is in debt. What is worse is that it has no support. Worse still, our investigations show a strange and possibly ominous unanimity of resistance to the new town.*

*The Fabian Society, which might have been expected to welcome enlightened progress describes the idea of a garden city as "futile and impracticable."*

*The business community, hard-headed and backward-looking as ever, ignores its possibilities. Of the 250,000 shares issued by the Company less than a third have been bought, perhaps because the rate of interest will not be higher than 7.5%! And that on a solid and long-term investment!*

*But it is from the politicians that we see the most studied indifference. The Government gives the scheme no funding and no support. The Opposition is equally ready to see the project fail. The reason is clear. There are as yet no votes in Welwyn Garden City. It has no decaying town centre, no mean streets, no traffic congestion, and above all, no voters! And so a new city that would bring housing and work and hope to the common man attracts neither the businessman nor the politician. It has no place in the conscience of the man who lives for profit or the man who lives for votes.*

*There is, however, a glimmer of hope. Last year the Government created a Ministry of Health. Under the Housing Act the Ministry is empowered, if not obliged, to direct funds from the Public Works Loans Scheme to assist state-aided housing schemes. With the New Year approaching let us pray that the Government will take an enlightened view of the building of a city worthy of the people of England.*

*Our readers may rest assured that this newspaper will keep its ear to the footings.*

They were a good pair, Maudie thought, Tony and Malcolm, one expecting the town to shoot up like a mushroom, the other believing it was doomed. In her opinion they were both a bit barmy.

Before getting into bed of a night she would look across the yard to where a small electric light illuminated a railed-off area that gave access to the boiler-room and fuel store, and then she would muse on the spear-pointed railings, the concrete steps down to the area, the light itself, clear and steady in the darkness. She didn't care that Bernard's face was twisted, that he was older than her and not the cleverest man in the world. He was comfortable to be with, and she rather liked it that he was married. She felt easy with him, could say anything she wanted to.

"You'll have to drop him a line," Rosie said.

"Drop who a line?"

She'd thought the little bitch was asleep.

"You know who," Rosie said. "And I hear he's married!"

"You must be daft! As if I've got the slightest interest in old Bernard!"

The two got chatting, not having seen so much of each other lately. Rosie asked if she ever heard from Tony. Sometimes, Maudie said. In fact she wondered if Tony wasn't partly in love with her.

"Oh, what part?" Rosie asked.

The part that wanted someone to live in Welwyn with him, Maudie said. Tony had put his name down on some list for a house. Not that she'd ever want to go and live there.

"What if his name was Bernard though?" Rosie laughed.

She said Peter had put his name down for a house too. She hadn't heard from him lately but he'd be here for the dance.

"Dance?"

The staff usually had a little get-together on the evening of Christmas Day when the rush was over. They played a few records, had a few drinks. It was a bit of a crush in the staffroom but it made a nice finish to the day. It was the best Christmas present Rosie could wish for, knowing Peter's name was on the list.

"He'll have to have his little reward," she laughed.

She asked if Tony would be coming. Maudie pulled a face. It wasn't Tony so much, she said. It was what came with him – all that palaver of meetings and committees and such.

"Oh, but his eyes!" Rosie said. "And those eyelashes!"

Maudie let it pass. She preferred to think of Bernard. Not that she had seen him to talk to lately, being busy all day long like the rest of the staff.

The days passed. Every night the light beckoned, the dimly-lit railings and the steps down to the area seemed a kind of comfort. Night after night the last thing she saw in her mind's eye before going to sleep was the low-powered lamp across the yard burning softly through the darkness.

One morning their paths crossed. A van had delivered a typewriter and Bernard accompanied the carrier as far as the office to get it signed for.

"I never came and helped you with that book," she said when the man had gone.

Bernard looked blank.

"That book you found – in the cellar," she reminded him. "Perhaps I'll pop across this evening."

Of course she wasn't about to throw herself away, she told herself. In any case, she was a woman now! But by the same token, she thought, she was a woman in a world of men and women, and if one meeting led to another she would be careful. Maybe she would confide in Rosie, take Rosie's advice. A half-remembered sentence from *Married Love* came to mind, about a man being able to judge from certain signs that the tide of physical passion was up. Then catching her face in the mirror she laughed at herself for having such a wild imagination. After all, she was only going across to see old Bernard about a book.

The hum and rattle of the boiler grew louder as she went down the steps. Light from where the door had been left ajar lay like a welcome across the area.

"C'min."

She closed the door behind her.

She loved the atmosphere of warmth and dust. Bernard was in his shirt sleeves, spanner in hand, attending to a brass tap on the side of the boiler. Light from a bare bulb overhead glinted auburn on his hair.

"Just having a look at this blessed drain valve." He watched it a minute, held a tin under the spout to see if it still leaked. "Soon have to have a new one. That'll please him, I don't think."

He put the spanner in the spanner section of his toolbox, wiped his fingers on a rag. It was a kind of conversation, him standing there, smiling at her, wiping each finger in turn, saying nothing. She knew he was pleased to see her, knew this was how some men were, conversing without words. How strange they were, she thought, men, at ease with a great black monster that growled and hissed, able to understand such a complicated metal beast, its curved back bristling as if about to explode, and yet be so naive when it came to ordinary things a woman would take for granted, like remembering what was said last time you met.

"You have a look at that book?" she asked.

"Ah!"

He went over to a tea-chest full of folded newspapers, knelt down and methodically removed them until he came to it.

"Here we are!"

He handed her the copy of *Married Love*.

She took it, held it while he replaced the papers. Images of that first evening in the hotel freshened in her mind, the smell of Maggie's room, the colour and patterns of covers and cushions, the excitement of reading what she had never dreamed could be written.

He hadn't got round to reading it yet, he said. Maybe he ought to have looked at it years ago. He'd never had much luck with love.

What about reading it through together? she asked. It might help to hear the woman's side of things. Especially if he were to marry again.

He looked doubtful, would prefer it if Maudie read it to him. He'd understand it better.

He sat on the newspaper chest, content to be read to. But seeing him sitting there, a married man, scarred by the war, so much older than herself, she lost confidence, knew she couldn't carry it off.

She glanced at a sentence, felt the colour rise to her face.

"It's too personal –"

"Don't matter about being personal."

But it mattered to her. She had pictured herself on his knee and him with his arm round her, the pair of them thrilling to a woman's idea of physical love. But with

Bernard sitting away, waiting as a child might wait to hear its mother, she couldn't do it.

"I thought it might help for the boy's sake," she said.

She felt foolish at the situation she had got herself into. It had been a daydream, being alone in the boiler-room with Bernard, reading the Marie Stopes book together. As always it had come to nothing.

"Read it then, Maudie," he said. "You thought it was good?"

It made it worse, having to admit what she'd felt.

"You'll think I'm awful," she murmured.

"Don't bother then, Maudie. The marriage is on the rocks in any case."

"But will you read it for yourself?"

She realised she really did want him to benefit from hearing the book's message, wanted him to benefit from a more understanding view of women. As well as the adventure of it, the flirting, she actually had wanted him to read it for his own sake.

The awareness gave her confidence. Just because a subject was intimate, she said, didn't mean it ought never to be mentioned. Maybe Bernard would marry again, settle down with some nice woman.

"If you do – well, I'd want you to be happy, old bean," she said. "You deserve it."

"Praps I'll get round to reading it."

She had her doubts.

"I'll just read a short bit. So you know the sort of thing it's about."

What she read urged a husband to take note of signs by which he could tell that his wife was ready for love. Many men, by ignoring the woman's needs, ended up destroying the relationship. A woman was less inclined than a man to say what pleased her sexually, though Dr Stopes suggested that kisses on the breast were a good way of stimulating a loving response. A woman's coldness was not so much part of her nature, more a result of the husband's thoughtlessness.

She was heartened enough by Bernard's interest to carry on a bit further. Society, Dr Stopes said, must see to it that women have easy access to contraception, the fear of pregnancy being never far from their thoughts. The possibility of having more and more children to provide for was a constant worry, especially for women who found it a struggle to provide for the children they already had. A marriage preceded by a pregnancy was a poor start –

She stopped, remembered Paddy.

She couldn't understand herself! An idiot would have been more discreet.

"I seem to have come here to make a fool of myself!"

"Sounds as if the woman's hit the nail on the head," Bernard said.

It was his niceness not to take offence. She had a moment of hoping the boiler would explode and take her to oblivion.

"Whatever you must think of me – !"

"It was a poor start," he insisted. "A poor start and a poor finish. Though I wouldn't not have had him. I mean, if the wife and I had settled down and then had a child, well, it wouldn't have been Paddy, you see."

She let the book drop to the floor.

It was always Bernard who was having to make allowances. If he hadn't been such a decent old stick he would have taken advantage of her by now, knowing what had been on her mind these last few days. She was an interfering bitch, no better than her sisters! Wanting to advise him how to live his married life! She, who had never been married!

"Do that doctor woman," Bernard asked, "tell you what to do about love when you come home from France with your face blown in?"

"I know one thing," she said. "If you'd been my husband and got injured, I'd never have deserted you!"

He drew her to her feet, kissed the top of her head.

"I'm too old for a girl of your age to bother about," he murmured.

"I don't care about your age!"

He squeezed her hand, let her go.

She scarcely knew what she felt. Everything she did turned out wrong. She had spent nights longing for him yet had misunderstood him. Perhaps had misunderstood herself.

"And there was this silly girl," she said, "trying to tell this lovely man how to be a better husband!" She picked the book up. "The fire's the best place for this!"

"I daresay I'll get round to reading it in a day or two."

But she hated the sight of it. It had brought little but trouble since the night she found it. "There's nothing my old bean can learn from this."

Bernard took a pair of metal prongs, twisted a lever in the fire door. Heat flooded out. Red and blue flames danced like liquid over the coke inside.

She pitched the book into the furnace. For a moment or two it lay unaltered. Then pages opened, curled, scorched, burst into flame.

She was glad to see it burn. It was one of Maggie's last possessions, perhaps one of her treasures. But it had come to nothing, like most treasures.

Flame and smoke were drawn to the back of the furnace. Glowing threads crept across pages that were already ash.

Bernard clanged the door shut, twisted the lever into place.

"I never read it, Maudie," he joked. "But I know how it ended."

She went back to her room, not sorry how things had turned out.

# CHAPTER 51

She liked dull days. She wanted the rest of her life to be dull, didn't want to get closely involved with people ever again. It was what she liked about hotel guests: you had their company, you could have a laugh and a chat, but you didn't have to know them, didn't have them banging into your thoughts half the night.

So when they said, dull days before Christmas, she was glad of it. Everything to do with people went wrong. She had met the Major countless times in daydreams, yet the day they'd met face to face she hadn't had the sense to stop and talk. Never mind that nowadays she'd have many things to say, if she met him again she doubted if she'd remember a word. And in the boiler-room with Bernard – poor old Bernard! What had she been thinking of!

Other people too! There was Maggie, who'd felt the best way out of her trouble was to kill herself. Bernard, parted from his wife and his son. Her brother Herbert, in love with his cousin, of all people! The Major's wife, out of her mind. Malcolm Steward, his head full of heaven knows what, and his wife in love with another man. And her dear Pa, looking for the shapes of his loved ones in the fire! When it came to people there was always something wrong. So if the days before Christmas were dull, she was glad of it. She hoped 1921 would be a dull year.

The hotel was full, would be full well into the New Year. As Mr Perkins had told them, the hotel didn't just accommodate guests, it had to persuade guests to accommodate the hotel. Unlike some staff she didn't begrudge guests enjoying what most people couldn't afford. She liked them to come, liked to be busy, didn't mind if the men smelt of cigars, and their wives of perfume and port wine. And she didn't take offence if now and then a coin was pressed into her hand for being such a nice young lady or that occasionally she was asked for a kiss under the mistletoe. As Mr Perkins said, it was guests that paid the wages. And if they kept you going early and late you'd sleep like a log come bedtime.

Christmas drew nearer. The mood of the guests was more urgent. People were frantic to enjoy themselves, determined to have a good time come what may. It was as though under the cheerfulness something was lying in wait. Everyone was saying the country couldn't go on like this. Trouble was on the way. There'd have to be cutbacks soon. Things had got out of proportion. Then they'd order another round of drinks and talk about something more cheerful. Maudie quite liked the feeling. It was like ghost talk in the country: it made sitting round the fire all the cosier.

She was glad not to be going home for Christmas. All you had to look forward to there was getting indoors at the end of the day – and then there'd be the coal to get in and the freezing cold dairy to be cleaned, let alone any other little joys her sisters would have in store for her. Give me London, she thought. London was the place for Christmas.

The dark green foliage of the Christmas tree was hung about with crackers and baubles and trimmings and lights. At home they hadn't bothered about a tree for years. Her

Pa used to bring home half a waggon-load of holly and ivy and deck it across the chimney piece and over the doors and behind the pictures till you hardly knew whether you were indoors or in the garden. Poor old Pa, she thought. She really ought to get round to sending him a card.

Christmas Day she got up as usual, pitched into her work as usual, treated it as much as possible like any other day. Not being interested in the get-together, she told Mr Perkins she would be happy to be on evening duty in reception. He told her she should go and enjoy herself. He and Mrs Critoph would take duty in turns. There wouldn't be much to do.

"You're only young once. Nobody knows what'll happen next year."

It was like joining a happy family, going into the staffroom. Nowadays, aware that she could give as good as she got, everyone welcomed her, and seeing that she could work as hard as the best of them they seemed to have forgotten the earlier hostility.

"Come on in, Maudie," they called. "The more the merrier."

The tables had been put into the corridor, the chairs drawn back to the walls, the bit of green lino polished and asking to be danced on. Mr Took was in charge of the gramophone, its rosy-pink horn curving out as open as a flower. He beckoned her over, told her he'd got just the record for her, and Mr Lexford took her on the floor. He was easy to dance with, light on his feet, finding spaces to dance into and out of, as if he was gliding round tables in the restaurant with her on his arm instead of a napkin.

*M- M-M-M-Maudie,* he sang, and the others joined in, *My beautiful Maudie!* and whirled her round till she felt happier and more at ease than she'd felt for ages. She was glad she'd come, grateful to Mr Perkins for persuading her, grateful to Malcolm and Nancy for getting her into the hotel in the first place. These six months, she considered, with all their ups and downs had been the best six months of her life, and this evening was going to be one of the nicest. There was dear old Bernard and Rosie and Iris and June and all the others – and Mrs Critoph in a lovely blue dress. She loved them all, wanted to reward them for being so friendly and nice, even though she'd kept herself to herself for so long.

There being more women than men she had a dance with Rosie. They chatted, chiefly about Peter and Tony. Very few men came up to scratch, they said. There must be a good one somewhere, they said. But though they were the best of friends again, when she saw Rosie's face close to she wondered whether there was something different about the girl.

Rosie murmured, "There's a sight!"

Mr Took and Iris were dancing, their fat stomachs touching, Iris's rough red hand on his suit, the pair of them bouncing their way round the floor, each enjoying the other's company.

"The next dance, ladies and gentlemen, is for Mrs Critoph!"

And Mr Lexford wound the handle, lowered the arm, and played *Alice Blue Gown,* and as the old lady and her partner danced, he was kind enough to lead the singing.

"The old cow's enjoying that!" Rosie remarked.

Maudie was glad the old girl looked so charmed, glad Mr Lexford had Christmas spirit enough to lead the singing. It was nice when people were nice, when they said nice things and did nice things.

"Here he is!"

A whisper, sharp, like a warning.

Peter had come in the other side of the room. Already in drink, he stood looking about him, faintly amused at what was going on. Rosie knocked back her drink, stood the glass down on the floor, her smile ready for him.

He seemed to gravitate towards her, had a few words with staff. Yes, he was still at Welwyn. No, he couldn't say when it would be finished. He wasn't in charge. He did what he was told and took the money. He didn't give a damn when it'd be finished.

It was as if someone had opened the door and let the warmth out.

He made his way closer, stood there, swaying a little, waiting to be made a fuss of.

"Get your coat off," Rosie said. "I'll get you some sandwiches. What'd you like to drink?"

"Whisky," he said. "Neat. Don't want none of that soda muck in it."

Rosie went to get it, Peter eyed her body as she walked. Then he turned, eyed Maudie the same way, as if she was an animal on a farm.

She said she was glad he'd got his name down for a house at Welwyn.

He gave her a sour look. "Why?"

Did he know when it would be ready to move into?

How the devil should he know? Did she want to move in with him or something?

Rosie came back with a whisky and a plate of sandwiches.

"Move into?" he mimicked. "She wants to know when it'll be ready to move into. They haven't picked the site yet, the silly bitch!"

"Never mind," Rosie laughed. "It'll get finished one day."

"Oh, well!" he jeered. "If you say so!"

"Like a dance, Maudie?" It was Bernard. She was glad to join him, was comfortable with him, the way he held her, his disfigured cheek against her hair.

*They fly so high, nearly reach the sky*
*Then like my dreams they fade and die...*

"Looks like Peter's had a drop too much."

Bernard didn't respond. He hardly ever gossiped or made a remark about anyone. It was a pity. It stopped her being as close to him as she might have been.

"What did Father Christmas bring you?" he asked

"Father Christmas?" It was the way he said it.

He didn't really believe in him, he said, but he liked the idea of a kind old man in a red cloak. And no-one could be sure he didn't exist somewhere, could they?

She squeezed his hand as they walked off. She liked him, didn't care what he believed.

Someone told her someone was in the corridor, wanted to see her.

Her heart sank. She went to the door. Too late remembered the mistletoe. Not that she minded a kiss under the mistletoe, but Tony kissed her woodenly, as if it was something he ought to do rather than what he wanted to do.

"Bring him in, bring him in," Martin Took said. "The more the merrier. On the floor, both of you!"

They found their way on to the floor. Maudie touched her hanky to her lips to get rid of the kiss.

"Tell you what," he said as they danced.

The new garden city was going to have a restaurant with a dance floor! And come Easter when it was due to open, there was going to be an application for a drinks licence! "Might take a year to come through. But there could be an opening for Rosie and Peter to run the drinks side of it! Think they'd be interested?"

Rosie would be, she said. It was Peter. Might be better to mention it when Peter wasn't there.

She knew they looked well together, Tony in his dark suit, his hair nicely trimmed, she in her dark blue dress. But he was so wooden! If only he'd let the music in and get his mind off being so serious!

"Something else I should have mentioned. The Company had been in touch with manufacturers such as Shredded Wheat, Palmers, Dawnays, Murrays, and there was talk of starting up a shirt and tie factory. There'd be work for hundreds – -"

The evening was passing, and here she was, stuck with Tony and his incessant dreaming.

"Did I tell you I'd got my name down for a house?"

"You did," she sighed. "So has Peter."

"Peter?"

"Weeks ago."

"Peter!"

He gave up his pretence at dancing, walked her towards the door.

She guessed from his face. "He wouldn't have made it up, would he?"

"Wouldn't he?" Tony was quite definite. All applications went to his committee. He himself kept a copy of the list, so he knew exactly who had applied. Anyway, he knew Peter! Would have been surprised if Peter's name had been on the list.

They watched Rosie and Peter dancing, perhaps the best pair on the floor, perfect with the music, Rosie leaning back, happy, Peter expressionless, intent.

"My name's down, though," Tony said. "So we don't have to worry."

It wasn't her he was seeing. He was looking at his future. She was merely a bit of its furniture.

"Tony. I'm not going to live at Welwyn. I live here. I like living here."

"But you'll want a change in a year or two. You'll want something better than this."

*But a voice in her heart was saying she'd seen the moonbow, the signpost to the best of heavens, being with the one you loved – -*

"Come over here."

She beckoned him under the mistletoe and kissed him.

"You're a dear friend. Always remember that."

She supposed it was extravagant of her. She didn't care. She knew what the future had in store for her, and felt extravagant.

Rosie was sitting the dance out. While Peter had gone to get more drinks Tony told her about the proposed restaurant, the application for a licence, the possibility of jobs.

Her face lit. "So there could be jobs for both of us!"

"Could be jobs for half London," Peter said, "if anyone wanted to go and live in such a dump." He had come back behind them, drinks and a half bottle of whisky on a tray. "No proper pub there for miles. Who'd want to go and live in a godforsaken dump like that!"

There'd be hundreds of jobs, Tony said. They were even talking of building a power station there.

"Power station! You must want your head felt! They can't build a piss-house, let alone a power station!"

"If Welwyn is a success," Tony said, "we could build a dozen new towns. It's what we need to make England a better place."

"If you think this country'll ever be a better place," Peter jeered, "you're a bigger fool than I thought you were."

"It's what the war was for. We've got to try to make things better. It's what all that killing was about – the chance to do it better."

Peter belched. "We went to war because we had to! That's why we went to war. All that talk about a land fit for heroes to live in! England'll always be the same for the likes of you and me, mate, same as it always was – a scrap-heap! Don't you kid yourself it'll ever be any different."

He opened the whisky, took a long swig, leered around for people to agree with him. "Bloody scrap-heap, this country!"

Tony ignored him, began describing the plan to keep some original trees and meadow land on a site to be called Meadow Green, which they hoped would remain unspoiled so children would have somewhere open to play on.

Rosie loved the idea. And Martin Took, having overheard something of what Tony had been saying, asked if he'd mind coming over when he had a moment and telling him and Mr Lexford a bit about the place. "Supposing the time comes when we have to leave here," he murmured.

"We used to have to play in dirty old alleys when we were kids," Rosie recalled. "Remember, Peter? Climbing on the railings – on the high pavement? And them old cellars?"

"If you say so, Rosie."

His eyes wandered over her femaleness.

"I do say so, Peter."

"Whatever you say, my love."

His eyes lingered over her, undressing her.

She sat round from him. "That's Peter!"

Where possible, Tony said, they were going to plant

lovely great avenues of trees across the town so the place wouldn't look too built up –

"Avenue heard all that before?" Peter asked around, chuckling at his joke. "Avenue heard all that before?"

"For God's sake! I want to hear about this place! I want a better bloody life than I've had up to now, and if you won't live there, I will!"

"Well," Peter retorted, "what the hell do you think I've been doing, working out there on a building site miles from anywhere, eating in a hut, sleeping in a hut! Who do you think I've been doing it for? Me? Because if you think that's my idea of life, you must want your head felt!"

"No, I don't want my head felt," she flared. "Nor anywhere else felt, if you want to know!"

Peter seemed to stagger, took another swig of whisky. "Now we know! Now we know! There's plenty more fish in the sea, old Rosie!" His eye lit on June. "Even if they are a bit scraggy."

He swayed towards the girl.

"As far as I'm concerned," Rosie called after him, "you can take your name off that list because I wouldn't live with you if it was the last house in England!"

He grinned round to face her. "Well, that's shot you up the arse, Rosie old girl! Because my name ain't on the bloody list and never has been!" He laughed, his teeth strong-looking, yellow.

"You said it was on the list!"

Peter smiled airily around as if a lie was no more than she deserved. "You said it was on the list," he mimicked, his voice squeaky high.

"I told *you*, didn't I, Maudie," Rosie insisted. "He'd written to say his name was on that list!"

Maudie knew how she felt. But it was over. It was only a dream, in any case.

"Last orders from the bar," Victor Lexford called. "Ten minutes till we close."

He closed the gramophone lid, put the records back in their buff brown sleeves, stacked them away in their case. Mr Took and Tony joined him.

Rosie took her glass of sherry, drank it down, banged the glass back on the tray.

"Said he'd put his name down! I was sure he'd got his name down! What's been keeping me going!"

She noticed Maudie's drink on the tray, drank it down as if she needed it, tried to bang it down as well but it missed the tray and fell to the floor.

"Give us a song, Peter," someone called. "Come on, Pete," others called. "We know you can sing."

Peter stood in the middle of the room, his cap on the back of his head, arm extended in the direction of the electric light.

"He's got to be the centre of attention!" Rosie was unsteady, tears down her face.

"Oh, no," Maudie assured her. "It was true, I'm afraid."

"You heard something I ain't heard?"

A few minutes ago, she said. Tony knew who was on the list and who wasn't.

"So you knew!" Rosie stared at her, her face hard. "You all knew! Except me!"

"I'm sorry -"

"Sorry? You're as bad as he is, you cow!"

The word bit down. After all the help she'd tried to give the girl! She turned away, hands to her head, overcome with the injustice of it.

It was a trick that had always put the bitches at a disadvantage.

Rosie glared, waited. In vain.

"What are you trying to tell me?" she demanded.

"Cow!" Maudie echoed. "Cow! When all I'm trying to tell you -"

She turned her back on the girl.

And let her wait.

"What are you trying to tell me?""

"How you could get a place at Welwyn." Maudie hardly looked at her.

"How?" Rosie asked. "How could I get a place there?"

Maudie let her wait, sighed "Oh, dear!" sadly to herself.

"You might as well tell me, Maudie."

Maudie noted the change, the bossiness gone.

"Not much point, you so crazy about his majesty over there!"

"Don't talk to me about him!"

"What I can't make out about you, is why you don't keep in with Tony. You'd have a thousand times better chance with Tony."

"And where would you live? In the attic?"

"Don't you be sarky with me!"

"What do you mean, then? Me run away with Tony?"

"You don't have to run anywhere. I told Tony I wasn't interested in Welwyn, but I said I knew someone who was. Tony knew what I meant, if you don't!"

"What did he say?"

"What did Tony say? It'll be up to you what Tony says. I just hope you treat him better than you do me!"

"Tony?"

Rosie tried to pick him out in the crowd. Her eye lit on Peter.

"Look at him!" she jeered. "Like a little gnome!"

Peter, eyes glazed, arm across his chest, drew a breath as if to start singing, then suddenly looked about the room. "Where's the whisky? Who's got the bloody whisky!"

Bernard held it up for him. Peter focused on it, lurched across to get it.

"You've got the -" He snatched the bottle away, tipped it up, took a long drink.

"Come on, old Pete. Give us a song before you go."

Peter turned. "Go? I aren't bloody going nowhere. I only just got here. I'm with Rosie, aren't I, Rosie?" His attention fastened on Maudie. He pointed her out, his arm unsteady. "Maudie Stelfox. That's who that is!" He seemed to trace her face as he pointed. "I'll tell you something about Maudie Stelfox," he grinned. "When I was alongside Rosie – know what I mean -"

"Shut up!" Rosie warned.

"Maudie come in the room – just the wrong moment, know what -"

Rosie was on her feet. "Keep your trap shut!"

"'Good God!' I said. 'Another one. I shall go blind!'"

Rosie flew at him, knocked him backwards. He fell against a table, slid to the floor, his cap upside down in spilt drink. Beer from an overturned mug trickled down his face.

Rosie, half laughing, half crying, snatched a glass of beer, emptied it over his head.

Someone pushed her in the direction of the door, others helped Peter to his feet.

"Whatever I saw in him!" Rosie cried, coming back. "I've got someone better than him now!" She picked up Peter's cap, flung it hard in his face. "Now laugh!" she howled.

"You wait, you whore!"

Maudie pulled her away, said she'd see her to the bedroom.

Mr Took came over, ordered Peter to clear off. "If you're still here in five minutes I'll call the police."

Peter swore, picked his cap up.

Rosie, crying, laughing, hung on Maudie's arm, unsteady from drink. "Hope I never see that horrible –"

Someone leapt at her from behind. A fury, a madman. His arm raised to strike her.

Maudie saw the jagged edge of the glass, tried to pull him away.

He swung round, tripped, fell towards her.

In the instant before Maudie's head hit the floor it was as though her thigh had been torn apart.

# CHAPTER 52

Her mouth was dry. She couldn't be bothered to get up and get herself a drink.

She slept again. When she came to her head ached. Was thirstier than ever. Rosie had got a scarlet blanket on her bed! Then sleep took her down, away from the pain.

Daylight! She'd be late for work!

Raised her head off the pillow, looked round the room. Scarlet blanket on her own bed too. On all the beds!

She was in hospital!

A nurse asked her how she felt.

Dry, she said. Her tongue was parched.

The nurse came back with a small white teapot with a spout on the side. Before she could give it another good suck it was pulled away.

Hours later the nurse let her drink a little more. It was the anaesthetic, she said. It got on your stomach and made you sick.

Her thigh didn't hurt much. Thick with bandages. All that blood, she'd have thought she'd be in agony.

Plates rattled. Smell of stuffing and potatoes and greens. Women were serving cold turkey for dinner. They looked at the foot of her bed, shook their heads and went past. A nurse came, fastened a rubber tube round her arm, pumped it tight. Felt Maudie's pulse and watched a thing like a barometer. Pumped the tube up again, something wasn't satisfactory. Maudie might be allowed a little supper, she said.

She was back in the staffroom, Peter and Rosie were arguing, both of them drunk. They turned on her. "All your fault, you cow!" He smashed a glass, came towards her, glass raised to slash her. Mrs Critoph calling, "Wake up! Wake up!"

"You have had a sleep," the nurse said.

Her leg stung like misery. Must be bleeding again. Pillow was wet with sweat.

Nurses drew the curtains round, sat her up. They bathed her hands, her face, let her have another drink. Gave her three pillows to lean against, then uncovered the frame and looked at the bandages, but didn't undo them. The younger nurse brought her some pills, the pain started to go away.

When she woke up patients told her how long she'd slept, told her what time the Sunday service was. Then they told her what time Matron's inspection was. It seemed Matron's inspection was the main thing, the way their voices went serious when they spoke about it.

Twenty beds each side in the ward, every bed with a scarlet blanket. The walls were dark green, a coal fire blazed in the fireplace opposite. At the end of the ward near the piano there was a Christmas tree. Almost as pretty as the one in the King James, except it didn't have candles.

Later, the ward sister, nurses and orderlies came round to check everywhere was spick and span. Cupboards were tidied, flowers removed, beds pulled straight, patients' belongings put away. Grown women all of them, flying about like schoolgirls. Sister walked back along the ward like a sergeant-major, her eye searching every bed as she went.

Matron came in.

Stern, strong face and iron-grey hair. She noted patients' names, read their notes, had a word with each. The patients, especially the older ones, thanked her for asking, nervous, as if their stay in hospital depended on her goodwill. Matron said nothing, moved to the next patient. Maudie noticed that while she might point out a rucked blanket to the sister, or indicate something out of place, she never remarked how tidy or well looked after anything was.

She stopped at Maudie's bed. Asked her if she was feeling better. The cool grey eyes waited. There was no knowing what those eyes had seen. Maudie looked a strong young girl. The leg should soon improve, but it was tricky where glass was concerned.

Maudie felt better. Matron had seen her, knew what to do. Matron was one of those people you could believe were related to God.

The matron's round completed, the chaplain came in to take Sunday evening service. Silly little man, watery face and watery smile. He kept his lips together as if his breath smelt. When he prayed he angled his face upwards, strained and screwed it up as if he was on the lavatory.

An elderly woman was in the bed opposite, yellow skin tight over the jaw, the jawbone like a corpse. When the chaplain prayed, the old woman prayed too, toothless mouth moving to the words of the prayer, lips tight as the rim of a cup. Maudie hoped God was listening to her. But the sight of him straining away as if he was on the lavatory made her want to giggle – and then she was crying. Sobbed aloud, because the only way God could help the old woman was to take her up into His arms, lift her away from her corpse and take her into heaven.

There were days and nights of pain. "You've got very low," Sister told her. "What you want to think about is getting better." Elsewhere in the ward women recovered and went home, other sick women took their places, an unending stream of disease and mishap.

One old woman came in with a broken leg. When she came round after her operation, an extension had been rigged up over her bed, her leg was in traction and a tin of lead shot hung from the extension to provide tension.

"They're trying to pull my leg off! What have I done to deserve that!"

A nurse explained what the apparatus was for, what they were trying to do.

"Oh, I see, dear."

The next minute the old girl had forgotten, called out to people to cut the thing down so she could get her leg back.

"If only they'd let me have my leg back! Just for a day or two! What do they want to cut my leg off for?"

Maudie was on the mend. One evening when she was chatting to the woman in the next bed she was aware of a visitor.

The same colourful cheeks, same tawny hair.

"I'll never be able to thank you. What you did." Rosie's eyes were kind, like a mother's. "What a mercy you saw him! Would have gone in my neck!"

Seemed to come from nowhere, Maudie said. It was a mercy he tripped.

"He's done his hand in," Rosie told her. "Glass went right through it. Dreadful! Right through it!"

Peter was in the men's ward, looked like being there some time. People were saying someone ought to bring a case against him. Mr Perkins had been to see him, so perhaps he was going to.

Had she seen much of Tony lately?

They'd had a chat, she said. What a relief to be able to talk to a man without him always alluding to sex! "No wonder you went out with him. He's so different."

"He asked me to marry him."

Rosie looked choked.

"What did you tell him?"

She took her time. Peter and Rosie between them had ruined what could have been a lovely evening.

"Told him to ask someone else. You'd suit him a treat, I should think. If you aren't pregnant, that is."

Rosie hovered between laughing and being cross. "About the only thing the little bugger was careful about."

"I didn't only mean Peter." It was something that had to be said. The girl had to face facts some time.

Rosie's face flamed.

"I can only go by what you tell me," Maudie told her. "You'd ruin it with Tony if you got pregnant."

They faced each other out, will against will. Maudie knew who would win.

Rosie turned away. "No need to think it's something I want to do."

Maudie lay back. She was tired. She had done her best. If Rosie wanted to make the worst of her life no-one could stop her. No-one was making the girl sell herself.

"Anyway," Rosie said. "Don't let's worry about that now." Her voice was kind. Maudie felt like being soothed. "There's me supposed to be cheering you up. First you save my life, then you try and find me a husband, and all I do is bring bad news."

Maudie gripped the bedclothes, her face cold.

It was Mr Perkins. Would Rosie like Maudie's job? Permanently.

Maudie felt sick with the shock of it, couldn't bring herself to look at the girl.

"I told him I couldn't do it. I told him I wouldn't take your job away even if I could do it."

"What did he say?"

"He asked me if I'd be seeing you. Said it would be better if you heard it from me."

"Heard what?"

Rosie leaned over, confidential. "He's got some old woman in!"

"In?"

"In the office! Doing your job, Maudie! She's awful. Worse than Beryl!"

The words rang round like dream words, nightmare words. If she woke up she might find it was true.

Rosie shook her arm. "Maudie!"

Maudie lay still, eyes open, couldn't believe, couldn't disbelieve. It was the end of the world.

"Oh, when d'you think you'll be out? Can I tell him you'll be back soon?"

Maudie closed her eyes, let the girl leave. Rosie had done enough.

The nurses were concerned, said she'd had a setback. Sister spent time with her, asked her questions. What she replied Maudie couldn't tell. She wanted to sleep.

She didn't blame Mr Perkins. She blamed Rosie. Rosie hadn't bothered to come till she could bring bad news.

When she got out of bed a few days later it was like taking all her weight on her wound. This was agony. This was what she wanted. This was what she deserved.

When she was able to walk she stood still to let the pressure build up round the wound. She wanted the pain to get worse, wanted it to hurt.

They told her to walk. Walking was what was needed now.

If it was only a matter of pain she could walk all night. She could walk all round London if she wanted to. What she needed was somewhere to walk to. Like her job.

One night she was walking back to the King James, heard someone walking with her. "You must get better, my dear. For my sake." Richard smiled at her for being so startled. He came close, walked close to protect her. "It's been so long," he murmured. "I miss you so much!"

She woke up. Alone. His voice was still with her. "I miss you so much!" She closed her eyes, tried to see him again, tried to remember the street, where it was he walked. "I miss you so much!"

"And I miss you, dear Major!" she whispered.

What a fool to wake up! Everything was empty without him!

But he had come to her again. Loved her as much as ever.

During the day she made her mind up. Losing her job was only pain. She would get over it, get another job, go out and meet Richard – and then it came to her that she hadn't lost her job. It was only what Rosie had told her. She'd have heard from Mr Perkins by now if she had. Yet even if she did lose her job she could bear it. For his sake.

The nurses were kind, helped her move about, helped her get better. Another shift came on, nurses she hadn't seen before. They were nice too. She liked their young faces, but there was no telling what they'd seen, what they'd had to look at, what they'd had to do.

Then she noticed her.

"I was hoping they'd keep you here till my duty changed. Didn't want you getting better and rushing off before I'd seen you." Kate was cleaning the cupboards, windowsills, bed rails. "A cleaner's ill – Matron asked me – so now I can come and see you."

Looked so pleased to see her.

She asked how Maudie had got injured, how she was feeling, she asked what her work was like, how the family was, how Muriel was enjoying married life. Maudie told her, but was more interested in Kate's white belt. Why all those different coloured belts the nurses wore?

The white belt was for first-year nurses, Kate told her. The next year it would be lilac, then dark purple, and after that, if she passed all her exams, she'd be State Registered. The colour of that one? Oh, navy blue, she thought.

She was generally too busy to stay long, but the night before Maudie was to be discharged she used her hour off to go and see her. She was happy enough to talk about nursing, and Maudie was happy to listen because it sounded a lot worse than working in a hotel.

According to Kate, student nurses had to buy their own uniform, which cost twenty pounds, had to pay for their own fares and books and exams. In return they got their training, their own room, they got eighteen pounds a year and almost enough to eat. Fortunately, patients smuggled them some of the food their visitors brought in, otherwise nurses could go pretty hungry. Harvest Festival, Kate told her, was an event they all dreaded. The first couple of days the bread and plaited loaves were very welcome; it was later on, when the hospital moistened and reheated the gift bread, then moistened and reheated it again, day after day. It was awful stuff. The day it was all gone they held their own service of thanksgiving.

If a girl didn't mind putting up with a few regulations, Kate said, she could recommend nursing as a career, though rules might vary from hospital to hospital. Here at the *Charles Lamb* hospital one rule was that the window of your room had to be open exactly six inches, and another rule was that no more than nine personal items were allowed to be visible in the room. Everything else had to be put in cupboards or drawers, and woe betide you if your room wasn't as tidy as it ought to be. If Matron didn't want two particular nurses to be friends she would tell them not to see each other or go out together. When a nurse did go out she had to wear a hat and stockings and turn her cape the scarlet side out rather than the dark blue. If a nurse broke a rule or displeased Matron she might be prevented from going out on her day off.

"Sounds like prison! And you're going to stick it for four years?"

The thing was, Kate said, most women were already in a kind of prison. Always had been. If she could help them improve their lives she didn't mind giving up a few years to do it. As she saw it, the curse of mankind was fertility. The human race continually overproduced itself. Villages grew into towns, suburbs expanded across the countryside, town merged with town. The only species that culled mankind was mankind itself, through war and starvation and global misery. She believed the relief of these evils lay in the control of fertility.

"If women were physically stronger," Kate said, "if a woman could knock her husband about, or lift him off her, fertility might not matter so much. But as things are, it's what the man wants that counts. If a man wants his pleasure he takes it, and leaves the woman to look after the consequences."

Almost every society favoured the male, she said. It was the custom for the eldest male to inherit, for the male name to be handed down, for a male to be paid more than a female doing the same work. Women, even in these 1920s, were not as eligible to vote as men, and hadn't been able to vote at all till 1918. A male priest asked the woman to obey the man in marriage; if a woman found herself with an unwanted pregnancy, male laws prevented her having an abortion safely or cheaply or legally; if ever she went to litigation she found herself facing a male judge and a male jury administering justice which was little more than a male point of view, having been framed over the centuries entirely by men. And the all-male staff of the Church from vicars to archbishops and the Pope preached the male view of morality, which was no surprise seeing that Jahweh and God and all their prophets were male as well.

"Somehow or other," Kate said, "society has got to be educated into a woman-view of life."

Few women wanted a bigger family than they could clothe, or more children than could feed, or so much childbearing that it ruined their health and reduced their ability to look after the children they already had.

"What on earth do you think you can do about all that?" Maudie asked.

"When I'm qualified, at least I'll be able to join those who're already trying."

It seemed a tall order. Didn't leave much room for a personal life.

"But what about you yourself, Kate?"

She had in mind that evening in her Pa's study, Kate's voice and Herbert's voice in the twilight, the way Kate had made sure it was Herbert and only Herbert who took her in the trap to Beckthorp station.

"Got any nice young man in view?"

But Kate had gone to give the patient in the next bed a glass of water.

"Poor dear!" she explained when she came back. "She gets so hot and bothered. What were you saying, Maudie?"

"I was wondering whether you caught the train all right that night."

"Train?"

"When Herbert took you to the station – after the wedding."

Kate looked surprised. "Didn't Herbert come back?"

"Didn't say much, though."

Kate agreed. Herbert wasn't a gossip. She'd noticed that in Yorkshire.

"Barbara tells me he's bought that butcher's shop back home," Maudie told her. "Looked a dreadful old shack to me."

"Oh, I'm sure he'll make a go of it. Once Herbert sets his mind on a thing -"

"What sort of thing, Kate?"

"Who can tell, Maudie?"

It was time she was back on duty. She hoped Maudie would make a good recovery. Asked her to give her Pa and family her best wishes when she wrote.

Maudie watched her move briskly away down the ward. Foolish bitch, letting herself be bossed about by a narrow-minded matron, working her fingers red raw just because she'd set her mind on being a nurse!

What she herself wanted was better than anything in the world. The promise of the moonbow was going to come true. One day she and Richard would meet, and when they did, they'd never part. Might not be yet, might not be soon, but one day it would.

With that in mind she slept soundly all night long.

"You *are* looking better!" Sister told her next morning. "I don't think you'll look back now."

"That I shan't, Sister. I've got something lovely to look forward to!"

# CHAPTER 53

"Mr Perkins is busy at the moment."

Mrs Adkins' silvering hair was swept back to a bun, her eyes framed by steel spectacles. "I can't think when he'll be free!"

"Busy or not," Maudie said, "I must see him as soon as possible!"

Mrs Adkins wavered over the appointments diary.

"I'd hate to be in your shoes," Maudie told her, "when Mr Perkins finds out you've stopped me seeing him."

Mrs Adkins, flustered at being spoken to in such a tone, shuffled the pages, got mixed up over which day it was.

"Everything here's in a muddle! Whatever that last receptionist was up to!"

"Today's Wednesday," Maudie read the diary upside down. "Mr Perkins can see me then!" She pointed to the first slot after lunch.

Mrs Adkins checked the day and the week. Checked again. At which Maudie sighed, drummed her fingers.

"Miss Stelfox, did you say?" She wrote the entry with an old-fashioned flourish.

"One l in Stelfox," Maudie told her after the woman had written it. And felt a thrill of revenge. "Never mind." She sighed, as if mistakes were all you could expect from such an old hen.

In the kitchen they made a fuss of her, said it was nice of her to pay them a visit. Rosie owed her her life, they said.

Peter was still in hospital. His hand was terrible. Glass had gone clean through it. Probably lost the use of it. No-one to blame but himself. Rosie was out somewhere. Her day off.

Bernard was the real welcome, his poor face twisted round in a smile at seeing her. Said the ordinary things in his stuttery old way, but she could feel the friendship in him, knew he was truly her friend.

It was almost two o'clock.

They wished her luck, called after her as she went out, hoped she'd make a full recovery – whatever the outcome of her meeting with Perkins.

Their voices! As if there was doom in the air.

Mr Perkins told her to sit down, asked her how she was, asked about her injury.

"Do they think it'll be all right eventually?"

"It's all right now!" she insisted.

Terrible affair, he said. He'd been really worried. When he heard she'd had a relapse after Rosie Durrell's visit he'd begun to wonder if she'd ever get better.

" Better? I'm looking forward to starting again. As soon as possible."

He told he'd been to see Peter in hospital. "Doesn't know what he'll be able to do. Probably lost the use of his hand."

"Serve him right. After what he tried to do."

Mr Perkins raised an eyebrow. He collected some papers from a drawer, put them in an envelope.

"I've given you a real good testimonial in with your papers here. And a list of some hotels you can try."

He handed her the envelope.

She was being shown the door! She couldn't move.

"You won't want to hang about without a job," he told her. "I expect you'll get one in no time."

"Why not sack that old cow instead?"

He looked surprised, his ferret-mouth open.

"Get rid of her," Maudie said. "Instead of me."

"Get rid of -"

Her meaning seemed to dawn on him. "Get rid of Mrs Adkins?"

It seemed a novel idea. Not altogether disagreeable. "We assumed - I mean, we didn't dream you'd be able to come back - or even want to."

"I'm a hundred times better than that old woman," Maudie told him. "I'd got everything going just right. I've worked night and day -"

Mr Perkins put a finger to his lips. "It couldn't be -" He stared at her, his eyes searching about for meaning. "Couldn't be that I've been misinformed? Could it?"

He went to the door, told Mrs Adkins to go and ask Mrs Critoph to come and see him. "Go now," he ordered. "Something unexpected's come up."

He closed the door, opened it again and snapped, "Urgent, I tell you!"

"My leg's practically better," Maudie was more than willing to correct any false impression he might have.

Mr Perkins put a finger to his lips, gestured her to sit down. "I want to tell you something, Maudie." He spoke confidentially, his voice no more than a murmur. "Your work here has been excellent. I never thought we'd get anyone so good - after poor Maggie. You're just what we want. If only I could see my way clear -"

He seemed as if he really wanted to help her.

"Tell me, my dear." He spoke gently. "Tell me the truth. It is true, isn't it?"

"What is?"

"That you want to leave because you're going to bring a case against Peter Masters. Or help the police to? Attempted murder?"

The notion astonished her.

"I quite understand," he said, "if you don't wish to discuss it. No doubt you've already been in touch with the police?"

"Oh!" she breathed. "Oh, no! You've got it all wrong."

He was patient with her, waited for her to collect herself.

"Wherever did you get that idea from?" She almost felt sorry for him being so misled.

"You mean, you're not going to prosecute?"

Though it would be the police who actually prosecuted, he explained, with her as chief witness.

"Prosecute? Good God, no!" She had her suspicions where that lie had come from.

Mr Perkins leaned back, the beard under his skin already darkening.

When he'd first heard of the Christmas Night affair, he explained, he'd assumed it was an accident. Which was what he'd told the hospital. And that was what he still believed it was. In fact, when he'd seen Peter in hospital he'd told him everyone assumed it was an accident, just a terrible accident. Then he'd heard there was going to be a prosecution, with all that that would mean for the hotel. "But now you're telling me, Maudie, you're not going to prosecute?"

"Never entered my head."

It was as bad as being in Beckthorp, she thought, these lies springing up out of nowhere.

"Let me get this clear." He was puzzled, wanted to get to the bottom of her intentions as much for her sake as for his. "You're telling me you're absolutely not going to prosecute Peter Masters?"

"Absolutely not." She was only too pleased to put the poor man straight. "It's the last thing I want to do, get mixed up with the police."

Mr Perkins sighed, smiled across at her, leaned back in his chair.

"If that's all you're worried about," Maudie told him, "you've nothing to worry about."

"Maudie." It was as if she was an old friend. He opened a drawer, took out another envelope, this one tied with red tape. He withdrew a document, smoothed it out. "Maudie. Not that I want to influence you in the least. You know me better than that. But the long and short of it is, if you'd like to sign this I'm pretty sure we could get you your job back"

She asked what it said. Not that it mattered what it said. Her job was all she was concerned about.

She was more than welcome to read it, he said. All it amounted to was a statement that she had no intention of going to court over the accident that occurred on Christmas Night. Or of saying anything to the newspapers.

"Newspapers?" She laughed, scarcely bothered to read the form in front of her. She felt at home in the room, felt quite at home with Perky. "I haven't the slightest intention of saying anything to anybody. I wouldn't even tell Malcolm Steward."

He seemed easier. His dark ferret-eyes shone as he smiled, no longer darting here and there on the hunt.

"I think you're wise. I think you're very wise. Of course, Peter might say you pushed him, made him fall and nearly cut his hand off." It wasn't what he was saying, he hastened to add. It was what some crafty lawyer might say in court. "You know how they wring these things round. You might even end up having to pay him damages. That's what been on my mind."

"Him? Damages? If I see that little -!"

He calmed her down, amused at her temper. "I tell you I've been to see him. He signed his form a week ago. In hospital."

Mr Perkins, she realised, was a lot more thoughtful than she'd given him credit for.

Mrs Critoph came in. Mr Perkins told her the news, that Maudie had decided to come back on the staff.

"I'm glad about that, Maudie. I really am." Maudie had a shiver of apprehension. Here she was, with the two most important people in the hotel, and both of them as pleased as punch to have her back.

"If you wouldn't mind witnessing her signature, Mrs Critoph?"

Maudie knew she was amongst friends. The room, in which she had been half terrified in earlier days, was quite a comfortable room now. Mr Perkins was more of a friend than an employer. As for Mrs Critoph, she seemed like a well-to-do old aunt, strict, but one who thought a lot of you deep down.

"If you'd just sign there, Maudie." Mr Perkins handed her his personal pen. She took it, felt honoured to hold it. In her best handwriting she signed where he told her. Mrs Critoph knew all about the document, didn't need to be told where to sign.

"Just one thing," she said. "If Maudie could start today? Mrs Adkins -"

She indicated the office. Mrs Adkins was no doubt throwing a fit.

"You can start today?" Mr Perkins asked her. "Now?"

Spoken like an order. But to Maudie it was music.

Mr Perkins stalked out. The rattle of the typewriter stopped. Maudie, her ear to the door, caught the gist of the exchange.

"You can collect your things, Mrs Adkins. You needn't finish that."

He didn't speak confidentially, didn't try to soften what he said to her.

"Engaged another secretary!" The woman sounded furious. She'd come to this hotel at short notice. How dare he just come out and tell her she was dismissed!

Her work wasn't up to standard. He didn't believe she'd had any experience as a secretary, believed she was there under false pretences.

"Go it, Perky!" she whispered.

"False pretences!" Mrs Adkins had worked at the Empire Hotel. A bigger hotel than this! The manager had begged her to not to leave. She knew how a hotel ought to be run!

In that case she'd soon find another job, Perky said. She'd made too many blunders. He wanted her gone in the next thirty minutes.

Mrs Adkins argued, Perkins ignored her, told her she should be glad she'd got money in lieu of notice. He'd send the porter to carry her things out.

Maudie sat herself back in her seat. glad he'd got rid of the woman, glad he refused to listen. She could picture his face, the ferrety mouth, the pitiless eyes. Mrs Adkins might as well have been a rabbit trying to argue with a weasel.

Mr Perkins came back in. "Maudie. I nearly forgot."

It amused her how forgetful men were.

"We've had an awful lot of expenditure over Christmas.

Got through a lot of pennies. I'm having to ask all of us, including myself, to take a wee cut in our wages."

In Maudie's case it would only be a shilling or so a week. She'd scarcely notice it. Mrs Adkins had been doing the job for less than he was paying Maudie. At least Maudie's job was safe. One or two might have to go but hers was as safe as houses.

"As long as I'm back," she said. "That's the main thing."

He said he was glad she liked the hotel so much.

"The day Nancy brought me here," she told him, "was one of the best days of my life."

Mr Perkins filled his pipe, lit up, was willing to chat. Maudie had done well, he said, had certainly done her bit towards getting the hotel back on its feet. "This Nancy you mention," he said, trying to remember. "A relation of yours, is she? Or is it Mr Vincy who's the relation?"

He seemed vague. It was right what Muriel used to say: men only half listen to what you tell them.

It was Malcolm Steward who was the relation, she explained, glad to be able to put him right. Nancy was his wife, and Mr Vincy was the man Nancy worked for.

She had a feeling she'd been over this earlier, somewhere. Not that it mattered. He'd be sure to have forgotten again in a day or two.

"This Malcolm Steward," he said, puffing away at his pipe. "He's the man on *The Daily Brief,* isn't he? I hadn't quite realised."

"It's only a shilling or so a week," she told them in the kitchen. "He said I'd hardly notice it."

"Hard job to notice what isn't there," Mr Took joked. "You've had a pay cut. Like the rest of us."

In the evening Rosie came back. She'd had a lovely day out over at Welwyn. Tony had shown her where the streets would be when they got built. And the Cherry Tree. And Tony's new house.

She was all Tony this and Tony that. "We just sat and talked. Making plans. It was lovely." She sounded relaxed, happier than she'd been for months.

"Pity it isn't Leap Year," Maudie laughed. "Then you could propose to him."

"Oh, I don't think we need a Leap Year," Rosie said.

# CHAPTER 54

It was the time of year for early flowers. In a corner of the hotel yard behind the stables a few aconites and crocuses had forced their way up. This area was once a garden, was still a marvel to see the flowers so bright amongst the rubbish.

The delivery men had come from the brewery. A young man lowered the barrel inch by inch. It reached the floor, was rolled into position by Bernard down in the cellar.

"That's the lot! Sign here, Bernard, an' we can be awa'!"

Ropes were coiled, gear was tidied away, Bernard came up to sign for the delivery.

"God, Bernard! Who's this dark-haired young lassie you've got here?"

He rolled the name round in his mouth several times, couldn't take his eyes off her.

"A wee pretty name for a lassie to go to bed with!"

She couldn't stay. But back in the office her thoughts were full of a young man with red-yellow hair and blue eyes full of the devil, repeating her name as if he loved the sound of it.

After work she went back into the yard. It was dark, the cellar doors were locked, the dray had gone. She looked at where he had stood, tried to see by the light from the outside lamp if his shoes had left their print in the dust.

She asked Bernard about him.

"Alexander MacAllister. Scotchman, o' course. Smart young chap!"

He wasn't a drayman at all, worked in the office, was helping out while someone was off with a bad back.

One day she noticed a white crocus in bud.

"Before you fade," she said, "he'll be back."

Next day it was open, a little white wineglass amongst the rubbish. She loved how white it was, how untouched by the muck it had grown through.

Soon it became a ruin. The yellow poker shrivelled, the petals died, were of no more account than the bits of tile and faded pottery in the soil around.

Night-times she would look out of the bedroom window in hopes he might come back to see her. Weeks passed. She couldn't be sure whether she was remembering him or just imagining a well-built young man with red-yellow hair and his eyes full of the devil.

Rosie hadn't seen him, couldn't think who on earth Maudie had in mind.

"I thought it was Bernard you were sweet on."

"I do like Bernard," Maudie agreed.

"I like Tony. And I used to like Peter. And one or two others. But I was never so round the twist as you are with this Alexander."

Her advice was not to let him know how she felt. Never tell any of them, she said.

"They'll only make a fool of you."

Bernard was forking clean dry straw in the stables.

The dray would be coming next day, he told her.

Tomorrow was a bad day for her to get away, she said. Couldn't Bernard find out something about him? Any sort of thing. She couldn't tell him what – just anything

– like whether he was married, for instance. Just find out anything? Old Bean?

Rosie got a letter.

It was from Tony, to the effect that the Welwyn project was short of money. So short that it was having to manufacture its own bricks. How long it could keep going he didn't know. Even the wages were sometimes late.

Same old Tony, Maudie thought when Rosie told her. A love-letter to warm any girl's heart.

Then she got a letter.

It was from Malcolm Steward. Could she come over to Upper Norwood? Nancy was poorly.

Hunter's Hill was off the Anerley Road. Large houses stood either side of the steep tree-lined road. There were secluded gardens, and public shrubberies with seats and flower beds. The road wound higher, past larger private properties with larger gardens, spiked gates and high ornamental hedges.

She paused for breath, looked back at the view. London lay below, vast and blue and beautiful in a bowl between where she stood and the distant countryside. She wished she was back in the city. Upper Norwood was too well-to-do, a posh onlooker, a neither-town-nor-country sort of place.

She found the house, rang the bell. Rang again.

The door was opened by woman who used to be Nancy.

"If it isn't Maudie Stelfox!" Her thin features lit with welcome.

The living-room was the other end of the hallway.

"Takes me a minute or two," Nancy explained. Maudie took her arm, helped her walk. "One of my less energetic days."

Back in her room she sank on to the chesterfield, her thin frame folding itself away even smaller.

"Malcolm's out." She said it humorously, as though the news might be a surprise. "But he's pretty good to me."

As well-dressed as ever, except that her clothes hung on her. Like a bag of sticks, Maudie thought. Even the way she looked about her had changed, as though she didn't take in what she chanced to be looking at.

"You've been unwell?" Maudie asked.

"My dear girl!" Nancy's fingers, always on the move, stroking her wrist, rubbing the backs of her hands, had worn themselves into bones. Maudie looked for something to do so she didn't have to sit and watch them.

"You could make us a cup of tea," Nancy said. "You may have to wash a couple of cups."

The sink and draining-board were full of unwashed dishes. She washed up some of them, made the tea and took it in.

"You pregnant?" Nancy asked. "Or still as God made you?"

Maudie hoped her face was answer enough.

"Then you stay that way, my dear. If you want a happy life." Nancy sipped her tea, asked how Maudie had come to call in.

Maudie told her, remarked that even the address on the envelope had been typed.

Presumably, Nancy said, because he didn't want anyone to recognise his writing. "Poor Malcolm. He still thinks it's all a conspiracy."

"All what?"

Nancy shook her head. Life, she supposed.

It had been a shock, Maudie admitted, to learn that Malcolm had got her into the *King James* to pass on information about Mr Vincy. "Just like you with your job as his secretary." She kept her voice friendly, but the remark about being pregnant had got under her skin.

In the grate smoke spurted out from a coal. It ignited, became a tiny jet of flame.

"The irony is," Nancy said, "I never told Malcolm anything about the firm or its owner. Information came my way, of course, stuff he'd have found interesting. But I only told him useless everyday things."

The flame died, leaving a jet of smoke into the room. Maudie pressed it away with her foot.

"I never knew what or who I was supposed to keep an eye open for," Maudie said.

"I kept an eye on James," Nancy said. "It was easy to keep an eye on James." Her wan face softened. She had finished her tea. Maudie didn't take her cup in case the hand-rubbing started again.

"Never let anyone tell you," Nancy said, "you can't love two men at once." Even her mouth was thin, the lips close against the teeth. "You don't love the old one less. Just different."

Words dribbled out. She sounded tired, tired to death, but the words came as if there was too much to be held back. Malcolm was the sort of man, she said, who wanted to make the world a better place. If Maudie had any sense she'd keep clear of men like that. They were no good to a marriage.

"What about Mr Vincy?" Maudie asked.

James was different. He didn't want to improve the world, just get a living out of it. He was easy to get on with. You could talk about ordinary things to James. "I never had to wash his shirts, you see."

Maudie took her cup. The hands were restless again, fidgeting with clothes, the cover on the chesterfield.

"I loved that little flat in Chelsea!"

Expensive for James, no doubt, but no more than she deserved. She'd been good for the business. Been good for James as well. "You should see his wife!" Not much support for James or the business there!

"I used to see Malcolm from time to time," she said. Sometimes she'd give him a snippet of news. Nothing confidential. "I suppose I was so happy I thought I owed him something. Maybe I thought James owed him something. Mind you, there were times when I wondered if Malcolm had noticed I'd left."

Her face was lit by firelight. Maudie remembered the devil-may-care look she used to have. Now it was a shadow under her jaw.

"The thing about men is, never give them anything. They get what they want, one way or another."

What, Maudie asked, was all this business about Welwyn Garden City that Malcolm was always on about?

The thin frame stiffened. "I hate the very sound – !"

She clasped herself, rocked to and fro on the chesterfield. "I knew one thing was going on." She glared at the fire, at the hearth, the mantelpiece. "I could have faced that. I was no longer young, and I wasn't married to him, but I could have faced it. That's what I knew was going on!"

She rocked herself, agitated enough for Maudie to sit close because of the open fire in front of them.

"If we'd had a row – or if I'd let him down! Then I'd have known why. But for James to tell me – half past ten in the morning it was – told me *It's got to finish, my dear. It's got to finish!*"

She lurched forward, stumbled to her feet, Maudie holding her arm.

"He was still fond of me. Probably still is. *I'm so terribly sorry.* Said it over and over. *I'm so terribly sorry.* I asked him why, why was it over. Was it his wife? Or me being pregnant? It wouldn't have been so bad if it was that. I could have understood it. But it wasn't. What I've been told, he said. Been told something – we can't go on, you and me. He wouldn't say what. But I insisted. Something to do with that new town, I gathered, something his business needed. 'If you ever loved me,' I said, 'If you ever loved me you'd tell me.' I know who your husband is, he said. I hadn't connected you with Malcolm Steward. Not that Malcolm Steward!"

Nancy clung to the mantelpiece, her head drooping. "I explained that my life with him had no connection with Malcolm. Asked him where he'd heard about Malcolm. Someone I know, he said. And I can't take the risk. I'm so terribly sorry!"

Nancy swung round, panting for breath. Maudie took her weight, tried to steady her back to the chesterfield.

"As if I would betray him!" She clawed at her throat. "That's what I – can't swallow!"

She had to fight to breathe. Maudie sat her down, lifted her legs on to the chesterfield, put a cushion to keep her head up.

Outside the window a grey-blue sky hung over the last of the day. Maudie wished she too was outside, with the ordinary things.

"So there it is," Nancy whispered. "Unswallowed."

The life had gone out of her.

"He'll always regret the abortion."

"What about you?"

The thin rib-frame lifted, fell. It was like a last sigh. Maudie wished she hadn't asked.

"Butcher! Supposed to be a doctor! Doctor Haemorrhage, I should think!"

It left her panting, her eyelids with scarcely the strength to blink against the glow of the fire.

"He'll regret it. Even when he's Sir James he'll regret the child."

The coals settled, flames crackled upwards. The hands fell still.

She opened her eyes, focused straight at Maudie.

"Maudie Stelfox," she murmured. She tried to touch the girl's hand, seemed pleased to have her for company. Her breathing quietened, she slid into sleep. After a while Maudie drew the curtains, made up the fire.

She had finished the wiping up by the time Malcolm came in. She put her finger to her lips, indicated Nancy asleep on the chesterfield. Malcolm went over to her, bent over, studied his sleeping wife a long time.

He was glad Maudie had come, he said. Nancy needed someone to talk to. It would do Nancy good to talk to someone.

Maudie watched him, waited for him to say why he'd written to her. It occurred to her that he'd hoped Nancy would tell her about being pregnant by Vincy, about the abortion, about being dismissed, so that he didn't have to tell her himself. It wasn't something she felt she could ask him outright.

Malcolm came away into the kitchen, fetched a white cardboard carton out of a bag, put it on the table.

Nancy used to like iced almond cake, he said. He bought her one most days, in case.

"She hasn't fancied one of them yet. There's half a dozen in the cupboard."

It seemed to amuse him, buying cakes that weren't needed.

"She'll make progress now," he said. "Now she's home."

"I got your note," Maudie said.

He didn't respond, didn't acknowledge how prompt she'd been, or ask how she'd got the time off to come. She wondered if it wasn't small-minded of him, getting her to come over to Norwood so she should hear from Nancy what he could have told her himself.

He had brought home bacon, eggs, sausages and bread for a mixed grill. And didn't protest when Maudie lent a hand, then took over. Nancy wouldn't have much appetite, he said. She'd do better to sleep.

He ate well, as did Maudie, but it wasn't her wife, she thought, lying more dead than alive in the next room. The more she had to do with Malcolm, she realised, the odder he seemed, his mind like a chest of drawers, the man able to rummage about in this drawer and be completely unaffected by what was in the other drawers. When it was mealtime he opened the hungry drawer, during the day he opened the work drawer, and now it was evening it was the Nancy drawer.

After the meal he went and sat beside Nancy, tucked a blanket round her in case she was cold, sat on and on beside her, like a vigil. He didn't seem to blame Nancy for deserting him – nor himself for causing her to. Maybe, Maudie thought, there was another drawer for that sort of feeling.

"Think it was worth it?" she asked him. "Getting her to work with Vincy?"

"When I was reporting the war," he said, still watching Nancy, "they'd risk a thousand men to gain a trench. So far as the High Command was concerned it was worth it. So far as the men were concerned, of course, it wasn't worth it."

It didn't seem much of an answer. Maudie supposed he loved his wife. But for herself, she wouldn't sacrifice someone she loved for anything in the world.

She went into the kitchen, washed up the tea-things. When she went back into the room he had scarcely moved, still sat with Nancy, holding her hand.

"Something I never understood," she said, "was what you meant about fruit and maggots, that time you were telling me about the new town."

Not that she particularly wanted him to explain, yet she felt sorry for him, seeing him with the wreck of a life beside him. But at the mention of the Garden City project he changed in a moment.

"Welwyn is a desirable fruit," he said, more than willing to explain. "The area designated for the new town is an enormous parcel of land, twenty-three thousand acres and only twenty miles from London. To succeed it'll require huge amounts of material, it'll need a transport system to distribute the material to where it's wanted, and it'll need a fortune of money to pay for it all. And that's where it's vulnerable."

Take the distribution question, he said.

Maudie didn't particularly want to take the distribution question, but she had opened the Welwyn drawer and would have to put up with the consequences for a while.

If the local authority wouldn't agree to the building of roads in its area, Malcolm was saying, the Garden City Company had no powers to build them itself, even though roads were necessary to the project. As for bringing the materials in from other parts of the country, that was best done by rail – and the Great Northern Line went directly through the building site. But the responsibility for providing a conveniently sited station for freight and passenger transport lay not with the Garden City Company but with the railway company. And regarding the finance, so far as he understood it, because the area where the housing to be built was local authority housing, the money should be available under the Housing Act from the Ministry of Health through the Public Works Loans Board. In fact a company called Labour Saving Homes Limited already existed to take advantage of the Act to build small middle-class homes.

"Now suppose," Malcolm said, his spectacles seeming to glint with more than firelight, "suppose that one of these utilities, the roads, say, or the railway, or the money, was not forthcoming. Obviously it would be impossible to proceed with any part of the project. Suppose a local authority wouldn't authorise the building of a road which was to form part of the town, or suppose the Ministry insisted on unacceptable conditions before granting a loan of money, or suppose the railway company ignored requests for a station to be built for the new town – even though land had been reserved for such a station, and even though the profits from passengers and freight from a new town so close to London would be considerable – if any one of these utilities didn't go ahead, everything would be at a standstill. That's what I meant about maggots, things that have a destructive effect on the fruit – or at least delay it growing."

He spoke quietly, cradling his wife as one might a child. But tired as he was, blotched and worn and greying as he looked, his eyes blazed. Maudie wondered if she might have misjudged him. He had sacrificed his wife for what he believed in, and had also sacrificed himself. And for what, she wondered. What was this outpouring of energy for. Surely anything you got in exchange could never be worth all that? There was Tony, living in those uncomfortable huts miles from anywhere, yet always on about what a wonderful experiment in living this new heap of bricks and mortar was going to be. And cousin Kate, prepared to sacrifice four years of her life in order to help women she'd never seen or heard of, so they could have a happier life.

Sacrifice, everyone was going in for sacrifice! Good luck to them, she thought. She'd had her share of torture, living with the bitches all those years! And as for Nancy – she knew all about the sharp end of sacrifice!

"But the curious thing is," Malcolm was saying, "it isn't just one of these utilities that's dragging its feet. All of them are! They're all at a standstill!"

The local authority was refusing to build the necessary roads, the railway board was saying there was no prospect of a Garden City station, and the Ministry of Health not only hadn't authorised the payment of any funds but as a condition of doing so was actually insisting that the Company permit ribbon development along the Great North Road edge of the proposed town. It was also insisting that there be no overall design for the town, and that all sorts of building firms be allowed to build there as they choose without reference to the design plan for the town.

"All of which," Malcolm said, "are precisely the abuses which the Garden City Company was set up to avoid. The Company, of course, can't and won't agree to such conditions, so the Loans Board hasn't awarded it a penny piece. And this despite the fact that other building projects have received millions of pounds."

"So that's what I mean about maggots. And what I mean by the effect on the fruit."

"But why?" Maudie asked. "Why would they want to wreck the scheme? How could wrecking it benefit anybody?"

Because, Malcolm said, and even though he was in his own house he lowered his voice, a local council, or a railway company, or a government ministry was run by *people*. And people with influence in a council or in a company or in a ministry might have influence elsewhere.

"Suppose a councillor happens to be a local builder, or suppose a company director has a piece of land he wants to sell for building – you can suppose all sorts of possibilities. You can have ninety-eight out of a hundred honest men and women in such posts, you only need one or two who're not quite so honest -"

"But if what you're saying about Welwyn is true," Maudie said, "it would mean that an influential person in a ministry, and an influential person in a company, and an influential person on a council would all have to know what each other thought. And then they'd somehow have to get together." It seemed improbable to her, if not downright fanciful. "And where would they all meet? These people who weren't sure what the others thought?"

"Be sure of this," Malcolm told her. "Maggots don't nibble for the good of the fruit." He sounded as if he approved of her question, had almost a smile in his voice. "What you're asking, Maudie, is where do the important decisions get taken?" Again he spoke as though he was afraid there was someone behind a nearby chair listening. "Well, some decisions get taken openly, in Parliament, or in an open council meeting. And others get taken – in hotels, say, or round a table in a restaurant, or in clubs, or lodges, or in small rooms behind locked doors."

"Deals affecting something as big as this? A town where thousands of people might go and live if it got built?" It sounded too far-fetched to Maudie. Those who ran England were surely people who had the good of England at heart. It would be crazy to think otherwise.

"That's where the Press comes in. To try to nose these things out -"

A choking, moaning sound from Nancy. Her eyes were staring, teeth clenched, lips drawn apart like an animal in pain. She shook in a kind of spasm, her breathing sharp, through the teeth, as if words were trying to form, as if she was trying to tell what she was desperate for them to know.

Malcolm laid her down more comfortably on the chesterfield. She'd had several turns like this, he said.

Maudie got some warm water, bathed Nancy's face. She wanted to relax the poor tight jaw. "There, my dear. Soon be better, dear."

She felt closer to her, seeing her so ill. And remembering her childhood she made sure to dry properly round her mouth and not leave dampness between the fingers.

She asked whether Malcolm was going to get a doctor. But he said the doctor was going to call round later so it wasn't necessary. These attacks didn't last long.

As if they were listening, the limbs relaxed, the eyes closed. Maudie stroked her hand, her arm, glad to try and comfort her for a while. As for self-centred men, she thought, they were no use to women, no use to anyone. If she came across one she'd steer well clear.

# CHAPTER 55

It was the time of year when leaves were unfolding, buds were flowering, gardens were turning colourful. But when she looked in the mirror she saw a face neither unfolding nor flowering.

If she was by herself in the bedroom she would angle the mirror and look at herself naked. She hoped the curve of her belly wasn't turning to fat, was relieved to be able to suck it in so that when she turned sideways it had disappeared. She liked looking at her body, liked the touch of her fingers on it. She could think of herself as a newly-emerged leaf naked in the spring sun, would sway herself about as if moved by breezes. But being a solitary leaf soon lost its charm. What she needed, she felt, was another little leaf to sway with.

Rosie too had lost her sparkle. No mention now of Tony or the house that was going to be their own little home. If Maudie asked about progress at Welwyn, Rosie would shrug, "It's all so slow!" But she was polite enough, and when she resumed her habit of coming in late she undressed and got into bed as quiet as a mouse. After a while it was like sharing a room with a stranger.

Malcolm's letter was brief. Nancy had died in hospital after another haemorrhage. He gave few details. Perhaps

Maudie would go and see him sometime. There was no hurry.

Maudie couldn't get the idea of the funeral out of her mind. She pictured Nancy being lowered into the ground, the sun shining, and Malcolm going home afterwards and Nancy not being there, nor expected.

Once or twice she dreamed she could see into the coffin. Nancy's eyes were open, neat blue eyes that widened at her as a warning to say nothing.

So that was the Nancy drawer. Not much more to be put in there.

The idea of someone else's funeral began to take shape. Mrs Dawson's coffin would be lowered, the Major would throw a pinch of earth, she would drop a rose. Across the open grave their eyes would meet, and there they'd stand, she and the Major, while the mourners departed.

"No-one ever saw such undying love," people would say.

They would not be unseemly, she and the Major. There would be no wedding till the grass had been cut on Mrs Dawson's grave.

The next envelope was bulkier. It was from Malcolm, enclosing an article he'd written for the *Daily Brief*. She read it carefully. It was the least she could do, seeing that the new town had been the cause of Nancy's death.

*Recent findings suggest,* the article said, *that far from there being official support for the building of Welwyn Garden City there is a level of opposition that a suspicious mind might believe was co-ordinated. Not that this paper entertains any such suspicion. The Daily Brief is well known for its belief in the uprightness of human nature.*

*It is clear that the successful completion of a town combining good quality housing, employment in modern locally-based factories, facilities for sport and leisure, with up-to-date schools and civic amenities, all within an inviolable rural belt, would represent such a model of the conditions in which British citizens ought to live that to delay its completion even by as much as a day would be outrageous. Yet delay there is, and from a quarter from which delay ought to be inconceivable. Certain facts have come to our attention that must be aired.*

*This paper has already noted a reluctance for road and rail links to the proposed new town to be provided. We now draw attention to the role of the Ministry of Health. This Ministry, staffed from top to bottom by politicians and officials paid out of the public purse, was set up in 1919 to promote and safeguard public health. For what other purpose, one might ask, would a Ministry of Health exist than to promote the well-being of the ordinary man and woman? A reasonable person might suppose that the building of reasonable housing and the provision of reasonable employment in a reasonable environment might be a reasonable concern for a Ministry charged with the health of the nation. Alas for reasonable hopes! The only concern the Ministry of Health has so far shown is that the Garden City shall NOT be built!*

*Along with many other housing projects across the country the Garden City has applied for loans from the Public Works Loans Board. The sanctioning body for such loans is the Ministry of Health. The reader may be therefore be interested in the attitude of the Ministry as revealed in the following conditions:*

1) *The Ministry wants the Garden City Company to build a residential estate only – with no industry, no commerce, and with few facilities and amenities.*

2) *Permission for the Company to buy land to the east of the existing site (this is land needed to complete the balanced planning of the town) is refused.*

3) *The Ministry urges the building of houses at the western perimeter of the site along the Great North Road. (It was to stem the ravages of ribbon development that the Garden City scheme was devised.)*

4) *The Ministry opposes the architectural control envisaged in the town plan (wherein building styles harmonize with one another and relate to the residential or commercial or industrial use for which they are intended.) The Ministry prefers an architectural free-for-all.*

5) *The Ministry insists that in the event of a loan being considered, a sum equivalent to each instalment of such a loan must already have been spent by the Company. This, of course, adds to the financial uncertainty of the project.*

6) *The Ministry would insist on the inspection of whatever aspect it wished of the new town before the release of any instalment of a loan, in the event of a loan being granted. (This condition gives the power of veto to officials who might well have little or no understanding of the concept of a Garden City.)*

*The most charitable view of such conditions is that the Ministry is concerned to keep a tight rein on public funds. Yet in the financial year ending April this year, 1921, loans approved for public authority building schemes have totalled £53,000,000, of which not one penny has gone to the Welwyn project. A less charitable view is that the Ministry is making every effort to destroy the Garden City scheme. This is, of course, absurd. It would run counter to the very reason for the Ministry's existence – the promotion of the health of the public. Nevertheless, if the destruction of the scheme WERE the intention of the Ministry, it would be difficult to conceive of more effective tactics.*

*We intend to pursue this matter to its conclusion.*

Nancy's death, it seemed, had changed nothing for Malcolm. Maudie could hear his voice reading it, the grinding down of detail after detail until everything was laid bare, she saw the glint of his spectacles, the blaze of enthusiasm when he knew he was seeing what others hadn't seen. What it was that kept him going, what it was that he really valued in this world were questions she couldn't answer. He was beyond her.

She looked in the envelope to see if there was any further message, any mention of Nancy. There was nothing. Perhaps little remained. Somewhere, Maudie hoped, there would be photos, mementos, things that had pleased her. She hoped Malcolm was treasuring them. Or was an article like this all her vivid life amounted to?

She folded the cutting, replaced it in the envelope. Later she wrote NANCY on the front to remind her what was inside. She kissed her finger, pressed it on the word like a kiss.

When she could she took to going for walks. One day she found herself on one of the Thames bridges, was reminded of Maggie's death. Now Nancy had gone too. There had been no great to-do when they died, nothing had stopped, no-one had screamed for the world to end. Like the river that passed under the bridge, life murmured on. Sooner or later all lives passed under the bridge, no matter where they had hoped their journey would take them, everyone, whether now, or gone, or still to come.

Another time she was in Trafalgar Square. Nelson's column leaned up into the clouds, seemed to lean further and further until she had to get her balance to stop herself falling over.

"He won't fall off, you know."

Peter, as cheerful as ever. He wore the large hat, he said, because of the pigeons.

"One of them makes a mistake, I'm in trouble."

He looked older, thinner, but she guessed most of him was unchanged.

"Buttons! Laces! Buy a belt and braces!"

He carried a tray of neckties, toy flags, belts and other small goods. He wore a glove on one hand, carried a small suitcase in the other. He had done pretty well since he came out of hospital, reckoned he could earn more at this game than at the building. It paid to stand in the sun, he said. People were readier to put their hand in their pocket in the sunshine. She recalled that Peter was always one to think about his work.

He asked after Rosie, hoped her house was coming on at Welwyn. "I couldn't have stuck it out there. Away from everyone you know. Besides, no-one would buy this stuff out there."

She asked him how his hand was.

"Like an elephant's foreskin," he grinned. "Hell of a drawback."

He spotted a prospective customer and made off to a strategic position.

"Give Rosie my love," he called. "Buttons! Laces!"

Alexander was taking a crate of soft drinks into the *King James*. It took him a moment to recollect who she was.

"Ah! I'll be back in a -"

After a while he reappeared. He put the empty crate in the back of the lorry, opened the passenger door.

"Jump in. I'll give you a lift."

It was her evening off. Without asking where he was going she got in.

The smell of the cab intrigued her, the way he stirred the engine to life and thrust the gear lever into position. She loved the way he mastered the engine, the vehicle shuddering, doing his bidding.

He'd come to the *King James* with an order, he said. Old Perkins had been in a fix. There'd been a run on soft drinks because of the weather, the men had knocked off, as had the office staff, and the draymen from the brewery weren't due till the morning.

"So out I came. Put a half dozen crates on the back, trundled over here. Way to get business! And see the prettiest girl of the week."

He leaned his head on the steering wheel to get a better look at her. "With a bonny wee name like Maudie!"

She loved it, the way he laughed up at her, his blue eyes full of the devil.

He'd just got to take the lorry back, and do a half-minute's bookwork. Then they could decide where to go.

He slowed down outside a large, run-down red-brick building, swung the lorry in through the gateway and parked alongside three or four similar lorries.

He leapt down, came round and opened her door. She took his hand, tried not to look excited. He'd got something to discuss with the boss, he told her. Wouldn't take a moment. She could make herself comfortable in his office.

His desk was strewn with papers, invoices, receipts. A map of London lay open on a table, the map covered with circles, some red, the rest blue. Some of the blue ones had a red tick beside them. On a chair under a portrait of the founder of the brewery was an opened box of half-pint glasses packed in wood spirals. From numerous hooks on the walls hung advertisements of London hotels and inns, some with a large red tick across them. This was a man's office, a young man's place, a man too busy and energetic to bother about putting things away. Oh, if she worked here, she thought, she could soon tidy it up, put those old papers in drawers, dust the tabletop underneath that heap of order forms that probably hadn't seen the light of day for months.

A door from his office led into the next room. It smelt of women. There were two tables, two typewriters, there were cupboards, trays, filing drawers. No doubt the women were a couple of gossips, their minds on Alexander and little else.

She could hear him in the boss's room, telling the boss this, telling him that. At last the door opened, the two came to the doorway. Alexander was on the point of coming away, was even looking in her direction. Then, "By the way -"and went back into the room again.

When he eventually came out he introduced her to Mr Turner, the managing director.

"I thought I was going to be introduced just now," Mr Turner said. "But you know our friend here!"

He left Alexander to lock up.

"Something to show you," Alexander said when he'd gone. He indicated his office, tipped the venetian blind against the evening glow, switched the light on. "These are our pubs. The ones we supply." He indicated the red circles on the map. "These blue ones are where we're trying to sell to. The ticks are where we've got a foot in. That's the exciting part, winning them over."

She smiled to herself. Another enthusiastic young man. But Alexander was nothing like Tony.

"The boss likes profit," he said. "And I like winning it. So I'm the blue-eyed boy."

He asked Maudie what she did, was impressed when she told him. "Brains as well as beauty!"

He wanted to know the details, how she got on with Perkins, what she did before she had this job. He had no idea she wasn't a Londoner. Perhaps he hadn't got that sort of ear. Maybe it was because she spoke like a Londoner.

He'd worked in England since he was eighteen. It was easy to get on in England if you were Scottish because of all the people here calling themselves managers who hadn't the least idea how to run a business. Many were afraid of work, more interested in cocktails than customers.

"Field's wide open. Just a matter of spending time in it. The English won't. They spend their time avoiding work. So I do it!"

She loved his cheerfulness, his confidence. And when she mentioned all the stuff lying around his room, he showed her what was under this paperweight, what was on that spike, what lay on that heap on the floor by the window. It wasn't a muddle at all. Tidiness didn't matter. Business mattered. Alexander knew what he wanted.

As when he asked her to have a look in his stockroom.

He unlocked the door, gave it a push with his shoulder, ushered her in and closed the door behind them. As to the stock on the shelves and on the floor she saw little of them. He drew her close, kissed her face, her eyes, her neck. She trembled, thrilled at his hand on her, wanted her body to be pleasing.

The telephone rang in his room. He left her, answered it at once.

No trouble, he said. Would be there within the hour. He asked how to find the place and rang off.

A free house along by the Thames had been let down, he told her. They wanted deliveries for a function. They'd been trying everywhere. No-one else would do it.

"Another red tick," he grinned.

Maudie helped him load soft drinks, wines, bottled ales. He locked the place up, they drove off. She'd got to be on duty soon, she said. He'd drop her back there now. Which he did, in time for a good kiss.

She watched him drive away before going indoors. The evening road was full of lights, Alexander's, in her opinion, among the brightest. When she got to bed she touched her tongue gently round her lips. Wasn't as nice as when he'd done it.

A few days later a letter came. Usually she could put a letter aside till she had more time. This one she had to read before her heart beat itself out of her chest.

But it was only from Kate.

It wouldn't be long, she said, before she'd be revising for the first-year exams. How quickly the year had gone! A couple of months ago she'd managed to get to the opening of Marie Stopes' first birth control clinic.

"Trust her to open it on St Patrick's Day!"

There was no doubt the clinic was needed. Almost every day women came to the hospital suffering the effects of haemorrhages, miscarriages, illegal abortions. And they were only the tip of the iceberg!

"If only abortions could be done legally! I was amazed to learn that the official rate of illegal abortions or miscarriages is one for every five live births – and Sister says she's sure the true rate is much higher. But of course the hospital can't say so publicly."

It was pitiful to see the suffering so many women have to put up with. Especially when it could so easily be prevented.

"I'm only thankful I'm training to be able to help. The disheartening thing about the new clinic – though Marie Stopes won't acknowledge it – is that it isn't yet being used enough by the women who need it most."

It would be nice for her and Maudie to meet, Kate added, when the exams were over. She hoped Maudie liked her job. If not, she could always apply to become a nurse.

Maudie read the letter several times, especially the bit about becoming a nurse. The public liked and respected nurses. And there was something very attractive about wearing a scarlet cape.

The drawback was, she didn't care for being with ill people.

# CHAPTER 56

She went across to the boiler-room as soon as she could.
"Is it true?"

She knew by the look of him.

His wife was going to live in Ireland. Her father and her new young man were going to run a taxi business in Dublin. They'd be taking Paddy as well.

"What am I going to do?" The twist on his face had got worse, the mouth muscle drawn up tight. "Maudie?"

She felt cross, him having so much bad luck.

When were they supposed to be going to Ireland? she asked. Wasn't his wife a Catholic? She'd never be able to marry this chap. Hadn't Bernard any relations who could bring Paddy up?

Be going in a few weeks.

It was a struggle to get it out of him, as if he could only bear a bit of the news in his mouth at a time.

"What does Paddy think of going away to Ireland?"

He was only a kid. Was looking forward to going. His mother had talked him into it. It was easy enough to do. "But I'm his dad. I want him to live here."

"Why do you think she's going?"

"She can't bear Paddy and me having a bit of fun together."

He clenched his fist, punched his open hand. If he came across the other man now!

"Paddy! My little Paddy!"

She felt fierce for him, wished she could seize the boy away from the woman and give him to Bernard.

Except for the sounds of the boiler the room was quiet. But this was where the world was, with this man breaking his heart.

"I – want – Paddy!" Almost crying, smacking his fist into his hand. "Paddy! Paddy!" A choked little sound, scarcely louder than the hiss of the boiler.

She could only watch him, hoped he could bear it. She wanted to help, would have given the world to be able to help.

His back was turned to her, head raised as if to heaven, arms twisting about. "Little Paddy!"

She was glad there was no-one else to see him, clutching up into the twilight as if trying to make the boy appear out of thin air.

"Little old Paddy!"

*But, my dear, we can't always have what we want!*

Her mother's words. She hadn't heard them since she was a child. She could hear her now, her mother, understood what was possible and what wasn't.

"We can't always have what we want!" she told him.

Bernard shot a look at her.

"I wouldn't have – if I'd been your wife and you came back from the war like that – I wouldn't have taken him away!"

He swayed towards her, gripped her shoulders, stared into her face, his face an inch or two from hers.

"What my mother used to tell me," she said. "We can't always have what we want, however much we want it. Before she – went to heaven."

453

"Your mother!"

It was a whisper. He hugged her, his face on her hair. She didn't try to push him away, stood there, her arms limp, let him hug her.

"If only your face -" She was ashamed of the thought.

"Can't always have what we want?" He pushed her away. "Can't ever, more like!"

He sat down, his back to her. The glow on him from a crack beside the furnace door made her think of hell.

Had his wife had the baby, she asked.

"You were right – what you told me. Says I can see Paddy more often. Till they go."

Trouble was, with Mr Perkins making his job up to full time he didn't have as much time to go and see the boy as he'd like.

Had his wife always been jealous?

Always, even when Paddy was a baby.

"Not if you weren't there, though?"

"Nobody made a fuss of him like me."

"But if Dad wasn't there, Mum wasn't so jealous?"

He might have been indicating no, might have been trying to shake the pain out of his head.

"If I know Bernard Smith," she said, "he'd rather have his little boy happy -"

She let it sink in.

He stared at whatever it might have been in front of him. "All right for you, Maudie!"

She knew it was true.

"You think I should let him go? Just let him go?" His voice was hard, unbelieving.

"If you thought he'd be happier, you could. Or would he rather see the pair of you fighting over him?"

Well, put like that, Bernard said. Put like that!

"There's another side to all this," she said. When the boy was older, he'd want to know about his father. All boys did. "She won't be able to do anything about it then. He won't be ruled by his mother then. He'll want to come and find his dad."

All Bernard had to do was be sure to keep in touch. "Get your wife to always tell you where he is. She'll have him a few years – you'll have him the rest of your life."

He put his hand out for her hand, absent-mindedly cradled it for comfort. He had little enough to cling to. "That's the ticket. I suppose."

He repeated it to himself. "She can have him for the time being – I can have him -"

"For the rest of your life."

He went over the point again. "She can have him for now – that's the ticket -"

"And you can have him the rest of your life."

"And I can have him -" He watched her mouth, needed the prompt.

"He'll be happy enough now," she said. "Not having his mum upset. And later on he'll want his dad more than he wants her."

"She can have him now." He was a child learning his lines. "And I can have him -"

"A few years for her," Maudie told him, "and a lot of years for you. So long as you keep in touch."

He seized her hands, his poor face almost relaxed. "That I always will, Maudie! I'll find up my old pen. I'll keep in touch. That I will!"

She kissed his hand. "That's a promise," she said. "Don't you break it."

There was a cough of disapproval. "Please don't let me interrupt."

"Oh, you aren't interrupting, Mr Perkins. I think things are easier now. Aren't they, Bernard?"

"Thanks to you, Maudie. Made me see sense, Mr Perkins. Made me see it her way."

"Her way?"

"That she has. About little old Paddy."

Mr Perkins looked from one to the other, unsmiling. "It's Bernard I want a word with."

He looked quite formal in his dark suit, sounded more distant. He opened the door for Maudie, watched her across to the main building before closing it.

# CHAPTER 57

Rosie popped her head round the door.
"The draymen are here."

All thought of the night before, all thought of breakfast, all thought being seen where she shouldn't be by Mr Perkins, these were as nothing to her longing to catch sight of Alexander again. She made her way to the bar, invented story after story in her mind as a reason for going there, in case she got noticed. The bar was empty, she opened the door Peter had shown her all that time ago – was almost face to face with Alexander. He remembered her, called her his bonny wee girlie, came over and murmured there was something particular he wanted to ask her if they could get a moment or two together.

She couldn't stay. She'd be back, she said. Had no idea how.

"I'll try and get away."

A moment or two! She'd have spent a hundred or two listening to what Alexander wanted to ask. But she was uneasy at being seen, because if she got the sack she'd never see him again. So she suggested to Mr Perkins that she collect the delivery note herself direct from the draymen rather than wait for Bernard to bring it into the office.

The idea seemed to suit rather well. He waved her away to go and get on with it.

In a daze she went downstairs, out into the yard, over to the cellar door.

"If you could – let me have – the delivery note?"

Her heart banged against her ribs, banged most of her breath away.

Alexander signed it, leaned close, touched her ear with his lips.

What was the name of that establishment in Welwyn, he asked, his voice as quiet as a kiss. The one that might get a licence in a year or so?

She frowned, racked her brains, couldn't remember.

"Could it have been the *Cherry Tree*?"

She was amazed how good his memory was.

How about going over there in his lorry, he asked.

Oh yes, she said. When?

"Soon as possible. Saturday afternoon? Just the two of us?"

She'd try and swap some time off. She'd swap three weeks off for the chance of half a day with him!

Didn't she know one of the chaps on some committee? he asked. Management committee?

She supposed so. And realized she'd forgotten Tony, let alone that he was on a committee, never mind what it was called.

Poor Tony. Yet she wasn't sorry for him. Compared to him Alexander was like a god come down from heaven.

"Don't forget your delivery note," Alexander laughed, handing it to her.

She loved sitting next to him, being jolted about, feeling the vibration through her as the lorry rattled its way towards Welwyn. She knew she attracted him, knew it wasn't accidental that his hand brushed her leg when he changed gear. She liked the sensation, let her leg rock with the motion of the lorry and sat so she showed to advantage. Alexander's attention was generally on the road ahead, but every so often he'd look and smile.

Presently they turned off the Great North Road into Brockswood Lane. There were the woods, the bracken, there were the roadside verges she'd seen with Tony – but now the smell of leaves, the whistle of unseen birds, the sunshine and daylight, everything around her was part of the excitement. Life was no longer passing her by. Life was inside her, she was part of it.

The site had altered since Nancy and Mr Vincy and Maundy Gregory had had their picnic. Now partly completed dwellings and staked-out plots alongside unbuilt roads formed outlines of the town; meadows and hedgerows had been replaced by rudimentary plots; what had been a vista of field and grassland had become churned earth covered by stacked bricks and sand heaps. Alexander was not impressed. He had expected to see streets, rows of completed dwellings. He'd have thought they could have made better progress than this. It was easy land to build on, flat, well drained. It looked to Alexander as though people needed a bomb under their backsides.

"Where are the workmen?" he wanted to know. "Hardly anyone about!"

And where was the site plan where he could find out where this Cherry Tree was? Alexander, she sensed, wasn't the sort to wait for a dream to come true. Alexander was NOW.

"Isn't that him!"

He stopped the lorry, pushed the window down. Over there, near a hut, in dungarees, not doing anything in particular was Tony.

She called him. Alexander called as well, asked him about the Cherry Tree, where it was supposed to be.

"Easier to show you," Tony said.

"Get in. Get up, Maudie, and sit on his lap."

He didn't notice her blushes, was too interested in asking whether any drinks contract had been signed, whether the Cherry Tree was going to sell soft drinks, mineral waters and the like.

Tony wasn't sure about such drinks. He usually drank tea.

"Here we are!" She could hear the pride in his voice.

They drew up on a circular gravel drive. The restaurant was of wood, with low white-painted verandas at the front and each side, and along the ridge of the low-pitched roof was a sign in modern lettering proclaiming THE CHERRY TREE RESTAURANT.

"There's a bowling green round the back," Tony said. "And tennis courts -"

"D'ye think the man I need to talk ta's inside? Could ye introduce me?"

Tony took him inside. When he came out he muttered, "Your Alexander could sell blood to a slaughterhouse."

She loved the way he called him her Alexander, and wondered if he felt hurt, seeing her with somebody else.

"Can't get the go-ahead to build," Tony said, surveying the site from the lorry. "So we can't make much progress. Hard to keep the workmen, what with the uncertainty. And all of us having to live in huts."

Alexander came out looking pleased with himself. He could start supplying soft drinks at the end of the month. The manager would let him know as soon as the restaurant got its licence.

"Now, where's this wonderful new town I hear so much about?" he asked Tony. They drove back through woodland along a track which Tony told them would one day be called Bridge Road. One day he hoped to have a house there.

"No-one's at work!"

Saturday afternoons was time and a half, Tony explained. The Company couldn't afford time and a half.

Why weren't they working at the ordinary rate? Alexander asked. Especially as some of the men were intending to live there. "I'd work for nothing if it was me!"

The men worked for a contractor employed by the Company, Tony told him. Matters weren't that straightforward. They were already doing more than was asked of them.

"Only one contractor?" Alexander exclaimed. "For all this!"

He'd have had five or six contractors, each developing a section of the town. He made a guess at the profit per house. Fifty pounds? A thousand houses? The houses could be run up in no time. The Company would make a fortune, and a thousand families would have a home. Who did this Company think it was to be so finicky and artistic?

Because they weren't just building another housing estate, Tony said. Nor a dormitory town with ten thousand people travelling away every day to work and travelling back home every night. They were building an experimental town, a model for better cities later on.

It cut no ice with Alexander. If people needed houses, he said, houses ought to be built. People wanted their own roof over their heads, not their mother-in-law's roof. And another thing people wanted, he'd have thought, were a few public houses so they could cheer themselves up of a night. From what he'd heard, pubs didn't figure in this Garden City.

Maudie knew if Alexander had been in charge the town would be almost finished by now, Rosie would have her house, all sorts of things would be different. Yet she liked old Tony, could understand his wait-for-a-dream outlook. But looking around at the roped-off plots, the undeveloped fields, the ruts where lorries had struggled over unmade roads, the rows of uncompleted buildings, she realised it was possible to wait too long. She took a good look round before getting back into the lorry, tried to imagine Welwyn as it might one day be – if it ever got built. She hoped it would be for Tony's sake. For herself she knew she would never see it again.

"I bet you've had no end of girls in your lorry," she teased.

He patted her knee. "Haven't had time for girls."

She pictured the stockroom back at his brewery, hoped his phone wouldn't ring this time. Not that there would be a this time. She wasn't going to consent to go in the stockroom this evening.

He had another call to make on the way back, and by the time he parked back at the brewery and was back in the office it was twilight.

"Two more!" He sounded delighted with his evening's work. Back inside he ticked the appropriate circles on his map. "No delivery's too small. Little ones turn into big ones."

The telephone rang. It sounded like a woman's voice.

"Can't discuss all that now. I'll have to think things over." No wonder he sounded sharp. It was a ridiculous time for someone to telephone. "Sort it out yourself. I've been rushed off my feet all day!"

He hung up. Maudie wasn't sorry. It showed how much he thought of her, putting others off to make time for her. "You hardly seem to get a minute to yourself."

He held her hand, kissed it. "As long as you and I can have a few minutes together."

They stood in the dusk, close together. He kissed her throat, her forehead, her mouth.

Later he suggested they go in the stockroom.

As Alexander drove her back to the hotel she felt a warmth that hadn't quite burst into flame, but it was enough. She knew she had joined the world. It was herself and Alexander now, a mated pair, as boys used to say of their pigeons.

No talk of marriage, of course. When she married it would only ever be to the Major. But the next time she and the Major met she wouldn't be such a childish fool. In the meantime it was nice to be admired, nice to be someone's loved one.

Alexander kissed her goodnight. Would seem like a lifetime till he saw her again, he said.

When she went in the bedroom Rosie was quietly removing her belongings from the drawers and putting them in a case.

"Going on holiday?" Maudie asked.

She felt like a chat with Rosie, Rosie being a woman of the world. But the girl was checking ledges and sills for stray belongings.

"Holiday?" She sounded detached, almost amused. "One way to put it, I suppose."

The suitcase was full. Rosie put a strap round it. Her coat was on her arm.

"Good-bye, Maudie." She held out her hand.

"When are you coming back?"

"Back?" Rosie gave the room a momentary, incredulous glance.

She had looked strained lately, slightly strange. Maudie wondered if she was fit to be out on her own. "What about Perkins? Your notice?"

Rosie opened the door. Her face was quite composed. Like a mask.

Already she was in the corridor. Then the corridor was empty.

It had been so formal.

# CHAPTER 58

Again no letter.
Day after day she searched the incoming mail. Nothing from Alexander.

She dreamed of him, thought of him, whispered in her mind to him. If she'd known his address she would have written to him, but she didn't know his address.

She held the envelopes in her hand, those destined for guests, for the manager, she examined the handwriting, thought how lucky they were, these people with envelopes to open, letters to read. She considered those who ought to write and didn't write were lazy. Or cruel. Or both.

Things reached such a pitch with her she made a point of going across to see Bernard.

She told him she wanted to know the latest about Paddy, wanted to know how Bernard was facing up to the prospect of losing him.

"It's only temporary, you know," she assured him. "She won't be able to influence him when he's a bit older. You might see him sooner than you think."

It wasn't a prospect she would personally welcome, she thought, having seen the child, but so far as Bernard was concerned it was what kept him going, the belief she'd put into his head that sooner or later his son would come back.

Bernard's thoughts seemed far away.

"Turned out to be true."

"Of course it was. I wouldn't tell you wrong, old bean."

"I mean over there." He indicated the stables.

A couple of workmen had spent the morning taking the pantiles off the roof of the end stable and stacking them to one side.

"What turned out to be true?"

What Mr Perkins told him that night, he said. The night he'd come into the boiler room unexpected. He'd been to a meeting with this Mr Vincy chap. And Vincy had told Perkins there'd have to be changes at the hotel.

"More changes!"

The stables were to be pulled down and garages put up in their place. "That's what he wanted to talk to me about."

There they lay, stacks of red and blue pantiles, piles of rafters and roof battens.

It meant more than the end of the stables. No more horses clip-clopping down across the yard, no more carriages to be washed and cleaned, no more horses to be looked after.

"Says they're the coming thing, cars. Says horses'll be a thing of the past, one of these days."

"So what's going to happen to you?"

"I've got to learn to drive. Mr Perkins is going to show me. In his own motor."

The idea was that instead of horses being stabled there, a car service would be offered to guests, the cars could be washed and waxed, tyres pumped up, and so on.

"That's if the guests want it."

"What if they don't want it?"

If they didn't want it, he'd be back to part-time again. Or laid off.

"You hadn't better tell Mr Perkins I told you. Won't be long before he'll be telling you not to book in any more guests with horses."

Why was it, she wondered, that people like Bernard were always unlucky. Why did people like him get the rough side of everything – marriage, jobs, accidents, the people they mixed with? As soon as you helped them with one thing, something else went wrong.

But her own troubles had reached such a pitch she had to come out with it.

"Ever see Alexander?" she asked. "Or hear about him?" She hadn't seen him since the visit to Welwyn, hadn't seen hair or hide of him. "Don't the draymen ever mention him?"

"Can't say," he said. "Don't rightly know." He scratched his head, wrinkled his forehead trying to puzzle it out. "Couldn't exactly say, Maudie."

She knew he had had a lot on his mind, what with Paddy and everything, but couldn't he be a bit more helpful? She always did her best for him, she told him. Surely he could just mention Alexander to them?

He looked unhappy. He'd do his best, he said.

"If I was a young bloke, I wouldn't need a lorry to come and see a girl like you. Not if I had to walk across London."

Then he remembered. The draymen were coming first thing in the morning. Why didn't she have a word with them herself? She'd know what to say better than he would.

"Alexander?"

The foreman let the rope out little by little, eased the barrel down the ladder, looked her up and down.

"One of his fancy ladies?"

"If I knew when he was going to call," she explained, "there was something I wanted to give him."

He leaned back, the rope across his vast leather apron.

"Alexander'd give *her* something, Lennie?" he joked to his mate. "If he got her in his stockroom?" He laughed, his eyes searching her figure. "He'd give her something all right, I reckon?"

Lennie was more helpful. "Bit of a charmer with the ladies, Miss. So they say. Wouldn't do to let him get too close. Take my meaning?"

A shout came from Bernard in the cellar. They took their weight off the ropes.

"Charmed that girl in his office, Lennie?" The foreman wiped his forehead on his bare arm.

"Oh, Lord!" Lennie said.

"Charmed her drawers off all right?" The foreman laughed. "Bellyful of arms and legs, I shouldn't wonder?"

Bernard shouted that the barrel was ready. The men hauled it up, Lennie rolled it towards the cart.

"Not that it matters." Maudie didn't care in the slightest. "Any time he's passing will do."

Not much chance of Alexander passing that way, the foreman said. Alexander was up in Newcastle. Been made manager up there.

They roped the next barrel for lowering. "All right, Bernard?"

"Righto!" Bernard called back.

She couldn't bear it. Even as they were doing it in the stockroom that night he must have known!

One of his fancy ladies!

And never a word since. And she had waited and waited for him.

A bellyful of arms and legs.

He must have known he'd got the girl pregnant. In that room that smelt of women?

That voice on the telephone?

One of his fancy ladies.

She couldn't bear to think of him.

Couldn't bear it.

She couldn't help it. It made her angry.

"You knew what he was like," she told him. "You should have told me."

Bernard stopped sweeping, leaned against the broom. "You'd have only told me to mind my own business."

"You could have dropped a hint."

"You wouldn't have taken any notice."

"I always take notice of what you say. You should have told me."

"I couldn't say things about someone you were going out with."

He pushed the broom a sweep or two for emphasis. Maudie put her foot on it to make him listen. "It's just what you should have done."

"He might have been all right with you," Bernard told her. "Girl like you. Might have treated you all right."

She knew she was taking her anger out on him. It wasn't like him to be argumentative with her. "Look! I can't stand here arguing. You should have warned me."

"As long as you're all right," Bernard said. "That's the main thing."

She tried to push the broom away but his grip was too strong. "Whatever do you mean by that?"

Bernard resumed sweeping, his attention on the ridge of rubbish in front of the broom. "You know what I mean. Are you all right?"

"Of course I am. No thanks to you."

He swept the rubbish into a wide metal dustpan. "Nothing to worry about, then."

"Well, if that's all you can say!"

She walked away. After all the trouble she had taken to help him, she thought, for him to be so matter-of-fact about it!

But later, when she had a chance to think things over, she wondered if Bernard's attitude wasn't best. It wasn't what she had or hadn't done that mattered to him, but whether she was all right. That was what was important in his eyes, whether she had got herself pregnant or not. And as she hadn't, what she'd done wasn't his affair. That was what was nice about Bernard: it was her welfare he cared about; not her morals.

And thinking about Alexander she realised she wasn't as heartbroken over him as she'd thought she'd be.

There was a tap on the bedroom door. It was Mrs Critoph. Sorry to come quite so early, she said, but could she come in for a minute?

"Mr Perkins wants to see you, Maudie. In his office."

She spoke quietly. Looked her in the eye as if telling her something.

"If you could get there as soon as you can."

She wouldn't say any more, let herself out quietly.

Maudie was washed, dressed and down in his office in no time.

She'd soon get another job, he said. He'd give her a good reference. She was an excellent worker, plenty of hotels would be glad to take her. And he was giving her a month's notice rather than the usual seven days.

But why? she asked. What had she done?

Mr Perkins' rodent eyes watched her, searched her over. That was his business, he said. He was sorry to have to tell her she'd got to leave, but there it was. If she found herself another job before the month was up she'd be free to leave then.

But please, she said, was it because she'd done something wrong? Or because of what someone had said?

Nobody that she need bother about, he said. More he could not and would not say. It wasn't what he personally would have wanted. He knew a good worker when he saw one. But that was how things were, and they'd both have to put up with it.

It was such a shock, she said. The hotel was like home to her. Better than home, in fact.

"I even like you," she said.

He took her arm, showed her to the door. He'd see she got another job, so far as he could.

She asked if it was really a way of giving her another pay cut. Because if it was -

He shook his head. Perhaps even smiled.

The news of her leaving had already reached the kitchen when she went in. Everyone wanted to find out more.

She knew no more than they did, she said. He'd given her her notice, and that was all. No explanation, no fault found, nothing.

Mr Lexford raised his eyebrows. Mr Took's forehead wrinkled momentarily and was smooth again. To do with the stables being altered, they hinted. Another piece of their jigsaw slotted into place.

Mrs Gibbs rubbed her knees, stared into space.

"A month's notice," she mused. "There's a reason for that, somewhere."

Eileen reckoned it was to do with Rosie's sudden departure. June had heard that one of Perky's relations was coming in to do the job.

"Not that she'll be a patch on you, Maudie."

Others gave her to understand they knew what the real reason was, and tapped their noses and gave a wink as if to say they could tell her a thing or two if only they were at liberty to do so.

Maudie didn't tell them what she'd heard from Bernard. They seemed now more like a loveable bunch of children, these men and women so worldly-wise when she'd started at the hotel all that time ago. Being with them was a comfort, yet they were the same now as the day she started, said the things they'd always said. Their lives were going to change, though, whether they knew it or not. Bernard's life had changed. So had Rosie's. And Peter's. Hers was about to change, God knows what to. Maybe this was how life was, sometimes an early morning knock on your bedroom door, sometimes someone falling on glass late at night, sometimes your friend walking away without a word. She couldn't understand it, what it all meant.

One person might be able to tell her.

She wrote to him that evening.

# CHAPTER 59

He looked as if he had suffered. His face was bonier, his spectacles more prominent. But his attention was as sharp as ever.

"A month's notice? And told you he'd help with another job?"

They were on the steps in Covent Garden, the air tangy with the smell of fruit. There was more to see in a busy place, Malcolm reckoned, less chance of being noticed.

Everyone had said how good she was at her work, Maudie told him. Mr Perkins was pleased with her, said she'd done as much as anyone to get the hotel back on its feet.

"And then this. Out of the blue!"

She was finding Malcolm less remote, easier to talk to.

"I don't think it's Perkins gave you the sack. Sounds as if he's done his best by you."

A market worker came past pushing a barrow loaded high with vegetable litter and broken crates, its wheels shuddering on the uneven surface. They watched it rumble across towards an alleyway the warehouse side of the market.

"So who did?"

Sounded like the *silent executive,* he said.

She tried not to smile. The barrow was rattling like thunder, and him talking about a silent executive.

"Haven't you noticed," he asked, "whenever there's a scheme for the good of the country – an idea for ordinary people's well-being – how time after time it goes wrong? As soon as someone tries to put a scheme into practice to benefit the public, something stops it happening? Might be shortage of funds, or the name of someone connected with it gets blackened, or a war comes along – almost without fail, things for the good of the ordinary person go wrong. That's what I mean by the silent executive – people behind the scenes, behind your back, behind the back of England – whenever there's a proposition to benefit the common man – there's a conspiracy to wreck it."

It hadn't occurred to her. It would be awful if that sort of thing happened.

"*If?* Isn't much *if* about it! You mean it's awful when it happens."

People think the electorate runs the country, he said. They believe the electorate votes a government in to do what the electorate wants. But does the government do what the electorate wants? Any government? Sooner or later good ideas get scuppered, whatever starts to benefit the people comes to nothing.

"Think so?"

"Look around you! Staring us all in the face."

The hundreds of thousands of British servicemen. Yesterday, fighting for England, they were heroes. The country awarded them medals, built statues to them, newspapers praised them.

Till they won the war for us and came home. Some of them. What are they now? These same men who need jobs and houses, what are they now? They're a threat. Won't be long before they're criminals, a danger to the state. And tomorrow, when the next war comes? They'll be heroes again, fighting the enemy, fighting for Britain.

"And what are they all the time?" Malcolm asked. "They're ignored. Your ordinary man – whether he works with his hands or his head – your ordinary man is ignored. He works a hard lifetime, his children have a hard childhood. His wife isn't worth a mention. Hardly worth a vote because nobody values a woman's opinion. The treatment your ordinary man or woman gets is shabby."

England's preference for England is the shabby. Shabby housing, shabby housing estates, shabby towns, shabby England. And behind it all, growing rich at England's expense, the silent executive.

She noticed his hands, a townsman's hands, different altogether to her Pa's.

"Ever wish you'd been a farmer? Instead of a reporter?"

They were suddenly close, suddenly really cousins. She could ask him what she wanted to know. "Seeing things grow? Sheep having lambs, getting the harvest in? You used to like that sort of thing, I believe."

"I used to love my visits to Beck Farm."

"Never wanted to be a farmer?"

"I am a farmer," he smiled. "I harvest snippets of news. Everyone's got an appetite for news."

"This silent executive," she asked. "You ever come across it in your work?"

"Saw what happened to Nancy?"

Maudie knew what had happened to Nancy. Mr Vincy had got her pregnant, then left her. Told her he didn't want to, but didn't have an alternative.

"You look surprised. That was the silent executive in action."

"But what about her pregnancy?"

"Remember what she said? *I can't take the risk!* That's what Vincy told her. *I can't take the risk!* But Nancy had taken a risk. For him. And Nancy was left to deal with it. And it killed her."

"Poor Nancy! And poor you, Malcom. Changed your lives."

"Made me realize life is quite meaningless."

"So unfair! No wonder you feel it's all hopeless."

"No! Never hopeless. I don't believe life has a meaning. No divine purpose or anything like that. There's no *meaning* to it. But life's never hopeless."

He could see she was puzzled.

"There's always hope. I hope one day mankind will solve mankind's problems. One day we'll use our brains and be kindly. That's my hope. It's our only hope."

"What do you hope for now?"

"I hope things are better in Canada."

He was going to emigrate. He too had been sacked.

"Like you. Like Nancy. Another victim of the silent executive."

Across the market the day was quietening down, the crowd had thinned. Beyond an edge of shadow on a warehouse wall the afternoon sun seemed particularly intense. The idea of foreign parts was in her mind.

She didn't want him to go away to Canada. She had begun to like him.

"Will you mind leaving England?"

"I mind for England. There'll be one voice the less to point things out. Not that I did much to help."

"But why did they sack you?"

Because a newspaper had to have financial backers, men with money. Sometimes such men influenced what was written, the line they wanted the paper to take.

"Someone behind the *Daily Brief* didn't want this new project at Welwyn to succeed. I supported it publicly – made a point of wanting it to succeed. So I had to go."

The prospect of a town like Welwyn Garden City that would benefit thousands of ordinary people wasn't on some people's agenda.

"And when I suggested the project was being strangled – I was silenced."

"Why Canada?"

He'd met this Canadian reporter during the war. They'd kept in touch, so he was going to start afresh there.

Did he think life would be better in Canada?

Be different, he said. After what was happening in England he didn't much care what it was like. Nancy would be with him in Canada as much as she'd been here.

"You saw how I neglected her. I burnt the core out of her life. She had to build what she could round the edges."

She realised how easy it is to bully a person with questions. Malcolm didn't need bullying. He didn't frighten her now, this large flabby cousin of hers who'd lost his wife, his job, and was about to lose his country. One thing he hadn't lost was his attitude of being a reporter. Even when talking about his own experiences he told it almost as if it had happened to someone else.

"I'm going to pay a visit to Beck Farm."

He hoped to stay a fortnight. Maudie's Pa and sisters were his only relations now. He wanted to see them before he went to Canada. "Any message you'd like me to take home? Anything you want me to bring back?"

He'd be seeing her again before he went to Canada.

She felt the colour rise in her cheeks.

Could be something, she said.

The old shyness returned, almost paralysed her. But

knowing what she'd lost through being a tongue-tied little fool, she told him about the Major. Told him her feelings.

"Anything you can find out. Where he is -"

The subject was too enormous. She regretted mentioning it. "Like you say – may all be meaningless. But I always hope."

She felt revealed. Yet if there was shame, she'd done it for Richard.

So if he could find out any little snippet. Or about Mrs Dawson. Anything. But people round St Matthew's were suspicious. They could sniff out a secret clean through a brick wall.

Malcolm reminded her he was a reporter, had been close to a few secrets in his time. Might be able to manage something by the time he came back.

He didn't condemn, didn't make a laugh of her, took her seriously, got it clear what she wanted him to do.

She wished she'd got to know him better. Wished she'd known him longer. He was as nice a man as she'd ever met.

He'd get in touch when he came back, he said. And Maudie must tell him what she was going to do when she left the *King James*. He'd like to know she was settled before he went to Canada.

# CHAPTER 60

The fair sprawled, bright as a nightmare. The park was a village of pinnacles, tents, booths. Other reds and blues, greens and yellows came briefly to mind, were forgotten under the noise and excitement, the smell of crushed grass, the sound of brassy music.

*Ha ha ha he he he ho ho ho ....eeeeh!....ha ha ha...*

Helmet askew, his thumbs hooked in his belt, his great red mouth laughing, gasping, laughing again, the laughing policeman greeted all who came in or went out.

*Ha ha ha he he he ho ho ho ....eeeeh!....ha ha ha...*

Paddy doubled up, held his stomach laughing, and Bernard laughed to see him laugh. It swayed round and back on its pivot. Maudie waited for its greeting, but the eyes, half hidden in folds of cheek, didn't focus, didn't welcome her, indifferent whether she came or went.

She pulled a face at it, took Paddy's hand and walked away. They wandered into the fair, the cackling not quite drowned by the music of a dozen booths.

It was Paddy's last night out with his father before going to Ireland.

"Our lucky night tonight," Bernard said. "What'd you like a go on, Paddy?"

Paddy had a go with the bow and arrow, Bernard had a go at the coconut. Another go. Another go.

"You have a go at something," they said.

Maudie tried the hoopla. The ring knocked against a jug, fell round a teddy-bear's neck. The woman didn't smile, handed a small toy bear over, her eyes anywhere but on the winner.

Maudie loved the grin on the child's face when she gave it to him.

"Told you it was your lucky night, Paddy!" Bernard said.

"Brown Bear!" Paddy hugged his new toy.

Bernard saw a fortune-teller's tent, wanted them to have their fortunes told.

"Oh, no! I hate fortune telling!"

Bernard laughed at the look on her face, told her she was superstitious. She tried to walk away but he grabbed her hand, pulled her towards it.

"Our lucky night. Might as well hear what's in store."

On the veil over the entrance to the tent hung new moons, stars, signs of the zodiac, dusty from years of bringing good luck. As her eyes adjusted to the glow from a small brass lamp Maudie noticed a stuffed owl, a plaster cast of a human face, a green glass ball partly covered with green velvet. Madam Kantell laid her cigarette still alight in an ashtray, took Bernard's coin, brushed ash from the tablecloth. A thin woman, a shawl over her head and shoulders, she wheezed, coughed in the child's face.

He was a lucky little boy, she said. Had he had his fortune told before?

Paddy shook his head, grinned round at his dad.

She took his hand, passed her fingers over his palm

He was his father's son all right, she said. He was going to have a very lucky life.

She studied a line on his hand, touched her finger along it, saw a journey.

Paddy grinned.

She looked closer. He'd be going on a journey soon.

"I know," Paddy said. "I'm going to Ireland."

She'd wondered if it might be Ireland. It would be a safe crossing. And he'd have a lucky time in Ireland. He'd grow into a big strong boy and have lots of friends there.

"I know. I'm going there with me ma!"

She also saw an animal. Maybe he'd have a horse in Ireland.

Paddy pointed to the bear.

Ah, she said. That was what had confused her. Horses were brown and so were bears.

Bernard asked her how long he'd stay in Ireland.

She bent over the palm again. Years, she said. He'd have many happy years in Ireland. She was Irish herself. She couldn't say when he'd come back to England. Young hands had so many possibilities. He might come back to England one day. Wherever he was he'd do well. He was his father's boy all right.

"She was saying what she thought you wanted to hear," Maudie told him. "She thought you were going to Ireland with him."

She was sharp with him. Had tried to warn him against having his fortune told, but go in he would! Now he was almost in tears.

"Believing what that silly old bitch tells you!"

"She saw it in his palm!"

"She doesn't know any more than I do. She was telling him what she thought you wanted to hear."

But Bernard was sunk. "I couldn't carry on if I thought he wasn't coming back."

"Couldn't carry on!" she mimicked. "You were soft enough to want to go and listen to her. Now you'll have to put up with it. You'll have to carry on. If you gave up on Monday and Paddy came back on Tuesday, you'd never forgive yourself."

Paddy came over from a side-stall where coins on a moving shelf seemed about to topple over from the impact of added coins. But though they watched for ages no coins toppled off the shelf.

"Can I have some more goes, Dad?"

Bernard gave him some coppers. The boy hurried back to the stall.

"What you want to do, Bernard Smith," Maudie said, "is cheer yourself up. Not let yourself be taken in by a silly old woman. After all, she said he was his father's son. Not his mother's son."

"That's true."

"This time next year he might be back with you."

"Might be, Maudie," he said, brightening. "Might be."

He suggested a go on the roundabout to cheer themselves up. They queued, but when it came to their turn he said he'd hold Brown Bear and watch her and Paddy.

Paddy sat in a racing car with a steering wheel and accelerator. Maudie chose a white steed with a flowing mane and staring eyes. She sat side-saddle, hoped her skirt would billow out like a hunting lady's to show she was used to horses.

The music sang. She felt the wind in her hair. Her horse rose and fell, the roundabout turned, onlookers became a blur. She followed the motion of the horse, not needing the reins, her chin up like a hunting lady's.

They were at full speed. The air brushed her face, the cars, horses, motorbikes lifted and fell, lifted and fell. She had the impression that the movement of the roundabout came from within her, that the energy of the music and colour was her energy. She felt in tune with some great force, galloping towards her future. In this whirl of brightness, weightless as a leaf, floating like a spray of flowers in the Major's arms, she was on the brink of a dream that would soon come true,

The gyrations eased, stopped. Her legs felt wobbly.

"Could tell you've ridden a horse," Bernard told her.

But his attention was for Paddy, at the wheel of his car, making car noises, accelerating, braking, the engine roaring. He laughed to hear him, paid the man for another go for the boy.

"Let's have a go at darts," Bernard said. "See how much we can win."

Bernard bought darts for himself and Paddy. They aimed, threw, missed, bought more goes. Maudie bought a go, two of her three landed unaimed on envelopes with money.

"She's won again. You never win nothin', do you, Dad?"

Maudie gave the money to Paddy. She knew she had only to breathe to be lucky.

They had a go on the chairoplane. The safety rail was snapped into place, and with Paddy holding the rail from between his father's knees the arms rotated, the seats floated upwards and outwards. She loved the sensation of being whirled about, shaken out of herself. The pace increased, the air caught her skirt up, and Paddy, his mouth smeared with chocolate, laughed at her shrieks. She couldn't withstand the force of the spin, was content to be pushed against Bernard, her head on his shoulder, captured by forces she couldn't resist. The night and its lights flew around them, the guffaws of the laughing policeman came and went. Life was at its sweetest, the three of them close, rushing under the stars through the darkness together, on and on to anywhere.

"I like a freak," Bernard said.

She was sorry to hear it. But to please them she joined the queue to see *The Smallest Man in the World*.

"He look like one of them gnomes." The man next to them in the queue had seen it before.

"Handy to keep the birds off the grass with," Bernard said.

"Don't know how he'd manage if he wanted to pass wind. He keep as still as them other gnomes."

The session was over, people were coming out.

"I spotted him straight away," someone said.

"You spot everything straight away," his wife said. "I don't know how he kept so still."

*See If You Can See Him* a notice said. *The Smallest Man In The World!*

"No good to you, Maudie," a woman joked. "Won't do you any good. Chap that size!"

Rosie looked more alive, her face colourful with rouge and lipstick. The man with her was old enough to be her father. He steered her away into the night, his hand low on her body.

The queue moved on. A man in the kiosk took their money, his fingers ingrained with dirt. They went through, found themselves a place to sit on one of the forms in the viewing gallery. This was separated from the stage by a partition of wire-netting across which a curtain was drawn. They sat down.

Waited.

Waited a long time.

When the proprietor was satisfied he'd got enough customers the door was closed, the lights in the grotto came on, the curtain was drawn back.

A scene as bright as a fairy story.

The grotto walls had been painted to represent a clearing in a forest in which were potted shrubs, a pool, a scattering of vividly coloured rocks, a number of clay figures painted to resemble gnomes. Two were seated at a draughtboard, one was about to capture a butterfly with a net, another was preparing to fell a tree with an axe, three more sat round the pool angling. It dawned on Maudie that they didn't just look like garden gnomes, they were garden gnomes, about the size of children. Or were they? Was there a movement in that hand? A quiver of that axe? It was as if a living scene had been suddenly stilled and turned to stone, and when no-one was looking they would all come back to life.

The little men were identically dressed, each with a long red hat, a green jerkin, blue trousers and red boots. But one of them was alive, the rest were make-believe. The puzzle was to identify which was the living man.

"That axe has dropped a bit," someone said.

Someone else thought one of the draughts players wasn't so upright now.

"Look at that rod! Him in the middle! He's the one!"

"Which one is the smallest man in the world, Dad?"

Paddy's little voice caused amusement.

Bernard didn't think any of them were alive. They were like ornaments, he said. They just stood where you put them.

"If you dropped them, would they break?"

"I bet he'd move if he got stung," a man said.

He brought out a pea-shooter, steadied it, blew a pellet through the wire-netting.

It struck one of the gnomes in the eye. He clapped a hand to the pain, the suddenness of the movement dislodged his hat into the water.

It brought a roar of laughter. Bernard, to Maudie's disappointment, was among the loudest.

"That's the one, Paddy," he pointed. "He's the smallest man in the world."

The little man snatched his hat out of the pool, stood with it in his hand, glared at his tormentors.

"Keep your hat on!" someone called.

"Did you get a bite?"

The man came to the partition, his body the size of a child's, his face the face of an old man.

"You like to wear this?"

He walked along the other side of the wire-netting, the hat across his hands, offering it to the jeerers.

"You like to be like me? Work with these?" He gestured to the painted figures behind him. "I do this to live."

He bowed. Put the hat back on and bowed again.

A man trapped in a Punch and Judy body, more noble than those who watched. Without thinking Maudie applauded.

His eye caught hers. The lights went out. The show was over.

*Constructed by George Ferris for the World Fair. Chicago. 1893*

They got in for their final ride of the night.

The safety bar was fastened, the gondola swung backwards and up, then hung still while other gondolas were being filled.

"Will you take Brown Bear to Ireland?" Maudie asked.

Paddy cuddled it to him.

"What day do you go?"

He looked to his father to be reminded.

"Monday," Bernard said. "You go Monday, Paddy."

"You'll come back and see me?" Maudie asked.

The child nodded. "And Dad."

Its gondolas full, the Ferris wheel began to move.

Hanging in the intersections of light and darkness amongst the criss-cross of girders, she had a sense of being part of something greater than herself, as though she and the night and Bernard and Paddy and the structure around her were one. She was part of it all, a part of everything. She would meet the Major. Things were going to come right.

The wheel turned. The gondola rose back and upwards over the fair. Higher it lifted them, above the booths and the calls of stall-holders, above the shouts of customers, the music, the guffaws of the laughing policeman. Below her the city lights, numerous as stars, spread as far as the eye could see. She wished George Ferris had built a bigger wheel, wished its rotations could lift her into the heart of the night, wished she need never go back to a town built by Punch and Judy, run by men whose hands were stained with money.

The wheel rose for what she guessed must be their last time. She wanted to be free from what was left below, wanted to ride across the sky and find the yellow-white arc of the moonbow. At the top of the turn she put her arm round Paddy and Bernard and kissed them. She loved them because life was more wonderful than she had imagined and, seeing their faces softened by distant light, because of feelings for which she had no words.

The ride ended. They made their way out of the fair. Paddy was asleep, his head on his father's shoulder.

Maudie was glad Mr Perkins had given her notice. She felt she had been absent from the world, had lived too long in familiar rooms. Now that she was about to be free she felt she wanted to comfort those less comfortable than herself.

"It's for the best, you know," she said, meaning Paddy.

Bernard sighed. "If you say so, Maudie."

"I do say so. You'll believe me one day."

Bernard leaned his head against the sleeping child. "I hope it's best for him."

"One day," she said, "he'll find out who really loves him. Then he'll want to find you. Love always finds a way, you know."

She knew it would be true in her own case, saw no reason why it shouldn't be true for Bernard. "Love always finds a way."

They had walked some distance from the fair on their way home. At intersections between rows of houses or where the wind cut across a factory yard came snatches of music, whispers of laughter.

*Ha ha ha he he he ho ho ho ....eeeeh! ....ha ha ha ...*

# CHAPTER 61

"And Herbert's making a nice job of doing that shop up. Looks as if it might do well."

They were in a pub not far from the Victoria Hotel where Maudie was working as a receptionist. The saloon bar was crowded, twenty or thirty people were chattering their heads off but Malcolm's voice was guarded as ever. Maudie leaned closer, watched his lips.

"And how is Herbert?" she asked. "I mean - in himself? How is he really?"

"He's all right."

She watched, waited for some further crumb.

"You don't sound very sure."

Malcolm took his time, had a sip of his drink, scarcely enough to need swallowing.

"Doesn't sound as if he's very all right."

He put the glass down.

"I think it's the war."

He'd talked to scores of other men who'd been in the war. Not that they told him much. Couldn't get it out of their system, relived it in dreams.

"All over England. Reliving the nightmare, night after night. Thousands of us. All supposed to be back to normal by the morning."

Maudie had her own opinion of what was in Herbert's dreams. Or who.

"I wish him luck, Malcom. I really do, now."

"Shop could be a gold mine," Malcolm was saying. "Good situation, good meat, good butcher."

She asked after her Pa. After Stanley. Heard what there was to hear about Muriel. And Barbara.

Waited.

He'd spent a few evenings in the *Hawk*, he said. Hadn't had to be particularly diplomatic. Anyone in a village who did the slightest thing out of the ordinary was talked about. The Dawsons were always being talked about. "Mrs Dawson, apparently, has been at death's door."

"Pity someone didn't open it." And when he looked surprised, added, "Well, that's the truth. I can't help what I feel."

Major Dawson had come home for a few days because of Mrs Dawson's illness. But thanks to the housekeeper looking after her night and day she pulled round, was now much as she'd always been.

"How that young woman managed to spend so much time with Mrs Dawson, and look after the baby, and look after her husband who by all accounts is elevenpence ha'penny short of a shilling, is an absolute marvel, they say."

She said she supposed he had heard that juicy little rumour. "Who the father of the baby might be?"

Malcolm didn't set much store by the rumour. "Rose Dawson may be mad, but she's no fool. If she'd had the least suspicion about that, Miriam and Raymond would have been sent packing ages ago. And another thing. They tell me the Major's a smart-looking man, whereas Miriam - well, you've seen Miriam!"

Maudie agreed with him there. Richard was the best-looking man in England, and Miriam the ugliest woman, so whoever started that rumour must have had a vicious mind.

"Though there's plenty of them in St Matthews."

Rose had more bird tables now, Malcolm told her. "They say she can tell one bird from another. Gets upset if any don't turn up. Goes round the parish looking for them."

Maudie laughed, circled a finger beside her head. "Born like it!"

"Some say it's the Major's fault. Neglecting her."

Someone else whose mind was in a bad way was the rector. Hadn't been too bad when he first came home, had got to the stage where he couldn't be let out on his own.

"Thinks the war's still on, thinks he's got to go out and comfort the wounded. Feels he's not doing enough to help.

Maudie stretched, looked out of the window, scanned the faces of the passers-by. "Be the asylum for him soon, I suppose."

Malcolm took his glasses off, polished them. "Regarding you know who."

She knew the moves of the ritual, the putting them back on, positioning them, making her wait. "I think there's something you ought to bear in mind, Maudie."

She heard it in his voice. It was the voice of her sisters, trying to close the door on what she really wanted.

"Whether you and he would have anything in common. Whether you wouldn't soon feel uncomfortable with each other. Different outlooks, different backgrounds."

Wished she hadn't asked him, wished she'd never mentioned Richard.

"Anything else you want to tell me?"

"Only that Richard Dawson was in France - a long time. Spent a long time at the front."

Was as likely to be as unsettled as the rest of us. There'd be times when he'd hardly know where he was or who he was.

"I was there. I know how it affected me. And I was only a correspondent. So if the Major ever gave you to understand - let you think it was anything more than a passing - maybe that's why he's gone - trying to sort himself out."

Before they went out to the front, Malcolm said, men had a pretty clear idea why they were going, what they hoped the war would achieve. By the time they came home- weren't clear about anything.

"Might not feel for you what you feel for him."

*But you didn't see the moonbow. You didn't dance with him that night in the barn, haven't seen him night after night in your dreams.*

She didn't blame Malcolm. She was even beginning not to blame the bitches. No-one knew what she knew, nor ever would, except the Major. It was the test, why she had seen the moonbow, she alone, that sign in the clouds. It had shown her that light, that message from the Major, that she alone, she would find him. *I knew you would, he'd say. His eyes would smile, "I knew you would, my dear."*

Malcolm smiled. "I had to give you my cousinly advice. Young girl, away from home, no-one else to turn to."

Maudie thanked him for what he'd found out.

It made sense now, all these difficulties, these clouds. They were what the moonbow meant.

"I shan't do anything in a hurry," she said. And felt quite light hearted.

It was time for her to start finding her way back to the Victoria. Malcolm walked with her to the bus-stop.

He held her arm. "I don't think I was told this in confidence, Maudie."

One morning when he was having a cup of tea with Muriel, chatting about days gone by, Muriel suddenly said she'd like his advice. "She brought out a long brown envelope. Wanted to know what I made of it."

It was tied round with red tape, addressed to Mr Stanley Chatham.

"She said it was the title deeds to Barn Field."

Mrs Dawson had given it to Stanley after the Major had gone to London.

"I told her I wasn't a lawyer. And I certainly didn't want to look in an envelope addressed to Stanley when Stanley wasn't there. She wanted my opinion on a little handwritten message under a loop of the tape. Said *In gratitude for my life, 1918. Richard Dawson.* She wanted to know what I thought it meant."

"I bet she didn't want Stanley to know she asked you about it," Maudie said. "Always a sly one, Muriel was. Bet she leads poor old Stanley a dance."

"The point is," Malcolm persisted, "it looks as though the land could have been a thank you for something Stanley had done. Must have been pretty significant. Giving him a great field like that!"

"Won't Stanley tell her?"

"Muriel says she can't make him out. He'll talk about anything and everything. Never a word about the war."

They'd reached the bus-stop. It was probably the last conversation she would have with Malcolm. She thanked him for the trouble he had taken finding things out, was sorry if she'd sounded a bit sharp once or twice.

"Muriel used to tell me I'd got a tongue like a viper."

She asked him if he'd be coming back to England one day.

He thought not. Didn't think he'd be able to stand a second upheaval. He'd have his memories wherever he was.

He gave her the address where he'd be living in Canada.

"I'd like to hear from you, Maudie. Don't let me down."

There was an air of departure about him. She regretted they'd never been close. Malcolm couldn't have had much of a life - the years in the war, trying to find out about Welwyn, Nancy getting pregnant by someone else. Dying. Him losing his job just as he was getting to bottom of things.

She knew her own life would be luckier.

Malcolm's bus arrived. It was strange to be saying good-bye to him for ever. She wished there could be a time they could meet again, when the whole family alive and dead could meet again. But things were otherwise, except in heaven.

When they shook hands his hand was warm.

She pictured the moment, wanted to remember him boarding that bus at that particular place, wanted to understand the everness of that step from the pavement to the bus. But she couldn't make it dramatic, couldn't get it to be more than an ordinary memory.

Around her came the roaring, voiceless traffic, coming from nowhere, going nowhere, patient, impatient, endless today as yesterday. She loved it, this river of people, the countless lives, the headfuls of ideas going past. As if all mankind came from a stream of life like this.

It may have been the shriek of a brake, or someone changing gear, and confirmed by something Malcom had said, the notion. By the time she'd returned to the hotel and changed into her receptionist's uniform for the evening stint it had strengthened, taken hold.

She knew where the next stage of her life must take her.

# CHAPTER 62

She loved the shapes of the animals, their unusual skins and furs. The seals were her favourites, enjoying themselves, their boneless bodies bobbing about in the water, sunning themselves on the concrete, scratching themselves with little flat hands. It was their eyes that were sad.

"I feel sorry for them," she said. "Brought all the way to London for us to look at."

Zoos did good work, though, Bernard said, saving the animals and that.

"Thing is," a bystander said, "there's thousands of zoos all over the world, all of 'em saving animals as hard as they can go."

The keeper arrived, made the seals do tricks, rewarded them with dead fish which the seals nosed about through the water and tossed into the air, pretending they were alive.

The air was rich with the smell of lions, elephants, giraffes, monkeys.

"Worse than horse shit!"

"Worse than pigs'," she agreed.

They wandered away, looked at animals, read notices outside cages about this animal and that animal, what the habitat was like where they came from, what they ate in the wild. Too much to take in.

They sat under a tree and had their sandwiches.

Bernard showed her a postcard. Moira had scribbled a note to say they had arrived safely and now looked forward to a happier life. Maudie said that when Paddy got better at writing Bernard would often hear from him.

"You always cheer me up," he said.

She asked how he liked looking after motor cars. All right, he said. He preferred horses, but cars, well, that was what Mr Perkins wanted him to do. It made a change. Was beginning to get the hang of them.

He asked her how she liked working at the *Victoria Hotel*.

"Something I want to tell you, Bernard."

She knew it was the right thing to do. Hadn't said a word to anyone. Wanted him to be the first to know.

"I know you always want what's best for me."

"That I do, Maudie"

"I'm going to give up hotel work."

"Don't you care for the *Victoria*?"

It wasn't that, she said. "I'm going in for nursing. I want to be a nurse." Someone she knew might need a nurse one day.

A look of concern came and went.

"You've done pretty well at that hotel job, Maudie."

"But what do you think, old bean? About me being a nurse?"

It generally took him a minute or two to make his mind up.

"Bernard?"

"You'll make a good'un. None better."

"Really think so?"

"Girl like you."

She'd written to the *Charles Lamb* hospital, she said.

Had had a letter back. Had an appointment to see the matron.

"Won't be an easy life," Maudie said. "But I've got a cousin there, training."

"You'll see some sights, nursing."

"You think I'll be able to do it?"

Bernard smiled. "Girl like you."

The shade of the tree had edged away, the afternoon was warm. Bernard rolled his jacket up, put it under his head.

Maudie lay beside him, knew it was unlikely they'd see much more of each other. She liked Bernard, better than almost anyone in the world.

"Girl like me," she said, "likes a man like you."

"That's it, Maudie."

He stretched, lay back, his hands under his head.

She compared the size of her arm to his, shivered and laughed at the tickle of his hairs on her skin.

They talked a little. Then less. Presently she noticed he was dozing. It would do him good, she thought, after all he'd been through.

His face was pale in sleep. Now and then he flinched. She wondered if he was back in the trenches, feeling the blast that changed his face.

So many men, it seemed, when they should have been at rest were back in the horror. Malcolm had told her as much. Richard had been at the front longer than most. Sooner or later what he'd been through would catch up with him. What form the crisis would take she couldn't tell. But one day he'd need her, and she' be there to help. Never mind that she couldn't bear ill people; if Kate could stand it so could she. And if it took four years to get herself prepared, that one moment would make it all worth while, the moment he came round in hospital and saw her, and she murmured, "So this is my invalid!"

Bernard was deep in sleep. Now and then he groaned. Maudie hated to think of him in pain. She leaned over him, her hair almost touching his face, wanted to share what he was seeing, knew she never could.

She pulled a grass stalk out of its sheath, pushed it between the buttons of his trouser fly, pushed it till it touched flesh.

He stirred.

She whisked the grass away, waited till he was back in sleep. She inserted the stalk again. The brittle end jabbed him. His hand flew to scratch himself.

He was awake, realised why she was laughing, and laughed too.

"Couldn't let you have bad dreams," she said.

He sat up, said he was sorry he'd dropped off. Seeing as how she was going to leave, he ought to be making the most of his time with her.

"Must think I'm a rum 'un."

"I know what to think of my old bean."

Bernard got to his feet, gave her a pull up. He checked his watch, said it was time they were making their way back. If they went now they could have a look at the river first.

She asked him if he ever worried about his face.

Not much, he said, though if there was a lady present he sometimes felt uneasy.

"What about now?" she asked. "Feel uneasy with me?"

"Never with you, Maudie."

It was when he saw the look on Moira's face after he was wounded. Realised he was like someone out of a freak show. She as good as told him, *What did you want to go and do a thing like that for?*

"That was the end of it, really."

"Poor excuse to leave a chap," Maudie said. "Specially one as nice as you."

She asked if he thought he'd marry again.

He'd have to find someone who'd have him first, he said. Though he didn't see how he could, being married already.

"What about Moira?" Maudie asked. "She's a Catholic, but she's got another man."

He couldn't answer for Moira. So long as she treated Paddy all right he didn't care what she did.

What did he think of two people living together who weren't married?

He didn't think it was fair to the children. If a couple liked each other enough to live together they should like each other enough to get married.

Maudie didn't argue. He was a simple old soul – straight as a die.

They reached the Thames, wandered across to the middle of the bridge. She felt free of the river now, the dread of what might come out of it. It was what Malcolm had said it was, the gateway between Britain and its empire, the best known river in the world, had a meaning beyond what sailed on it. But what that meaning was she couldn't find the words to think it.

"Always did like the river," Bernard called to her above the noise of the traffic.

"By the way," she said. "You needn't tell anyone about me trying for a nurse."

"If you say so, m' dear. You'll make a good'un."

"Whatever I do, the one I'll miss most will be you."

"And you, m' dear," he said. "And you."

She stood close to him, put his arm round her shoulders.

One day, she thought, a scarlet cape.

They watched the river traffic, the small craft, the barges, the criss-cross of pleasure craft, the great river beneath. She was fascinated by its surfaces, its colour here, loss of colour there, its movement under the bridge, its stillness between the banks of the city further off. Ceaselessly it slipped away beneath the bridge, ceaselessly it was replaced. From bank to bank the river was in motion, from bank to bank it remained. She wanted to point it out to Bernard, wasn't clear what she wanted to point out.

They wandered back the way they'd come, chatted about things that caught their attention, their jobs, ordinary things. Bernard checked his watch.

"Well, I suppose we'd better be getting back, Maudie. Been a lovely afternoon out."

# AFTERNOTE

1) The mainline railway station at Welwyn Garden City did not get built until 1925. One of the conditions on which the railway company insisted was that the company should be able to buy 69 acres of land at the original price paid by the Garden City Company. It also insisted on having advertisement hoardings, despite this being contrary to the architectural policy of the Garden City.

2) The first loan from the Public Works Loans Board towards the building the Garden City was not received until April 1922.

3) The loan debt repayment was completed in 1946.

4) The Cherry Tree obtained its licence to sell alcohol in 1922.

5) The original wooden structure of the Cherry Tree remained a popular community centre until 1932. It was then replaced by a permanent and less well-liked building.

6) The average "going prices" for honours arranged by Mr Maundy Gregory were:

   knighthood – £10,000

baronetcy – £40,000

peerage – £100,000

7) in 1932 an open verdict was returned on the death of Edith Rosse, a lady with whom Mr Maundy Gregory lived. It was widely believed she was poisoned by Mr Gregory.

For the setting of the novel I acknowledge with thanks my indebtedness to the following sources amongst others:

*The Office of Population and Census Surveys*;

*Garden Cities of Tomorrow* by Ebenezer Howard, published by Faber;

*The Building of Satellite Towns* by C B Purdom, published by Dent;

*Marie Stopes* by Ruth Hall, published by Deutsch;

*The Carlton Chronicles*, the diaries of Canon Reginald Bignold, published by Norwich Union;

*The Honours System* by Michael De-La-Noy, published by Allison and Busby.

I must also thank Mrs Winter, a lady who chatted with us in Welwyn Garden City during my researches. Hearing that I'd like to look inside one of the first houses built in Welwyn, she immediately invited us into her house. As we walked through the rooms, there was, open on a table, a map of the town as it was first envisaged.

I should add that my father George Bower, after three years as a soldier on the Somme in the First World War, worked as a carpenter at Welwyn Garden City during its construction.

The moonbow described in the story is as the one I saw when travelling by car late at night from Saxmundham to Debenham, with a full moon to the south and rain clouds to the north.